Carol Smith, formerly a leading London literary agent, now concentrates full-time on her writing career. She is the author of the highly successful *Darkening Echoes*, *Kensington Court*, *Double Exposure*, *Family Reunion*, *Unfinished Business*, *Grandmother's Footsteps* and *Home from Home*, all published by Time Warner Books UK. She lives in Kensington, West London.

Grandmother's Foot...
'*Grandmother's Footste...* ... ; and guessing all the way t...

'With its teasing insight .... of a serial killer, *Grandmother's Footsteps* keeps you guessing until the end' *Sainsbury's Magazine*

Unfinished Business
'If a pacy thriller is your thing, *Unfinished Business* will suit you to perfection . . . an addictive read' *Sunday Express*

'A thriller which certainly keeps you turning those pages . . . gripping right to the end' *Daily Mail*

Family Reunion
'A gripping read' *Family Circle*

'Full of action, twists and surprises, this intricate suspense story offers a fascinating new take on the nature of family ties' *Good Housekeeping*

Double Exposure
'Totally fascinating' *Express on Sunday*

'A hugely enjoyable book' *Woman & Home*

Kensington Court
'Skilfully sustains the suspense until the closing pages' *The Times*

'*Kensington Court* . . . will have you racing through the final pages for the brilliant, twisting climax' *Company*

CAROL SMITH

Hidden Agenda

timewarner
paperbacks

A *Time Warner* Paperback

Published in Great Britain in 2004
by Time Warner Books
This edition published by Time Warner Paperbacks in 2004

A CIP catalogue record for this book
is available from the British Library.

ISBN 0 7515 3635 0

Typeset in Berkeley by Palimpsest Book Production Limited,
Polmont, Stirlingshire
Printed and bound in Great Britain by
Clays Ltd, St Ives plc

Time Warner Paperbacks
An imprint of
Time Warner Book Group UK
Brettenham House
Lancaster Place
London WC2E 7EN

www.twbg.co.uk

For Sheila Lynford (née Thomson), Mary Walbank (née Hoskins), Alison O'Neill (née Cripps), Jane Hastilow (née Brown), Eleanor Grey (née White) and Old North Londoners everywhere, in memory of Dame Kitty.

Acknowledgements

Thanks to everyone involved in this book; my editors, my agent, my schoolfriends and Time Warner, who never fail to do a superlative job.

Prologue

The heat was so heavy it weighed everything down. The city seemed to be sleeping. On the bank of the sluggish Mississippi river a car drew up so close to the water that the backwash from a passing steamer lapped around its front wheels. The driver, having checked the windows, locked the doors and headed away, leaving the engine quietly ticking over. Anyone watching might have seen from the slight shift that the handbrake wasn't on but, at four in the afternoon, there were very few people about. In New Orleans they take a lengthy siesta.

The water was dense and grey with mud as the heavy Buick inched itself slowly forward. Because of the slope it gained momentum until it nosedived beneath the surface. Within the car, two small stricken faces were just perceptible against the glass. Four tiny hands with scrabbling fingers raked the closed windows as it sank.

Beneath the trees, still as a heron, the driver watched till the ripples had ceased then turned and walked briskly away.

1

Even this early the heat was wicked and Judge Dee Saunders groaned as she buttoned her jacket and steeled herself for the ordeal that lay ahead. In her years as part of the state judiciary she could not recall any case that repelled her more; a mother, supposedly legally sane, on trial for the slaughter of both her children in a particularly blood-chilling way. The fact she wasn't a native of the state in no way detracted from the horror of the crime; if anything, made it worse. For this was no trailer park trash to contend with but premeditated murder by a middle-class Brit who was so far showing no remorse.

'Honey, I'm off now,' she called up the stairs to Jackson, rehearsing in his vibrant bass as he spruced himself up for the Union. Tonight was a church supper at which he'd sing solo. She prayed that she would be there in time to provide the support he so richly deserved. In the pecking order of candidates for sainthood, her husband was right there at the top.

'Good luck, baby. Up and at 'em! Show 'em what yo're made of, girl!' Razor in hand and suspenders dangling, he stood on the landing, his face half-eclipsed by foam. Dee's whole career had been heading towards this day. Having listened with patience to her account of the accumulated evidence, her husband knew just how much this trial meant to her. To consign a sane woman to the certainty of death or else find some way to reprieve her; Jackson Saunders was heartily glad that such a burden did not rest on him. He bounded down the stairs to embrace her, creasing her jacket and mussing her hair.

'The best you can do, hon, is listen to your heart. The Lord will show you the way.'

If only. She smiled and wiped away the suds then stretched to kiss him full on the mouth. 'I know that,' she said, with more confidence than she felt. 'Now finish getting dressed, lover boy, or else they are gonna whup yo' ass.'

On the road into town, she ran the sparse facts once more through her overtaxed brain. Two children had drowned in the family car while alone with their mother one afternoon. There had been no witnesses; they had not been seen again till their sad little bodies were dredged from the river and their mother had been arrested for murder. No other person seemed implicated. Their father had not been there. He had been, as usual, at his place of work which several of his colleagues could confirm. Cut and dried; in cases like this it was, more often than not, a domestic affair. And the mother was offering no kind of defence; had, by her total silence, declared herself guilty. All that was lacking was a motive. It didn't add up.

The headlines worldwide were virulent, a witch-hunt was under way. There were crowds besieging the courthouse building while mounted state troopers, batons at the ready, warned them to keep the peace. A lynch-mob in the making, Dee sensed, as four armed guards escorted her from her car. What kind of a monster could have acted that way? It went against all the laws of instinct and nature.

She certainly didn't look like a monster as she stood there frailly in the dock. Slimly built with a boyish figure, she appeared to have shrunk since her first appearance in court. Susan Victoria Lockhart (née Palmer), thirty-nine, a UK citizen currently domiciled in New Orleans where the incident had taken place. No sign today of the quiet, supportive husband who had ended his visits so abruptly. Yet together they had lost two tiny children and the marriage was relatively new. A tragedy of such immensity should have drawn them closer together instead of driving them apart.

'Name and occupation?' intoned the court official, robotic as a speaking clock, perhaps out of self-defence. She went through the familiar legal procedure of checking in the prisoner who just stood there, showing no emotion, engulfed in the regulation overalls. Susan Victoria Lockhart (née Palmer) looked nice in an understated way, or would have done before the nightmare began. Short brown hair with natural sun-streaks and skin that, despite the sultry heat, was still only slightly tanned. Wide hazel eyes that had glinted with laughter until the cops came and took her away, and a generous mouth, well accustomed to smiling, compressed now into a tight line. No matter what the prisoner had done, Dee's heart went out to her. To have lost her children must be punishment enough without the additional agony of a trial.

But the court's business was Dee's domain. On her lay the task of seeing that justice was done. A bailiff called the assembly to order and the prosecutor took the stand. The facts presented were both stark and brief; a mother had perpetrated the most heinous crime of all, motivated, it would seem, by petty vengeance. Two helpless children, too young to fight back – Holly, two, and her baby brother, Jonah – had been left to drown in the Mississippi river because of a marital spat.

Medea could not have been hated more; the public gallery erupted into anger, and were sharply called to order. From outside, the rumblings of the crowd could still be heard, with the occasional whine of a siren. There was nothing worse than the murder of a child, even here, in Louisiana, where such things were not unheard of.

This, thought Dee grimly to herself, was the toughest case she'd encountered yet. She prayed for the strength to see it through and ensure that true justice was done.

'I'm afraid that poor soul is destined to die,' she confided to Jackson as they sat on the porch. She'd arrived at the church minutes before he sang but with little appetite for the supper. The day's events had sickened her. Sometimes she wondered why she had chosen this path.

Her husband leaned over and gripped her hand. 'Honey,' he said, 'you are not to fret. The Lord knows you're doing your level best to save this miserable sinner. Thankfully, soon it will be out of your hands and up to the jury to decide.'

To his mind any mother who harmed her own children deserved to be strung up on the nearest tree. A God-fearing man, he abided by the rules by which his ancestors had run their lives. An eye for an eye, so the Good Book said, though in this case it was a double whammy. Two bitty children, too young to understand, not even when the waters sucked them down. At least by now they would be with the angels. But Dee was in no mood for theological debate. Jackson pulled her on to his knee and set about the process of relaxing her.

Andrew Lockhart was deeply sedated, his spirit completely broken. One moment he'd been the happiest man on earth, the next he was sunk into such black despair that only the doctor's intervention had stopped him following his children into the river. Luckily there had been another person there who'd assessed the situation and called for help. Now he sat passively in his chair, blankly accepting whatever was offered, unable even to think. His life was over; deep down he knew that, but the sedatives stopped him from totally falling apart.

Of course the Palmers had offered to come, despite their personal agony, but Andrew had known enough to put his foot down. Family they might be but he couldn't face them now, had even asked his own parents to stay away. Until he could come to terms with the truth, he wouldn't see anyone at all. Except, of course, for the obliging friend who vowed to stay at his side till the trial was over. That agreed, the doctor ticked it off, and swiftly and gratefully took his leave. His casebook was crammed as it was.

In any case Gwen could not possibly have travelled; that was out of the question. She'd already experienced once in her life something so dreadful she had feared for her survival but this, she had to admit, was infinitely worse. So bad she could not properly take it in but clung to her husband instead.

'Tell me it hasn't happened,' she begged. 'This cannot be going on. My darling daughter, she could never have done that. There has to be some other explanation.'

Guy, her husband, merely shook his head. It was finally beyond him. All he could do was hold her close and watch her endlessly crying. Yet again he felt he had let them all down and this time there could be no going back.

The defence attorney was a mild-mannered man, not at his ease in a high profile murder trial. He wore a formal vest and old-fashioned spats, uncomfortably overdressed for a hot spring day. From his watch-chain dangled his Phi Beta Kappa key, which he absent-mindedly fidgeted with as he talked. Silver hair sloped in wings above his ears; he had the long-nosed look of an amiable hound. Despite, however, his flowery oratory, Horace Cutts was stumped to come up with anything convincing. There had been some kind of an altercation, after which the defendant's husband had left the house.

'And did not return?' Dee's gavel was poised in case of further interruption.

'Apparently not.' He referred to his notes, then slowly removed his glasses and eyed her squarely. A neighbour had reported voices raised in anger and the sound of a car driving off. Nothing else.

'Do we know where he went?'

'To his office, I'm told.' Having replaced his glasses, the lawyer was back in his notes. 'Where, he claims, he passed the rest of the night alone.'

'And what is his profession?' asked the judge.

'A botanist, ma'am,' was the reply. 'Mr Lockhart, I am reliably informed, is a world famous expert on trees.'

The hint of a snigger ran round the crowded courtroom; not what many would have thought of as man's work.

'Silence,' rapped Dee, 'or I'll have you all for contempt. A serious crime has been perpetrated. We are here to establish the truth.'

The facts, it transpired, were unnervingly simple. When her husband had failed to return the next day, the defendant had driven the children to the river and drowned them. *Their* children, mind, not anyone else's. Or so the prosecutor claimed. He was younger, more famous and far more flash but, had they known it, not remotely as experienced as the defence attorney. Dee knew it, though, and so did the bailiffs.

'Old Horace takes his time,' whispered one, 'but usually gets there in the end.'

Dee's gimlet eye was instantly upon him. Reprimanded, the man closed his mouth and settled back to hear what was coming next.

When it came for her to take the stand, the defendant mumbled and stared at the floor, unable to meet the prosecutor's eye. From her blank expression and lack of emotion it seemed she might be on drugs, though Dee knew for certain that not to be the case. She was under a twenty-four-hour suicide watch;

they refused to allow her the more humane option of seeking her own way out. The State of Louisiana took homicide seriously, evidenced by its draconian penal laws.

She answered monosyllabically, as though lacking the energy to fight. The court reporter would interpret this as indifference but the judge, with her deeper compassion, detected more. The prisoner was crushed by the loss of her children as any parent was bound to be. Face to face with her at last, even Dee was having doubts.

'Speak up,' she directed, gavel poised, 'and let the court hear what you have to say.'

Which wasn't much. She barely responded to the barrage of questions thrown at her so that, time after time, her elderly counsel was obliged to struggle to his feet in protest. The prosecution was too hard, he claimed, on a mother deranged by shock.

'Have pity,' he urged when his turn came to speak. 'And imagine yourself in her shoes.' Thus provoking further hissing from the crowd which obliged Dee to bring them to order. Any more interruptions and she'd clear the courtroom.

Patiently Horace drew answers from his client; there had been a row, she had lost control. Such things were not unheard of in a marriage. She was tired, she was fraught after many sleepless nights, the result of having a child with persistent earache who almost never stopped crying. The rest of what happened that night she had blanked. Understandable in view of what happened next.

'It sure doesn't look very hopeful for her,' Dee told Jackson that night. The absence of any kind of defence, apart from her unstable state of mind, was likely to go against her. Unless a reliable witness could be found to throw light upon what had occurred.

'Was he playing around?' Jackson was curious. He had rarely seen his wife so ignited.

'So the oily Orville would have us believe. Horace seems less convinced.'

The police had been in there in their usual clumsy way, yet turned up no dirt about Lockhart. At the botanical gardens, of which he was director, he could not have had a better press. Dedicated – almost visionary – he had brought real flair to the job. New Orleans was lucky to have him, he came so well qualified.

'Which still don't mean he ain't screwin' around.' The guy, after all, was only human and two small babies, only months apart, had probably driven him to his limits.

'Maybe. Yet still there is no hard evidence.' No illicit sightings, nor lipstick smudges; no phoney alibis, zilch. Apart from which, a woman like that, so calm, so controlled, so ultra-British, was unlikely to act out of character, even if provoked.

She'd been making quite a name for herself with

her delicate paintings of flowers. Did this fit the profile of a hardbitten killer? Dee still had her doubts.

'Yet she's not talking?'

'Not a word. She appears to be utterly shell-shocked. I doubt she knows what happened herself. I don't believe she is bluffing.'

'And how about him? What does *he* have to say?' Surely he should be up there, at her side.

'He seems scarcely more compos mentis than she is.' Although he could be faking it. Dee had not yet been able to talk to him. The doctor had him heavily sedated and under round-the-clock care.

'Then you can't convict her.' Jackson rolled himself a spliff. He always reasoned best when he was mellow.

'Only with proper evidence,' she said. There were still things that didn't quite add up. 'It's those children I can't get out of my mind. What kind of crazy lunatic could have done it?'

2

In London Rabbi Deborah Hirsch stood in her Belsize Park kitchen, straining the beans. It was a glorious golden Friday evening and she was preparing the Shabbat supper while listening to Sean Rafferty on Radio 3. They were just returned from their Easter vacation and the kids were scattered about the house, supposedly writing their holiday essays, due in on the first day of term. Neville had not yet resurfaced from the office.

'Why go there at all?' she had asked, once he'd brought in the luggage.

He needed to sort out his desk, he explained. The first day back was always chaotic. So she'd left him to it and got on with the meal, aware she would face a backlog herself when she turned up at the synagogue next week. Besides, life at home was inclined to be simpler without him under her feet.

The programme broke for the news which was when she heard it. Loud and clear and it froze her to the core; one of her former classmates from school was in trouble. Prize-winning artist Suzy Palmer – surely there couldn't be more than the one – was accused of murder in New Orleans, facing trial for her life. Horrified, Deborah flicked on the TV in time to see it confirmed. The family had only been gone two weeks; how had she missed the brouhaha that accompanies such a press story? There was a blurry shot of someone who might have been Suzy, almost eclipsed by a wall of meaty armed cops. All that muscle to control one frail woman; the Americans always did take things to extremes.

Rinsing her hands, Deborah grabbed the phone and punched out the number of Lisa Maguire, still, after all these years, her closest friend.

'You're back!' said Lisa, who was on the point of trying to get through to her.

'Last night,' said Deborah. 'Too late to call. There were hold-ups at the airport. I was going to ring you in any case and then I heard the news. Tell me it can't be our Suzy, can it?'

'I've checked already,' said Lisa, 'and it is. I'm afraid there isn't any doubt. I've been following the case through a New Orleans website and it's starting to look pretty bad. Which,' she added, 'doesn't just mean the kids.' In the American south they took the crime seriously; it was one of the last places in the world to put murderers to death.

'No way is she guilty, not our Suzy.' She had to be

one of the gentlest creatures alive. And how she had doted on both those babies, having waited so long to conceive. It had taken her till her mid-thirties to meet Mr Right.

'What does Andrew have to say? Have you spoken to him?' At least Suzy had a fine strong man at her side. Andrew Lockhart was the answer to her prayers; they had met by chance at Kew where he was working, hit it off immediately and were married within a few months. A happy ending for a lovely couple; everyone who knew them had agreed.

'That's the strange thing, I've tried repeatedly to reach him but he seems not to be picking up. Once someone answered but didn't speak, simply replaced the receiver.' Lisa was worried; it didn't make sense, though, of course, you could never be sure. It was possible that a fly legal adviser had warned him not to speak off the record. They were in trouble enough without talking to the press. She could not disagree.

'Poor man, he must be out of his mind.' Deborah still hadn't quite grasped all the implications. 'And so must her parents. I'll ring them right now.' At such a time they might well feel the need of some pastoral propping up. Although of a different faith, if they had one, Guy and Gwen Palmer were wonderful people with whom Deborah and Lisa had spent much of their formative years. She thought fleetingly of Kit, with the familiar pang, then shoved him out of her mind. All these occurrences in one family; it didn't bear thinking of. 'And after that I will email Helen. It is only fair she should know.'

'Probably does already,' said Lisa. 'Even in South Africa, these days, they do have television.'

'The Famous Five' they had styled themselves, after the Enid Blyton books, the year they first met at school aged eleven, to bond for the rest of their lives. Suzy was slightly younger than the rest, and had come up from the junior school; the others were part of the eleven plus intake and, within months, they had all become close friends. Intense, dark-haired Deborah, fiercely bright, and perky Lisa with her wild Irish blarney. Serious Helen, nose forever in a book, and ethereal Miranda who was not quite of this world, sang like an angel and looked like one too; perhaps just a little too perfect, they later agreed.

Helen Kruger had indeed heard the news, was as shaken as the others. Was even thinking of flying over to give what support she could to poor Guy and Gwen. One major tragedy in their lives had surely been more than they deserved but now this too; there weren't enough words to describe it. 'Or should we all be going to New Orleans?'

Lisa was the one with the legal training. 'It wouldn't make any difference,' she said. 'They would never permit us to see her. Not at this stage.' If she was to be convicted it would mean death row, which was notoriously hard to crack, especially by a bunch of out-of-towners whose presence would simply cause aggravation and do nothing to forward the case.

'I'll do what I can,' Lisa promised Helen, 'by taking things right to the top.' Before they could pass sentence, she meant, which might be uncomfortably soon. Since President Bush had been in the White House, the judicial processes had speeded up. The world now knew that the man was a killer; after the invasion of Iraq, things didn't look promising for Suzy.

The school had taught them from an early age that if one were in trouble, the others would be there for her. It was an ethic that they all shared, like telling the truth and putting their friendships first. They'd been taught to believe there was nothing they couldn't do; one of their number, after all, had been the first woman up Everest.

The following week they met for lunch, the two who still lived in London. Deborah had cancelled her afternoon appointments while Lisa, by a stroke of luck, was not due in court that day. She looked very trim, thought Deborah with envy, as she strode into Christopher's in her well-cut black suit and cripplingly stylish high heels. As slim and toned as she had been at school and at least ten years younger than her actual age; not, of course, that anyone was counting. Her auburn curls formed a halo round her head and her ivory skin was luminous, without a perceptible wrinkle.

'I hate you,' hissed Deborah, giving her a hug. No

matter how drastic her own regime might be, she still had a very long way to go to catch up with her friend. Also, she'd lately been indulging herself; the point of any holiday was to unwind.

'It's the bike,' explained Lisa cheerfully, 'plus trying to keep up with the boy.'

'How is he?' asked Deborah, studying the menu. 'Is everything in paradise still perfect?'

Lisa grinned and asked for the wine-list. 'I wouldn't go quite as far as that,' she said. In recent years, she'd preferred younger men and these days lived on a painted canal-boat with a jazz musician she had picked up at Ronnie Scott's. She rode her bicycle daily to her chambers and worked out rigorously three times a week. How she fitted in all that work as well remained a mystery to Deborah.

'I don't know where you find the energy,' she sighed, wilting at the thought. 'These days I fall asleep straight after the news.'

'It's sex,' said Lisa, with a complicit wink. 'The fact is, he can't get enough.'

'Lucky you.' Deborah pondered the merits of salmon carpaccio then gave in and ordered the pasta.

'Go for it, girl,' said Lisa approvingly, ordering the same. No matter how much she indulged herself, she seemed never to put on so much as an ounce. 'How are the kids getting on?'

'They're fine and really enjoyed the trip. As well they might; it cost us a bomb.' Instead of Israel, this year the Hirsches had splashed out and gone to Mauritius. More relaxing and less of a headache, with all that was happening in the Middle East. And lately Deborah had been worrying about Neville, whose working hours seemed to be growing so much longer that these days she hardly ever saw him at all. They had definitely needed that break together; besides, could hardly describe themselves as hard up.

'Abby must soon be doing her GCSEs.' The daughter had followed the mother to the school.

'Next year.'

'God, I can't say I envy her. All those tedious hours of revision. How many subjects is she taking, poor kid?'

'Nine,' said Deborah, secretly proud. 'They are all so brainy these days.' The fact she'd got four As with distinction herself was something she now seemed to overlook. And she'd gone on to Cambridge to get a first, which was what her fond father had expected.

The pasta arrived, with salad on the side, plus a bottle of chilled Pinot Grigio.

'Usually I try not to drink in the day,' said Deborah, helping herself liberally to cheese. 'But this counts as an exception, wouldn't you say?'

Which brought them sharply to the subject of the lunch: what could they possibly do to rescue poor Suzy?

'I am horribly afraid they'll go through with it,' said Lisa, who was now in regular contact with a Louisiana law firm. 'Unless some new piece of evidence emerges to put her firmly in the clear. If only she would be more forthcoming; it seems she has genuinely blanked. Not surprising, considering what happened; losing two babies would drive anyone insane. She won't even open up to her own legal team. Not good.'

'Have you any idea who's in charge?' Deborah asked.

'Someone called Horace Cutts,' said Lisa, who'd been hot on the case since the news had first broken. 'An old-style radical, now semi-retired but in whom my American colleagues have absolute faith. He's inclined to be slow and a tad pedantic but gets there in the end, they say, and, more than that, believes in Suzy's innocence.' The only reason he had taken the case; everyone else approached had refused to commit.

'Ought we go out there and interfere?'

'And end up in the clink ourselves? You're joking.' It had been Helen's suggestion but what did she know? Her bright, incisive mind was fogged with research, though she claimed to have a theory that might just hold water. 'All we can try to do is talk to Andrew who, it appears, isn't answering his phone.'

Andrew Lockhart, the most decent man on earth, had always been so amenable in the past, seemingly not threatened by their closeness. They had known him only a comparatively short time but what they had seen, had all liked. He'd had the intelligence to marry Suzy which showed he had excellent taste.

Why wasn't he, then, beside her now, holding her hand?

'There could be any number of reasons,' said Lisa, though without much conviction. 'By the way,' she asked, 'did you manage to reach the parents?'

Deborah nodded. 'As you might expect, they are devastated with worry and pure terror. Can't take in what is going on and, as usual, blaming themselves.'

'For what?'

'They feel they have somehow let her down. Like Kit, all those years ago.' Suzy's brother had died in his twenties and his name wasn't mentioned much these days. Deborah fell silent, having disinterred his ghost. 'Do you realise he'd be in his forties by now? I'd really love to know how he'd have turned out.'

Lisa considered it thoughtfully. 'I hate to say it,' she eventually said, 'but probably paunchy and balding. You know how those tall athletic types go to seed.'

Sacrilege, the Palmers would have thought, but at least it had helped to improve the mood of the meal.

Christopher Palmer, golden boy, star of the local cricket club and one of the reasons, though they'd die before admit it, that Suzy's friends had so much liked visiting her home. The Palmers lived in a rambling house with crooked oak beams and whitewashed walls, in Pinner, a prosperous North London suburb, just thirty minutes from the school. Behind the neatly-trimmed privet hedge lay a wilderness garden with a

22

frog-infested pond, the whole place a riot of dragon-flies and wild flowers. Suzy's mother, the inestimable Gwen, had presided over it like a magic kingdom, encouraging her children, from the time they were small, to develop their own imaginations. A teacher herself before her marriage, she had thrown her energies wholeheartedly instead into being an exemplary parent. She thought up exciting holiday projects to entertain and inspire them and also help develop any latent talent. It was she who had been responsible for encouraging Suzy to draw and she'd also helped Kit with his maths and Latin when boning up for exams. She'd imbued both children with a sense of fair play, along with consideration for others. She encouraged them both to bring home their friends, was at her most fulfilled baking cakes for their tea.

'Your mum's a marvel,' was the general consensus and, indeed, she seemed very content. A close family unit, happy and secure, was all she aimed for once she'd made the decision to put her teaching career on hold and allow her children to come first. At the time it had seemed the right thing to do; later she may have been less sure. But her husband had his own accountancy practice so that money was never a problem and the children thrived from knowing she'd be there when they came home for their tea. Neither was ever sent away to school; one of the benefits of where they lived was access to the very best education.

'I wonder if she resented it,' said Deborah. 'Sacrificing her career to put family first.' It wouldn't ever happen now, certainly in the Hirsch ménage where Deborah ruled and made most of the major decisions. But she also worked long hours, like her husband, repeating the precedent set by her own mother.

'I don't know,' said Lisa, who still kept in touch. 'She has certainly never said so. It was Gwen's example that influenced Suzy, another reason I can't believe this has happened.'

They had all loved Gwen who'd been like a second mother, one with the time to listen to what they said. At her instigation, they had started their regular teas on the final day of every holidays, before they went back to school. 'The Eve of Waterloo' Guy had dubbed it and, right up until their final year, they never missed out on it once. But only ever at Suzy's house, under the watchful eye of her caring mother.

'Did anyone think of contacting Olivia?' asked Lisa as the bill arrived. They hadn't made any decision yet as to how they should proceed except that Lisa would take care of the legal side while Deborah would do all she could to comfort the Palmers. They would keep in email touch with Helen who'd be over in a flash if she were needed. She had offered to come but Lisa had told her to wait.

Deborah was startled by the mention of Olivia; hadn't thought of her in years. She remembered now she had seen her at the wedding and on one occasion since. For reasons she wouldn't go into now, they had never really got on. Lisa, aware of the situation, tried firmly to push home her point. Like it or not, she'd been part of their set and had every right to know what was going on.

'She was one of us, you can't exclude her.' She dropped her credit card on the bill; they took it in turns to pay. 'And, furthermore, whatever you may think, in a way she was Suzy's closest friend.'

3

'What *does* the poor child look like?' thought Gwen Palmer the first time Olivia came to the house. The occasion was Suzy's thirteenth birthday party; Olivia had only been at the school a couple of weeks.

The teacher had had a quiet word with Gwen. 'Her father's away in the forces,' she'd explained, 'and her mother, sadly, is dead.'

Whoever was now taking care of the child had decked her out like a yellow meringue in layers of couturier organdie on a stiflingly hot afternoon. Teamed with white socks and brown Clarks sandals, the outfit looked more appropriate for a garden party than for just a school chum's birthday tea. It was a Saturday in mid-September at the end of the hottest summer in two hundred years. Gwen's usually luxuriant garden was looking decidedly droopy, despite the recent lift of the hosepipe ban. But the front door stood invitingly open and someone had laced fairy lights through the trees. The Palmers were good at this sort of occasion, each one a lavish celebration.

'This is Olivia Fernshaw,' said Suzy, still not certain why the new girl was there. Her mother, where lame ducks were concerned, was a law unto herself. Outside a cab was pulling away as Deborah's father's Daimler drew up and deposited his daughter on the doorstep. Deborah was wearing the statutory jeans, with one of her mother's exotic silk shirts knotted below her impressive cleavage, and sporting new contact lenses. With large hoop earrings and hair piled high, she looked at least seventeen. As the only child of indulgent parents, she succeeded in staying one jump ahead. Her classmates crowded around her now, ignoring the new girl completely. 'Can you really see as well as with glasses? Don't you find it yucky sticking them in?'

'Let's go and find you a glass of fruit punch,' said Gwen, propelling Olivia by the shoulder. It wasn't just that the dress was dreadful but also it didn't fit. It was far too loose for her scrawny body and, against the pallor of her complexion, the colour killed her stone dead. Her mousy hair hung lank and straight; no effort at all had been made to pretty her up. And her spectacles, which were National Health, were mended on one corner with sticky tape.

'Have you come far?' Gwen manoeuvred her away from the shrieking throng still besieging Deborah.

'From Stanmore,' said Olivia politely. Twenty minutes' taxi ride along the Uxbridge Road. Her voice was

27

low with a Scouse inflection that instantly betrayed her roots. Poor little soul, thought Gwen with compassion, she could hardly be more of a misfit. But the school was adept at bringing them on, an excellent melting-pot. And she must be bright to have got in at all, though they certainly wouldn't give her an easy ride.

A trestle table had been set up under the trees where Suzy's father, whom they rarely saw, was ladling out alcohol-free punch. Wearing a long white apron like a chef, he was playing the role to the hilt. A mild-mannered man with a diffident smile, he threw himself into this kind of occasion provided he wasn't expected to do too much. By the time he came home from the office most nights the kids had been fed and were doing their prep. They'd emerge around nine for *Rock Follies*, Suzy's favourite, or *Starsky and Hutch*, which was Kit's.

'In my day,' he was always telling them, 'we weren't allowed to watch at all on school nights.'

Things, however, had changed fundamentally, as demonstrated by the arrival of Lisa Maguire. She and Deborah were sparring partners when it came to hogging the limelight. Today she was dressed in true punk style, complete with torn T-shirt, fishnet tights, and strategic safety-pins. Her normally pretty ginger curls were contorted grotesquely into ugly spikes and her face was plastered with flat white makeup from which her eyes burned like coals. If pretty Deborah looked seventeen, Lisa could pass as a tacky twenty-five.

28

'Gracious,' thought Gwen, almost doing the un-thinkable and inquiring if Mrs Maguire was aware that her daughter was out dressed like that. Instead she simply asked Lisa how she'd got there, not on a bus she hoped.

'My brother dropped me off on his bike.' The older, tearaway brother that would be who, from all they had heard from Suzy, managed to stay just this side of the law. Which, since his father was a cop, must involve him in treading a very fine line. Though Gwen tried never to be judgemental. Other people's children weren't her business.

'And will come to collect me if I call him at the pub.' Lisa had the number scrawled on the back of her hand.

'No need for that, dear,' Gwen said hastily. 'Suzy's father will happily drive you home.'

These girls. They had all been so sweet when she first knew them, endearing in their tunics and flannel blouses, in those days obsessed with lacrosse and net-ball and comparing their collections of Barbie dolls. But now they had reached the cusp of their teens; what a difference a couple of years made. Gwen looked from Deborah and Lisa to the new girl, and could scarcely credit they could be the same age or even the same generation. One thing they had in common, though; they were all quite exceptionally bright.

There was a sudden commotion from within the house and Miranda Sinclair came tripping out, face

29

lit up and all aglow with excitement. She flew like a frail little bird to Gwen, burying her face in her skirt. 'I wanted to bring the pony,' she whispered, 'but Mummy wouldn't let me.'

'Probably all for the best, dear,' said Gwen, fingering the child's amazing hair. 'Think what the neighbours would have said if he'd started eating their hedges.'

Miranda giggled but kept her face hidden. Despite the off-the-shoulder top and scarlet bandanna worn Woodstock-style, she might have been several years younger than the rest, even as little as ten. Gwen was fond of the delicate child who looked like a porcelain figurine. Exquisitely pretty and bright as a button, she possessed the most amazing voice which was always much in demand. Also she could dance like a dervish. There seemed to be no limit to her talent.

'Are you going to sing?' asked Gwen, privately fearing that too much use might strain the child's vocal chords. But the parents, both out-of-date showbiz professionals, loved to show her off, decking her out like an old-style hippie, which was where they were permanently rooted.

'I've brought my Abba tapes,' said Miranda, 'so everyone can join in.'

All too soon, thought Gwen with regret, it would get to be boys and dating. Let them remain at this innocent stage at least for another few years.

* * *

Olivia stood at the edge of the group, observing them all with mistrust. Another posting, yet another school; she was sick of having to move around and never putting down roots. Of course they'd worn jeans but her aunt wouldn't listen, thought for a party she ought to dress up. And although Aunt Sarah worked in fashion, she still made horrendous mistakes. Like this yellow monstrosity she'd brought home from the shop without first checking Olivia's size or if the colour would go with her sallow skin. Olivia cringed when she saw the pity in Suzy's mother's eyes. Still, she supposed, her aunt and uncle had been good to take her in though she still hadn't figured out why.

She had only been with them a couple of weeks, knew them no better than this bunch of new classmates, and assumed that before too long she'd be moving on. This was the fifth school she'd been at already because of her father's lifestyle. Whenever she started to make a friend, off he would go to another distant posting, trailing her behind like unwanted baggage. Usually he stuck her in boarding-schools where the other pupils were snooty and posh. It might have done things for her speech and veneer but had not made her feel secure.

This time things were different, though. Her aunt had opted for a day school. Suddenly, out of a clear blue sky, her dead mother's sister had intervened despite the fact that they'd hardly met and had had little contact in years. She had no idea what had caused the change of heart, except that Stanmore was convenient for the school which, as her aunt kept reminding her, was one of the best in the country. But now she was with them it was only too plain that they hadn't really wanted her at all. If they had really cared about children, they'd have surely had some of their own.

She was sick of having to make new friends, though Suzy's mother seemed nice enough and Suzy was more approachable than the rest. They didn't seem interested in getting to know her, being far too involved with themselves. She wished she could slip away and go home but her aunt would not be pleased. She insisted Olivia should try to fit in and, while she was living beneath her roof, her word was what went.

'Now, just you behave,' her father had told her, forgetting to kiss her, just patting her head. He never had shown her much affection but, then, she saw him so little. These days she hardly knew him at all, his absences abroad were so extended. And this time he hadn't worn uniform, just gone off as he was, in his tracksuit, with his few possessions in a canvas roll.

'Come away from that window,' Aunt Sarah had said sharply when the unmarked van came to pick him up and he hadn't even turned for a final wave. Olivia knew little about his profession; he was some kind of jobbing soldier, she thought, who seemed to be always on the move. Sometimes she fantasised that perhaps he was a spy which might account for his reticence when he was home.

The house was quite nice, she granted them that, close to the common with spectacular views, though it did mean having to trudge up the hill after school with a heavy satchel. She even had her own room, a first, furnished for her specially with a built-in desk, a bookcase and a reading-lamp. She had lined her glass animals along a shelf to make it feel more like her own. There was a spacious closet, though she hadn't many clothes, as well as a chest of drawers. And downstairs two television sets, one in the kitchen they said she could watch after she'd finished her prep.

Aunt Sarah and Uncle Gerald worked hard, running their own exclusive dress shop. They had given Olivia her own set of keys and each afternoon, when she got home from school, she had to get her own tea. There was usually something left in the fridge – her aunt took seriously her role of guardian – but Olivia was growing bored with healthy eating. Her classmates often went out after school for pizzas or burgers, which sounded more fun, but Aunt Sarah said that was vulgar. They weren't spending all this money, she said, to raise Olivia like a guttersnipe. She had left all that behind in Merseyside.

Occasionally she asked about her mother but her aunt's responses were oddly vague. They had never really kept in close touch, had always lived too far apart and, besides, there was the age gap. Olivia had been born in Liverpool after her uncle and aunt had left. These things happened in families, said Aunt Sarah. People went their separate ways; you couldn't expect to live in each other's pockets.

Which wasn't at all how things seemed with the Palmers who were close and obviously liked each other a lot.

Guy lit the barbecue then, while he was fanning the flames and the girls were crowding round to watch, Suzy's brother and a bunch of his pals came strolling into the garden, clutching beer cans.

'Hi!' said his father. 'Are you going to join us? I could certainly use some extra hands.'

'Sorry,' said Kit, with an engaging smile. 'We have just dropped by on our way to the Rose and Crown.'

Olivia had heard the girls giggling about Kit, who was five years older than Suzy. Tall and athletic with sun-bleached hair, he looked more like his father than his sister. Suzy was more or less average height with freckles and a happy-go-lucky grin. She grabbed her brother by the arm to stop him leaving.

'Stay,' she begged. 'Miranda's going to sing.'

Olivia saw the way Kit looked at Miranda, with growing warmth in his light blue eyes. She might be childish and young for her age but there was something about her fragile prettiness that hinted at what would come in a handful of years. Envy gripped Olivia;

she was sick of being ignored, by boys, in particular, who never seemed to see her.

'She is awfully pretty, isn't she?' said Helen, with frank admiration. The nice thing about Miranda was her seeming unawareness of her charm, one reason people took to her so quickly. When they made Miranda, they broke the mould; that's what the other girls said.

'So what are you singing?' asked Kit fondly, ruffling her shimmering hair. To him, like Suzy's other friends, she was little more than an endearing kid but he'd known her most of her life and found her cute.

'"Dancing Queen",' said Miranda. 'And "Waterloo".'

Kit glanced round at his friends for approval and they shrugged. The pub could wait; they had all evening and the real action wouldn't start for a couple of hours.

'Have you got enough food?' Kit looked at his father.

'Enough to feed an army, old chap.'

After they were done with the sausages and burgers, Gwen popped inside for the cake. Pink and silver with thirteen candles, which Suzy blew out in one breath. Everyone clapped and kissed her then and Miranda led them in singing 'Happy Birthday'. There were gifts to be opened but not till later, to avoid embarrassment.

Suzy's friends, the so-called Famous Five, were grouped around her in a huddle. All were outgoing with an ease of manner Olivia doubted she could ever attain. Most of her life she had felt invisible; people tended to look round her rather than at her.

'Dance with me,' said Deborah provocatively, swaying in front of the boys, arms outstretched. With her luscious body and undulating hips they could hardly take their eyes off her. That one's going to be trouble, thought Guy, relaxing with a beer having finished his chef's bit. He had known them all for the past two years and was watching, with interest, them growing up. Not his little Suzy, though, who continued entirely unspoilt. Perhaps because of the older brother, she had so far shown no interest in boys. The house was invariably full of them so that they were an integral part of her life.

'I am sure that's the right way to bring them up,' Gwen was always saying. 'Let them rub along together and develop at their natural pace. There's time enough in the future for that sort of thing.'

She was surprised when, on Wednesday afternoon, she had a phone call from Olivia, the sad little shrimp in the ghastly yellow dress.

'Aren't you in school, dear?' It was not yet three-thirty. Normally they didn't let them out till four.

'It's a study period. I'm allowed to work at home.' She had, she explained, rung to thank Gwen for the party. 'I really love your house.'

'Then you must come again,' said Gwen, wondering how Suzy would take it. At this age they were inclined to be territorial; she was never quite sure who was in and who was not.

'What on earth was she thinking about, ringing you?' asked Suzy, predictably indignant.

'Being polite,' said her mother crisply. 'It would do you no harm to pick up some manners from her.' It said a lot for the child who appeared to be otherwise neglected. 'Why not ask her for the weekend?' she said. The uncle and aunt worked Saturdays, which meant she'd be all alone in the house. Not a nice way to bring her up; Gwen wondered if they knew what they were doing.

Reluctantly Suzy did as she was bid though a stranger would ruin the cosiness of her home. Olivia arrived in a taxi, as before, wearing an ugly unfashionable dress at least two sizes too large.

'I wonder if she even looks at her,' thought Gwen, stirred to pity once again. The aunt had formerly been a model which was why, in middle age, she still looked good. But the dress was dreadful and the child looked really unhappy. 'Lend her some jeans and a T-shirt,' she said. 'She might as well be comfortable while she's here.'

Olivia's visits became regular; she'd phone Gwen, sounding fragile and dejected, and get invited to lunch. She wasn't much fun and desperately needy, seeking Gwen's attention all the time. She even helped in the kitchen, which made Kit and Suzy groan.

'Be kind,' warned Gwen when she heard them mock her. 'Remember she's not had much of a life of her own.'

Despite her affection for Gwen, however, Olivia was reserved towards Guy and Kit. It was clear she wasn't used to male company, seemed relieved when both were out of the house. Yet Kit, when he was around, was friendly and generous with his time. He really enjoyed their girlish chat and taught them underarm bowling on the lawn. In the street, however, it was a different matter; he would walk straight past as if he didn't know them. Boys his age would not be seen dead acknowledging little girls. Suzy, well-used to it, hardly noticed but Olivia's pride was stung.

'That's just boys for you,' Gwen explained. 'Wait till you are a few years older and you'll have them eating from your hand.'

'Can't you get rid of her?' asked Deborah ruthlessly, who wouldn't have stood it for a second. An only child, she was used to being indulged.

'No,' said Suzy miserably, 'my mum would never allow it. Olivia's taken a shine to her which she's just too stupid to see.'

They were lazing around in the memorial garden, teaching themselves to smoke. Lisa was posted on staff alert, perched on the back of the bench. Should anyone in authority approach, she'd be able to see them in ample time.

Suzy had tried to talk to her mother but Gwen refused to listen.

'Don't be so mean,' was all she would say. 'She has not had your advantages.' The uncle and aunt sounded chilly and withdrawn, had never even bothered to thank the Palmers. And the father, it seemed, had disappeared. Olivia had no inkling of where he was. 'She's a sad little soul who could use a bit of spoiling. The least you can do is make her feel at home.'

So Suzy was stuck with Olivia at weekends though she knew it wasn't her she came to see. Normally she went to the tennis club on Saturdays but Olivia only wanted to stay at home and follow Gwen pathetically round the garden. She had never known a mother of her own and was abnormally clingy until even sunny-natured Suzy started to resent her. 'My mum can't resist a charity case. We are always putting up with waifs and strays.'

At school they were now perceived as best friends but Suzy's set knew better and all agreed they would never allow her to butt in.

'Thanks,' said Suzy, glad of their support. It was good to know they were on her side and saw Olivia for what she was, a pushy interloper.

'She wouldn't fit in,' declared Deborah flatly. 'Besides, who ever heard of the Famous Six?'

4

The New Orleans police were out in force, dredging the river where the car went in, searching for what evidence they could find. It had taken a crane to raise the waterlogged Buick and recover the sad drowned bodies of the children. Within hours the story was all over the news, being milked by the world media for all it was worth.

'This is the woman,' said the TV reporter, beside a mugshot of a happier Suzy, 'arrested this morning in the Garden District for the brutal slaying of her children.' The strange thing was, she had not resisted which seemed to proclaim her guilt. Also she was an artist which went against her. Drugs and booze and no moral code; foreign, too, which made her even more suspect.

'From what I hear,' Lisa told the others, 'it's a media frenzy and getting worse.' In England there would have been legal restraints until after the case had come to trial. In New Orleans they were baying for blood and talking about execution.

'I still think we should be there,' emailed Helen, already arranging to park the boys. She was having a problem with her conscience because she'd done nothing to forestall the crime. It was clear from what she had heard already that Suzy was suffering from post-natal depression which can develop into psychosis with terrible consequences. She called herself an expert on the subject yet hadn't intervened when she might have done. She wanted to go there as a witness and use her formidable qualifications to help to sway the jury in Suzy's favour.

'Leave it,' said Lisa, 'until we know more. If we go there now, we will only be in the way.'

The police had talked briefly to Andrew Lockhart who was still under heavy sedation. He was not compos mentis enough to say much, too devastated by the children's deaths to think very clearly about anything. But his colleagues at the botanical gardens had given him a firm alibi. He had been there, working, since the early hours and not been out of sight since. The first he knew about the accident was when the police arrived. They were on their way to arrest his wife, they told him.

Andrew, of course, had rushed to her side, arriving just a little too late. She was already handcuffed and in the car and he hadn't been able to talk to her. She had looked quite ghastly, with flat glazed eyes, and had shown no sign of even recognising him. She had not denied that she'd been driving the car or that the children had been with her all the time. When they asked her why she had gone to the river, she couldn't even remember. There had been a row, she admitted that, but from that point her memory was a blank.

The nanny, Bonnie, was interviewed but had been off duty that day. There had been some woman who was sometimes there and stepped in to help with the children. The baby had been suffering from earache for days which meant the parents had gone without sleep. When asked what sort of a mother Suzy was, Bonnie had sung her praises. It wasn't easy, as anyone knew, to raise two children just months apart especially when she was not in the first flush of youth.

'Also, she had a career,' said the news, implying dereliction of her duty. Her fame was widespread, she was much-acclaimed in England. If she'd given her children her full attention, this tragedy might have been avoided. Women who worked were anathema to many of the New Orleans townsfolk.

A neighbour, a writer, had heard raised voices late in the evening before the car drove off. She'd been reading by an open window. No, she hardly knew the Lockharts but had heard they were very nice. Very much in love, was the general opinion. She'd been planning to invite them over for dinner as soon as she had finished her latest book.

'So where did it all go so wrong?' Deborah asked but Lisa could give her no explanation. They had grown up together as close as sisters and would stand by Suzy whatever the outcome might be.

'If only they hadn't moved to New Orleans.'

'Or had the babies so close together.' Helen was already hinting at possible post-natal causes which appalled them.

'If she had stayed at home,' said Lisa, 'Gwen would have known how to cope.'

5

Three of them – Deborah, Lisa and Helen – had all been exemplary students. Deborah, when she wasn't clowning around, took her future the most seriously of them all. Her economist father and stage designer mother both encouraged her to study hard, alongside which she showed definite leadership promise.

'Once she is over the boy phase,' said her teachers, 'that one will run the full mile.' It didn't help that she'd got physical assets which her mother's flair for fashion only enhanced. But her teachers weren't worried; they saw her potential. Girls as bright as Deborah Greenberg usually took their schooling in their stride, gathering along the way straight As and lasting friends.

'I predict she'll end up Prime Minister,' said one teacher. 'She certainly has the brains and application.'

'Not to mention the chutzpah.'

Which was not altogether a definite plus, certainly

not at this age. There were those in the staffroom who felt the odd slap would not be entirely out of place. Precocious was the word most often used, not always with admiration.

Lisa Maguire was more of a sprinter, distracted from her studying during term-time then swotting frenetically through the run-up to exams to cross the finishing-line with flying colours.

'There is something about Lisa that thoroughly exhausts me.' Nevertheless, she was a favourite with the staff. She came from a rowdy family of kids where survival was an essential skill picked up at a formative age. Her frazzled mother seemed to shell them out; how they coped on a policeman's salary was a subject of much discussion in the school. Luckily Lisa was a scholarship girl. For now, at least, her education was ensured.

Helen Goddard was altogether quieter and, in some ways, more erudite. Science had always been her thing. Her mother, a former lab technician, on a whim had married the professor. And brought forth Helen with her straight dark hair and slightly preoccupied smile. At thirteen she seemed almost middle-aged. She dressed primly, both in and out of school, with her pleated skirts and round-necked jumpers over spotless shirts with neatly turned-back cuffs.

'Can't you just see her in forty years?'

'Probably winning a Nobel Prize.'

'But never, ever off duty. Not for a second.'

Suzy Palmer was a slightly different case, academically undistinguished but developing quite a flair for drawing and getting a lot of support from her teacher, Miss Holbrook. At forty-one, Maggie was an established character, a fellow of the Royal Academy, yet one who preferred to remain a teacher than take her chances in the cutthroat arena of fine art. Nobody's fool, she had seen them come and go and acquired from experience a personal modus vivendi. She enjoyed the anonymity the school provided, which also gave her space to do her own work. She was more prestigious than many parents knew; the school could be very discreet when it came to such things. And she was certainly expert at spotting raw talent and doing what she could to help it thrive.

What she primarily recognised in Suzy was her visual intelligence, a quality not easily defined. It had less to do with her draughtsmanship and more with the way she perceived things generally. Though lacking in basic confidence, in her art she was meticulous. She came from a solid home environment, with parents who encouraged and praised her, but she wasn't even interested in aiming for the fast track, as opposed to Deborah and Lisa. Nor did her father's flippant attitude help. He doted on his younger child, would do anything at all to make her happy, yet fundamentally failed to comprehend what all this drawing nonsense was about.

'Instead of just sitting there doodling,' he would

say, on his frequent evening forays to the fridge, 'you'd do better to work a bit harder at your maths.' Which, to his mind, was the ultimate qualification and should stand her in good stead for the rest of her life. Though secretly he also assumed that his daughter would marry well.

Suzy, at the kitchen table, doubtless damaging her sight, would turn on him her thoughtful smile, while still absorbed in the piece of work in hand. She had glossy brown hair and green-flecked eyes and a smile that radiated charm. Less than pretty, she was nonetheless engaging, attracting people with her natural warmth, inherited from her mother. Right from the start she had been little trouble, a placid baby who was rarely cross and had grown into a quiet and biddable child.

'I'm no good at maths,' she reminded him, not for the first time. 'I can't get my head around fractions and things.' All that close figure-work gave her headaches which had nothing to do with straining her eyes. It was all about the left side of the brain but she was too absorbed in her drawing to try to explain to her father, who wouldn't have listened.

'Whatever you say, dear,' was his stock response. Then he'd amble back to the living-room where Gwen was engrossed in television, knitting needles clicking as she watched. Their life was calm and uneventful. They existed in a state of quiet harmony.

At school, however, Suzy came into her own, especially in her free time. Miss Holbrook was giving her extra tuition which had nothing to do with the regular syllabus but more with free expression and dexterity.

'No need to involve your parents yet,' she said. 'But I think you have an unusual talent.' She also enjoyed the child's quiet presence, found her company restful. While Suzy drew, she'd stretch canvases and refill the little pots of poster paint. And as she did, she would reminisce about the wilder escapades of her youth. There wasn't a husband but there had been lovers and the stories were lurid and intense. While Suzy was still in her early teens, her teacher maintained a modicum of decorum, but as the child grew older and the friendship deepened, so the raunchy confidences spilled out, to Suzy's private delight. Miss Holbrook became the pivot of her life which soon had the rest of her circle on to her case.

'I reckon you've got a crush on her,' taunted sex-obsessed Deborah. 'Why else would you rather spend time with her than hanging out with us?'

Suzy said nothing, merely smiled. There was no way Deborah would understand the rapport she had with this older woman who gave her so much of her time. She was well aware that her parents loved her but Miss Holbrook believed in her talent and that meant more.

Occasionally Suzy had tea with her, at her cluttered studio in Finchley Road. The place smelt deliciously of turpentine and paint and you had to shift piles of canvases in order to find anywhere to perch. Miss Holbrook, who had travelled extensively, brewed fragrant tea in a samovar and Suzy would sit cross-legged on the ottoman, soaking in the atmosphere along with the colourful tales. Though by no means good-looking, the teacher had a definite flair and a restless energy that kept her on the move, endlessly pottering with this and that and shifting things around. She slept in a narrow bed in the next room, covered with a dusty Turkish rug and also crammed with assorted pictures and books. She swore like a trooper and smoked like a chimney. She was by far the most exotic being that Suzy had ever known.

'Sometimes I'm up all night,' Miss Holbrook told her. 'I find the grey matter is at its most potent once the rest of the world has gone to sleep.' She shared the cramped space with a sinuous grey cat, who disapproved when she lit up, flicking imaginary ash from his fur as he waited to be fed. It was a way of life that Suzy envied. Her family home in conservative Pinner seemed dull by comparison. She longed for the day she could get away and have some adventures of her own.

Miss Holbrook allowed her to look through her sketches, flattered by the girl's intelligent interest and an awareness beyond her years.

'I'd die to be this good,' said Suzy.

'You will, I promise, if you work hard enough. You have two great gifts, a natural eye and the patience to get it right. Also you're brave enough to start again if you think you've made a mistake. All good qualities in an artist. I have absolutely no doubt that, in the future, the world will hear more of Suzy Palmer.'

While Suzy was dreaming of a life as an artist, somewhere Bohemian like Paris or Prague, and the other three were assiduously swotting, Miranda was being groomed for eventual stardom. She was at the school because her mother was an Old Girl and was hoping to transfer to a classy stage school. She'd been having voice coaching since the age of eight and showed every promise of making it to the top. The looks were a mix of the glamorous hippie parents but the voice was a throwback to a famous forebear who had once sung *Tosca* in Milan. At thirteen, Miranda was allowed no spare time. Outside the school curriculum, which they rigidly made her stick to, every single second she had was crammed with private tuition. She had tap-dancing classes on Saturday mornings, followed by piano in the afternoon, while her voice coach arrived on the dot of five to put her through her vocal exercises. Wanda and Cedric, her besotted parents, stood listening, spellbound, just outside the door.

'I think they work that child too hard.' Gwen, as a former teacher, disapproved. 'You are only young once and she's a mere scrap of a thing.' Thoughts of Judy Garland's mother added to her disquiet. To her mind, talent was more likely to emerge when treated with appropriate respect. Little Miranda was bright as a penny but her fragile frame was not strong enough yet to support that miraculous voice.

'The school would intervene,' said Guy, 'if they felt she was being overstretched.' He liked the Sinclairs who were excellent value, both of them larger than life. Cedric had once been a Black and White Minstrel while Wanda had danced with Lionel Blair. They had stayed thin and lovely, as show people can, and could usually be relied upon to spice up any gathering.

Miranda's pixie prettiness, however, belied a razor sharp brain. If it weren't for the voice, she'd have excelled some other way and secretly had a desire to train as a doctor. She liked the school, it suited her well; was reluctant to have to move on. 'Voices wear out,' she explained to the others, 'whereas letters after your name you never lose.'

'Then do what Jonathan Miller did,' said practical, down-to-earth Helen. 'The doctor bit first and the singing later. That way you'll be covered all round.'

'My parents would never allow it,' said Miranda. She knew they had her whole future already mapped out.

When, the year they turned thirteen, Olivia was suddenly dumped in their midst, no-one took much notice of her once the novelty had worn off. She was thin and nervous as a jumpy cat and not at all outgoing. Kept to herself and didn't make waves as though always expecting the worst from life. The consensus: not much fun.

Deborah viewed her with pitiless scorn. She could never respect a weakling. 'What does she think she looks like?' she said. 'Her clothes don't fit and she's always slightly grubby.'

'She lives with an aunt who works late in town.' Suzy felt it her duty to defend her. 'What used to be known as a latchkey kid. She doesn't have a mother.'

Deborah, as always, was airily dismissive; her mother, too, worked long hours. At a school like this there were certain standards that really should be upheld. She could stick her clothes in the washer, for heaven's sake, or even rinse them out in the sink as people on holiday did. To Deborah, everything was cut and dried but she had never known deprivation, the upheaval of having to follow when her father moved on. All Suzy knew had been gleaned from her mother in whom Olivia increasingly confided. Which didn't make Suzy like her any more but helped her glimpse the sadness beneath the veneer.

'She's just a poor little waif,' said Gwen, 'who has never in her life come first with anyone.'

Her constant presence got on Suzy's nerves and in the way of things she wanted to do. When Olivia was there, no more Finchley Road; she was never going to share Miss Holbrook with her. But her mother expected her to play the role of hostess. Olivia, after all, was Suzy's friend.

'Show her around the neighbourhood, dear. Remember, she is your guest. Take her down to the tennis club and introduce her to people.'

'But she doesn't play,' objected Suzy, who had private coaching at weekends.

'Well, take her to the pictures, then. There must be something on you'd both like to see.'

Olivia, however, had other ideas, preferring to stay in the house and talk to Gwen. It felt good to be part of a real home at last, with the warmth and stability she had always lacked. The cooking smells, the family chat, the distant hum of the mower on the lawn. Gwen tried to probe but without success. Olivia had been just too young.

'What exactly happened?' asked Gwen.

'I really don't know,' said Olivia. Neither her father nor her aunt would ever open up.

'It must have been a considerable blow, to be left like that with a baby.' As a regular soldier, always moving on, small wonder he'd had to farm her out. Olivia talked about the foster homes, mostly with distaste. Sometimes there'd been other children there too with none of whom she had stayed in touch. It was so depressing it made Gwen want to cry. When Christmas approached and she asked about her plans, Olivia said she had none. The uncle and aunt would be working late. The sales began on Boxing Day; it was their busiest season.

'Come here,' said Gwen and so it was fixed. Kit

and Suzy rolled their eyes but all to no avail. She would check with the aunt that it was all right, even though Olivia told her not to bother. They were used to being on their own, she said. Had still not yet adjusted to having her there.

'Better to be on the safe side,' said Guy. You never precisely knew. And Olivia, despite her perfect manners, was still a bit of a dark horse. Even now, after all these weeks, Guy still didn't feel he knew her. He was also aware that his children weren't pleased and how much it took to upset that equable pair.

But when Gwen made the call, Olivia was right.

'We are glad,' said the aunt, 'that she's making new friends.' And quickly rang off, without any further comment.

'Perhaps she checked with the school,' said Guy. Even in areas like this these days, you could not be too careful with your kids. One of the pluses of paying those steep fees had to be peace of mind. Every parent was carefully vetted before a child was admitted to the school. As with any exclusive club, you got only what you paid for.

The afternoon was practically over and Deborah still had her shopping to do. Holidays were all very well but went by far too quickly; she had put on a second load of washing before she even went out. Tomorrow she would be back at work, in full rabbinical swing; meetings, committees, a memorial service for a child who had died far too young of leukaemia. Sometimes it seemed there was death round every corner. She shuddered as she drove back to Belsize Park. If they were to act, it must be fast. Beyond that she dared not think.

Lisa was having similar thoughts as she walked the few blocks to her chambers. Suzy was one of life's innocents, accepting everybody at face value. Who else would have picked up a man in Kew Gardens and married him in two months? He had seemed nice enough but you couldn't always tell and, since they had then gone to live abroad, Lisa had not got to know him enough to form a more clued-up opinion. Just one further meeting, which she'd organised herself, but they'd all been there and the wine had flowed and all they had really done was enjoy themselves. From her years spent as an East End lawyer, she had learned a lot about the criminal mind. Things were not always what they seemed. You could never totally be sure.

Which brought her back to Olivia whom she'd always rather liked.

6

Markus was practising when Lisa got home and she stood for a while on the towpath, quietly listening. The eerie lament of the soaring tenor sax added a piquancy to the atmosphere of this quiet corner of Little Venice where they moored their boat. She waited until the conclusion of 'Blue Train', then wheeled her bike across the gangplank and secured it to the handrail at the rear. Markus was standing in the cabin doorway, wearing only combat trousers, low-slung.

'Exhibitionist!' She loved the way he looked, understood whenever she caught him like this what men saw in nubile girls. He lowered the instrument and carefully wiped the mouthpiece, exchanging her mock lascivious stare for a smouldering one of his own.

He grinned. 'You're back early.' He glanced at his watch. Usually Lisa worked until all hours and he ended up doing the cooking, which didn't faze him. Frau von Hagen had done a great job in raising a truly emancipated son though, of course, it might also have something to do with the age gap.

Lisa unlaced the track shoes she kept for the bike and peeled off her elegant jacket. It was a muggy evening, far too hot for formal clothing. All she wanted was to shower and change and then a big glass of something chilled before they even thought about anything else.

'I wasn't in court. Just had lunch with Deborah. Trying to figure out what we could do about Suzy.'

Markus's eyes were like chips of sapphire in the tanned perfection of his face. At times he reminded her faintly of Kit with his chiselled nose and humorous mouth, even the cleft in his chin. He laid the saxophone carefully in its case and drew her into his arms. He smelt of a mixture of sunshine and sweat so that all her instincts went on alert, even after that energetic bike-ride.

'Come inside while I take a shower. I can tell you, I could use a bit of a backrub.'

'At your service, ma'am.' He massaged her shoulders with pliable fingers then slapped her lightly on the rump and followed her inside.

Later, over dinner, she brought him fully up to speed. They sat out on deck and ate lightly-grilled steaks with Markus's speciality, shoestring French fries, which he'd developed into a fine art. He had opened a bottle of Chilean Cabernet and kept replenishing her glass.

She leaned back in the dimming light and gradually unwound.

'No need to get me pissed,' she said. 'There's still life left in the old dog.' She told him more about the Suzy situation and Markus listened sympathetically. He caressed her cheek with the back of his hand and asked what she planned to do. He rubbed his thumb lightly across her lined brow to relax it.

Lisa shook her head wearily. 'The truth is, I don't have a clue. We all assume Suzy is innocent, with nothing at all to back it up except that we've known her so long.' Before she dared talk to the New Orleans lawyers, she needed some real ammunition. The fact that she'd been at school with the defendant amounted to nothing in a capital trial with, so far, all the evidence stacked against her. Added to which she had virtually confessed, a pretty dire situation. Lisa was hoping to talk to Andrew, but had still been unable to reach him by phone.

'She left the kids in the car and they drowned which seems the sole basis of their case. The engine was running and the handbrake off. She is therefore, in their eyes, the obvious suspect. There were no eye-witnesses – none so far – and Suzy has made no attempt to defend herself. When the cops came to get her she didn't resist, just mutely allowed them to hand-cuff her and preceded them into the car. Put at its mildest, it doesn't look good.' How in the world it had happened, she couldn't imagine.

'And you've no idea why she might have done it?' Markus had met the Lockharts just that once and then only fleetingly. By the time he'd come into Lisa's life they were already married and living abroad. He didn't know Suzy but knew a lot about her. A man less secure might have grown resentful at how much Lisa talked about her friends. But in Markus's eyes that was just another virtue in this tough little package he had grown to adore. Lisa was feisty, courageous and bold as well as the most exciting woman he had encountered in his twenty-seven years. From a casual pickup she had become an obsession, the reason he lingered on in London instead of returning to Hamburg and his career.

'Absolutely none at all,' said Lisa. 'Nothing makes sense.'

She remembered how thrilled Suzy had been when she found out she was pregnant, wasting no time in spreading the news to her friends.

'I'd almost given up hope,' she confessed, on arrival back from China for the birth. 'Thought I had already left it too late.' Her fortieth birthday loomed horribly near and she had been desperate for a baby, though kept it deliberately secret from Andrew for fear of hurting his feelings. He might believe he had somehow failed her, which couldn't have been further from the truth. Just having him in her life was enough but now that she held baby Holly in her arms, her happiness was complete.

'See,' she said to her friends as they crowded round.

'She has Andrew's eyes and definitely Christopher's smile.' Kit, by then, had been dead thirteen years; it was touching that she believed that he might still live on. How they had laughed; only two days old and she reckoned she could see all this already?

'If you're thinking of sending her to the school,' said Lisa, 'you'd best put her name on the waiting-list right now.'

'Your parents must be over the moon,' said Deborah, joint godmother with Helen and Lisa. 'At last, a grand-child for them to spoil. How they must have longed for this day.' Then caught, with surprise, the sudden shadow that flickered for a moment in Suzy's eyes.

'Yes, well,' she said, her attention on the baby. 'Lately they've been through a spot of bother.' She said no more, just fiddled with the fringe of the exquisite shawl her mother had hand-crocheted. 'But you're right, of course.' The smile returned and her green-flecked eyes glowed with pleasure. 'If they had their way, they would camp here all night but the hospital won't allow it.'

When, in only eleven months, Holly was followed by Jonah, Suzy had been similarly over the moon. By then the Lockharts were in New Orleans but she kept in regular touch via email and sheaths of jpeg photo-graphs to show what marvels she'd produced. And, indeed, on that point she could not be faulted; both babies were indisputably gorgeous, the boy a clone of his older sister with the same huge soul-searching eyes.

'What's the husband like?' Markus was suddenly

curious; he had met him just once but that hardly counted. He knew Deborah's Neville and had private reservations which he'd never voiced, even to Lisa. He knew the strength of their pack devotion, would not risk ruining this perfect relationship by uttering a single ill-judged word. But the absentee Suzy was surely fair game; besides, his concern was for Lisa. He hated to see her so tormented by a situation she couldn't control, something she wasn't used to.

'Oh, the dearest of fellows, ideal for Suzy, a marriage made in heaven. It's sweet.'

As were the parents yet it hadn't saved Kit. Lisa kept trying to block him out but he always returned to haunt her. Recalling the blissful childhood they'd all shared, it seemed unbelievably cruel of fate to have dealt the Palmer parents two such blows. How she had envied that calm oasis created by Suzy's mother, in total contrast to the turbulent chaos in which she herself had grown up. She remembered their Eve of Waterloo teas, held at Suzy's place. They would laze around and listen to records while Gwen was quietly there in the background, ready with sandwiches and cakes and homemade lemonade. She had always been remarkably tolerant towards this gang of excitable girls, shrieking their heads off and interrupting, laughing at each other's fatuous jokes. One of Lisa's fondest memories was of Gwen, in the kitchen, ironing to cricket, a woman entirely at ease in her own skin. Then Suzy's dad would arrive home from work and valiantly chauffeur the lot of them home before even bothering to change his clothes or stop for a drink. Lisa had longed for parents like that, pulling in tandem to give their children the best advantages in life.

'It was always Suzy's house we went to. Her mum never seemed to mind.' She recalled the faded, chintz-covered sofas, strewn with cat-hair and gardening journals, with Gwen's knitting left on her favourite chair, to be worked on sporadically when she had the time. It was a sprawling, comfortable barn of a house, straight from a children's storybook; Enid Blyton, Arthur Ransome, the images all entwined. The Maguires lived cheek by jowl with their neighbours in a noisy, danger-ous urban street, sharing three to a bedroom, with only one bathroom. If she ever thought about a haven of peace, it was the Palmers' house that came to mind, with its privet hedge and jigsaw puzzle garden with hollyhocks and lupins growing wild.

'So why did it take her so long to settle?' Suzy had thought she had missed the boat until that chance meeting with Andrew had changed her life. Lisa stayed single entirely from choice; the idea of having babies left her cold. With her family background, the last thing she needed was a bunch of boisterous children of her own. At least not now, though Markus had plans; if she'd only stop thinking of him as just passing through. But Suzy had always got on with her par-ents, liked spending time with them and Kit, who had been as much a friend as an older brother.

'I guess she was too much cocooned as a child. Never felt the urge to get away.' Guy and Gwen treated her always as an equal, more so as she grew older. They'd been wholly supportive when they'd finally understood that her passion for art was far more than just a hobby. After they'd been to talk to Miss Holbrook, they had never again stood in her way. 'When the rest of us went on to university, Suzy chose art school and living at home. She never wanted to leave until she met Andrew.'

Abby was already home, eating an apple at the kitchen table, when her mother staggered in with her Tesco bags. As usual, there was no sign of the boys apart from muddy football boots on the floor.

'Be a dear and bring in the rest.' She tossed her daughter the car-keys. 'Had a good day? How was economics?' To be greeted only by the sound of a slamming front door. She grinned. Her daughter was so like herself at that age; what a way she still had to go, poor sweet, before she discovered what life was really about. There was a message from Neville to say he'd be late, plus a pile of niggling inquiries from the parish. Deborah sighed as she shrugged off her jacket; what was the point of expensive vacations if it meant returning to this constant backlog of crap? Her feet were aching, her ankles felt swollen, yet all she had really done today was have lunch. And so far without any positive result. She filled the kettle and switched it on. She would have a quick coffee and five minutes' zizz before she even started tackling supper.

There were women she knew who did little all day except diet, work out and complain. She had met too many in this opulent neighbourhood with nothing to talk about except themselves. Deborah sighed. Despite her resolution, she riffled through her messages then poured the coffee and dragged herself up to her study. Best get it over with now or disrupt the evening with needy people anxious to talk and categorise their woes. She sometimes wondered why she'd chosen this calling, then remembered the early ambition she'd had and grinned. The biter bit; she had done it to herself, perceiving it in her last year at Cambridge as the fast track to a political career. Though why she could ever have wanted that, she now no longer remembered. Suddenly Deborah felt tired and defeated, middle-aged and overweight. She thought about Lisa's racy lifestyle – the bike, the boat, the much younger man – combined with a most impressive legal career. At thirty-nine she was a celebrated barrister who had recently taken silk. From a background like hers, that was doubly commendable. Deborah slumped into an armchair and kicked off her shoes.

Twenty minutes later she woke with a start. The phone downstairs was urgently ringing yet no-one was picking up.

'Abby,' she shouted, stumbling to her feet, but the house remained resolutely silent. Kids, she thought, as she hurried down the stairs. How did they come to grow up so self-obsessed? And neither of the boys had yet put in an appearance.

The voice seemed so close that she thought for a moment it was local. 'Helen?' she said, with dawning hope. 'Can it be that you are here?'

Helen, relaxing in her Constantia garden, laughed. 'How could you possibly think that?' she said. 'It's just a good connection. I'd never turn up without letting you know. You know me better than that.' Although she joked, she meant it sincerely. Tight-assed was how she described herself. As the only child of an elderly father and a mother preoccupied with seeing to his needs, she had never really learned to let her hair down.

She had rung, she said, to find out about Suzy and update herself on the trial. The *Cape Times* had touched on it only briefly; living so far away, she felt cut off. Deborah recounted the gist of the lunch, told her what Lisa had had to say and warned her that the prognosis wasn't good, which was putting it at its most benign.

'She doesn't think we have a hope in hell without some miraculous intervention. Though has no idea where that's coming from, just believes we must give it a try. And fast.' The alternative was too horrible to consider but Helen was one of the original five. And by nobody's standards a fool.

Once she had said it, Deborah felt better. No more clouding the issue. Suzy was up to her neck in so much trouble, it would take the Virgin Mary to dig her out. Which, from a rabbi, was somewhat extreme but they needed all the assistance they could get.

'Should I come over?' Helen was ready, had dug out her passport and checked her current account. Had consulted Piet and gained his support and warned the maid that she might be coerced into working double time. She felt the way the rest of them did, devoted to the Palmer family for what they had always been to them in the past. Without even mentioning lovely Suzy who had never, in all the years they had known her, had so much as a mean thought.

'Lisa says no.' Deborah was primed. 'At least, not until you are really needed. She feels you could carry more weight over there, the scientific voice of feminist reason.' Helen's doctorate was in anthropology, her specialist subject motherhood. An academic as senior as she was might help sway the world to their cause. Provided, of course, they could reasonably show that right was on their side.

'Oh, just one more thing before you go. Olivia,' said Deborah. 'Do you happen to know where she might be?'

Almost imperceptibly, Helen faltered. 'Strange you should ask that,' she said. 'She was with us a while back, staying here. Surely I told you at the time? It was after we'd seen her at Suzy's wedding, she just turned up out of the blue.' She laughed, drawing Deborah into the joke. 'All a bit of a fiasco really. Although, of course, it was great to see her, she did rather catch us on the hop.' They all knew what Olivia was like, chaotic in the extreme. Thoughtless and needy, demanding attention. Her stage success hadn't helped to calm her down. Because of her lifestyle, perpetually moving, she'd acquired the habit of dropping in then staying as long as it suited her, not always to everyone's convenience. Still, all things considered, she'd done well for herself. Even Deborah granted her that.

Olivia had taken the garden route from Port Elizabeth, just on a whim, Helen explained. Called the Krugers the minute she hit town, then moved in, without a by-your-leave, and stayed for several weeks. Longer than she was really welcome, as Deborah would know and understand; now it was funny but then it had been slightly awkward.

'You know what they say about fish and house-guests?' The laughter had gone from Helen's voice.

'After three days they stink.' Deborah grinned; how like Olivia to turn up unannounced. She never had been a diplomat, as Deborah knew to her cost.

Helen, relieved to have got it off her chest, was happy to spill the beans. She had only been married herself a few months and was still getting used to that state. The family had been on their best behaviour, trying to get along together, tiptoeing round each other and making no waves. The boys made an effort to tidy their rooms and even came in for meals on time, while Piet was still at the honeymoon phase, relieved and grateful to have found the right woman at last. What they hadn't needed at that time was a stranger in their midst.

'So?' said Deborah, keen to hear more, suddenly hugely cheered. She loved to hear stories about her friends, it helped take her mind off her own quiet despair, of which she hadn't divulged a word to a soul.

'So,' said Helen, warming to the plot. 'In bursts Olivia, just like that. I think you can more or less imagine the rest.'

Indeed Deborah could, better than most. She still hadn't quite forgiven Olivia for Neville. She could well imagine the glowing eyes and breathless admiration, directed at Piet. Piet was no fool; she hardly knew him, but was certain he'd see through the act much quicker than Neville had. Men could be such idiots but now was not the time . . .

'Hang on a sec,' she said, crossing to the fridge and pouring herself a hefty glass of wine.

'You'd think,' she said, once she had heard the rest, 'that if she could splurge on the garden route, she could also afford a hotel.' From what she knew of Olivia now, she could not be short of a bob or two yet she always had been something of a skinflint. Suzy's mother, bless her heart, had tried to explain it succinctly; as a child she had never really known her own roots so was always trying to compensate. Deborah and Olivia had long been at odds, though now they were adults things hopefully should have improved.

'I think she's probably lonely,' said Helen, all the old guilt flooding back. 'She never seems able to settle down, though I think she genuinely longs for a permanent home.' There was still something wistful beneath the charm that never failed to touch her. 'Just a weekend,' she had promised Piet but somehow, when it came to the crunch, their guest had shown no sign of moving on. She loved Cape Town with its mellow climate, was knocked out by the scenery. She signed up for all sorts of bus excursions, some scheduled alarmingly far ahead. Dutifully Helen, with the boys in tow, had driven her out to the winelands one morning and then on for lunch in Simon's Town, which she'd loved.

'I wouldn't mind living here myself,' she had said, soaking in the quaint atmosphere, surrounded by people with cut glass accents who could have come straight from home.

But pressures of work allowed Helen little leeway to relax. On top of the usual academic demands, she now had a home to run.

'Don't you have work to get back to?' she asked but Olivia merely shrugged.

'This and that,' she said somewhat vaguely, closing her eyes to enjoy the sun. 'A gig at the Edinburgh Festival – who cares? And a voice-over in L.A. Neither exactly Oscar-winning stuff. Soon I'll be back on the dole.'

'Well,' said Deborah, glued to the phone. 'Did you manage to get her to spill the beans?' Olivia had always had some mystery about her; whole areas of her life remained a blank.

'We did sit up for a late night drink after Piet and the boys had gone to bed. The following morning she upped and left. I've not heard a word from her since.'

'You mean she didn't even thank you for her stay?' Even Deborah was startled. She had never been one of Olivia's fans but remembered she'd always had excellent manners. Plus the sly little smile and mordant wit that always cracked them up. 'Did she tell you anything about the missing years? What happened when she disappeared?' At the time it had caused a huge scandal at the school, the way she had let them all down.

Helen, having warmed to the subject, was keeping the best for last. 'Better than that,' she said, waiting a beat. 'She told me about her marriage.'

7

She had chosen Zurich more or less at random, wanted to leave as fast as she could, and this was the first flight out with empty seats. Olivia splurged on a club class ticket and only then could relax. Once airborne she would have sufficient time to decide on her ultimate destination. She hated herself for destroying the calm she'd experienced staying with Helen. They had made her so welcome in their comfortable guest-suite that she'd felt no urge to be moving on, enjoyed being with them and part of their life, considered herself a new honorary aunt to the boys. That was the thing about visiting friends; for a while you could enter their private world as easily as a chameleon changes colour. At school she hadn't been close to Helen but had liked them both when they'd met at the wedding and decided impulsively that she would pay them a visit.

Helen had evolved from a slightly priggish school-girl into a confident, articulate woman whose obsession with her chosen field Olivia found compelling. On the subject of motherhood she waxed almost lyrical, an odd reversal from the uptight feminist Olivia remembered from school. Though scant on small talk, when it came to her research she positively radiated commitment. Something Olivia especially envied; she had little in her own life to crow about.

She'd been very drawn to the husband, too, with his quiet reserve and courteous habit of hearing you through to the end. She gathered Piet Kruger was highly respected and envied Helen for what she had got. They were, quite obviously, good together with an easy intimacy as well as shared interests that made them a pleasure to be with. Olivia experienced the familiar pang at never having been in such a relationship, nor even once come close. Somehow, it seemed, she always missed out, though still couldn't figure out why. Her school contemporaries had all done well while she remained unsettled and groping for something, she wasn't sure what. Even her career as a performer was progressing only sporadically. Endlessly having to live off her wits did not make life any easier. She was growing weary of the whole charade but had no idea how to escape it.

What was bugging her now was her crass stupidity at having told Helen about Klaus. Till now she had tried to put that business behind her and almost succeeded in doing so. The Richthofen family were no longer on her trail. Only once had she ventured to use his name. Life in Constantia had been so soporific she had fallen into the most obvious of traps, entrusting a confidence to an acquaintance who wasn't really close.

Hardly even an acquaintance really, just someone who'd briefly featured in her past. And the way those women seemed to thrive on gossip, it would be all over the airwaves by now and the rest of them would have learnt her sad little secret. They had been so cliquey at school, that set, she had never really belonged. A mist of rage clouded Olivia's eyes; whenever anything started to go well, invariably something intervened to spoil it. It wasn't fair, she did not deserve it. She gritted her teeth and closed her eyes and willed the plane to take off.

The uniform had been second-hand but Aunt Sarah's fitter had taken it in and given it a proper pressing. There had been no point in buying it new; by the end of the year she'd have grown so much, it would only have been a further waste of money. Aunt Sarah studied Olivia with critical eyes; even despite the alterations, she still looked a sad little thing. Her hair was colourless rather than fair and never looked properly clean. And her nose was pinched, with a shiny red tip that constantly seemed to be running. How her pretty sister had produced this little runt was something she had never understood. It couldn't even be blamed on the father; whatever his flaws, there was nothing wrong with his looks.

'Poor kid,' said Aunt Sarah behind Olivia's back, her conscience pricking her again. 'She's not had much of a life up till now.' At least, with the father out of the way, she stood a chance of making some friends and getting a decent education. She had turned out surprisingly well considering she'd been fostered by strangers and shifted around all her life. She was bright, that had never been in dispute, endorsed by the fact the school had agreed to take her so quickly. They'd be pleased to offer her a place, they had said, despite the fact she was two years late for her year.

'She'll soon settle down,' the head had assured them and, sure enough, by her second year, she seemed to be finding her niche. Suzy's set still remained quite aloof but Suzy herself had accepted her as a friend. Her main source of comfort, though, remained Suzy's mum to whom she turned whenever she needed a hug. Despite a certain standoffishness from Kit, Olivia felt that theirs was her natural home. Aunt Sarah's house was just somewhere to sleep; she hardly saw her uncle and aunt at all except at meals. Throughout her life she'd been searching for a mother; Gwen Palmer filled that requirement admirably.

'You know, dear,' said Gwen, once she felt she'd earned the right, 'you might look better with a different haircut, something shorter that doesn't droop. I'll treat you to an appointment.' It was tricky to do things behind the aunt's back but so far she hadn't objected. Probably too busy to look at the poor child and at this age, facing adolescence, looks were important to a girl. If only she'd put on a bit of weight; she was still a scraggy little thing.

'Don't get too involved,' warned Guy, used to his wife's lame ducks. But he had to agree that Olivia looked better and, once she got over being scared to death, she could be quite amusing. Because she felt safe in the Palmer house, she gradually dropped her guard until she even had Kit laughing at her jokes. She had a lightning fast tongue. Gradually, as the year progressed, she came more into her own so that even Suzy got used to her constant presence. In Suzy's cast-offs she looked quite good and allowed herself to be taken around and shown off.

'You see,' said Gwen. 'She's a nice girl really. All it ever took was a bit of a hug.'

They were lolling around in the gym one day, listening to Miranda rehearse. She'd been picked as a soloist in the carol concert which meant a lot of practice. Her own choice, the *Pié Jesu* from Fauré's Requiem, would challenge a voice more resilient than hers but she wasn't worried at all. The aching purity of her flawless treble stopped even Deborah in mid-sentence. They all fell silent, hugely impressed. No doubt about it, Miranda was good. The fuss her parents made was justified.

'Amazing,' said Lisa. 'I wonder where she gets it?'
'Don't know,' said Suzy, 'but she's going to be a star.'

The nice thing was that it hadn't spoiled her. She remained the sweet child they all adored, good-natured and unassuming. She was still very small, like a delicate elf with a cloud of silvery hair.

'She looks like the fairy off a Christmas tree,' Gwen had often pointed out. So fragile that, if dropped, she'd probably break.

Helen, perched on a vaulting-horse, reluctantly closed her book. 'I only hope she won't leave us soon for the Guildhall.' Which was one of the plans her parents were discussing to develop her formidable talent.

'We mustn't allow that to happen,' said Deborah. 'Nothing must ever split us up.' No-one could ever take Miranda's place, on that all four were agreed.

Unobserved by the other girls, Olivia stood listening. She was mesmerised by the soaring voice yet still too reserved to let them know she was there. Though she'd only admit it to herself, she was slightly in awe of their tight little clique, particularly Deborah's viperish tongue, so often directed at her. Yet she also knew she was quite as bright as they were. Of them all, she liked Miranda best because she was smaller and posed no threat, while Suzy and Helen were also okay and seemed not to mind her tagging along. If only she could sing like that, perhaps they'd respect her more. For hours at home she would stand and mime silently in front of the mirror to songs playing on the radio while her aunt and uncle were still out. Often enough she had heard it said that her looks were unprepossessing yet found, when she worked herself into the mood, that she had other attributes that animated her face. Simply by miming to her favourite singers, she lit up from within. And her voice, when nobody else was around, was steadily growing stronger. Miranda's was great but she'd had all those lessons; Olivia's wasn't trained but was richer in pitch. One day they'd see, she would show them yet. There was nothing she couldn't do if she really tried.

The parents came to the carol concert, a highlight of the winter term. Except, of course, for Olivia's aunt and uncle who were working, as usual, in the shop. Secretly Olivia was glad they weren't there; Aunt Sarah could be very pretentious and she didn't want her letting her down at the school. Suzy told a story of her mother snipping plants whenever she was let loose in the grounds but, Gwen protested, it did them no harm and see how well they were flourishing at home. And, when they'd grown, she passed cuttings to her friends. 'What goes around, comes around,' she said.

'She's the Robin Hood of the gardening world,' said Suzy's father with a twinkle. 'Robbing the rich to help the poor. Every gardener's patron saint, provided she doesn't get caught.'

Aunt Sarah, however, was another matter. In Olivia's eyes, they were much better off without her.

The programme began with the uplifting strains of 'It Came Upon the Midnight Clear' and the audience rose, as one, and all joined in. Olivia, who'd wangled a place next to Gwen, felt for the first time ever that she belonged. Her voice, Gwen noticed to her surprise, was confident and mature. She nudged her husband who listened too, equally impressed by the girl's singing.

'That was very good, dear,' said Gwen when it was finished. 'I didn't realise you could sing like that.' It was Miranda, however, who carried the night; beside her nobody else at the school stood a chance. She stood in the spotlight, fully at ease, and the audience held their breath as she started to sing. Faultlessly she hit each note, and when it was over blew kisses to the crowd. Not quite the thing for a solemn occasion but this was Christmas and these were her friends, roaring out their appreciation and calling for an encore. Next came the thunderous opening chords of 'Once in Royal David's City' and the audience were back on their feet.

'Really moving,' said Gwen, at the end. 'Quite as good as King's College Chapel. I must say, the school puts on an excellent show.'

Later, as they filtered out, she slipped her arm through Olivia's. 'Where did you learn to sing like that?' What impressed her most was the girl's shy reticence.

'My mother trained to be an actress,' Olivia explained. 'I guess it must be in the genes.'

'Then you should do something about it,' said Gwen. It was a shame Miranda always stole the limelight. 'Why not audition for the choir?'

She was pleased for Olivia; it would do her no harm to put herself forward for a change. Despite her shyness, the girl was bright and her looks were perceptibly improving. All she lacked was confidence or she'd hold her own against the rest.

But the idea of auditioning filled Olivia with horror. 'No way!' she said, appalled at the idea. The only singing she would do was in the privacy of her bedroom. She would not risk making a fool of herself in front of her critical peers. All her life she'd put up with such slights, her skin was only just beginning to thicken.

'Well, think about it. I'm serious,' said Gwen. 'Don't be so hard on yourself. Now come along and we'll drop you off on the way home.'

Twenty years had passed since then; it seemed a whole lifetime away. And Gwen's advice had been very sound and spoken from the heart. Olivia shifted in her comfortable seat and suddenly altered her plans. From Zurich she'd thought of going on to Lucerne where some of her formative years had been spent. But acute nostalgia was beckoning her and she knew what she wanted to do. Instead of Lucerne she would go to London where she still had unfinished business.

8

The tablecloth hung low on the mountain which meant she couldn't go for her afternoon hike. Helen was disappointed. One of the perks of living in this great country was the mind-blowing scenery that cradled the city, creating the illusion of being closed in on all sides. She loved to explore the easier trails; it helped to keep her physically fit besides providing quality time for thinking. A ready-made family was all very well; had, at least, saved her from the messy business of raising babies of her own. But little boys were a shock to the system for anyone coming to it cold. When she'd married Piet and moved to Cape Town, leaving her friends and the lifestyle she was used to, she'd already had strong private qualms. No matter how welcoming her new stepsons were, she knew she could never replace their real mother who had died from an aneurysm, tragically young, at the age of thirty-one. Piet, she suspected, was still quietly grieving while the boys, though polite, maintained a distance which meant that they all got along very well. On the whole.

But, then, she had never been used to children, raised, as she was, as an only child by parents whose age-gap was even wider than the seventeen years that divided her and Piet. She had spent her childhood very much on her own, since both of them worked long hours at the lab, cocooned in their exclusive world of science. Solitude had made her self-sufficient with a voracious appetite for reading. Right from the moment she first learned to read, invariably her nose was stuck in a book. Her tastes were unashamedly eclectic; fiction, biography, popular science, textbooks of all kinds. School had been a glorious awakening; because you had to be bright to get in, most of the natural selection was already done. She had found a group of like-minded spirits and fallen on her feet.

Deborah, Lisa, Miranda and Suzy – the Famous Five, as they'd dubbed themselves. Helen looked back with nostalgia to that time; what fun they had had since that very first term, the forging of a bond that had strengthened over the years. She blessed the advance in electronics that made communication so much simpler these days. Without regular emails from her friends, life here in this alien land would have been a lot more daunting. Boston had been a different matter; there she had fitted in. She loved the campus, enjoyed her research and was able to get home a lot more often. And the girls, of course, had all been over, Lisa several times.

South Africa was different, though; here she still felt an outsider. She loved her husband, got on well with his boys, but like-minded girlfriends were what she really craved most, the hardest thing of all to replicate. Olivia's visit had stirred all this up, made her realise the depths of her isolation. Also, at work she was acutely aware of the veiled hostility aimed at her from many of her male colleagues. They hated the fact that she was female, married to a university VIP, which gave her status they felt she hadn't earned. They made things as difficult as they could and sneered at her chosen area of research, implying it wasn't a serious subject, just more of that feminist claptrap. And then she had stumbled across the book club and life had immeasurably looked up.

They met every month in each other's homes and took turns to choose a book to discuss that they felt would appeal to them all. And there, in a very short space of time, Helen discovered new friends. Not just new but ones she could talk to about her more intimate feelings. Jackie, Shirley, Annie and Pat, although from widely disparate backgrounds, were all essentially her kind of women with whom she found she had a surprising rapport. They'd begin by discussing the chosen book then quickly move on to more general things and later go out for a meal together plus a few more glasses of wine. These regular meetings were a breath of fresh air, away from the pressures of jobs and relationships, where they could frankly discuss their problems, which is what they inevitably did. Helen found it a welcome catharsis. Because of her lack of experience with children, she would sometimes seek advice from the others and they never failed to boost her confidence and make her feel abler to cope. They found it amusing that she was studying the subject yet had little hands-on knowledge of motherhood. Jackie and Shirley both had children; Shirley, recently remarried, was hoping for more. Annie and Pat were absorbed in their careers, Annie a freelance film-editor, Pat a statistician. Helen looked forward to these monthly meetings, the highlight of her social life.

And yet, if she were honest with herself, it was her schoolfriends she still mainly missed. Connections forged at the age of eleven stayed with you for the rest of your life, with shared memories and references and the same quirky jokes. Olivia's visit was an unexpected tonic. Helen regretted now that she hadn't stayed on.

Harvard graduate school, even in the eighties, was still a hidebound institution, especially where the sciences were concerned. After school and three years at an all-women college, Helen had found it a shock to the system to be working, indeed competing, mostly with men. Her chosen area of research was one that had long obsessed her, a quest to comprehend her own beginnings and the slow evolution from the start of mankind that had led, over nearly two million years, to this precise moment in time. Out of her own mother's myriad egg-cells, hers was the one to be fertilised and, against inconceivable odds, the foetus had managed to crawl through gestation to be born, indeed, to survive. Which, looked at from almost any angle, was a pretty miraculous thing. Her physicist parents had been so work-obsessed they'd had very little time for her, which had led to her insatiable reading habit and turned her into a scientist herself. Considering the origins of the species was somewhat like gazing at the stars. The more you looked, the more you saw. From an early age she was enthralled.

Piet Kruger, when their paths first crossed, was Professor of Investigative Medicine, working just down the corridor from Helen. A man with a glittering array of awards for the work he had done on infectious diseases, he was grave and withdrawn, with those striking dark eyes that looked as though they could peer straight into your soul. Although she didn't realise it then – nor, in fact, for several years – Helen was profoundly moved by the man. His students held him in high esteem, respected his attitudes towards the underprivileged when he could have been living on a fatter ticket and not working nearly as hard. It was fate intervening, she believed now, the same fate that had decreed that her egg should survive, considering the infinite millions that did not. And fate that had led her to Harvard in the first place, instead of doing her post-graduate work at home. Dad had been failing, her mother anxious and Oxford reluctant to let her go. She missed the girls, doubtless always would, but compared to what she now had with Piet, it had all been well worth the price.

Tonight the book club was meeting at the Table Bay Hotel which made a nice change from the norm. Annie was there, already waiting, in the chic, wood-panelled, softly-lit bar with maps and travel posters on the walls. She had long, fair hair in a thick unravelling plait and a smile that instantly put people at their ease and made them want to hug her. They embraced.

'No-one else here yet?' Helen glanced round.

'Shirley is parking her car.'

Helen ordered a local wine, recommended by the waitress. She was black and smiling and impeccably groomed, would not have looked out of place in a Knightsbridge hotel. Helen thought of the townships she had visited and the awful conditions in which black people lived. Four families crammed into a two-bedroom shack, obliged to sleep in shifts. And this young woman would be living there, returning each night to that squalor. Small wonder the national crime rate was soaring and white people once again starting to get out. It was a subject she tried not to dwell on too much although, now that she had those boys to consider, it was difficult not to worry. Four quite separate people she had met had been held up at gun-point in their homes, an experience now so wide-spread they gave counselling for it. She ordered glasses and mineral water; the others would be here soon. And later those without prior commitments would go out together for a meal.

Piet was especially good about that, liked to feel she was making friends and finally settling down. They had worked in close proximity for years before Janine had died and, though nothing had happened between them all that time, she had always been slightly in awe of him and sneakily found him attrac-tive. She liked men like Piet, with his courteous manner and the close-cropped beard that added a touch of distinction. She also discovered she preferred older men, perhaps because of the pattern set by her parents. When he'd made the decision to return to his roots, he'd persuaded her to come with him. It hadn't exactly been love at first sight, not the euphoria Suzy described, but rather a gradual deepening of affection, based on shared interests and mutual respect. And, of course, there were the boys.

'Why choose motherhood as your area of research?' Olivia was curious. For someone like Helen, with her strongly held views, it seemed the very antithesis of all she preached. Even as long ago as school she had boldly declared her decision never to marry, way before such a view was fashionable. Her parents behaved more like workmates than lovers until her father grew older and started to fail. Then her mother had shown alarm but already it was too late. Deprived of a family life at home, with regular meals and open discussions, Helen had turned instead to the Palmers, become their surrogate child. Which was something, she realised, she shared with Olivia; both had grown up feeling like intruders though she hadn't ever thought of that till now.

Olivia repeated her question. 'Why motherhood?'

'I guess it just kind of crept up on me,' said Helen, speaking of a time before she'd met Piet. She tried to explain the miracle of birth, resulting from all those evolutionary millennia, and the huge satisfaction she derived from her wide-ranging exploration of the subject. 'It's like a detective story,' she said. 'You never quite know what you'll turn up next. You can't imagine how thrilling that is.' She explained her analogy of studying the stars and Olivia listened, enthralled. 'It's like peering through a gigantic telescope; the more I see, the more I understand.' Going right back to the Pleistocene epoch whence man's ancestors came.

They were eating lunch at the River Café, relaxing under the trees. It was hot and still and the food was first rate, with an accent on local cuisine. Helen's guilt at taking time off eased with the wine and the conversation. After all, it wasn't every day that an old friend turned up out of the blue and the more she saw of Olivia, the more she liked her. The transformation was still quite startling; she'd forgotten the sudden bewitching smile and brilliant mimicry. She wasn't pretty but was certainly striking and could twist her mobile face into any shape.

'It's ironic, really,' said Helen, with a laugh, 'that I'm now the mother of two strapping lads. Me, with my po-faced views about sisterhood.' Total commitment, no turning back, though she wouldn't have it any other way. 'Haven't you ever thought about children yourself?'

Olivia adeptly sidestepped the question. 'But you're really great with them,' she said. She made no bones about envying Helen and the lifestyle that obviously suited her so well. Helen looked tanned and fit and far prettier, even though her hairstyle hadn't changed since school. She wore sensible cords and her husband's plaid shirt, sleeves rolled up neatly to above the elbow, reminiscent of the monitor she'd been, solemn, tidy and well-scrubbed.

'No credit to me,' said Helen with a shrug. 'They came as part of the package. Though I swear that now I could not get along without them.'

On the short drive back to Constantia, Helen asked about Olivia's career. 'It's amazing how well you have done so quickly. It seems like only yesterday we were larking about in the gym.' Which brought her neatly to the question of the hour; what had happened to her since she dropped out of school? But right now Olivia wasn't taking the bait. She smiled and changed the subject.

'I was lucky,' was all she would say. 'Though the early years weren't easy, I had a few breaks.' She had worked as a barmaid in Covent Garden and later in shifts at the National Theatre until a chink had appeared in the curtain which she'd managed to wriggle through.

'It's a genuine rags-to-riches story.' Helen was impressed. Though if Olivia had been in London all that time, how odd that none of them had seen her.

'You are glamorising it,' said Olivia. 'All I was, was in the right place at the right time.'

It seemed that she still wouldn't open up; Helen had grown frustrated. Here she was, sharing her life with Olivia just as they'd all done in the past, yet getting very little back. Despite the gifts she had lavished on the boys, at heart Olivia was that same wistful waif with her nose pressed firmly to the glass. Helen, however, was far too nice-natured ever to bear a grudge. She had lucked into a lifestyle that she loved and constantly counted her blessings. Olivia's life might be one long adventure yet she still seemed unfulfilled, which was sad. She determined not to allow her to leave without cracking through her reserve. After all, they had been friends all these years and that's what friendship was about.

That night they did have a heart-to-heart; in the morning Olivia was gone.

'I've no idea,' she said when the others asked her. 'I don't believe it was anything I said.' Piet's reaction had been relief; he hated to share his happiness with a stranger and Olivia had long outworn her original welcome. The boys, too, were callously unconcerned and rarely ever mentioned her again. Poor Olivia, thought Helen with compassion. Now that she knew a bit more about her, she felt she had possibly let her down. At school they had rubbed along well enough, allowing her into their private clique regardless of Deborah's objections. Helen had rather taken her for granted; perhaps that was what had gone wrong. Olivia's neediness had become all too apparent after she'd told her depressing story and left. Helen might have tried tracking her down, had she known where to look, if it weren't for the many other pressures on her time. At that time the marriage had still been new and her colleagues were unreceptive. She had to admit she had given Olivia very little further thought.

But that was then and this was now. Suzy had got to be rescued. Lisa was keeping Helen fully informed of every bit of evidence she could glean.

'There was some sort of row and he just went off. They don't know what it was about. The neighbour heard their voices raised and then, a long time later, a car driving off.'

'And nobody's heard his side of the story?'

'Not so far,' said Lisa.

'I would have thought they'd arrest him too. Surely he must be implicated.'

'No. As it happens his alibi is sound. He was at the botanical gardens at the time.'

Poor Suzy, thought Helen after Lisa had rung off. Olivia had always been a bit of a kook but Suzy's recent behaviour was aberrational. Two babies born in eleven months must have been a colossal strain, especially since she was old to be starting a family. On top of which, she had all that work. Her fame as an artist had suddenly taken off and demand for her paintings was huge. It couldn't have been easy, with just the nanny, to deal with all that sudden extra pressure.

She would think it through carefully before talking to the girls; anything she could contribute might well help. Though she hesitated, before she spoke, to imply, in any way, that Suzy was liable. It was a hard one to crack and she'd give it considerable thought before she did anything at all that might not help.

She was still thinking as she swung into their drive and waited for the security gate to open. Some of their neighbours kept huge angry dogs but that would be dangerous for the boys and, in any case, out of keeping with the way they wanted to live. Piet had returned here as a native South African, to try to right some of the terrible wrongs being wrought by the present regime. Saving lives from AIDS was to him more vital than any number of awards they might heap on his head in the States. He was waiting for her in the kitchen doorway when she emerged from the underground garage.

'Had a good night, love?' He held out his arms and, gratefully, Helen went into them. She was home, she was safe, that was mainly what mattered. She had Piet and the boys and a brand new life. She would think about Suzy and her own private theory later, when she wasn't quite so tired.

9

The kids had eaten and dispersed and Deborah was thinking of turning in when Neville finally came home. He looked tired and harassed, with his collar-stud undone, and had loosened the knot of his expensive silk tie. He seemed mildly surprised to find her still up; he dropped his briefcase as he stooped to kiss her.

'Have you eaten?' asked Deborah from the depths of her chair, where she'd been trying for hours to catch up on the papers. 'There is leftover chicken cacciatore in the fridge. I can easily heat it up.'

'Don't bother,' said Neville and she smelt the whisky. 'I grabbed a bite after the meeting. There were odds and sods that needed sorting out.' Despite his obviously stressed-out state, her husband still looked terrific. The lean good looks that had initially hooked her had weathered remarkably well; at forty-two he was still in his prime with only the merest hint of grey in his hair. He could pass for younger, which could not be said of her. Over the years the pounds had crept on and the lissom teenager who had once wowed the boys was only detectable now in her gorgeous daughter.

'How was lunch?' He shrugged off his jacket and helped himself to another drink.

'I'm not really sure,' said Deborah thoughtfully. 'Great to see Lisa – it always is – but I can't pretend we accomplished anything much. The Suzy situation is quite horrendous. I don't know what we can do to help. As things stand, she faces a possible death sentence.'

For a moment Neville stared at her blankly, his mind still on other things. 'As bad as that? I'm sorry, I hadn't realised.'

'So bad,' said Deborah, rubbing her eyes, 'that it's given me a migraine.'

'You're wasting your time,' he said brutally. 'To start with, what makes you so sure that she didn't do it? You are all up in arms about it, yet you still don't know the full facts. To me it sounds like the classic revenge of a woman done the dirty on by her husband.'

'By killing her children?' Deborah was outraged. There were times she almost hated him. More so since Suzy was his favourite of her friends, or so he had always led her to believe. He admired Suzy's talent, found her company relaxing; even declared her pretty, in her own way. Had also, that evening they had spent together, come down in favour of the husband too, something he didn't do without careful thought.

'Calm down,' he said, flicking on the news. 'Don't go getting into one of your states. The truth is, it's years since you knew her properly. There's no telling how she may have changed. People do, you know, when they're under pressure.' He gave her a cynical sideways look. 'Marriage can do strange things to us all, not always for the best.'

'But not turn Suzy into a killer. Leopards don't change their spots.' Deborah was energised by her rage; she wanted to smash him in the face. How dare he come home like this and upset her, shattering what peace of mind she still had. 'The Suzy we know wouldn't hurt a fly. It just isn't in her nature. And, what's more, I would testify to that in court.' She plumped up the cushions and shook them into place, then furiously gathered up the papers.

She would round up all the others fast and they'd go to New Orleans. No matter what it took, they would stop the trial. Proper justice had to be done. They would tell the world about the Suzy they knew and prove she would not be capable of doing such a thing.

'There's no way you're going without me,' said Markus. 'If you go, I'm coming too.'

After all, New Orleans had been his stamping-ground long before he'd been halted in his tracks by meeting Lisa and ended up staying in London.

'To do what?' asked Lisa, hunched before her screen, checking out flights and reservations while she waited for the lawyers there to respond. She respected Deborah's sudden decision yet didn't want to risk acting too hastily. Her contacts there were better placed to test the emotional climate. The trial was still in its opening stages; full evidence had not yet been presented. And she'd still been unable to raise Andrew on the phone, something she didn't understand.

'Be with you. Hold your hand. Give you strength. Do some gentle sleuthing.'

Lisa looked up. He was serious; his eyes were worried and for once he wasn't smiling. She stretched out and touched him; what a dear boy he was, so eager always to put her well-being first.

'That's sweet,' she said, 'but I'll have the others. Deborah definitely, possibly Helen and we still haven't found Olivia.'

There she went, brushing him off again, but Markus, now he had made up his mind, stood his ground. He wished he could make this woman understand that his love was entirely authentic, but because she was so much older than him she refused to commit in any way. Which was steadily driving him crazy. She had gone so far as to let him share her home but even that was subject to her whim. They had moved in together yet the boat was hers. He hated being a kept man. It didn't sit well on his proud Teutonic shoulders; he wanted a lot more than that.

Seeing the resolution on his face, Lisa returned to her screen. 'We'll talk about it later,' she said. 'Once I know for certain that we are going.'

Still incensed by her husband's cynicism but with a clearer head, Deborah realised there was something she must do that shouldn't be put off any longer if she planned to make the New Orleans trip. She must go and see the Palmers right away to find out how they were coping. On the phone Guy had told her they were still hanging in but she needed to see that for herself.

10

The drive out to Pinner was relatively simple. Deborah chose to go by the North End Road. It was ages since she had last come this way; it alarmed her even to contemplate how fast the years had scudded by. She skirted Harrow-on-the-Hill, where Byron had spent his schooldays, and shot through the meaner suburbs until she hit open countryside. Pinner still had a quiet, pastoral feeling, belied by the busy carriageway, with real cows grazing on pastureland and the healthy, open air smell of fresh manure. The Palmers had lived here throughout their marriage and liked it too much to move when the children grew up. She navigated the steep main street of the four-teenth-century village and pulled in under the chestnut trees that shaded the gateway to the church. The Palmers' house, with its spacious garden, was one of the finest features of this spot. Deborah switched the engine off and sat for a moment, just looking. Here had been enacted so many scenes of her youth.

There was no sign of life inside the house; the curtains were all half drawn. The white wooden fence was in need of some paint; otherwise everything seemed much the same as it had when they'd played here as kids. She tilted the driving mirror towards her to check out her appearance. Even on a sombre occasion like this, she wanted to look her best. She stretched back and picked up the flowers she had bought at the station. Peonies, she'd finally settled on; lilies had too funereal a connotation. She took a deep breath, then set out on her mission. They were expecting her, she had called them first, but her heartbeat was unnaturally rapid as she let herself through the front gate. She had no idea what she would find, just hoped she might be of some constructive service. Her rabbinical training had made her adept at bringing comfort to the bereft. And the Palmers were both close as family to her; the very least she could do was be there for them.

After a fairly lengthy pause, the door was opened by Guy, a weary-eyed man whose thinning hair was suddenly heavily greying. For a moment he stared blankly at Deborah as if trying to recall who she was, then the old familiar smile appeared and he crushed her fervently to his chest. She was shocked by how thin he had become.

'You came,' he said, ushering her into the house. 'You can't know how grateful we are.' He seemed to have lost a few inches in height but it could only be her heels and his slouching posture. In gardening trousers and shabby cardigan, he looked uncharacteristically scruffy. There was a smudge of leaf mould beneath one eye that he hadn't bothered to wipe away so Deborah did it for him. She halted in the wide, low-ceilinged hall, breathing in, with appreciation, the familiar aromas. It smelt of beeswax and lavender; despite the terrible tragedy, someone had clearly been keeping things well up to scratch. She dropped her car-keys on the cedarwood chest, just as she'd done since she first learned to drive, then ducked before the antique mirror to check that her hair was in place.

'You haven't changed,' said Guy with a smile. She always had been a vain little thing. She was heavier now but her skin was still flawless and the extra pounds did not detract from her looks. What a cracker she'd been in her teens and twenties; Guy, an admirer of feminine beauty, had always been slightly disturbed by her, not that he ever let it show. Being surrounded by teenage girls had been both a delight and a strain. There had been moments, of which he was not proud, when he'd had to admit to himself that he could have been tempted. Fortunately though, in this house, his son had ruled supreme and the girls had been oblivious of the father's envious lust.

Gwen was seated in an armchair by the window, too desolate even to rise to her feet, all the old sparkle gone from her eyes, looking shockingly older. Deborah kissed her and gave her the flowers.

'I'll put them in water for you later,' she said. 'First

tell me how you are.' She perched on a footstool close to Gwen's chair, a pose she had often affected as a child, and gazed around with nostalgia as all kinds of ancient memories flooded back. The furniture was still much the same, faded and saggy but comfortable, indicative of a lot of leisure time. A cat she hadn't encountered before was fast asleep on the sofa and yesterday's papers, which Guy was still reading, were strewn untidily on the floor.

'We're in a bit of a mess,' said Gwen, on the edge of cracking up.

'I'll put on the kettle,' said Guy, keen to get out of the room. There was a feeling of death and hopelessness here. Even the pot-plants were wilting.

'Please don't go to any trouble,' said Deborah. 'Not on my account. I'm here to check how you're bearing up and if there's anything you need. Just say the word and I'll be glad to do it. Anything at all.'

Gwen turned red-rimmed eyes to her; it seemed the tears would never stop. She clutched Deborah's hand, mutely shaking her head. She looked like a woman broken with sorrow. 'I can't believe this has happened,' she said. 'Those two adorable babies.'

'Let's make it sherry,' said Guy briskly, even though it was barely four. Drastic measures in a hopeless situation; the little gestures designed to keep them both sane.

Deborah followed him into the kitchen and looked in all the cupboards for a vase. She felt so at home here, even after all this time, that she didn't feel the need to ask if she might. She filled a crystal bowl with water and started snipping the stalks. Guy arranged glasses on a tray and filled each one to the brim.

'There are biscuits out on the dresser,' called Gwen but Deborah, deciding they didn't need them, pretended she hadn't heard. She tried not to snack; it was ruinous to the figure, though drinking at this hour was fair enough. It was part of the duty of a spiritual adviser to help provide solace where she could and sharing a glass of sherry was a ritual of which she entirely approved. They looked like a couple of shipwreck survivors. She felt true remorse at not having come before.

With the peonies arranged on the mantelpiece, Deborah moved to a corner of the sofa, kicked off her shoes and settled herself down to hear what Gwen had to say. Before she mentioned the US trip, she needed to know how the land lay. Slightly embarrassed, Guy stood and fidgeted, then settled beside her, displacing the sleeping cat. Deborah sensed he was glad she had come. Things were bad and might get worse and poor old Gwen showed imminent signs of collapsing altogether. Most of the information she had, Deborah knew already; Lisa had her hotline to New Orleans and was keeping the Palmers informed. But Deborah, the trained listener, knew how important it was for people to talk. Gwen had a lot to get off her mind so she settled back quietly to listen.

* * *

While Gwen gave full range to her terrible grief, Deborah's eye was roaming the room, summoning ancient memories. Beside the flowers on the mantelpiece, family photos were displayed. A beaming Suzy with both babies in her arms and a slightly self-conscious Andrew. A younger Suzy in her riding hat; another, holding a cup, in tennis whites. What a cheerful, guileless schoolgirl she had been before growing into a poised and serene young woman. Deborah found her own eyes misting as she heard the crack in the mother's voice as she tried to face the unthinkable. Whatever had happened, the children were dead. That was the indisputable fact that no words in the world could ever put right. Deborah's sole wonder, at the outpouring of pain, was that Gwen could discuss it at all.

On a corner table, on an embroidered cloth, further pictures were displayed: Suzy radiant on her wedding-day; Kit at his graduation. The sight of his beaming good-natured face, even after all these years, resounded in Deborah's heart. He must have been twenty-two at the time; a few years later he was dead. Yet not even after all this time had anyone ever found out about those frantic clandestine weeks that they had shared.

It was Deborah's final year at school; she had just completed her As. A place at Newnham was provisionally hers, assuming her grades were sufficiently good, but studying had never been any sort of problem to Deborah. Kit, having spent some months in Australia, was also now in his final year, coasting along at St John's College, Oxford, having himself a ball. He'd already got a cricket blue and was aiming for another for squash. What concerned him hardly at all were his exams; he had never been a worrier. He had chosen the diplomatic corps which he felt would suit his lifestyle best; now all he required was a reasonable pass, a two-one or even a two-two. He was six foot four with an amiable disposition and a truly heart-stopping smile. Girls in general, especially Suzy's schoolmates, unanimously voted him a knockout.

His proud acquisition, bought with his earnings from tending bar on Bondi Beach, was a vintage Morgan sports car in fire engine red. Even Suzy was proud of him when he turned up at the tennis club, though cricket, of course, remained his number one sport. 'Your brother is gorgeous,' the girls all told her as they vied for a ride in his car. Kit, however, took none of them seriously; in his eyes, at seventeen, they were still small fry. There were women aplenty back in Oxford more than willing to go the whole way but sport remained his principal obsession. That and his fabulous car.

Deborah had never been one to resist a dare. At that age she was spunky and bold with challenging eyes, a provocative mouth and hair as black as a gypsy's.

She curved voluptuously in all the right places and boasted a twenty-four-inch waist. She brazenly borrowed her mother's clothes when she thought she could get away with it which, since her mother was rarely home, was often. Though still in her teens, she acted mid-twenties and was thoroughly bored by the boys of her age, who found her intimidating. All the nice Jewish boys she met at the synagogue, whose families liked the thought of a Greenberg alliance, were, in Deborah's opinion, weedy and dull. On Saturday evenings, bored out of her mind, she would sometimes borrow her father's car (again, without permission) and case the Hampstead hostelries, searching for some action. Often she took Lisa along; they made an effective team.

The papers were hinting at a royal engagement. It was high time the Prince of Wales settled down; he'd been playing the field for too long. But these girls' minds did not run to such things. They still had university ahead and were having far too much fun. In their skin-tight jeans and colourful kickers, they considered themselves the bee's knees. Deborah tended to dress exotic, with dangly earrings and armfuls of bangles, while Lisa, having moved on from punk, now wore denim and cowboy boots; all she lacked to be properly turned out was a gun.

But deep in her heart, secret even from Lisa, Deborah nurtured a flame. Since those far-off days when they were little more than kids, she had always carried a bit of a torch for Kit Palmer. Of course, the fact he was strictly off limits was part of the attraction. She imagined with relish her parents' reaction were she ever to bring him home as their future son-in-law. She liked his height and athletic good looks and the way his confident smile lit up any room. She knew they would make an eye-catching couple, just longed for the chance of putting it to the test. But she didn't know how to see him, let alone date him. The obvious way was via Suzy but Deborah was shy of ever letting her know.

Gwen, seeing Deborah studying Kit's picture now, picked it up and gently dusted the glass. 'Next week is his birthday. How time does fly. It is difficult to believe it has been so long.'

Deborah took it gently from Gwen's hand. That smile, the mischievous glint in his eye, told of a life lived always in the sun. Nothing bad had ever darkened Kit's life, certainly not like the present situation. He'd been big and good-hearted and essentially kind, as on the day she had dropped by Suzy's house and found she wasn't home.

'Hello, Deborah. Did she know you were coming?' Gwen was clearly surprised when she opened the door. It seemed a long way to have come just on spec, particularly by public transport. Suzy hadn't known, actually, though Deborah didn't say so. It was the start of the summer holidays and she'd called in the hope that

Kit might already be home. Her exams were over and she knew she'd done well; all that remained was to wait for the results. She had no doubt at all she'd be going up to Cambridge. Now what she wanted was fun.

'She's at the tennis club,' said Kit, appearing. 'If you wait while I throw on some clothes, I'll run you there.' His hair was spiky and damp from the shower and all he wore was a towel.

'Thanks,' said Deborah, eyeing the towel. 'She's clearly forgotten I said I might drop by.'

The car smelt of leather and linseed oil from the cricket bat under the seat. The top was down and the breeze blew her hair so she tied it back with a scarf pilfered from her mother. When they reached the lane that led to the club, she placed her hand on his knee. 'Let's not bother after all,' she said. 'Take me for a spin instead. I really love this car.'

Kit, who needed no urging to show off, revved the engine and put his foot down, heading for the motorway where he could put the Morgan through its paces. Despite all Deborah had been through since, the memory still made her shiver. At just eighteen, she had all the right equipment, not least the bouncing pneumatic breasts flamboyantly displayed. He could scarcely keep his eyes on the road and soon had his hand on her thigh. He drove to Harefield and parked in a field with the traffic roaring past, fifty yards away. She was wearing a flouncy, full-skirted dress with a bodice that slid off one shoulder. Almost before he had killed the engine she was out of the car and spread-eagled in the corn. When he unzipped and she saw what was inside, she had sudden doubts about what she was doing. Kit was large in every way; she feared he might split her in half. But when he carefully entered her she could tell, with relief, that he'd done it before and was grateful for his gentleness and patience.

She never told Suzy in case it affected their friend-ship, and enjoyed the delicious sense of sin that gave her. Nor did she ever tell Lisa either, which was harder to explain; normally they kept no secrets from each other. All that summer, till the start of the new term, Kit and Deborah met secretly, which added to the thrill. Looking at his portrait now, in its stylised studio pose, she remembered the scent of sweat in his hair and the prickly stubble against her bare skin as they lay together in the cornfield. If it wasn't love, it came very close. Nothing she had experienced since, not even with Neville, had been like it.

Gwen had stopped talking and was watching her. Deborah wrenched her thoughts back from the past. Kit, for now, would have to keep; she still had the long drive home. She was here today with a job to do. Both Palmers were deeply traumatised; she longed to be able to ease their pain without falsely raising their hopes.

'Have you managed to speak to her?' She knew it was unlikely.

'They won't allow it,' replied Guy bleakly, putting a strengthening arm round his wife. 'They are treating her like a dangerous criminal who has forfeited all her rights.'

'And what about Andrew? What does he have to say?' The poor man must be living through hell. She did find it strange that he hadn't been in touch since he knew how much they all loved Suzy. Even in his appalling grief, she'd expected him to call.

Guy shook his head. 'I know nothing at all. There appears to be a conspiracy of silence.'

'We'll see about that,' said Deborah grimly. The three of them would not be thwarted. 'Lisa, Helen and I are on the case. And hoping to rope in Olivia.'

'I don't suppose *you* know where she is,' Deborah asked Guy as he walked her to her car. 'Has she been in touch with you lately? She seems to have slipped through the cracks.'

'Not for quite a while,' he said, sounding faintly peeved. 'I've no idea what she's up to these days. She never was very good at keeping in touch.' It made his blood boil when he thought about it but he wouldn't go into that now. Those endless meals she had cadged from Gwen, as well as the overnight stays. To this day, the guest-room was still referred to as hers. The very least she could have done was given them some support; the others were rallying round as in the old days.

'Well, if she should be in touch, please have her

call me. And I'll do the same for you if I hear from her first. I am certain she'd want to be with you now. After all, you practically brought her up.' Certainly in the years that mattered when they'd been like surrogate parents. Deborah was struck by a sudden thought.

'Do you have a local directory?' Stanmore was just a few miles down the road; she had the time and felt like doing some snooping.

'Can you remember their name?' she asked, flicking through the pages, and Guy, with some effort, managed to summon it up.

'Standish. I think his name was Gerry.' He hadn't thought of either of them in years. A chilly woman, that once they had met, with a haughty demeanour and carefully-coiffed hair but, beneath the plummy tones, a hint of the Scouse roots she tried hard to hide. She had never so much as thanked the Palmers for all they had done for her niece.

Deborah located them easily enough and keyed the number into her phone.

'Thanks,' she said, handing him back the book. 'I'll let you know if I come up with anything.' She'd be late home for supper but that was okay, she'd call Abigail from the car. It was time that idle little madam did something for a change.

11

The best time to talk to New Orleans, Lisa found, was either early afternoon or else around two in the morning, which suited her better. Markus grew used to lying in bed, hearing the murmur of her voice, still with its faint hint of brogue, from behind the closed door. He would burrow deeper into the pillows, waiting to help her unwind when she finally came to bed. On nights he had gigs he would frequently find her still hunched at her makeshift desk, her sole source of light the computer screen as she doggedly worked at her notes.

'Still at it?' he'd ask and she'd silently nod and then he would know it was all to do with Suzy. Interest in the case had flared up with the fiftieth anniversary of the hanging of Ruth Ellis, the last woman in the UK to be executed. The sister was fighting to get the sentence quashed; in these more enlightened times, the consensus was that she had been a battered woman who hadn't deserved to die. To accomplish her aim the sister, now old, was vowing to stick around to see justice done. For, what had been barbaric even then, could not happen now. Which hardened Lisa's resolve to fight on and get an acquittal for Suzy.

'Come to bed, please,' Markus beseeched her. 'You will think more clearly when you have had some sleep.'

'Can't,' said Lisa, 'there isn't time. They seem hell-bent on finding her guilty and the deadline is getting very close.'

She had found, in one of her student box-files, some grainy old black and white snaps of them all, grouped on the terrace at school in brilliant sunshine. She must have shoved them into the file the day she'd finally left home and set off to start her next phase at the foot of the legal ladder. After Oxford, with its spacious rooms and silent libraries where she could study, the prospect of having to return to that bedlam appalled her. Eight adults and a noisy baby shoe-horned into a terraced house; there was no way Lisa could contemplate that again. Even though Dermot and Connor had moved out, she still couldn't handle the noise.

'I need total quiet for my studying,' she explained to her ma, who took it as a personal affront when any of her progeny attempted to leave. Seamus and Billy, in Lisa's absence, had bagged their own separate rooms, meaning she now had to share with Roisin, the second youngest till the new one had come along. At fifteen,

Roisin was a trainee hairstylist with a passion for strident rock. It wouldn't be fair on her either, said Lisa. After working so hard in the salon all day, she had earned some space of her own.

'Aw, don't fret,' she reassured her ma. 'I'm a big girl now and can stand on my own feet.' The sooner she got away from Kilburn, the more liberated she'd be. She had learned a lot at Lady Margaret Hall and was anxious now to progress to the next stage, which would lead to joining one of the Inns of Court. Her first rented room was in Tottenham Court Road, noisier and grimmer than even she was used to but only a stone's throw from Chancery Lane and the Law Society Library. She promised to bring her washing home and turn up for Sunday lunch, but pretty quickly moved further out, to Rotherhithe, not yet on the way up, where she could afford to rent on her own. It also appealed to her socialist conscience; the working people in this part of the East End needed the services of well-trained lawyers at fees they could afford.

The first thing she did, once she'd spruced the place up with cushions, pot-plants and scented candles, was summon the gang round one Saturday evening to celebrate her newfound independence. In their different ways, all were moving on; Deborah to her rabbinical training, Helen to Harvard for her Ph.D. Olivia had vanished and Miranda was dead. Only Suzy, having finished art school, was happy to go on living at home with her parents. In a way, it was a final Eve of Waterloo only this time they were off in different directions, not knowing when they were likely to meet again.

'We must definitely stay in touch,' commanded Deborah, always their natural leader. 'We will make new connections but what matters most is to stick with the ones we already have, for the friends you make at school you will keep for ever.' Wise words, as usual; they knew she was right. Life without each other was unimaginable.

Her New Orleans contact was an attorney called Nathan Blumberg whom Lisa had located via the internet. A criminal lawyer in a thriving practice, he had leapt at the chance of becoming involved in this prominent murder trial. He was younger than she was by several years and she liked his sharp mind and laid-back manner, felt that with him on board she might yet get results.

'Ought I be coming over?' she asked but the answer was always no. If, at this delicate stage in the proceedings, she attempted to interfere, she would without doubt, he warned her, be shown the door. To start with, the fact she was Suzy's friend would certainly go against her; she might even end up in custody herself. In the southern states they took murder seriously. It paid not to meddle with the rules.

'I feel so helpless,' she fretted to Markus as he held her close in his arms. 'Poor Suzy is such an innocent,

I can see her confessing to something she didn't do.'

'Why?' he asked. He barely knew Suzy but it sounded far-fetched to him. Though double murder didn't quite fit the picture Lisa had painted of her. Innocent, maybe, but it didn't add up. The children, after all, were dead. That was the only fact that had been confirmed.

'Because she trusts people too easily and maybe was somehow led astray. I'm not entirely sure what I mean, just know without doubt that there's no way she can have done it.' Her voice was failing; he hugged her to him. All this was taking its toll.

'By what?' he asked but she didn't know. It was all so horribly frustrating. Unless there was someone she was shielding, but who? Certainly not Andrew; they were his children too and he'd loved them every bit as much as she had.

'She must be out of her mind with it all, unable to get her thinking straight.' What couldn't have been more than a macabre accident had put her on trial for her life. In a foreign country, away from her parents, with a husband who seemed to be ignoring her. Which was why, if they went, they might possibly help. Just for Suzy to have friends she could talk to, if only the legal system would let them in.

'Stay away,' Nathan continued to tell her. 'There is nothing you can do.' But still Lisa fretted and went without sleep, frustrated by her own ineffectuality.

'Stop beating up on yourself,' said Markus, hating

to see her suffer. 'You have done what you can; now listen to him. At least she knows she has you behind her, which must be a comfort of sorts.'

Assuming the messages were getting through, another source of uncertainty. If they weren't, poor Suzy might feel she had been abandoned. Several times Nathan had been to the prison but came back with very little news. At least the judge was a woman, which was something, respected for her humanitarian stance.

'She is black,' he reported to Lisa. 'And stern. But the word also is that she is fair.'

Perhaps she was the person they should try approaching but Nathan was dead against it. 'Interfering with the process of the law,' he told her, 'can only go against you. And she wouldn't be able to talk to you, anyway, while things are sub judice.'

'What else can I do?' bleated Lisa in panic.

'Wait,' said Markus. 'And sleep.'

When Lisa had passed the school entrance exam, police caps were hurled in the air, and when she further compounded her triumph by winning a scholarship too, Paddy bought all his mates many drinks which had him staggering home. Colleen, for once, was prepared to overlook it; it wasn't every day, after all, that one of their children excelled. Most of the boys had been in and out of trouble and even Lisa, in her wilder moments, was not the little angel she sometimes seemed. But a scholarship to such a prestigious school was way beyond their dreams. For this had Paddy risked his life on the streets and Colleen scrimped and saved. The uniform would be hard to provide but they'd manage somehow even if it meant the two of them working extra shifts. The older boys could get jobs in the market and the rest could walk to school. Despite the roughness of the neighbourhood, there were enough Maguires, if they stuck together, to present a united front.

Not Lisa, though, in her smart new blazer and the satchel her dad had brought home. She could take the tube down to Canons Park and walk through open fields to the school, provided she always joined up with other girls.

'No loitering, mind,' said her mother firmly. She knew her daughter only too well and you could never be quite sure in those wide open spaces. Colleen had been married to a cop far too long not to have raised her children to be streetwise. Nevertheless, on that very first morning she had waved Lisa off with a lump in her throat. Despite the jaunty strut and fiery red curls, only a mother could understand how scared she must be inside. It meant certain sacrifices in all their lives but she knew that Lisa was worth it. For if any Maguire had a secure future, she was unquestionably the one.

At the start she and Deborah had not hit it off. Deborah was confident, bossy and brash and made rude fun of the other girl's Irish brogue. She taunted her, whenever she could, about her carroty hair and way of speaking. But she quickly dropped it when it had no effect; Lisa was far too canny ever to rise. She had grown up rough on the Kilburn streets and would not be terrorised now by a spoilt little rich girl. Instead she turned her attention to Helen, whose bookworm instincts and plain commonsense she found infinitely more attractive. Both had a single aim in sight, to work hard and pass their exams, whereas Deborah had always had everything easy and was used to queening it over her peers, which she took as a matter of course. At her prep school she had been top of her class but here was just another of the new girls and it irked her to see the easy friendship springing up between the other two.

They began by sharing each other's books and sat in adjoining desks. And then started travelling home together; Helen lived in Cricklewood which was not that far from Kilburn. Neither was ever in a hurry to go home; Helen's parents would be working late and Lisa's house was always knee-deep in children. So they'd go to the library or a coffee-bar or even to the pictures after school. Deborah, thwarted, had to make do with Suzy who had come up from the junior school and knew her way around. And also knew Miranda through their parents.

The situation couldn't last; Deborah and Lisa were too much alike and, sooner or later, things had to come to a head. Not only were they the brightest in the class, they were also the most vocal, so that, after only a matter of weeks, a mutual admiration took over and they gradually dropped the banter. Lisa was far too good value to waste, whereas Deborah was also shrewd enough to want her on her side. After a period of cautious assessment during which they sized each other up, commonsense finally prevailed and they became friends. It was then signed and sealed by Suzy's mother who invited them all home for tea.

Markus was startled when Lisa started crying; it seemed to have come out of nowhere. He hugged her tightly and felt her shoulders heaving, stroked her hair until she calmed down, glad to be there at such a time and transfer some of his strength. She was the gutsiest woman he had ever known, yet still possessed a vulnerable side which only added to the powerful allure that prevented him ever leaving. His parents in Hamburg kept ordering him home but he could not tear himself away from London.

'Hush,' he whispered, as though she were a child, uncertain what had brought on this sudden grief.

'It's Gwen,' she said, sniffing and rubbing her eyes, looking for all the world like a waif in her T-shirt and skimpy briefs. 'After what she did for us all, she didn't deserve any of this. She dropped her career without a second thought the moment she knew she was pregnant. At a time when women her age were fighting for equal pay and shorter hours. She would have made a brilliant teacher, that has never been in dispute. But instead her energies went into her marriage and making sure that both her children had the best start in life. And we, as Suzy's inner circle, got to share in her wisdom too.'

She blew her nose and mopped her eyes. Markus had never seen her as shaky as this.

'So why,' she asked, as if he would know, 'have all these horrible things started happening to her?' Kit, the kids; now Suzy herself. Things couldn't be any blacker. 'Now I know for certain there isn't a God. Something, I confess, I have long suspected.'

12

There was nothing in the world Markus wouldn't have done to help make Lisa feel better but, on this occasion, he wasn't sure what he could do. He loved her more than she possibly knew but feared to make it an issue. She was always intolerant of emotion and turned up her nose at soppiness. She was tough and feisty with an unrelenting heart, which only added to his pain. Women had never been a problem to Markus; he could pick up anyone he liked. Only Lisa continued to resist him; he sensed that beneath her diamond-hard shell, she was nursing a secret hurt.

If ever he raised the subject, she laughed it away. Too young, she said, at this stage of his life to contemplate any sort of permanence. Besides, the age gap could never be got round. Helen and Piet were a different matter; he was much older but that was more socially acceptable.

'You've got your whole future ahead of you,' said Lisa. 'By the time you are ready to settle, I'll be too old.'

'Is that what you really believe?' asked Deborah, envious of Lisa's lusty sex life. That side of things between her and Neville had long ago faded away.

'It is,' said Lisa. 'He would soon start to hate me if I let him tie himself down at this stage in his life.' Besides, in her heart she remained a good Catholic even though she no longer believed in any god. If she'd planned to marry, she'd have done it by now. The only one she had wanted had let her down.

Markus, however, would not be deterred. Although he tried not to mention it, in his heart he swore he would never give up on her. He watched her fretting and tossing in her sleep and wished there was something positive he could do. But she failed to take him seriously; he was only a musician, passing through, and she an eminent QC.

And then he had a stroke of good fortune he couldn't quite believe. Out of the blue he had a call from a man he'd played with at Ronnie Scott's who was taking his band to New Orleans for Jazz Fest and was short of a saxophone player.

'Six days,' said Artie, 'if you're really pressed. Longer than that, if you're not. We're planning to tour the southern states and end up in Savannah.'

Markus was instantly so elated, he scarcely knew what to say. It seemed so meant, he thought he had misunderstood.

'New Orleans in the States, *ja*?' he said, wondering

how Lisa would take it. It might look awfully like interference but he couldn't turn it down.

'Where else, you dope? The jazz capital of the world. You can't afford not to come. You never know who'll be there to hear you. It could very well change your life.'

Four heady days of solid playing with some of the greatest jazz legends in the world. Plus all the major labels would be there; he couldn't hope to find a better showcase.

'Okay, count me in,' he said, though it would mean having to cancel a London gig.

Lisa, still up to her eyes in it, was delighted and impressed. 'Terrific!' she said, embracing him. 'Maybe it will turn out to be your big breakthrough.'

'And you won't come with me?'

'I can't,' she said, too stressed to pick up his nuance.

'You could meet Nathan Blumberg face to face and perhaps get into the trial.'

'I mustn't, you know that. And you mustn't either.' She saw the determined glint in his eye but decided to overlook it. 'Now I must really get back to work. We'll talk about it later.'

13

Maggie Holbrook emerged from her studio, wiping her fingers on a turps-soaked rag. At sixty-seven, she was still impressive; not, by any means, a beauty but with strength and character in her face. She was tall and spare, with a shock of iron grey hair and dressed in a paint-spattered work-shirt. Her skin was weather-beaten from living by the sea and, as usual, her bony feet were bare. When she retired she had left Finchley Road and moved to this picturesque fisherman's cottage in Hastings, close to the harbour. Although she had given up regular teaching, as a painter she was even more acclaimed than before, just finishing a clutch of new canvases destined for the Summer Exhibition. It was half-past one; she'd been at it since dawn.

She poured herself a glass of red wine then returned to the Sunday papers. She still couldn't quite believe what she was reading; Suzy Palmer, a former pupil, was in court in the States, on a charge of first degree murder. It couldn't be true, not that gentle child, though the accusation screamed from all the head-lines. In confirmation, her photo was there, with the same shy smile from happier times before her world turned completely upside down.

Maggie's family of cats had increased to five – she could never resist a stray – and these now circled around her ankles, reminding her it was time that she thought about lunch. When she was on a painting jag they knew, to their cost, that she might go on working all day. Their union spokesman, a feisty red tom, was making their grievances all too plain. He was rangy and unremittingly vocal as he repeatedly butted her arm.

'All right,' she said absently, scratching his ear, absorbed in the horror of what she was reading. Although she hadn't seen Suzy since the wedding, she had recently grown quite close to her mother who was rapidly turning into a cherished friend. Poor Gwen, what agony she must be enduring. As soon as the light went she would call her and see what she could do. Mother and daughter had always been close; much of Suzy's determination was derived from the loving support she received at home.

Maggie had spotted Suzy's potential when she'd first started teaching her and realised how committed she was to her art. At the school there were many gifted pupils, a reason she'd stayed there for so long, but the highest fliers were mostly academic. Year after year the school topped the league in the contest for

Oxbridge places but art was rarely more than an also ran. It used to be understood in the staffroom; the brainy ones studied calculus or Latin, the duds learned to cook or paint. A throwback to an earlier age when girls were raised to be wives. Only this school was more forward-thinking. It was years since cookery had been on the syllabus and art was only a tail-end choice when putting together a package of O level subjects.

It had suited Maggie to be on the staff, less because she cared about teaching than for more selfish reasons. It provided an income and structure to her life and allowed her to do her own painting, the only thing she had ever been passionate about. But, on those rare occasions when she unearthed a nugget, she went instantly into action. There was far too little real talent in the world for it not to be nurtured from an early stage and drawing, like poetry or an ear for music, was something that could wither without proper care. And Suzy, entirely without pretension, had not even realised she had such a gift.

Maggie opened some tins for the cats, then made herself a hefty sandwich to keep her going till the light began to fade. She ate on the patio, among the geraniums, and pushed back her sleeves so her leathery skin could soak up more Vitamin D. She loved living here on the edge of the sea with the cry of the gulls as her dawn chorus. She missed the bustle of Finchley Road, though not the pollution and traffic noise, and was daily becoming more hermit-like. Cats were important but she didn't miss people, only a handful of cherished friends. She closed her eyes for a ten-minute nap but couldn't stop thinking about Suzy. It made no sense at all that such horror should touch the life of someone so essentially good.

But the facts were there in black and white even if she couldn't believe them. If all that was claimed had really occurred, then the poor child's life was at stake. Whatever the truth, it was vital she be saved, which meant immediate action. She scrabbled around to locate her address-book; the call to the Palmers would have to wait. She slipped on her horn-rim reading glasses and scrutinised its battered pages in search of a number she remembered scrawling down. Weddings were often a source of delight; she loved to catch up with the past. It was interesting to see what changes time wrought and this particular pupil, not a favourite, had turned out much better than she might have guessed. Liking her more, Maggie had taken her number with a vague idea of keeping in touch. Which hadn't, of course, happened, they were both so busy, but now she knew she'd been justified. For if anyone from the old days could help Suzy, this was the one she would nominate. And, since she was rarely wrong, she felt vindicated.

Deborah was pleased to get Maggie's call, touched and grateful as well. At school she had never really known Miss Holbrook, had viewed her with a degree of caution because of her celebrity status as an artist. The teacher, famed for her lacerating tongue, was known not to suffer fools gladly. Deborah, sensing that they wouldn't get on, had managed to steer clear of her which wasn't hard because she was lousy at art. They had briefly spoken at Suzy's wedding but, other than that, hardly knew each other. Now she was touched by the teacher's concern and brought her up to date on what she knew.

'It's really Lisa Maguire you should talk to. Remember her? She was at the wedding too. She's the one with the legal training who now has a foot in the enemy camp. I am certain she'd love to hear from you. We need all the support we can get.' They chatted awhile then agreed to stay in touch. Maggie, an experienced peace campaigner, pledged her support for whatever they chose to do. She liked the way these girls had grown up, amply fulfilling the school's expectations by giving something back to society. She remembered what rebels they once had been, smoking in the memorial garden, messing about on the way home from school and trying to pick up boys. Little had got past her eagle eye. She had been, after all, that rarest of creatures, a teacher with a colourful past and the crusading spirit of someone much younger. An ardent pacifist, she still loved a fight. Hastings was all very well but had its limits.

'Perhaps we should organise a protest,' she suggested. She wouldn't mind making the banners herself. 'Outside the American Embassy. We need to make our presence felt before they can do her any harm.' She remembered telling poor Suzy once that the world would one day hear more of her. This hadn't been what she'd had in mind; she still couldn't really believe that it wasn't a dream.

'If you do get a message through to her,' she said, 'tell her I'm thinking about her.'

Deborah promised and made a note. Maggie's signature on any petition should add considerable weight. She still occasionally hit the headlines, when receiving an honour or reviewing an exhibition, and her caustic remarks about the Turner Prize were always widely reported.

'She sounded terrific,' said Deborah to Lisa when they had their daily catch-up call. 'Feisty and youthful, just like old times. Though by now, I suppose, she must be well over sixty.'

Lisa laughed. 'You make it sound like a hundred. Haven't you heard that sixty is the new forty-five?' Which was just as well; the big four-oh was closer than either would admit.

'I don't suppose there's any news of Andrew?' Lisa had Nathan Blumberg on the case.

'No,' said Lisa, 'it's really odd. You'd think he'd do anything at all to help his wife.'

'Have you any idea what his legal status is? They haven't taken him in?'

'Not yet. He isn't under any suspicion. They seem determined to pin it on her and since he has a cast iron alibi, for the moment they're leaving him alone.'

'Do we know yet what the row was about?' It had been in all the papers. It seemed unlikely but the woman next door had reported raised voices and the sound of a car driving off.

'Just a domestic tiff is all they'll say. It doesn't sound remotely like Suzy and Andrew.' Their domestic bliss was still legendary; even the neighbours in New Orleans had described them as very much in love.

'So what happens next? Should we go there?' asked Deborah. Helen kept ringing to find out.

'Nathan says no. It would not be productive. If we stir up bad publicity it could all blow up in our faces.'

'But we have to do something. This waiting is hell.' Deborah kept thinking of Gwen and Guy and their rapidly diminishing hope. 'Perhaps if we went we could talk to Andrew. Find out his side of things.'

'If he'd see us. He might not want to. From all accounts, he is hugely angry and seems to believe in her guilt.'

'That can't be true. He knows her too well and how much she doted on them.'

'He's deranged with grief, as you might expect, and probably not thinking straight. Besides,' added Lisa, who'd been submerged in it all week, 'there isn't anyone else for him to blame.'

'If only the cops would get up off their backsides

. . .' The same old lament they had heard so often before. Lisa's father was strongly on their side and so were his Kilburn colleagues. The life of a policeman had never been easy but, for once, they were rooting for the accused.

Talking to Deborah had brought back so much. Once she had finished her evening's stint, cleaned her brushes and changed her clothes, Maggie poured herself a whisky nightcap and settled down to go through her bulging files. Which wasn't easy since the whole of her small space was crammed with canvases and her painting paraphernalia. This time, however, she knew what she was after; somewhere amongst the accumulated dross was a faded portfolio from long ago of Suzy's early drawings. She had made a point of keeping them since she'd always hoped they might one day be of value. Value to her, if not to the world, because she had been Suzy's teacher. Eventually, after several false trails, she found them at the bottom of her chart chest, carefully preserved between sheets of pristine tissue and labelled in Indian ink. In the natural course of things, of course, she'd have kept them for Suzy's children; as it was, she'd continue to keep them safe and then maybe give them to Gwen. What a terrible waste it was; she still couldn't quite take it in.

Here they were, those exquisite sketches of celandines, primroses and other wild flowers, executed in minutest detail precise enough for a textbook. She remembered clearly the solemn child, tongue protruding in concentration as she carefully laboured to get them exactly right. And here was the date – spring '76 – when she would have been in the Lower Fourth. Maggie held each one close to the lamp and marvelled again at the workmanship, good enough for public display even at that age. She'd inquired about the origins of the talent; such a gift rarely came out of the blue. Gwen generously credited her, as the teacher, but things were rarely that straightforward; draughtsmanship this good could not be taught.

In the old Finchley Road days, when Suzy came to tea, they talked about a wide range of things which might have surprised Suzy's parents, had they known. Always a free thinker, Maggie despised the stuffy conventions about what was appropriate for discussion between teacher and pupil. 'If you're old enough to produce work this good, then it's time you knew about the other stuff too.' She had travelled extensively and lived to the full, throwing her energies into her art which had greatly benefited from her wide diversity. Some of this she was now passing on to her highly receptive listener.

Suzy adored her and absorbed every word. Never in her life before had she met such a colourful character. And Maggie, in turn, was drawn to the child because she sensed from the start that she was special. There were many noisy extroverts in the school, always flinging their weight around, like Deborah whose parents neglected her while pampering her with their money. Maggie had always preferred the quiet ones, those with something going on inside, who took the time to think before they spoke.

As Suzy grew older and more aware, she started confiding in Maggie. Her brother, the fabled Christopher, had long been the talk of the school. On the few occasions he had actually been there, most notably once to the sixth form dance, his reputation had preceded him, lending him rock star status. Because of the age gap, their paths rarely crossed but he dated a string of the older girls in his lackadaisical way.

'My brother never has problems with girls,' said Suzy to Miss Holbrook. 'He doesn't take them seriously yet they just won't leave him alone.' She had often heard him talking about them and his cavalier attitude shocked her. Despite their shared upbringing, she knew she could never treat anyone so lightly.

The teacher laughed. 'It's his age,' she said. 'Wait a few years till he matures and the boot will be on the other foot.' She knew the father slightly from the school and found him attractive and respectful. A nice-looking man with a load of natural charm; if the son grew up anything like his dad, he'd do well.

Suzy, however, remained unconvinced. She didn't think much of boys. The ones she knew were pimply and horrid with filthy minds and smutty talk. 'I don't intend to marry,' she said, colour-washing a delicate fern.

'You will,' said Maggie, 'when you're older. I promise. Look how well-matched your parents are.' She liked the Palmers, both of them, could see why the daughter was so sweet.

'But you never did.' And her lifestyle was brilliant; in Suzy's eyes Miss Holbrook had it all.

'I'm different,' said Maggie. 'Don't use me as a yard-stick. I've always been too selfish to compromise.' There had been moments but even she knew where to draw the line. The thing about life was to live it to the full but Suzy was still a shade too young to be led astray by her fairly outrageous opinions.

'I want to be like you,' said Suzy.

'Nonsense,' said Maggie. 'Now come and have tea before you get a crick in your neck. Your mother would never forgive me.'

14

Preservation Hall was densely packed but Jackson Saunders was a happy man. After his family and his Maker, in that order, most of his waking hours were devoted to music. He had sung since childhood with the Baptist choir, progressing, when his voice matured, to being their resident bass. On church occasions, he was usually there, an imposing figure and champion of his people which was why he'd become a union official, a position he'd proudly held for many years.

This Thursday night, the eve of the Jazz Fest, the town was packed with fans from all over the world, with not another bed to be had there for love or money. On Sunday he'd be performing himself, doing his gospel bit; tonight he was out on the town alone, relaxing. Preservation Hall served neither food nor drink so he carried beer in a paper bag and stepped outside into St Peter Street to catch a breath of fresh air. The joint was jumping, the way he liked it; though largely out-of-towners, he loved their spirit. Next he'd move on to Fritzel's Jazz Pub, another of his favourite nightspots, but he liked to keep his finger on the pulse by watching the crowds and tapping his toe to authentic traditional jazz. As he strolled he was greeted from left and right by smiling familiar faces. Jackson had spent his whole life in this town; both he and his wife were much respected within the black community.

A tall young man was lounging in the doorway when Jackson re-entered the hall. Warmed by his obvious enthusiasm, Jackson smiled and attempted to be heard over the cacophony of sound. Not a local, he could tell that right away from his chic leather jacket and the fervour in his eyes, someone who obviously took his music seriously.

'Y'all new to N'awlins?' asked Jackson between sets and the young man stared at him blankly for a moment, baffled but polite. But after two repetitions, he got it and smiled.

'I'm here for the Fest,' he said, in accented English, and they fell into conversation about the bands. The stranger, who was German and quite obviously knew his stuff, was part of a combo over from London and played the tenor sax. He introduced himself as Markus von Hagen and the two men solemnly shook hands. One thing led to another, as happens, and pretty soon they'd discovered acquaintances in common. The world of jazz is like a club with everyone speaking the same language. So Jackson invited Markus to join him for a meal and led the way down Bourbon Street to Fritzel's.

The room was dark and pulsating with life; the door stood open to let in the steamy night air. Once they were seated, with bourbon chasers alongside their foaming beers, Jackson expanded and talked about his life. He spoke of the town that he ardently loved and his work as a union official. Of the two bright sons who were both away at college and his wife, the light of his life, who was with the judiciary.

'She doesn't like jazz?' Markus couldn't believe it. To this man, like him, it was clearly a religion.

'She just doesn't have the time,' said Jackson and mentioned the trial that was ruling her life. No going into details, of course, except that she was working so hard, he feared her health might suffer if she didn't let up.

Markus knew exactly what he meant, had been there himself all too often. 'Your wife's a lawyer?' he asked, impressed. This gnarled, benevolent man seemed a real rough diamond.

'A judge,' said Jackson proudly, smiling broadly. 'One of the best in the state.'

'How many black judges can there be?' said Markus later, on the phone to Lisa. 'And of them, how many women?'

'Now just you be careful,' said Lisa sharply, though she felt her heartbeat quicken. She couldn't have

Markus interfering when Nathan had warned her to stay out of it, though she did trust him not to do anything too rash. The men were meeting again that night for beers with a bunch of musicians. After which, they planned to jam a little. Markus was clearly having a brilliant time.

'I'll just keep my ear to the ground,' he said. 'This community is so inbred, there's no telling what I may pick up.'

15

It was seventeen years until Maggie Holbrook's prophecy for Suzy finally came true. When they all left school and moved on to the next phase, Suzy enrolled at Harrow art school, just a couple of railway stops from home. Her friends were amused but it suited her well, handy for town and the tennis club and involving no major upheaval or any expense. Her foundation course was for twelve months only, so real decisions about the future could wait. She got on with her parents well and enjoyed their company; whereas Kit had wasted no time in moving out, Suzy was quite content to stay where she was. She and her mother were genuine friends and, as she grew older, this closeness grew. In the evenings they often did social things together; the occasional film, a concert at the church, even cookery classes. Not that Gwen needed to learn how to cook; she enjoyed refreshing her repertoire and found it fun to do so with her daughter. Guy had his golf and his friends at the pub. It was good, for a change, to have female company more stimulating than Wanda.

They shared a quirky sense of humour, too, laughing at jokes that left Guy totally baffled. TV ads, the sort with jingles that instantly leech into the brain, had the pair of them falling about in delight. They often added verses of their own and sang along until Guy was obliged to change channels.

'You're both daft,' he would tell them benevolently, loving having his family intact at a time when children were more often fleeing the nest. Both the kids were doing well. Kit had chosen the diplomatic corps, in which he was already excelling and would soon be posted overseas.

'Don't you ever get claustrophobic?' Deborah asked Suzy at lunch one day. Her father had joined her to the English-Speaking Union, deeming it an appropriate place to entertain her friends. She was up from Cambridge for a fleeting weekend and fitting in as much as she could. Shopping and Suzy were today's agenda; later her parents were hosting a dinner for some influential contacts. Her Cambridge life was rapidly expanding; she spent less and less time at home.

'No,' said Suzy, 'I really don't. Which must make me sound very wimpish. I enjoy being with my mum and dad and they're great about not getting in my way. I can do what I like, come and go as I please.' She had bought herself a second-hand Beetle which was handy for getting around.

'Boyfriends?' asked Deborah, with her single-track mind.

'Nothing you'd notice.' Suzy shrugged. A couple of local Lotharios, neither of them serious. It wasn't something she gave much thought to though the flaw, if there was one, in living in the suburbs was the dearth of suitable males. Like Kit, the young ones had mostly moved away leaving, apart from the halt and the lame, only the newly-married. Which didn't bother Suzy at all since all that really concerned her was her course. If all worked out as she hoped it would, in a year she'd move on to St Martin's. And after that she'd see; it was early days yet.

Deborah laughed; Suzy might not have changed but Cambridge had widened her own horizons. School had been challenging but allowed her to coast whereas college was finally stretching her. It was clear she had grown more responsible, had shed her adolescent loucheness. Even her appearance was modified. Most of the old flamboyance had gone; she was quieter and more restrained. No more hoop earrings and gypsy scarves nor kohl-rimmed eyes like an Indian dancer; she was dressed demurely in a simple grey suit with a single strand of matched pearls. Her hair, which she'd always worn long and dishevelled, was now neatly parted and tucked behind her ears.

'You look like someone's PA,' said Suzy, secretly admiring her friend's new panache. She still wore the same baggy jeans, with a patchwork jacket she had thrown together as part of a college project. But that was what it was like at art school, a bunch of students who had not yet grown up, vying with each other for the spotlight.

'Smart is good,' said Deborah seriously. 'It adds to your overall clout.' For someone still in her junior year, she had certainly polished her image. What she wasn't revealing was her latest ambition, to train to be a rabbi. It had occurred to her during a philosophy tutorial that, female competition being sparse, it might make a handy shortcut to the fast track once she had got her degree. She had only recently told her father who had been so pleased there was no turning back. He had always considered her a bit of a wastrel, though confident that she would eventually turn out well.

'My daughter, the rabbi.' It rolled smoothly off the tongue. At last, maybe, she would settle down and fulfil the dreams he had had for her since she was born.

In place of the Eve of Waterloo, these days the girls met for cocktails. On Boxing Day, the year they left school, it was drinks and nibbles at the Palmers' house from noon. There were a handful of neighbours invited as well who stuck together at one end of the room, allowing the youngsters to mingle. Kit was there with a couple of friends while Suzy's guests were Deborah, Lisa and Helen. They were so excited, they all talked at once, just as it had always been in the old days.

The neighbours felt they were almost intruders since only the parents were paying attention to them.

It was a full three months since Deborah had seen Kit and she shot him quick glances when she sensed his back was turned. He still looked wonderful, with slightly longer hair, and was sporting a fancy cravat and cashmere sweater. He had also put on a bit of weight which gave him an air of maturity. She found herself still drawn to him, though less since she'd been up at Cambridge.

'Christmas presents,' said Suzy, giggling, noticing the focus of Deborah's gaze. 'Now he's at the Foreign Office, we thought he could do with a bit of sprucing up.'

He still had the same red Morgan parked outside and the friends were his flatmates from Baron's Court, both of them with him at Oxford. Deborah found herself lost for words, suddenly feeling gauche. Once she'd have been in the centre of things, flirting and getting on everyone's nerves. Now, in her sharp little tailored suit, she had reinvented herself. Guy, from the sidelines, watched her spellbound, intrigued by this latest new role she had assumed. She always had been a flirtatious little minx but whatever it was she did apparently worked. Her eyes, he noticed, were fixed on his son which was something he'd had to put up with for years. He went around topping up everyone's glass, feeling horribly passé. It was one thing having all the young things around but now they were growing up fast and moving on. In the hall he paused to consider his reflection. He had to face it, he was middle-aged; even his hair was thinning and dusted with grey.

Eventually Deborah found the courage to join them and was rewarded by Kit with a fleeting kiss, as though he vaguely recalled her from somewhere, just couldn't remember her name. His main attention remained focused on Lisa with whom he was acting very cosy. They were swapping Oxford anecdotes; they had numerous friends in common. Helen, of course, was up there too, though not included in their conversation. She had hardly changed at all since school, looked lost without a book. Lisa, however, had gained in grace, having toned down her wilder excesses. Her hair, having lost its fiery red, had deepened into elegant auburn; she was dressed from head to toe in black, which set it off to perfection. She was slender and trim and a careful listener; all good attributes for an aspiring lawyer.

Deborah quashed a jealous pang and turned instead to the flatmates. One was a doctor, a houseman at St Thomas's; the other, to her surprise, a trainee accountant.

'What on earth persuaded you into anything so dull?' She had always been outspoken.

'The romance of figures,' he replied without a flicker. 'Plus a desire to retire before I'm fifty.'

Nice, she liked that; she was studying PPE and found that, after all, he was witty and bright. Besides, it took her mind off Kit, still glued to Lisa's side. But she couldn't blame her best friend for that since Deborah'd never said a word about her fling with Kit. Even now it seemed too private though she knew, as she always had, that it couldn't have worked. The family fallout would have been too great, especially in view of her latest ambition. So she closed in instead on the trainee accountant who was spending Christmas in Highgate. Deborah, who had the Daimler outside, cut her losses by offering him a lift, knowing how impressed he would be when he saw it. She hasn't changed, reflected Kit, who was more on her case than she knew. That crazy summer was something he'd long cherish but in the past three months he, too, had moved on.

Lisa, however, was quite transformed, from raucous schoolgirl to thoughtful adult, in addition to which she had grown into a real looker. She still retained a touch of the brogue but her madcap behaviour was gone. A shame in a way, reflected Kit. He would bet that, fired up, she would be stupendous. Then remembered this was his parents' home and Lisa his kid sister's friend. Diplomatically he moved away and crossed the big divide to talk to the neighbours. Nice boy, was the considered opinion, with lovely manners for his age.

'Do you fancy Lisa?' asked Suzy later as her father carved cold turkey for a late lunch. The guests were gone and the glasses had been cleared. All that remained was to wash them up and hoover the living-room rug.

'Not especially.' Kit was non-committal but she knew him well enough to detect when he lied.

'Or Deborah?'

'No.' He spoke too fast. Anyone more clued up would have got it in one. 'She is far too pushy and in your face. Not my kind of girl.' He felt ashamed of denying her this way but it was better than having to fend off the family's jokes. What he said was also true; she was too ambitious for him. All he wanted was an easy life. Oxford had been paradise; he had sailed through without a care. The girls were willing, the booze had flowed; he had got two blues and passed with adequate marks. He liked his job and the heady freedom he got from sharing a flat. He missed his mother's home comforts, of course, but the time had come to move on.

Gwen understood. She had never been a clinger and had known that very soon he would leave the nest. She was lucky that, in addition to Guy, she still had her daughter at home. 'Soon,' she had cheerfully told a neighbour, 'we'll be shot of the pair of them. And then, who knows what adventures we may have. I fancy doing a spot of exotic travel.'

Gwen is a marvel, was the general consensus. Whatever she puts her hand to, she always does well. Perfect marriage and beautiful home plus the nicest couple of kids you could ever hope for. Sneakily, now she would like a grandchild but that might be counting her chickens a little too soon.

On social occasions, like the Boxing Day drinks, Suzy was all too aware of her limitations. She had never excelled at trivial chitchat at which Deborah, in particular, was so adept. She had always been a dreamy child, head firmly in the clouds, drifting through life on an alternative plane, looking at things with a draughtsman's eye, absorbing minuscule detail. Her father called her his wise old owl and loved having her still at home. Gwen, however, was increasingly anxious, wondered if they were doing her harm by not kicking her out of the nest.

'You know you could always move out,' she said, afraid of being possessive. 'We wouldn't object. Would even help you. You might prefer to live somewhere closer to town.'

'What, am I boring you?' asked Suzy, feigning shock. She could see through her mother every time.

'Of course not, darling. The very idea. I just wouldn't want you to feel we were cramping your style.'

'She'll leave when she's ready. They usually do. Now don't you go driving her out ahead of her time.' Guy was grateful that his little girl had more in her life to think about than boys.

Harrow School of Art was great but St Martin's better. Suzy lapped it up. She travelled daily to Leicester

Square, almost every night returning late. There were all kinds of diversions to detain her, extra classes, visiting lecturers, even a fortnightly jazz club. Guy worried about her walking home from the station but Suzy pointed out it was only a few minutes and also extremely well lit. He begged her to phone him and he'd meet her off the train but she told him, fairly sharply, that she could cope. She could use her own car but it wasn't worth the trouble. Just two minutes' walk, three at the most; it was high time he learnt not to fuss.

'I am not a child,' she told him sternly.

'You will always be my little girl.'

Apart from that slight inconvenience, Suzy was totally content. From the moment she first climbed those wide stone steps and inhaled the aromas of charcoal and paint, she knew she was in the right place. The students came from a wide spectrum of backgrounds and the lecturers were an assorted crew, many of them distinguished. She was thrilled. The moment she could, she trekked over to Finchley and regaled Miss Holbrook with her first impressions.

'They all seem terrifyingly talented,' she said.

'I've no doubt you'll hold your own.'

Maggie was delighted with her protégée's success; had overseen her foundation course, then guided her to St Martin's. She knew several of the teaching staff well and managed to drop the occasional word. They were, she was pleased to hear, as impressed as she was. There were other options that Suzy might have chosen but she stuck to her original plan. Drawing flowers was what she liked best. She saw no reason to swerve from that.

'Like Audubon?' said Maggie, amused, when Suzy attempted to explain.

'Or Elizabeth Blackadder.' Her current idol. What that woman was doing in paint Suzy hoped to emulate, though she knew she still had a very long way to go.

'You have the time.' It made commercial sense. Work for new artists was hard to come by but this one seemed to be set on a winning streak.

As indeed she was: the galleries loved her. Before she had even completed her course her work was becoming known.

16

Miranda had been serious when she said she wanted to train to be a doctor. She hated always being treated like a child; even her friends talked down to her just because she was small. What she lacked in inches, though, was more than made up for by her brain. She could hold her own with the rest of the class when it came to passing exams. And she didn't want to be singled out just because she could sing and dance. Voices fade and faces sag, boobs droop and stomachs barrel. Even at just fifteen she knew it was vital that she do something to safeguard her future. A wise head on a pint-sized body; but still they wouldn't listen.

'The world is full of clapped out actors and singers whose voices have passed their prime.' Before her always, as a chilling reminder, were her own parents, Cedric and Wanda. Both had toiled hard for longer than most yet their bookings had spiralled relentlessly down until they'd been forced to hang up their dancing shoes. From the London Palladium to Blackpool Pier, then inch by inch down the slippery slope to Butlins and cut-price cruise-ships. Which was not at all what Miranda wanted; she hoped to do better than that. And refused to squander this superlative education by simply treading the boards. If she couldn't make it straight to the top, then she'd rather do something quite different. Something in which she could use her brain instead of relying on her physical assets; her voice and her tippy-tappy shoes.

She talked it over with Helen, who sympathised.

'I must have real qualifications,' she said, 'if only for that fabled rainy day.' Even this young, it made sound sense. Helen was on her side.

'What do your parents say?'

'They won't even listen. Where I'm concerned, they're away with the fairies, refusing to face up to facts.' Their dream for her was Covent Garden, progressing in time to Hollywood, but her voice was too thin and reedy for opera; also she was too small. Musical comedy was a likelier bet; it was said Elaine Paige, of the hit show *Evita*, was an inch below five foot. Likewise Piaf but she was long dead, besides which, legends don't count. The truth was, Miranda was not that outstanding and she dared not risk trusting her whole future to fate.

'My parents' dreams are for themselves, not me.' At times she was almost bitter. They still lived in a celluloid world where bouquets were thrown and audiences roared, where you kept coming back to take curtain-calls and your name was perpetually in lights. What they failed to understand was that the world had changed and if she was ever to be a star, she should by now be cutting her first disc.

At Junior Guildhall, on Saturday mornings, they gave her the juvenile roles. Puck or Ariel or Dorothy from *Oz*, nice for those with stage aspirations but, even so, restricting. The cold truth was that, sooner or later, everyone has to grow up.

'Peter Pan's about as good as it gets. Over the hill by twenty-nine like a sports star or ballerina.'

'Couldn't you teach?'

'You're joking! *No way.* Too dreary and soul-destroying.' The staff at school exemplified that. Worthy, maybe; inspiring too, but nothing she'd ever do herself. The lure of show business was its glamour; some of her mother's vanity had rubbed off.

'Suzy's mother was a teacher,' said Helen, who had always idolised Gwen.

'And quit,' capped Miranda triumphantly. I rest my case, said her smile.

Thus turning her back on a worthwhile career in order to stay at home and raise kids. A betrayal of what women for decades had fought for, occasionally even with their lives. Helen, the feminist, saw Gwen as a martyr, overruled by a self-serving husband. She ignored the fact that they were very well-matched; was still too young to appreciate that. Saw only the example of her own parents where one was repressing the other's natural gifts.

'Do you realise Marie Stopes was here?' Helen was slavishly devoted to the cause. There was nothing about her own parents' marriage that made her want to have children of her own. Her mother only had eyes for her dad while his were invariably peering at slides or engrossed in learned papers. While Miranda basked in her parents' adoration, Helen had a dismal belief that her own conception had probably been accidental.

'What I want,' said Miranda, 'is a normal life. Doing the things that the rest of you do instead of all those blasted extra classes.'

'But why a doctor?'

Miranda shrugged. 'It's what I've always wanted. Don't laugh, but I'd like to save lives and do good. Hope to make a mark for myself in something that really matters.' Pretentious maybe but Helen understood. She felt much that way herself.

Miranda was thoroughly sick of her life, a prisoner not of her own volition. Her voice coach, her trainer, her dance instructor regarded her purely as promising material, failing to see the real self, a needy teenager, struggling alone with pubescence. She had cramps, she had spots, she was cranky at times but nobody bothered to find out why. She was sent to bed with a mind-numbing pill and if she had a headache, they gave her another. She yearned for the freedom the other girls had, to get away from this gilded cage to which they wouldn't even allow her a key.

Her carol concert triumph was the talk of the staffroom.

'That wee girl has the most miraculous voice.' Miss McLeod, the new chemistry teacher, was almost breathless with awe. 'She ought to be having it properly trained. Or else it's a terrible waste.' She was herself a devout choir member who sang at the church every Sunday.

'Don't worry,' said Miranda's class teacher grimly, heartily sick of the subject by now. 'Everything doable is already being done. The child has more tutors than you've had hot meals. It's a bad case of overkill. The sad thing is, they are planning to move her. The Guildhall has offered her a place next year as soon as she turns sixteen.'

'Is that wise?'

'I doubt it. We know the pitfalls. But all we, as teachers, are empowered to do is offer her parents advice. And they won't listen to anything we say. I think they perceive her as their pension in their old age.'

The Sinclairs quite often came up in conversation when the staff were jaded or needed a laugh.

'Don't start,' warned the class teacher wearily. 'It might be funny if it weren't so sad. I often wonder where the poor child got her brains.'

* * *

The next big event would be the summer show. This year they were ambitiously staging *Oklahoma!*. They had a new drama teacher, fresh from provincial rep, who was ultra keen and certainly knew her stuff. Any girl from the fifth form upwards was invited to audition; the older leading parts would be taken by staff. Because of the choruses and dance routines, the eventual cast would be huge. In addition to which there'd be backstage work, scenery to be painted and costumes made.

'Great,' said Suzy, 'we can all get involved. I fancy learning those square-dance routines my parents used to do.'

'Rather you than me,' said Deborah, who'd consider nothing unless she could be the star. And since singing and dancing was not her forte, she refused to get drawn in. Typical Deborah; she walked away, pretending to have higher things on her mind.

'Well, there's plenty of scope for you, Miranda. You can take your pick of the parts.' Suzy's generous heart overflowed with goodwill. 'A great way to end your school career.' Miranda was going to Guildhall next term. 'It will make a brilliant swansong. Which we'll none of us forget.'

Olivia was with them, on the sidelines, so quiet they might not have known she was there. Her hair looked better since Gwen took a hand but she remained pale and undernourished. She said not a word as they talked about the show but when Miranda turned up to audition, she was astonished to find her there.

'Olivia!' she said, in genuine delight. 'I wasn't aware you could sing.'

Olivia flushed and shuffled in embarrassment. 'I'm not sure I can but thought I might give it a go.'

'Quite right,' said Miranda. 'Do you know the songs?'

'I have the record at home.'

More than that, though they didn't know it, she was steeping herself in live theatre. Since most of her Saturdays were spent alone these days, she had started going to matinees and was working her way through the London theatre scene. At first Aunt Sarah did not approve, was worried about her safety. But, as Olivia pointed out, she was now fifteen and old enough to take the tube on her own. She didn't add that, after all, she'd been taking care of herself for much of her life.

'Besides,' she said, 'you never know. I may decide to go on the stage myself.'

For a fraction of a second Aunt Sarah froze at this unexpected announcement. Anyone less equipped to perform it would be hard to imagine. Olivia rarely opened her mouth and, even when she did, only ever mumbled. She was also skinny and colourless; the idea was ludicrous. Though, at least, it showed fighting spirit, which was something.

'Where did you get that idea?' asked her aunt, trying her hardest to be kind.

'Well, my mother trained as an actress,' said Olivia. 'Maybe it's in my genes.'

Her aunt was speechless, did not know what to say. 'Where did you hear that?' she finally asked.

Olivia shrugged. 'I have always known. Don't say it isn't true.'

'She was a drama student,' her aunt said stiffly. 'Who worked part-time in a bar. She did have talent and might have made it if circumstances hadn't intervened.'

'What circumstances?' It was time she knew. She was sick of always being fobbed off like a child. Fifteen was almost grown up these days; in a year she'd be old enough for marriage.

Her aunt attempted to leave the room but Olivia blocked her way. 'What circumstances?' she asked again, with sudden authority in her voice. Her cheeks were flushed and her fists were clenched; she looked in the mood for a fight.

Aunt Sarah sighed and fingered her pearls, feeling a headache was coming on. When she spoke, her voice was shrill and her pale blue eyes were frosty. 'Circumstances? Why, your father, of course. He came into her life and totally wrecked it.'

Everyone joined in the choruses at first, to get them in the mood for the auditions. Most of them had seen the film and knew the words off by heart. Because of the popular choice of show, there was an amazing turnout. Over a hundred girls were keen to take part. Most leading roles would go to the seniors, which seemed only fair, but when it was her turn, Miranda stole the show. Though small, with her silvery curls and sweet smile she looked exactly right for Laurey, the lead. She also danced as well as she sang, a star in the making already. Everyone clapped and the drama teacher was impressed.

'I don't think there's any doubt,' she said to the rest of the selection committee. Fifteen was young for the leading role but the school was democratic.

But the biggest surprise came when Olivia stood up to audition for Ado Annie. Falteringly she stepped up on to the stage, the pianist struck up with the opening chords of 'I Cain't Say No' and Olivia was away. Before their eyes she transformed herself from sorry waif to voluptuous vamp whose morals were no better than they should be. They no longer noticed her pink-rimmed specs or the cold sore on her lip. Her scrawny frame seemed to flesh itself out and her glances were provocative and saucy. And her voice, when she sang, fairly rocked the hall. How she achieved it, nobody knew; she just opened her throat, like a song-thrush, and out it came.

The applause was deafening and they all stood up while Olivia, suddenly bashful, slipped away.

'Now that,' said the drama teacher, scribbling notes, 'is acting.'

* * *

Deborah couldn't believe it when she heard, furious that Olivia had done so well. But the others were there and vouched for it. Miranda had been her brilliant self but Olivia was outstanding.

'It's a shame,' said Helen, 'that the part isn't larger. Ado Annie only gets two songs and one of those is a duet.'

'Even so,' said Lisa, 'it is the big hit. The one the audience comes away still humming.'

'So you're playing a slut,' said Deborah, when she heard. 'Not exactly typecasting, I wouldn't think.' She looked at Olivia, in her dowdy gingham and sensible Clarks sandals, with her chalky skin and prominent cold sore, and laughed.

'Don't be so mean,' said a radiant Miranda. 'Wait till you see her perform.'

'I'm not sure I'll have the time,' said Deborah.

Bitch, said Olivia to herself.

Rehearsals took up a lot of time but Olivia loved every second. At home, on her own, she mimed to the record, then adapted the performance into her own. She learned the words of the other songs, too, and had all the parts word perfect. Anyone watching would not have believed that the gawky schoolgirl in her frumpy clothes could mutate so effortlessly into a shameless flirt.

'Was that you singing?' asked Aunt Sarah, disbelieving, one night when she came home early.

'No,' said Olivia, deadpan. 'Gloria Grahame.'

'She's a natural,' said the drama teacher, watching her in rehearsal. To think that, without the show, they might never have known.

'Tell me more about my mother,' Olivia pleaded with her aunt.

'There isn't any more.' Which was all she would say. If Olivia wanted her questions answered, then she must apply to her father, assuming she could find him. She had not heard a word in the past two years since he'd left without kissing her goodbye.

Excitement rose to fever pitch as the day of the show approached. The cast rehearsed every afternoon and often in the lunch-break as well. The dance routines were sophisticated but the teacher kept putting them through their paces, over and over until they'd achieved perfect sync. Miranda had one that was all lassoes, rather like doing skipping games. The faster the music, the wilder it got until she collapsed in help-less giggles which usually caused the chorus to crack up too.

'Think of it like a hula hoop. Swivel your hips,' said the teacher.

'I can't,' said Miranda, mopping her eyes. 'It makes me feel such a fool.'

'You won't once you've mastered it,' said the teacher. 'And it goes so well with the lyrics.'

Suzy was singing in the chorus as well as doing

scenery. Things grew so fraught she would sometimes appear with paint stains still on her hands.

'I cannot wait to see it,' said Gwen. 'It's certainly a step up from Gilbert and Sullivan.'

And then the terrible thing occurred that blighted all their lives. No-one at the school at that time would forget it. It was nobody's fault, a freak accident, but it shattered everyone's confidence and meant they almost cancelled the show which, it was agreed, would be a pity. An urgent top level conference was called and the headmistress intervened.

'The show must go on,' she told the school. 'It is what Miranda would have wanted.' It was part of the learning curve, she felt, to have to face up to such things. The sooner they came to terms with it, the better.

Only one person could replace Miranda and that, of course, was Olivia. She knew the part and could sing all the songs; also, with minimal alteration, could fit into her costumes.

'Are you certain you feel all right with this?' the drama teacher asked her. The girl was pale, but she always was, and rarely showed any emotion.

'Sure,' said Olivia, unnervingly calm. She'd been privately rehearsing Laurey's songs for months. It was sad about Miranda, of course, but sometimes these things do happen. She shouldn't have been messing around in the gym on her own. Jubilation swept over her though she didn't let it show. Something at last had gone right in her life and this time nothing was going to get in the way. But when she got home from the dress rehearsal, a nasty surprise was waiting. Aunt Sarah stood there, ashen-faced, while behind her in the living-room lurked a virtual stranger.

'Get your bags packed,' her father said, after a perfunctory hug. 'We've a plane to catch in a couple of hours. We are leaving.'

'But the show,' protested Olivia, appalled. 'I can't possibly let them down at this late stage.'

'Noble sentiment. I'll drop them a note. Now get your skates on, we don't have very much time.'

17

It was one of those magical April mornings that England can do so well. Suzy, having risen early and driven against the traffic to Kew, was in search of the Princess of Wales conservatory, where the orchid collection was located. All she knew about these exotic plants was that the flowers were exquisite and hugely varied. Exactly the sort of subject for her; she had made her name with her delicate flower paintings and her books, a sideline, were now a staple seller. With this in mind, her publisher had shrewdly commissioned a specialist volume aimed at the upmarket connoisseur. It was almost complete, with delivery date pressing, and all that was left now for Suzy to do was track down one final rare species. Which, she'd discovered, could be found at Kew if only she knew where to look.

She stopped for a coffee in the morning sun, feeling marginally guilty. The great advantage of the freelance life was working elastic hours and fitting the rest of her various commitments around them. Her one real pressure was meeting deadlines, and she prided herself on always delivering on time. Miss Holbrook might be responsible for fostering her creativity but she owed her precision to her accountant dad. Friends teased her about still living at home but it suited her lifestyle well. She had the freedom to come and go as she pleased and space in which to spread out. She loved the house and her parents too, aware they all needed each other. That was the bit she couldn't explain to less than intimate friends. For, in a way that was never discussed, they were welded together by what had happened to Kit.

She could not forget that appalling call and the nightmare flight to Strasbourg. They had never discovered what had actually gone on and had long ago given up wondering. Except for her mother who she knew still fretted; whenever she caught her gazing into a pram, Suzy experienced a spasm of guilt and felt she had let them both down. Kit would have made a brilliant father; she could see him right now out there on the lawn, teaching her how to catch a cricket ball. He had had the patience and extreme good nature to have given his children the sort of upbringing their parents had lavished on them. It wasn't fair the way things had worked out. If anyone would have made a great granny, it was Gwen.

She finished her coffee. Time to get going; she still had to find that blasted plant. Nose in guidebook, she headed for the glasshouses; this place was so vast, she still hadn't worked it all out. She had thought about bringing her mother along but she'd only have slowed her down. She needed time and concentration to capture this elusive little beauty in paint. She'd prefer not to have to make a second visit.

'Can I help you?' asked a voice. Her lostness obviously showed. 'Are you looking for something?' it inquired. And, glancing up, she came face to face with the man she instinctively knew that she would marry.

'How could you possibly have known?' asked Deborah, who had settled for only second best. And, even then, he'd taken over a year to decide.

'I just did,' said Suzy. 'I don't know how.' She had no experience of such things.

'Did you hear a fanfare of celestial trumpets?' Lisa, who didn't believe in love, hoped she was not missing out.

'No,' said Suzy, feeling slightly foolish. 'I just knew the instant I saw him.'

He was slim and brown-eyed, with close-cropped curly hair, in wellingtons and jeans and with mud on his hands. He was standing in one of the inside beds smiling at her obvious confusion. A shaft of light through the glasshouse roof lit him up where he stood, which was when she had recognised destiny. Just like that.

'Is he gorgeous?' asked Lisa, who hadn't yet met him.

'Rich?' asked Deborah, the materialist.

'Neither of those things. He is just . . . well, Andrew. I know it sounds daft but we just sort of recognised each other.'

'So what did you say?' They were starting to enjoy this, quizzing her over lunch. Their little Suzy, who was such a late starter. They could tell from the sparkle in her eyes that this was the genuine thing.

'I asked where the *Epidendrum ilense* was. And he told me.' In fact he had put down the seedlings he was holding, wiped his hands on his jeans and led the way.

'So the whole thing happened over an orchid?' said Lisa. 'How romantic is that!'

'Did he feel the same?' asked Deborah, impressed by how Suzy had suddenly bloomed.

'I guess so,' she said. 'Though it took him two weeks before he let me know.'

Deborah, in her pastoral role, held out her arms to embrace her. Things with Neville weren't good at present but over the years she'd become an expert at putting on a good face.

Later, Andrew had sought Suzy out again and admired her exquisite draughtsmanship. It was noon, he had asked her to join him for a drink and she, without hesitation, had accepted. And that, she confessed, had been it, more or less. From that day on they had scarcely been apart.

* * *

'I feel we have known him all our lives,' said Gwen, the first time Suzy brought him home. 'He's the sort of boy who could have lived next door.' Then laughed when she saw her daughter wince. 'Well, you know what I mean, he is really good news. How come he doesn't have a wife already? I can't believe no-one has snapped him up before this.'

'I don't know, Mum.' But of course she did. In the short time they had been together, they had told each other most things. At heart, they discovered, they were natural soul-mates who needed few words to communicate. He hadn't married because he'd been too busy, mostly trekking across the world, seeking out rare trees. He was, by profession, a botanist, as absorbed in his own world as she was in hers, a perfect matching of talent and dedication.

'So what happens next?' asked Gwen, as she basted the joint. 'You'll be crazy if you let this one go. Even tree experts don't grow on trees.' And you're not getting any younger.

'Relax,' said Suzy, hugging her. Her mother at times was transparent. 'Whatever it is, it won't be bad.' She trusted him absolutely. 'Those days are over, I promise you that. From this point on, it is all going to be all right.'

For some odd reason, seeing Suzy so happy reminded Gwen of Olivia. She had never understood why she'd not stayed in touch. In seventeen years, not so much as a postcard, not even when Kit had died. She seemed to have totally disappeared, yet they knew she hadn't as Deborah had seen her. That, more than anything, offended Gwen. She had always hoped she'd meant more than that to the girl she had treated like a daughter. Now and again they saw her name in print; against the odds, that awkward child was making it as a performer. Not yet a star but a strong supporting actress, specialising in character parts. What with that and her cabaret act, she seemed to be doing well. Which didn't solve the mystery of why she'd dropped out of their lives.

'It does seem odd,' said Guy to his daughter, as they strolled down the lane to the pub. 'Whatever her reasons for leaving the school, the least thing she might have done would be tell your mother.' He was angrier than he cared to show; his feelings for Gwen went deep. And he, more than anyone, knew how much she had suffered from losing her son.

'I know,' said Suzy, taking his arm, 'I've wondered about that too.' At the time she'd resented Olivia's intrusion though, looking back now after all these years, viewed her with slightly more compassion. She had never properly fitted in, either with them or at school. But Mum had been such a brick to her and given her all the support she could possibly need.

'Watch yourselves,' Gwen would tell them sharply whenever she heard them ridiculing her. 'Remember Mrs Do-as-you-would-be-done-by and thank your stars that you have a nice home and parents as tolerant as us.'

What Olivia had been was now clearer to Suzy, the unwanted child who had nothing, nose forever pressed to the sweetshop window. Whatever they'd got, she wanted too. Now it was clear but then Suzy had found it annoying.

'Deborah bumped into her several years ago. I don't know if there have been any further sightings.' It had been in Harrods, Deborah's regular haunt, and Suzy's reaction when she heard was annoyance that Olivia still hadn't called Gwen.

'We ought to be getting back,' said her father. Their meal would be ready by now. He had always had reservations about Olivia, had never been able to work her out. But his wife's propensity for social misfits was something he was well-used to. To throw all her kindness back in her face had been pretty shabby behaviour.

They could always track Olivia down; she was probably listed in *Spotlight*. Suzy, planning her own hen party, considered going to the library to look but then decided against it. Olivia had not proved a loyal friend, had ended up letting them down. Not just her defection from the summer show but mainly for snubbing her mother like that and entirely ignoring Kit's death. There was no point in chasing bad memories. Instead she telephoned Deborah.

Deborah, up to her eyes in congregation business, was nevertheless delighted to hear her voice. She was tired, despondent and overweight and, furthermore, feeling middle-aged. And here was Suzy, the soon-to-be bride, ringing, no doubt, to extol the virtues of romance and everlasting love. She glanced at the clock; it was almost five and she still had a load of work to get through. But, what the hell, she could do with a break and friends came first with her every time. The selfish creature she once had been had vanished years ago.

'So,' she asked, massaging her neck, 'what gives? How are the plans progressing?' They had spent many hours discussing the dress and come to a mutual decision. Suzy was euphoric about their choice, giving much of the credit to Deborah. 'But that's what friends are for,' she had said, which was true.

'Tell me about Olivia,' said Suzy. 'And whether you think I should include her in my hen night?'

'Goodness!' said Deborah, genuinely startled. 'I'd forgotten all about her.' She hadn't, of course; the memory still stung but she hadn't told Suzy about that. Even now, after all these years, Deborah still assumed the role of pack leader. Olivia had never been her favourite person; right now there were very few people she would less like to see. But it was Suzy's big day so she must tread carefully and not say anything to upset her.

'Why would you want her, in any case? I thought you weren't friends any more.'

'Because she used to be part of our set. Remember?' She wanted a last Eve of Waterloo, longed to recreate the closeness they'd shared.

'Not really,' said Deborah sharply, tiredness overwhelming her like a cloak.

'It was just a thought.' Deborah was probably right. The only one Suzy desperately missed was Miranda.

'I have no idea where she is,' said Deborah, having ripped that page from the book. She suspected Neville might have her address somewhere but was certainly not going to ask. 'She lived in Covent Garden, I believe, but I'm not sure we ever knew where. She seemed to be going places fast. Nice of her to stay in touch. I really don't think we need her at your party.'

'You're right,' said Suzy compliantly, crossing out the name. She would keep it to just the four of them like old times.

18

The rain was sheeting across Lake Lucerne as Olivia battled up the hill. She was late for the first of her morning classes because she hated getting out of bed to face those numbskulls with whom she now shared her days. She was well-accustomed to misery but Switzerland was dire. She regretted bitterly being taken from the school on the eve of her big stage breakthrough. Life wasn't fair; she was used to that now and was close to giving up hope. Each time she found something she could love, it was brutally snatched away. First, her mother, whom she didn't remember; later a string of foster homes, some better than others but none of them up to much. The house in Stanmore had been an improvement, the first proper home she had ever really known. Her aunt was sharp and her uncle distant but at least they had seemed to have her interests at heart. Then, as usual, her father had interfered as he moved to yet another foreign posting. Why he dragged her along with him, she still didn't understand. It wasn't even as if he missed her; years could go by without any contact at all.

She realised now he couldn't be a spy which was merely a childhood fantasy to give herself a little vicarious glamour. Now she was older, the holes in the make-believe showed. He was, she'd found out, a mercenary soldier who went to fight other people's wars in order to keep his daughter in fancy schools. Or so she'd deduced from eavesdropping on Aunt Sarah who seemed less than pleased with the way things had turned out. It was she, after all, who had paid for the last school, so why had he uprooted her just to dump her over here?

The ladies' academy, overlooking the lake, was antiquated, second-rate and ruinously expensive. No more Latin or economics; instead they supplied a tasteless fare of dancing, deportment and culinary skills, with basic French conversation. Learning to be a lady; it was several years too late for that as well as a social anachronism that would have had Helen snorting. Where in the world could she use these new skills unless she happened to marry a duke or run a Parisian bordello? Olivia groaned every morning when she woke, faced with another mind-numbing day. She longed for the friends she had left behind, except for Deborah with her viper's tongue, but didn't want them to know what she had sunk to. Through no fault of her own, she had let them all down when stardom was just within her grasp. Worse than that, though, she had failed Gwen Palmer, by far the hardest part of all to bear.

Occasionally she thought about Miranda, usually in the early hours when she found it hard to sleep.

In addition to the set syllabus, she had opted for acting lessons which did, at least, provide something to brighten her week. They were taught by a Frenchman with a very short fuse but he brought those twice-weekly sessions to life and kept Olivia constantly on her toes. For him she spruced up her appearance, too, by trying to eat more and take care of her skin. As she grew older, she put on a little weight; she couldn't do anything about her small bones but was at last developing some sort of shape. She also took private singing lessons which was, she felt, the least her father owed her.

Before the start of the summer term, she was summoned by the principal. At last she was beginning to settle in, was due to perform a song she had written herself. It was 1979, she was sixteen, prettier and more confident than when she had first arrived, with a flair for drama and an ear for French that were earning her excellent grades. So what was the problem now? She would soon find out.

Fräulein Fischer, looking tired and harassed, was seated behind an antique desk overflowing with documents and ledgers. She was right out of an earlier era, with her greying hair twisted into a knot and rimless spectacles perched at the end of her nose. She acknowledged Olivia and motioned her to sit, then shuffled her papers with thin, nervous fingers until she uncovered the one she was searching for. She studied it for a moment or two, as though learning it off by heart, before raising chilly eyes to meet Olivia's.

'Miss Fernshaw,' she said, in her accented English, 'I'm afraid we have a slight problem here.' Which was, put bluntly, a drying-up of funds. Her father had failed to pay next term's fees and was not responding to her letters.

'Do you happen to know where he is stationed now? I seem to recall he said he was a soldier.'

Olivia nodded. 'But I've no idea where he is. Due to the secret nature of his profession, he is constantly on the move.' Argentina or Angola, it made little difference. He had never been one for staying in touch as she'd known, to her cost, all her life.

'Is there anyone else, then, to whom I might apply?'

For a second she thought of Aunt Sarah, then shook her head. No way could she turn to her; her aunt had already done more than her fair share. And the thought of having to return to the school brought on a panic attack. She would not return to England again, certainly not in disgrace.

'No problem,' she told the principal. 'I am more than able to take care of myself.'

'But have you money or somewhere to stay?' Fräulein Fischer was clearly concerned about the liability though unwilling to be out of pocket. That was the thing about these cut-price charm schools; scratch the surface and underneath was pure tat.

'I'll get a job,' said Olivia bravely, in Judy Garland mode. 'I'll be just fine. I can speak the lingo. And I have just turned sixteen.'

She had never imagined it would be easy but was shocked by how hard it actually was. No-one wanted an English schoolgirl who knew how to set a table properly and had conversational French. She left her things in the academy's care while she miserably tramped the streets. There were plenty of openings in the tourist trade but not for someone as young as her and it had to be somewhere she could live in, in order not to pay rent. She also knew it was on the cards that Fräulein Fischer might inform the police and that was something she definitely didn't want. From this point on she was resolved to fend entirely for herself. She had no-one in the world to turn to, was now absolutely on her own.

It wasn't till the end of the third fruitless day that her eye was caught, as she trudged up the hill, by a vacancy sign in a newsagent's window for a care worker in a retirement home. She stopped to read it; it seemed within her grasp. Assorted duties for an unskilled worker: changing bed linen, clearing tables, tidying up and generally lending a hand. Minimal wages but what attracted her was that accommodation was provided.

She washed her hair and polished her shoes then, prompt on the stroke of nine next day, presented herself on the doorstep of Alpenhaus, now in Mary Poppins mode. Yes, she agreed brightly to every question and no, she was not afraid of hard work. References? Sadly, she had recently been orphaned and needed the job to survive. The manageress was quite clearly overworked and nearing the end of her tether. She hesitated over Olivia's age – insisted on seeing her passport as proof – but agreed that she did look mature for sixteen and would, with time, get older. In the end, because she was so hard-pressed and Olivia so persistent, the woman said she could have a week's trial and, perhaps, if it worked out, stay on.

Relieved, Olivia retrieved her bags and moved into the attic. It was small and cramped and would be cold in winter but the only thing she cared about now was having a roof over her head. A home of her own for the first time ever; she was almost cheerful as she unpacked her few things.

The work was hard, unremittingly so, but Olivia didn't complain. She was glad to be independent at last, away from the rules and regulations and those tediously boring other girls who were Fräulein Fischer's pupils. Middle-class and mainly from the Midlands, with daddies who'd made their money out of muck, they really believed all the rubbish they were taught and saw themselves engaged by the end of the course.

Cramped in her draughty little shoebox of a room, Olivia was nonetheless exultant. Not quite an adult yet already self-supporting. She wondered what Deborah and the others would say if they knew.

The weeks crawled by and then the months and still she kept to herself. The tedious work was so exhausting she found herself, at the end of each day, grabbing a snack in a fast food joint before going early to bed. Her skin grew roughened, her lips wind-chapped, her knuckles were swollen and aching. By the time she was seventeen she looked several years more, with her hair scraped back beneath her cap and not a scrap of makeup on her face. She no longer thought about her previous life; all her energies went into just surviving.

Alpenhaus was a discreet establishment, more a private hotel than a home, on a windy corner of a lakeside street with a garden running down to the water and truly magnificent views. It catered for forty residents at most; in the several years that Olivia worked there it was almost always full. The majority of the inmates were widows, eking out their twilight years on the nest-eggs left by their husbands. A few were bedbound and a handful senile; those were the ones who needed special care that Olivia wasn't qualified to provide. Her days were spent running up and down stairs, stripping beds and remaking them, emptying chamber pots and doing a little light cleaning. She also worked regular shifts in the kitchen, which had totally ruined her hands. Peeling potatoes without protective gloves, scrubbing down tables and rinsing out cloths in addition to washing dishes, all took their toll. Her mind would flick back to those Palmer weekends and how she had loved helping Gwen. Ironic, really, that an act of love could also be a soul-destroying chore.

The other staff were pleasant enough when they had the time to chat, which wasn't often. Few spoke English and, even then, not well though Olivia was becoming proficient in German. She looked upon this period of her life strictly as a learning experience. Her schoolfriends by now would be up at university, a dream she, too, had once shared. She cursed her father for his neglect but grabbed the chance to extend her experience by any means that she could. Knowledge was power, she knew that now, so threw herself into the job. She was allowed to mingle with the residents at last, tidying and putting things away. She also helped with the afternoon tea, pushing the trolley and passing round plates. In her neat white overall, with squeaky-clean hair, she became a positive fixture in their midst. The old ladies told her she cheered them up; the management, too, seemed pleased.

And then, after three years of back-breaking toil, fate intervened and Olivia suddenly lucked out.

There was consternation among the staff; a VIP was arriving. He was taking the best suite of rooms in the house, which had to be thoroughly aired. Rugs were beaten, cushions replaced, even the curtains were sent away to be cleaned.

'Who is he?' asked Olivia curiously, carrying in armfuls of towels and fresh linen and helping the housekeeper make up the canopied bed.

'Count von Richthofen, a relative of the proprietor. Recently he suffered a small stroke and requires total rest.'

'Why here?' A count could surely do better. Though clean and well-run, it was scarcely the Ritz.

'Because we have the nursing facilities. He no longer needs to be hospitalised but requires professional care.'

'When will he be arriving?'

'Tomorrow.' Hence the rush. It was all that anyone could talk about, the biggest excitement in years.

Olivia was strolling back from the lake, where she went for her afternoon break, and saw the ancient Landau drawn up with all its doors standing open. Staff were lifting out bags and boxes and lugging them into the hall, then, as she watched, a tall, stooping figure slowly emerged from the passenger seat and was helped by a nurse up the steps and into the hall. He was thin as a whippet with flowing hair that had once been blond but had faded to grey. Count von Richthofen, dressed like Sherlock Holmes. At last, some action; Olivia perked up. She could hardly wait to be introduced. These days she was feeling much more at ease with herself.

Their meeting took place the following day when

Olivia took up his tea. Sugar and lemon on the side, and make sure you fold the linen napkin correctly, fussed the housekeeper.

'Do I curtsey?' asked Olivia, mindful of the academy, and wouldn't have been surprised had the answer been yes.

But, no, said the housekeeper, distracted as always. She had as much on her plate as she could handle without this new resident chucking his weight about. 'Come straight down,' she ordered Olivia. 'I need you to take the trolley round.'

When he answered her tap and she went inside, holding the tea-tray carefully with both hands and closing the door with her bottom, Olivia found him stretched out on a recliner in a velvet jacket and matching monogrammed slippers. He looked younger than she had taken him for, unless he was just well-preserved. She asked him, in her flawless German, where he would like the tray and he indicated the bedside table, if she'd shift it a little closer. As she did his bidding and then poured the tea she was conscious of his detailed scrutiny.

'You are English,' he said, a statement not a question. 'Why in the world are you here?'

There were all sorts of answers Olivia might have given; she had a whole glib repertoire which she used as invention struck. But when she met his discerning eyes, she knew she couldn't lie. He was elderly and ailing and hated being there, an autocratic man of means unused to needing to be helped. She gave him his tea and told him the truth and watched him lighten a little. Something about her appealed to him; he liked her youthful defiance. He invited her to take tea with him but she said she was needed downstairs.

'Then join me later for a glass of schnapps.' He was clearly a man accustomed to having his own way.

She wasn't supposed to drink on duty but saw no reason to mention that. She liked his style and the cut of his clothes and resolved to do what she could to brighten his stay.

It was the start of a sprightly friendship that would alter Olivia's life. The count, or Klaus as he asked her to call him, was widely read and had travelled far; he hated this temporary sedentary state imposed on him by his doctors. He grew to rely on Olivia's visits and the titbits of news she regularly brought. There wasn't a lot going on in the home but she usually managed to find bits of gossip to keep him entertained.

'If only I could get out,' he sighed but he wasn't supposed to walk. The stroke had affected him down one side which meant, with a stick, he could hobble as far as the bathroom. But not any further; the nursing staff were adamant about that. Any unnecessary exertion now could hamper his chances of recovery. Olivia came up with the obvious suggestion of borrowing a wheelchair and taking him out. There were several on the premises, of course, not all in regular use. She checked with Matron, who seemed not to mind. Anything that helped keep a resident happy meant less for her to worry about. Not to mention her personal standing where his cousin, the proprietor, was concerned.

Olivia altered her schedule in order to take him out in the afternoons. By now, after several years' solid slog, she could more or less make her own rules. At first he argued, though with little conviction, and gave in like a lamb when she persevered. He was bored and petulant and sorry for himself; being an invalid was diminishing his spirit. He was a man accustomed to being active; he hated feeling helpless.

'A young girl like you should have better things to do than hamper herself with a sick old man.'

'Nonsense,' she'd say as she helped him into the chair. 'I'd be going for a walk in any case. It's far more fun having you along to talk to.'

What she said was true. Once she got him outside, Klaus turned out to be a fun companion. Till now she hadn't realised quite how lonely she had been; three years of menial drudgery had drained away much of her spirit. He, in turn, was touched by her kindness when she should be spending time with friends her own age.

'I have none,' she said and then explained why. 'I blame it all on my dad who never loved me.'

'Well, that's not how it is with me. I enjoy your company too much.'

Klaus, who was seventy-two and a widower, found

himself touched by her pathos. The girl was appealing, with her honest eyes and perfect cheekbones that gave her occasional beauty. With time and money invested in her, she might realise her potential. Besides which, she was sassy and bright and kept him laughing as they bowled along with her wicked impersonations of people they knew.

'You don't need acting lessons,' he said, weakly wiping his eyes. 'You are good enough as you are to go on the stage. You shouldn't be wasting your time in this dump. Get out there and grab life by the throat. You only get one shot at it, don't waste it.'

From that point on he began to plot and Olivia was thinking on similar lines. They got along; he was youthful in spirit and, now that he was improving, enormous fun. She liked his lean ascetic looks and imperious aquiline nose. He looked every inch what he was, an aristocrat.

'If I could have one wish,' she said, as they paused for breath at the top of the hill admiring the view of the lake, 'it would be to stay with you all the time. I mean it.' And she did. Pushing him round in a heavy wheelchair was peanuts compared to her usual routine. She had been in this deadly job too long; her youth was passing her by. She glanced at him shyly through windblown hair. 'I feel closer to you than a father,' she said. 'Certainly than my own.'

He took her hand and squeezed it hard but continued to sit in silence. Apart from his two disagreeable children, who popped in briefly to check him out, there were, she knew, a handful of grandchildren, not one of whom had ever bothered to visit.

'We could travel the world. I'd take care of you.' Not as a servant, as something more. Olivia felt she had love to give; all she had ever dreamed of was to be wanted.

'You are crazy, child,' he said, drawing her to him, and she felt his heart-rate increase.

'No longer a child. I am almost twenty.' And she stooped and kissed him boldly on the mouth.

Thus it was settled. 'Marry me,' he said and she felt no need to reply.

Despite the matter of her not being Swiss, the licence proved no stumbling-block, perhaps because he pulled strings. It was all arranged in a matter of weeks and she simply asked for the afternoon off, being due lots of overtime.

'It feels like we're eloping,' she said, glad he hadn't told his children who might well have stood in her way. She liked the idea of being a countess, looked forward to introducing him to her friends.

'I haven't bought you a ring,' he said. 'You'll have to choose one yourself.'

'A ring doesn't matter,' she told him shyly. 'All I want is you.'

They toasted the marriage in champagne by the lake, then started slowly back up the hill. It was growing chilly; she should get him home. He was still officially sick. Now that he had a legal wife, she hoped the doctors would let him go. They were free to travel wherever they chose and no-one could stand in their way. At the top of the slope she paused for breath, tired from the effort of pushing the chair. She attempted to light a cigarette but the breeze was so strong, it took both her hands to manage it.

She only let go of the chair for a second but when she reached out, it had gone. All that was left was an empty view and an abyss of dread in her stomach.

19

Deborah looked up from the Royal Doulton show-case and there she was, large as life. After all these years, Olivia Fernshaw, and, from the way she was dressed, with cash to throw around.

'Well, hello!' said Deborah, blocking her path so that Olivia, startled, was obliged to stop.

'Deborah?' she said doubtfully, after a pause. Olivia was chic and well-groomed and looked fit and well, with a new-found confidence that disconcerted Deborah.

'What a lovely surprise. It must be, what, seven years?'

'Eight,' said Olivia, looking her up and down.

'Fancy that. You haven't changed a bit,' said Deborah, smiling falsely.

Olivia, recalling their old sparring days, regarded her with suspicion.

Deborah was arranging her wedding list, a pretty exhaustive business. 'Let's go down for a coffee,' she suggested, steering Olivia towards the Dress Circle bar.

Once settled with coffee and Black Forest gateau, Deborah prepared herself for a good old gab. Eight whole years, could it really be that long? What a lot of ground they had to cover. She updated Olivia on the doings of the Five. Lisa was working as a trainee lawyer, specialising in welfare cases somewhere in the depths of the East End. Helen was at Harvard, doing her doctorate, having graduated with honours in anthropology. Suzy was just through art school and living at home. Olivia already knew about Miranda.

'And you?' asked Olivia carelessly, lighting a cigarette. Deborah looked sleek and prosperous, like the cat who got the cream.

'I'm getting married!' she said with shining eyes. 'Was upstairs sorting out my wedding list.'

'Who's the lucky fellow?' Despite herself, Olivia felt the familiar twinge of envy. Something about Deborah had always managed to rile her; whatever she did, she managed to come out on top. Nothing ever went wrong for her which stemmed, perhaps, from her pampered childhood. Even the first time they'd met she'd arrived in a Daimler.

'Neville Hirsch. A financial adviser in the City. I met him at Cambridge in my final year. And you; tell me about you,' Deborah said. 'We've all been dying to know why you disappeared.'

Olivia exhaled a thin stream of smoke then stubbed out the cigarette. It was a habit that lately she'd been trying to give up but she'd needed the hit in order to cope with Deborah. 'I've been travelling,' she said offhandedly, 'and have only recently returned.' Her nails were neat and her hands were ringless; she appeared unwilling to say much more but that was how it had always been in the past. Shy and withdrawn, mousy really. At least she was looking faintly chic.

'Where are you living?'

'Oh, here and there. I haven't been back in the country long enough to have put down any roots.'

Deborah, now a fully-fledged rabbi, beamed at her with benevolence. She was rounder, fuller, but it suited her; her cheeks were flushed and her eyes were bright, the very image, Olivia thought, of smugness personified.

'Here's my number,' said Deborah, producing her card. 'You must promise to call and come over soon for a meal. And why not,' she added, as she gathered up her shopping, 'call Suzy and her parents too? I know they'd be pleased to hear from you and catch up. We have often wondered what happened to you and why you didn't stay in touch.'

'How are they?' asked Olivia carefully, feeling the familiar lurch that came whenever she thought about the Palmers.

'They are fine,' said Deborah. 'Really well. And Kit has this posh diplomatic posting in Strasbourg.'

Kit. Sooner or later he'd been bound to come up. Olivia burned to remember those weekends and how disparaging he had always been, treating her like a kid and never listening. Walking past her in the street as though she were something nasty on his shoe; ignoring the fact she was even there and going off to play cricket without saying goodbye. His mother had tried to make excuses for what was plain bad behaviour. Some of Suzy's sillier friends had found him dead attractive; Olivia simply considered him a pig.

'I have to go,' said Deborah, hovering but keen to get back to the china department to add more items to her list. 'Now, promise you'll call as soon as you can. Apart from anything else, you must meet Neville.'

The last few weeks in Lucerne had been hell. To start with, of course, there had been an inquiry as to how the wheelchair had got out of control and rushed backwards down the hill. It had been very windy, Olivia explained, and she'd turned her back for just a split second to light her cigarette. Klaus had been unable to struggle free and his neck had been broken by the fall. When the police found out about the sudden marriage they had taken Olivia into custody and his horrible children, both after his money, had come and screamed abuse at her. Olivia, however, stuck doggedly to the truth. She had loved him, yes, and knew he had loved her too; to her that was all that really mattered. The accident was a tragedy from which she would probably never recover. Barely twenty and already a widow; she still couldn't quite believe it had occurred.

They had let her go. There was no reason to hold her once it came to light that his money was all tied up. Years before, he had put it in trust for his grandchildren, leaving himself just a modest annuity to see him through his old age.

'It won't hold water,' his daughter had screeched at Olivia's threat to take it to court. 'A few hours married? What rights does that give you? You are going to tell me next it was consummated.'

In the end, to avoid bad publicity, they had come to an out-of-court settlement. For a lump sum of twenty thousand pounds, Olivia would sign away all her rights and leave the Richthofen family alone. She would also agree not to use the title; she found that hard but eventually gave in. Though adequate, it wasn't a fortune but at least meant independence at last without having to work at menial jobs for survival. She packed her bags and left Lucerne, leaving no forwarding address.

Deborah was faintly surprised when Olivia called. She had so much on her plate right then that the last thing she needed was to have to entertain, but she'd made the promise and wouldn't go back on her word.

'Come to lunch on Sunday,' she said. 'We usually have a bit of a crowd.' She tried to get hold of Suzy, too, but she was off on a sketching weekend and wouldn't be back in time. Lisa also had other plans, playing tennis at Lincoln's Inn and afterwards lunching at the law-courts.

'Everyone's so ambitious,' grumbled Deborah, as though she were innocent of that. It was a shame the others would miss Olivia but that, she supposed, could be rectified. Presumably now she was back, she'd be sticking around. There hadn't been time to catch up properly but on Sunday, no doubt, all would be revealed. Deborah started phoning her friends to rustle up some willing volunteers.

At that point she was living near Regent's Park, at the foot of Primrose Hill. She invited an assortment of local acquaintances as well as some of Neville's friends who were mainly from the City. The room was packed when Olivia slipped in, demurely dressed in a starkly plain dress while most of the others wore jeans and training shoes. Deborah had an instant flashback to Suzy's thirteenth birthday party when the gang had dressed pretty much as today and Olivia had been grotesquely decked out in layers of fluorescent tulle. Then she had looked an utter fright; today she was elegant and understated, could have passed in any company at any time.

Deborah introduced her round.

'Which one's Neville?' asked Olivia.

'He's in the kitchen, opening bottles. Wait and I'll introduce you.'

'No need,' said Olivia, 'I can do that for myself. You get on with entertaining your guests.'

Neville was dark and sleekly good-looking, with olive skin and straight black hair and a nose that could have almost passed for Italian. He was in his shirt-sleeves and pulling corks; he looked up and smiled as she stood in the doorway and said: 'Hi, you must be Olivia.'

Olivia, suddenly shy, held out her hand. 'I don't know a soul,' she said in a whisper. 'Except Deborah, of course.' Neville glanced at her without much interest; he was only newly engaged. In any case, she was not his type; too pale and insipid for him. But, remembering his manners, he talked politely, asking anodyne questions as he continued wrestling with his corks.

'And what do you do? As a job, I mean.' (*Tell me how you like school, little girl. Here, let me show you how to throw this ball. Underarm does less harm.*) He wasn't even looking at her; she might have been anyone at all.

'I work in Covent Garden,' she said. 'In a job connected with the arts.'

'Great,' said Neville, not even listening, concentrating on opening a bottle without getting wine on his shirt.

'Oh, you've met,' said Deborah, appearing suddenly and grabbing him from behind. 'Don't you think he's delicious?' she drooled and all of a sudden Olivia could see her, back in the garden when Suzy turned thirteen, making a similar ass of herself, putting out to all the boys. She remembered how often she had imitated her in the privacy of her own bedroom; could almost have repeated the routine now.

'Here,' she said, snatching a couple of bottles and disappearing into the throng to replenish glasses.

She hadn't known where to go at first; whether to stay on in Switzerland and chance her arm at finding a proper job, or to investigate some other European city while she still had the money to fall back on. Even at twenty she realised it wouldn't last very long, so had kept her expenditure in check, resisting the urge to fritter. She went to Paris where she did buy clothes and got herself a stylish haircut. She wanted Klaus to be proud of her; her affection for him had not been entirely feigned.

She moved on to Berlin and then Amsterdam, all the while looking for something, she wasn't sure what. She worked occasionally in random bars but avoided making friends. She wasn't ready to settle yet, needed to sort herself out. She had lost all touch with her absentee father but no longer gave a damn. In the end, somewhat weedily she felt, she had headed back to London, uncertain whether to let people know of her return. She found a job as a barmaid in Covent Garden, across the road from the opera house, where she passed long hours pouring drinks for the theatre crowds. Still conserving her ill-gained inheritance, she stashed it away in a savings account and rented a seedy room in Drury Lane. Once she had found her feet again, she'd decide what she wanted to do. But first she needed to reorientate; she had left the city as a naïve child, returned as a wellish-off widow.

It was in this frame of mind that she'd bumped into Deborah, at first appalled at coming face to face, then rapidly seeing a possible benefit there. Deborah, on occasion, could be loathsome but they did have a lot of shared history and now that she was grown up (and a rabbi) perhaps good nature would outweigh the spitefulness. Olivia could only wait and see. And when she heard that Deborah's intended worked in the City as a financial adviser, her ears pricked up and she acted docile. Since she had got her hands on it, she'd been wondering what best to do with Klaus's money.

At lunch Olivia was seated next to Neville. 'Be nice to her,' Deborah had said. So once he had checked that everyone had wine, he settled back and gave her his full attention.

'So where did you emerge from?' he asked. 'Somewhere abroad, Debs said.'

'Switzerland,' said Olivia smoothly. 'My father sent me to finishing-school. A bit of a bore but it's over now. And the skiing was terrific. After that I just travelled a lot till I got homesick.'

Skilfully she guided him into talking about himself. A few well-placed questions and Neville was off, spouting on about the City and how the markets were currently bullish and everyone raking it in. She left it long enough not to sound greedy, then shyly asked if she might pick his brains.

'I've come into a small inheritance,' she said. 'From my mother's estate.' She was conscious of his sudden awakening interest. 'Mine, at last, now that I've come of age.'

Dead mother Deborah had mentioned; how sad. He steepled his fingers like a much older man and gravely inquired in what way he could help.

'I have it in a savings account but naturally want it to grow. Is this something, perhaps, you could help me with? I know absolutely nothing about finance and haven't a clue where to start.' She gave a slightly flirtatious giggle and fluttered her lashes a bit. 'I don't expect any special treatment. Would naturally pay your normal commission, if you can spare the time.'

Mentally groaning, Neville put his mind to educating Olivia in money matters. The more he talked, the closer she listened; men, in general, were simple souls, unbelievably easy to con. Deborah, watching from the far end of the table, was alarmed to see the apparent rapport growing between her man and her former schoolmate.

'I hope he's not boring you,' she said intervening, offering salad and trying her best to break up their tête-à-tête.

'Not a bit,' said Olivia, starry-eyed. 'He is giving me excellent advice. What a man! How astute of you to have snapped him up.'

Charmed by her open admiration, Neville grew even more expansive. She hadn't stated the precise figure but he'd certainly got her drift. Not a fortune but enough to have fun with; he thought he might quite enjoy the task of enlarging this little lady's legacy. Before he went off to fulfil his hostly duties, he slipped Olivia his business card.

'Call me at the office,' he said, 'and I'll set up a meeting in town. I've a pretty shrewd idea of what you need.'

'What is she like now?' asked Lisa curiously, sorry to have missed the Sunday lunch.

'Totally changed,' said Deborah. 'You'd hardly know her. Far more stylish and more outgoing. Not at all the scared little thing we knew.'

'Interesting?'

'Neville seemed to think so.' Try as she might, Deborah could not conceal the hint of asperity in her tone. She was used to Neville coming on to other women but Olivia Fernshaw? Surely not. She might be more chic but she still didn't sparkle and hadn't a lot to say for herself. Not to women, at least.

'She is working somewhere in Covent Garden. I am not sure at what since we barely spoke. She was quite well turned out and has beautiful manners. Her father put her through finishing-school.'

'How archaic,' said Lisa with scorn, every bit as disapproving as Helen. 'When are you going to see her again?'

'I'm not.'

'Not at all? Not ever?' Deborah thrived on entertaining and had long been the fulcrum of their social set. Lisa had expected her at least to throw a party to welcome Olivia home.

'Don't get me wrong. She left no number, is constantly moving about. Isn't even certain she'll be staying very long, seems to have perpetually itchy feet.' She suspected, though, that Neville would know how to reach her. 'She just came into some money,' said Deborah. 'From her dead mother's estate.'

'How weird. I thought she was a welfare case. Which was why the aunt had to take her in.' Lisa had a sudden desire to see Olivia herself and catch up. Especially on those missing years they had wondered about for so long.

Suzy was curious too, though less so. With all that was happening in her life, commissions for paintings and an exhibition, she had rather forgotten the hanger-on who had tried so hard to infiltrate her family.

'Don't worry,' said Deborah, 'she said she'd call. There is no way she's not going to pick up her friendship with you.'

'With my mother, more like,' said Suzy with a sniff. 'I don't imagine she cares either way if she sees me.' Even gentle-natured Suzy still felt miffed at being dropped after the school had perceived them as being best friends.

* * *

Neville was unusually unforthcoming when Deborah asked about Olivia. 'Not especially interesting,' he said. 'Out to pick my brains for investment tips.'

Deborah knew Olivia had been to his office at least twice. She didn't make more of an issue of it because of the pressure of wedding plans which were starting to overwhelm her. Lists, lists, lists . . . that was all she could think of; even her needy parishioners took second place. Food and flowers and bridesmaids and guests, plus places for them to stay. Seating plans and wedding-cars and endless debate about the dress; and who was to sit with the bridegroom's widowed mother and organise the toasts. Olivia was forgotten in the general mêlée and, since she never did call the Palmers, no-one ever found out where she was staying. Undoubtedly Neville knew where she was but Deborah never got round to asking him.

The wedding took place in early May, with the bride at her radiant best. All was perfect, even the weather, and Deborah's parents pulled out all the stops because, once again, their daughter had come up trumps. On top of her triumphs at Cambridge and beyond, Deborah was now rewarding them by making an excellent marriage. A prominent Rabbi, a family friend, presided and later there was a ritzy reception at the Dorchester.

The gang were all present, except for Olivia who Deborah pointed out hadn't really belonged. They stood in a group round the bride, holding hands, and posed for a picture that each would long cherish, a memento of the close friendships they'd made at school. It was a day that none of them would ever forget.

The more so since, just a short while later, they heard the shocking news that Kit was dead.

20

The birds were making an unholy din but Suzy, who hadn't slept anyway, didn't care. It was the morning of her wedding-day; henceforth she would always awake to find Andrew beside her. A feeling of such rare contentment swept through her that she thought about diving beneath the covers and trying to snatch a few minutes' sleep before the events of the day kicked in. But the sun was rising, the grass was dewy; in just nine hours they'd be meeting at the altar. She sprang out of bed and stood in her pyjamas, studying herself in the mirror. Despite the light-headedness she'd experienced all week, on the surface little had changed. She was still the same unexceptional-looking woman, slight of figure, brown of hair, with a short, straight nose and a too wide mouth which brightened up her face whenever she smiled. Which she was doing now all the time; she had never been happier in her life.

On her closet door hung the dress she'd had made

from fabric designed by herself. She'd originally meant to make the whole thing but Deborah had vetoed it.

'You can't possibly get married in a homemade dress. Not at your age,' she said. And with a rising reputation to consider; there might be press photographers at the church.

'No chance,' said Suzy, who'd deliberately kept it small, but Deborah stuck to her guns. Since, as a rabbi, she was expert in such matters Suzy, in her usual way, gave in. Besides, Deborah had an ulterior motive; Abby, her eldest, was flower girl and she wanted her looking her best. Secretly Suzy could see the logic; nothing designer for the seven-year-old if the bride were frumpishly dressed. So she'd left all the details to Deborah to take care of and here was the result, this shimmering masterpiece in swirling silk with her flower design, almost too exquisite to put on. She would need to do something about her hair but there'd be time enough for rollers later, once she'd had her bath and completed her packing. It was a strange realisation that never again would she have the privacy of being on her own without the constant presence of a man. Intrusive, maybe, yet also liberating. For far too long she had lived a spinster's life.

Right on cue, the door opened a crack and there stood her mother with tea on a tray and a hopeful expression on her face.

'Something told me you'd be up already, so I thought I'd join you in a cuppa,' she said. Their last one alone, she meant, though didn't say it. Gwen was wearing her floral housecoat and an old-fashioned hairnet to protect her wash and set. They sat side by side on the edge of the bed, drinking in companionable silence. Had she known it, Gwen's own thoughts ran parallel to her daughter's. After thirty-three years of sharing a home, both faced a radical change. But she didn't want to mention it and risk reducing them both to tears. Instead she looked around and said briskly: 'You know, I've always liked this room.'

Suzy, surprised, surveyed the clutter, an eclectic mix of childhood and now. Her nursery favourites were lined up on the bookshelf, along with *Gone With The Wind* and Philip Roth. Plus a fat art encyclopaedia, gift of her parents to celebrate starting at art school. On the bed-side table, against the lamp, slumped Marmaduke, her beloved bear, with one eye missing and a fraying ear, bloody but more or less unbowed. Right now Gwen felt a bit like that too. She had put her all into raising her kids and very soon would have lost them both. Right now, an empty future stretched ahead.

'Aren't you taking him?' she asked as a joke; Suzy gave it grave thought.

'I think he may be more useful here, keeping his eye on you two.'

Both were verging on the wobbly now so Gwen made a business of topping up their mugs, then wandered over to the window and peered out. I'm leaving her, thought Suzy, slightly panicked, just when I thought it was never going to happen. I wonder how they will manage in future without the need to put on an act. She was startled by this unexpected thought, not entirely sure where it had come from. But, right from her earliest memories, the house had always been packed with strays; for Sunday lunch and, of course, at Christmas, their door had always stood open. Recent widowers from the golf club, cousins from abroad. A couple of tedious former colleagues from Gwen's teaching days who popped up at intervals. Without Suzy there to help or discourage, she wondered how her mother would cope. It seemed she was quite incapable of saying no.

She's really going, her mother was thinking, seated by the open window, smelling the freshly-cut grass. She had known that, inevitably, this day would come; for Suzy's sake had wished it. But a dream was one thing, reality another, and now she was facing a void that, right now, she didn't know how she would fill. It was sheer indulgence that had stopped her thinking ahead; she was used to having her daughter around, a friend to confide in and do things with, a buffer between her and Guy. Part of the secret of their long, happy marriage was that they were rarely alone. With Suzy gone, she was terrified they might finally run out of conversation, with nothing much in common any more.

'Come along, you two,' said Guy from the doorway. 'Stop nattering like a pair of old tarts and let's get this show on the road. Before you know it, the Lockharts will be here. You don't want them catching you like this.'

'It's hours before they are due,' said Suzy. 'They are probably still asleep.' Andrew and his parents were staying at the pub, despite the fact there was quite enough room in the house.

'Not good karma,' Gwen had said and would not be dissuaded. She liked the Lockharts, Jessie and Walter, but there'd be time enough to spend with them once the wedding was out of the way. Bunkum or not, she wouldn't jinx her daughter's future by ignoring an ancient superstition.

'Really, Mum,' Suzy had told her fondly. 'You get dafter by the minute.' But she'd meekly gone along with it since secretly it suited her too. She felt jealous of time spent alone with her parents; after a lifetime of being a threesome, it would be odd not to have them always there.

From habit, she put on the same shabby jeans she wore each day for her work. The dress and elaborate underwear, another of Deborah's extravagant follies, would keep until the very last moment. The church was just across the road.

'I hope you aren't having second thoughts,' said her father, aware of a sudden lull.

'You'd better not be,' threatened Gwen from the stove. 'I won't have you changing your mind at this late stage.'

'Why not?' asked Suzy, pretending to rise. 'It's my life. I'll do what I like.'

'No, you won't. It's not allowed. I am planning to turn your bedroom into my workroom.'

They gawped. This was news to both of them but at least it showed that Suzy's leaving was not going to get Gwen down.

'What will you do there?' asked Suzy, curious. She loved her mother's resilient spirit after all she had been through.

'Who knows,' said Gwen, casually flipping eggs. 'I may even take up painting as a hobby.'

'Hurry up,' said Deborah, 'we can't be late. Suzy needs all the backup she can get.'

'Why?' asked Neville, as usual hardly listening, glancing through the financial pages, privately wishing his attendance wasn't required.

'Because I'm her best friend,' said Deborah. 'And, in case that has slipped your mind, your daughter is flower girl.' As if it could; he'd already seen the bill. So much money on a fancy frock for a child who would rapidly outgrow it. But he didn't comment, it wasn't worth it. Debs expected, and usually got, her own way.

Also, Deborah was thinking to herself, because of what Lisa had said; that she'd run into Olivia quite by chance, who, on hearing about Suzy's imminent wedding, had wangled an invitation cool as you please.

'What on earth did Suzy say about that?' The nerve of it, after all these years, especially when she'd so thoroughly snubbed the Palmers. But, then, Olivia had always acted oddly. Deborah had never really forgiven her for Neville.

'Don't know,' said Lisa cheerfully. 'I heard it second hand from Helen. But she's invited herself to sit next to me in church. I'm as curious to see her as you are.'

Helen, in her more restrained way, was similarly excited. She wouldn't dream of stealing Suzy's thunder but was glad of the chance to catch up with her friends and demonstrate her own domestic bliss. She had had, by default, a low-key wedding after Piet had persuaded her to join him in Cape Town and decided that, for propriety's sake, they should marry before they moved there. There was also the delicate question of the boys. They had lost their mother at an early age and Helen still felt she needed to treat them with care. Although they'd had time to get used to her, it was more in the role of university associate than as their father's future wife. As it happened, they'd settled down very well and the Kruger family was once more a complete unit. But they were all still on their best behaviour and had only come on this sudden trip because of Helen's closeness to Suzy and also so that Piet could meet her mother. The distance till now had been too great to warrant such an expense.

It was odd how life sometimes mirrored itself,

repeating scenarios exactly. Her parents had had an even greater age gap, although now her father was dead. Also, both couples had met through their work, in different branches of science. Helen wondered what the future might hold. More for herself, she devoutly hoped, than the loneliness of her mother's diminished existence.

'Hurry up, girls!' shouted Guy from below. 'Chop, chop. It's time we were off.'

Suzy, surrounded by a bevy of handmaids, stood transfixed by her own reflection; the gown was even more fabulous than she had thought. The delicate intricacy of her design worked perfectly on the fragile silk which flowed like mercury round her slender figure. With its classic lines and tiny waist, it made her look pre-Raphaelite. All she lacked was the garland of flowers for her hair.

'I'll get them,' said Deborah, racing down the stairs, ignoring Guy who had fretfully started to pace. Both bride and flower girl had identical blooms, full-blown roses woven artfully together to intertwine with their hair. The only jewellery Suzy wore was an art nouveau pendant in opals and pearls that had once belonged to Jessie Lockhart's mother.

'You look a picture.' Gwen kissed her cheek, unable, because of the lump in her throat, to say more.

'Come along,' said Deborah, herding them before her. 'Poor Andrew will think you have changed your mind. Let's all go and put him out of his misery. Good luck,' she whispered, embracing Suzy. 'If anyone deserves happy ever after, it's you.'

The music that was playing softly, as they waited for the bride to arrive, invoked in the old girls of the school immediate nostalgia. 'Jesu, Joy of Man's Desiring' . . . trust Suzy to have come up with that. Helen and Lisa, in their separate pews, both had an image of portly Miss Merton pumping away for all she was worth on the organ at assembly. Deborah, scurrying late up the aisle, nodding and blowing kisses left and right, caught Lisa's eye across the church and grinned. Only Olivia, at Lisa's side, failed to understand the allusion and instantly tensed up.

'What?' she whispered, intercepting Deborah's grin. Just as always in the old days, she felt excluded.

'The music,' said Lisa. 'You must remember. From school.'

Olivia didn't, which wasn't surprising. Few of her memories of that period had been good and, in recent years, she'd succeeded in blocking them out. Especially the events of that final term. Now she suddenly wished she hadn't come.

Seated further back in the church was a tall, gaunt woman with a shock of grey hair, dressed in what looked like a Persian rug, with a monocle on a black string. Apart from the colour of her hair, Miss Holbrook appeared to have hardly aged. She was now quite eminent in art world circles – had been even in their day. It was good of her to have travelled so far but she'd always been special to Suzy.

Maggie Holbrook, knowing no-one except a handful of former pupils, amused herself by looking around and trying to figure out who everyone was. There was Deborah, late as usual, making the maximum commotion, tripping up the aisle on three-inch heels as though it were her day, not Suzy's. She'd always been keen on the limelight, that one, right from her earliest teens. Spoilt and precocious but brilliant with it. Now she was a high profile rabbi who often appeared in the news. She slipped into the second pew, next to a man in a well-cut suit who looked like the Godfather's favourite son. She had clearly done well for herself. There were two small well-behaved children there too, with their father's saturnine beauty. Maggie, with her painter's perceptive eye, wondered if Deborah were really happy. Things were often not as they appeared on the surface.

There was quiet Helen Goddard, with a silver-haired man who looked nice. She had always been such a swot at school as well as a bit of a loner. It was good to see her looking so well, confident and much prettier. There was nothing like love to bring out the best; Maggie looked forward to meeting the husband later. Nearby was feisty Lisa Maguire, trim as ever in sage-green linen, her riotous curls now darker and tamed; definitely a head-turner. She had been a favourite amongst the staff, who'd admired her grit and determination; against the odds she had got into Oxford and was now a respected QC. Next to her, chic in understated grey, was someone who rang no bells at all until she suddenly turned her head and Maggie caught her profile. It still took a minute but then she got it, the waif entirely transformed. The child for whom she had always been sorry, whose clothes didn't fit and never looked quite clean, and whose pasty skin was usually covered in eczema. How she had changed and much for the better; talk about duckling into swan. She groped for the name but could not recall it, just that there had been some sort of bother in which she had been involved. I'm growing old, thought Maggie wryly, turning instead to the Order of Service sheet.

She remembered fast enough, however, when a late-arriving couple pushed in; a man still with matinee idol looks and a faded beauty, peroxide blonde, so skeletal she was hardly there, looking as though, with a puff of wind, she might crumple into ashes. Cedric and Wanda Sinclair, Miranda's parents; instantly it came flooding back. What a joke they had been, this ridiculous pair, with their posturing and unrealistic ambitions, strutting around like theatrical royalty, getting themselves a bad name. Clear as daylight Maggie could see it, the ghastly accident that had altered their lives and thrown a blight over that summer. It must have been nearly twenty years ago; now she felt even older.

But now the organist had switched to Handel; the bride was finally here. She tripped up the aisle on her father's arm, as sweet and guileless as she had been then, light on her feet as a mountain deer, brimming with happiness and hope. She took her place by the waiting groom and the look that passed between them touched Maggie deeply. She wished them all the happiness in the world for Suzy had always held a special place in her heart.

Out on the lawn the crowd was swarming as bride and groom, both with shining eyes, circulated slowly amongst their guests. They had been so lucky; the weather was perfect, without a cloud in the sky. Waiters flitted with laden trays, hired for the afternoon from the pub, and beneath the trees was a groaning table bearing a buffet fit for kings. The Palmers were always exemplary hosts who never stinted their guests.

I have been here before, thought Olivia, convinced for a second it was déjà vu. But then she recalled the birthday party, the first time she'd ever set foot in this house or met the family en masse. How needy she'd been; it embarrassed her now to remember how she had always clung to Gwen.

'Penny for them,' said a voice close by and there stood Suzy's father.

'Guy,' said Olivia, stretching up to kiss him as though she had ever called him by that name or even had the right to be here at all. She had phoned on an impulse when she'd heard about the wedding and asked if she might come and Guy, the consummate gentleman host, had told her the more the merrier. But she strongly suspected that he hadn't told his wife who was definitely keeping her distance.

'Where have you been?' He came straight to the point. They had all been stunned by her disappearance and twenty years was a very long time without a single word.

'Abroad,' said Olivia, accepting champagne. 'My dad came and took me from the school. It happened so fast, I couldn't let any of you know.'

'Why?' asked Guy, slightly mollified. She was looking good and he liked her new-found poise. From what he remembered, the absentee father had not played much of a role in her life. Which was why she was always at their house instead, looking for someone to love her.

'Because he was always a bastard.' She spat out the words. 'Who never considered my feelings once or what might be best for me.' Her eyes, when she raised them, were bruised with pain; for a second it even looked as though she might cry. Good God, he thought, she is still a child, as needy and insecure as she was then. She must have been through so much in those last awful weeks. Perhaps after all they'd misjudged her. On impulse he turned and beckoned to his wife.

'Gwen,' he called, 'come over here and see who I have found.'

Gwen, who was chatting to Jessie Lockhart, had spotted Olivia already. She looked so different from the child they'd once known, whom she'd taken into her home and also her heart. Soon she'd go over and say hello; for the moment, let her wait. It was well in the past yet she couldn't forget the way Olivia had disappeared and never been in touch again, not even when Kit died.

'He seems nice,' said Maggie, when Suzy embraced her and thanked her for having come.

'He's lovely,' beamed Suzy, 'the answer to my prayers. Everything that you've always had, I hope to find with him.'

Maggie smiled and touched her cheek. In many ways Suzy was still such a child. 'You are doing so well in your career,' she said. 'Don't let him ever hold you back.' She spoke from the heart; she'd been through it herself and knew that the real price of art was self-denial. The freedom to stand and observe and think without domestic intrusions. Yet she also envied this innocent trust. One of the things she admired in Suzy was her determination.

'He won't. He understands,' said Suzy. 'For the first time ever, apart from you, I have found a genuine soul-mate.'

She looked so untouched in that gorgeous dress, aglow with her new-found love. The solemn child was now an established artist, already with an enviable reputation. Maggie experienced a small glow of pride at having helped her talent to develop.

'Be happy,' she said, 'and make sure you stay in touch. Remember I'll always be watching out for you.'

Lisa and Helen had found each other and now stood quietly talking while Olivia, as in the old days, had wandered away. Suzy was still not entirely clear how she came to be there at all; someone must have invited her and then forgotten to mention it. Which was all right with her; what she wanted today was for everyone to get on. And to welcome Helen who had flown so far and the husband who seemed really nice.

'He's great,' said Lisa. 'Where did you find him?'

'Work,' said Helen, which made perfect sense. 'And you?'

Lisa shrugged. She was far too busy even to think about settling down. Though she had to admit that at times like this, she did have the odd private pang. If she were honest and less work-obsessed, she would quite like a permanent partner too. She had once been very badly hurt, which had helped put her off commitment, and the thought of all those children at home had stopped her from ever being broody. She was one of the youngest women barristers in the country to have already taken silk yet, on the whole, preferred male company and envied the sort of enduring love that her parents still shared after all they had both been through.

'And what do you think about her?' asked Lisa, deftly diverting Helen's attention to Olivia, now in conversation with Piet.

'Hasn't she changed,' said Helen, 'and for the better.' They had chatted briefly outside the church and she'd been impressed by Olivia's poise as well as the cut of her clothes.

'She seems to be making quite a name for herself. You can hardly turn on the radio these days without hearing Olivia's voice.'

'Did she say anything about what happened?'

'No. There hasn't been time.'

Together they strolled across to join them just as the Hirsches also descended, their children trailing behind. Much hugging and kissing around the group. The Hirsches had not met Piet before nor seen Olivia as a couple since just before they got married themselves. She had not been invited.

'Suzy looks in seventh heaven. I couldn't be happier for her. The dress is a triumph; what talent she has.' Deborah, downplaying her own involvement, was fulsome in her praise. The others agreed. 'She waited ages but it seems to have turned out really well. From the little I've seen of him so far, Andrew is a terrific guy who doesn't appear to be carrying much extra baggage.'

All of them laughed and Neville rolled his eyes. 'My wife, the rabbi,' he said.

Piet was introduced around and passed with flying colours. Good for Helen, once so drab, to have hooked herself such a striking man, with an international reputation plus kind and humorous eyes. Olivia, as in the old days, felt excluded. No-one had asked her about her career or shown much interest in the missing years. Even Gwen was cutting her, the part that hurt the most.

'Attention!' shouted Guy and they all stopped talking. 'We are delighted to welcome you here today as our guests.' In his morning coat, he looked dashing and distinguished, towering over his daughter who stood at his side. They were doing away with traditional speeches, keeping things simple and low key.

'I give you the bride!' And they raised their glasses, then Suzy took her father's place and proposed a toast to the guests.

'To all of you,' she said sincerely. 'And thank you for being here today. Especially those who have come so far.' Next she introduced her groom who also offered a toast.

'I join my wife in thanks,' he said, 'for loving her as much as I do and letting me take her away. I promise,' his toffee brown eyes were sincere, 'to love and cherish her always.' He stooped to kiss her and the guests applauded. Gwen had to turn away to hide her emotion.

'One last toast,' said Suzy seriously. 'I wish my brother might have been here today. Miranda, too, one of my dearest friends whom all of us miss so badly. Kit and Miranda.' She raised her glass and the crowd, more soberly, raised theirs too. Guy slipped a comforting arm around Gwen who was unashamedly crying.

A hush ensued, to be horribly rent by a cry that was barely human. Through the crowd stumbled an ashen-faced figure, making her way towards the bridal group. Wanda Sinclair, more than half-cut, wobbling on her too-high heels, unsuitable for walking on a lawn.

'Murderers!' she screeched, pointing wildly at them all until her husband took her arm and rapidly led her away.

21

'He seems a decidedly okay guy,' said Markus, bursting with news. 'Has even invited me home to meet the wife.' The jam session had been fantastically good and turned into a spontaneous performance, with six of them playing in Preservation Hall with Markus as solo sax. He had even done a vocal spot, too; once he'd got into the swing of things, he was really rather good. And he'd certainly enjoyed it.

'Now just you be careful,' warned Lisa, alarmed. 'Don't go sticking your nose in too far and buggering up the defence.'

'I won't.' He laughed. 'I'm too fly for that.' She smiled at his easy assurance. There were times when the twelve-year gap didn't count. She was, increasingly, heartily glad she had got him.

With her permission, reluctantly given, he had gone in search of Nathan Blumberg; had boldly been to his office and made himself known. He found a pale young man with owlish specs, lanky as a teenager yet with a college professor's thoughtful mien. After a bit of initial fencing, Markus won his trust. Nathan temporarily shut up shop and they moved across to Jackson Square for coffee and doughnuts in the open air.

'Have you got hold of the husband yet?' Markus came straight to the point.

'Not yet,' said Nathan, fidgeting. 'He's not taking calls, nor returning them. The few times I've driven past the house, the shutters have all been closed.' Which did make sense since he must be in deepest mourning. It was perfectly understandable if he wouldn't talk.

'Maybe he's left town,' said Markus.

'He can't without police permission.'

'And have they got anything out of him?'

'Not a lot, I don't think. His alibi means that they cannot take him in.'

Markus wished he'd seen more of the Lockharts and got to know Andrew better. In their single meeting, he had instantly liked him but straight after that they had come out here where they'd been for almost a year.

'And what do his colleagues have to say? The botanical gardens or wherever?'

'They haven't seen him since it happened, which isn't surprising. They say he is still under heavy sedation. Poor guy, what a thing to go through. It's amazing he's hanging in at all. I'm certain I couldn't do it.' Nathan took off his glasses and polished them hard.

'Do you have kids?'

Nathan nodded. 'A couple. Two small ones, four and two.'

'Then you empathise with the situation?'

'You bet.'

Then was he, Markus privately wondered, the best choice of lawyer to be on Suzy's side? Nathan ran slender fingers through his hair, looking like a college kid. 'The oddest thing of all,' he said, 'is that she appears to believe she might really have done it.'

'Then maybe she did.' Markus felt guilty yet had never entirely accepted Lisa's belief. Friends they might be but that didn't mean she was automatically innocent of the charges. Circumstances can alter things; they had lived separate lives for many years. And under strong pressure, there's no telling what people will do.

'Where do we go from here?' asked Markus as they strolled back across the square. The morning was bright, with the heat just rising. Outside the cathedral, musicians were already in full swing. Markus's fingers itched to join them but first he had serious work to do.

'I'm hoping to get to talk to her defence.' It was clear that Nathan was not including him.

'Horace Cutts? Is he any good?' Markus had read the file behind Lisa's back.

'Once he was the best,' said Nathan, 'though these days is virtually retired. He only took the case out of sympathy.'

Markus came boldly to the point. 'What's the chance I could meet him too?'

'None,' said Nathan. 'He is very much a loner. Who plays his cards close to his chest.'

But who did like jazz, though Nathan wasn't to know that. It was going to take Jackson Saunders to fix Markus up.

22

The Palmers and Sinclairs lived near each other so Suzy and Miranda had grown up as friends. Their fathers knew each other from the golf club; their mothers occasionally had coffee together and sometimes the four met up for Saturday night bridge. Miranda was often at the Palmers' house where Gwen was inclined to mother her and Kit behaved like a tolerant older brother. At weekends the girls would ride together, sometimes competing in point-to-points. Though always inclined to be over-protective, even Wanda realised that her daughter needed friends.

'There comes a time when you have to let them go,' said Gwen, accustomed to frights from her son who was regularly getting into scrapes. Over the years he had had some close shaves, yet so far had managed not to damage his looks. 'You can't tie them to your apron-strings. Sooner or later they have to fend for themselves.'

In principle Wanda agreed, of course, yet nothing

could keep her from worrying. Riding was excellent exercise but Wanda fretted that Miranda might be thrown and damage her neck.

'Miranda's got one of those stupid hats,' Suzy reported to Gwen. 'Makes her look like some kind of spaceman. Grotesque.'

'You should be wearing one too,' said her mother, who knew enough not to lay down the law. They mainly rode on fields and quiet lanes and the ponies were very docile.

'Rubbish,' said Kit, who thrived on taking risks, seeming to bounce when he hit the ground. He had left school and was off back-packing in Australia, and although Gwen begged him to stay in touch, she knew there was nothing she could do. He wanted a sports car, had done so for years; the good thing was that, until he was earning, he wouldn't be able to afford one.

The girls, meanwhile, were still continuing their regular Eve of Waterloo teas. Gwen kept suggesting they include Olivia but Deborah, their leader, disagreed.

'She isn't one of us,' she said. 'She simply wouldn't fit in.'

'My mum feels she's part of our family now.' Suzy weakly stood up for Olivia though her heart wasn't really in it. She saw quite enough of her as it was without her also crashing their tight little set.

'I think you're mean,' was her mother's comment, content to leave it at that. As a former teacher, she knew about such things and the mysteries of the selection process that was part of belonging to a clique. She made a big fuss of Olivia, though, seeing how needy the poor child was. It seemed that no-one had shown her much affection; the aunt and uncle, though they'd taken her in, appeared oddly uncommitted. They were not, in any respect, a caring family. Gwen wondered what the father must be like.

At their coffee mornings, Gwen and Wanda naturally talked about their girls. Wanda was featherbrained and slightly fey but Gwen found her often amusing. Her stories about her days as a dancer frequently had Gwen in stitches. Beneath the slightly starchy veneer she'd assumed to fit in with her Northwood neighbours still lurked the heart of the spirited showgirl who had never quite made it big time.

'It was a tough life but a merry one,' she said. 'The stories I could tell you. I confess I'd prefer something better for my daughter.'

'Then how wise you were to have sent her to the school.' Gwen was always plugging it, aware of what Miranda really wanted.

'She's only there because I was too.' Which really astonished Gwen. In her youth, Wanda must have been a real looker but no-one now could remotely describe her as bright.

'I was only there till fifteen,' said Wanda, instantly picking up on Gwen's gist. 'Then I left and joined a dancing troupe. The Lavender Girls we called ourselves, long before I worked with Lionel Blair.'

225

And this was what they were planning for their daughter, albeit via a classier route. It would not make the future any more secure though obviously Gwen couldn't say that; not only wasn't it very polite, it was also none of her business. She knew Miranda had plans of her own but it wasn't her place to mention them. What she overheard when the girls were together was strictly off the record. In any case, Wanda had another ambition; she was determined Miranda should marry well. She often told stories of how she'd met Cedric, in the chorus at the Palladium when the Black and White Minstrels topped the bill.

'It was love at first sight,' she said coyly, fluttering her lashes. 'He sent me roses every single night until I agreed to go out with him. And we've stayed in love ever since. Have hardly spent a night apart in the seventeen years we've been together.' But, she was honest enough to add, she might have done better had she waited. Some of the girls had married really well, one to an international newspaper magnate, another to a well-known nightclub owner. 'I want my daughter to have everything and more, including loads of money. Never to have to work once the voice starts to go.'

They moved on to Suzy, which seemed only polite. What were Gwen's hopes for her?

'Provided she's happy, I don't much care.' At just fifteen, she had years to decide; no need for any life-changing decisions now. Too much pressure wasn't good for a child, not at this impressionable age. Gwen intended to take a back seat and see how things worked out.

They touched on Olivia, whom Wanda had just met because she was busy rehearsing with Miranda.

'She's a strange little creature with no presence at all. I can't believe she can sing.' No contest there then; Gwen was amused. Wanda only saw what she wanted to.

'She can, you'd be surprised,' said Gwen, remembering the carol concert and Olivia's reluctance to audition for the choir. 'She isn't good at projecting herself, that's all.'

Clearly considering Olivia of no interest, Wanda dismissed her out of hand. But Gwen remained curious to see how she'd shape up. It could be the making of the girl if she pulled this off.

As the rehearsals for *Oklahoma!* gathered pace, Miranda was still having trouble with her dance steps which, for such a pro, was quite surprising. She could handle the square-dance stuff without a thought; it was the twirling ropes that literally tripped her up.

'It doesn't help having you watching me,' she said, convulsed with laughter. The gang were grouped in the gym while she practised, Helen, as always, engrossed in a book. Miranda was trying her best but just couldn't get it right.

'Didn't you ever play skipping games?' asked Lisa, doyenne of the Kilburn streets, but Miranda simply shook her head, having no idea what she meant. 'Here,' said Lisa, scrambling to her feet. 'Two of you take an end each and I'll show you.'

She coerced Deborah and Suzy to turn the rope while she dazzled them with her Irish dancing.

'Wow,' said Miranda, mightily impressed. 'You ought to be in the show yourself. Why ever didn't you come to the auditions?'

Lisa shrugged; it was not her scene. 'Because,' she said, 'I can't hold a tune.' And, in addition, had far too much studying to do.

'But we could have used you in the chorus,' said Suzy. 'All we really do there is dance. They might have given you your own solo spot.'

'Come with us tomorrow,' said Olivia, whom no-one had noticed was even there. She had this uncanny ability not to be seen.

Deborah, pushed out of the limelight for once, was already growing impatient. 'Come on,' she said, 'let's give this a miss. I can't be bothered any more with this stupid show.'

What a bitch she had been, for sure, in her teenage years, aggravated by the slightest thing that kept her from centre stage. Deborah looked back to those days with remorse. For reasons she no longer recalled, she'd had it in for Olivia big time which sometimes spilled over on poor Miranda because she resented their friendship. She'd been selfish, conceited and

228

insufferably vain. She blamed it now on her father, who had spoilt her.

'I sometimes wonder why you married me,' she occasionally said to Neville.

'Because you were a great lay,' he'd reply, his mind as usual on other things, answering purely by rote. 'Plus the best-looking girl in your year,' which didn't actually improve things.

She wanted to ask if he still felt the same but no longer had the courage. Things between them had not been good for a while. But if then she had only thought before speaking, Miranda might still be alive.

'Would it help,' asked Olivia, after the break, 'if the two of us worked on your dancing?' As Ado Annie, she had a far smaller part with only that major solo and a duet to perform. Miranda was almost constantly onstage, with barely time to change costumes between numbers. She sang like an angel and looked the part, too, with her hair in ringlets and glowing cheeks. If she could only get the dance routines properly worked out.

'It might,' said Miranda. 'Just having you there without the others scoffing and making fun. I'll be in the gym at the three-thirty bell. If you have the time, I would love it if you would join me.'

She liked Olivia, who had turned out to be fun. One to one she could really be quite a scream. It was Deborah's acid tongue that inhibited her; when she was present, Olivia rarely spoke.

'Okay,' said Olivia, 'I'll see what I can manage. Provided I don't have to stay back for extra maths.'

When Miranda didn't come home her mother immediately phoned Gwen. Had Suzy any idea where her daughter might be?

'I think she was staying late,' said Suzy, 'to work on her dance routines. I heard her asking Olivia if she would help her.'

Since she had no number for Olivia's aunt, Wanda instead phoned the school. It was after hours; few people were about. The caretaker said he would check the gym, though by now it should be locked up.

Alarm gripped Wanda and she wanted to go there but Gwen, who had come straight round, tried to calm her down.

'There's no point getting in a state,' she said. 'You know what these girls are like, they lose track of time.'

Suzy reported that both girls were brilliant. Unbelievably, Olivia's voice matched Miranda's in strength. 'I think it's really great,' she said, 'that they seem to be palling up. Olivia's always tended to be reclusive.'

With luck it might mean she'd become less clingy; let the Sinclairs have her at weekends for a change. Though Suzy no longer objected to her, was now accepting her as a friend, she could certainly do with a break. For one thing, she'd like some time alone with her mother.

Wanda fretted but the phone didn't ring so Gwen insisted on pouring them each a large gin. It wasn't yet six but she knew the signs; it took very little to put Wanda into a state.

'We've got Olivia's number,' she said. 'I'll get Suzy to check in case they went back to her place.' Wanda's problem, she privately thought, was having too little else to worry about. They had enough money and a comfortable home and she hadn't had to do anything since she stopped dancing. Which meant Miranda had been horribly over-protected. She was now fifteen, well able to take care of herself.

But when Suzy rang back, she sounded subdued. Olivia was home but hadn't seen Miranda.

'I couldn't get to the gym in time,' she said. 'Miss MacIntyre kept me in for extra maths.'

'So where is she now?' asked Wanda, distraught. At which point the doorbell rang.

It was fortunate Gwen was there because Cedric was not. He had gone into town for a fitting with his tailor and hadn't yet returned. The two police officers were gentle and discreet. The woman helped Wanda into a chair while Gwen put the kettle on. A horrible accident, was all they could tell her. The child had been hanging from the parallel bars. The noose had tightened around her neck; it was probable that she hadn't even screamed before the fall snapped her neck. They found her looking like a broken doll, her pretty eyes staring like organ stops, her tongue protruding from her mouth.

'She was always delicate,' Gwen told them quietly, while Wanda was being sedated. 'I thought her mother was over-protective. Now, it would seem, I was wrong.'

An accidental death, the coroner said. Unpremeditated asphyxiation while playing around on the parallel bars without being supervised.

'Not playing,' protested Suzy, when she heard. 'She was working on her rope-twirling act for the show. If only she hadn't been there on her own.'

'It was all my fault,' Olivia sobbed. 'I ought to have been there for her but I wasn't.'

23

Olivia's room in Drury Lane was dreary in the extreme. Though it was larger than the Lucerne attic, she had to share a bathroom, and cooking smells from other floors perpetually seeped in. But at least it had a door she could lock and few people knew where she was. It was also close to the bar where she worked, which was handy on the nights she came home late. More important, it was relatively cheap which meant she could conserve Klaus's money, vital until she had got herself properly sorted.

She worked long shifts which she didn't mind; she enjoyed observing the various types that dribbled in and out of the bar, swarms of people in from the suburbs as well as bunches of rowdy twenty-somethings. She found watching people a useful study for the repertoire of usable characters she was gradually putting together. Even now she could switch personas as easily as other people change their clothes. The lighting in the bar was red, lending a diabolical hue and making her face, by contrast, ghastly pale. The tarty uniform was black and skimpy and she'd taken to wearing heavier makeup and glossy scarlet lipstick. If anyone she knew should happen to come in, which wasn't remotely likely, the odds were they wouldn't recognise her. She was rather banking on that.

All it was intended to be was a stepping-stone into the world of the theatre. She had known for years what she wanted to do and was determinedly working towards that goal. School and the Lucerne singing lessons had fired in her a fierce ambition; she was sure she could do it, convinced she had the talent.

The season's hot ticket was *Phantom of the Opera*, recently opened and playing to packed houses. Tickets were almost impossible to get but Olivia queued on her afternoon off and achieved standing-room at a matinee. Sarah Brightman had a wonderful voice but Olivia felt she'd have done it equally well. She wasn't a beauty but neither was Brightman; it was far more of a character role and there were, of course, the songs. She continued the habit she'd acquired at school of spending as much of her time as she could going to every production she could get into. She bought the music, took copious notes and then went home and rehearsed. She might not be an original singer but had a faultless ear, combined with a lively talent for mimicry.

She didn't tell her aunt she was back. The thought of having to return to Stanmore filled her with the utmost gloom, although she also had doubts that they would want her. They'd already done more than they needed for her, paying her fees at the school; for that, if for nothing else, she would remain grateful. But she knew Aunt Sarah would not approve of her working in a bar, even though her mother had done it before her. Some time in the future, perhaps, she would let her know where she was, but only when she had a proper job and could look her in the eye. She would never tell her about the marriage; for reasons of her own, she felt ashamed. The money was hers legitimately, which wouldn't make it any easier to explain. That episode in her life was over. She intended it should remain so.

For the same reason she didn't call Suzy, now studying art in London. At first she meant to but kept putting it off. Their lives had diverged so radically, she doubted they'd have much in common any more, not after all this time. Gwen was the person she missed the most but she lacked the courage to contact her. She still wasn't sure why she hadn't stayed in touch; shame, she supposed, at what had gone on, but the longer she left it, the harder it would be to pick up connections again. She was lonelier now than she'd been in her life, even in Lucerne. Until that fateful morning in Harrods when she bumped into Deborah.

Having completed her year in Israel, studying the basics of Judaism, Deborah enrolled in the Leo Baeck college to start her rabbinical training. Her father was funding the Regent's Park flat, keen that she shouldn't live anywhere seedy. He would have preferred her to remain at home but recognised her need for independence, after a year on a kibbutz. In his eyes Deborah could do no wrong, having sailed through Cambridge with flying colours and chosen such a commendable vocation. There had been times when he'd had his doubts; at school she'd been something of a rebel. But that was long behind her now and, to crown it all, she was getting married. And no prospective father of the bride could have chosen a more acceptable suitor than the smart, smooth-talking and very high-flying Neville Hirsch. Anything she wanted she could have. Part of the deal, unspoken of course, was babies before too long.

During her year in Israel, Deborah thought often about Kit. Those few wild weeks they had spent together remained fresh in her memory and, even though it could never have worked, he still held a place in her heart. A very special place; she knew now she had loved him and wasn't sure she could feel that way again. These days they only ever met at Suzy's where it seemed as though, by tacit agreement, neither had any wish to rekindle the past. Both had moved on, she understood that, though on her side, at least, the attraction was still powerful. For her he would always be forbidden fruit and, accordingly, all the more enticing. If she happened to see him unexpectedly, her heart would miss a beat. But now she had Neville and shiny new horizons. He was handsome, sexy, all she could want; best of all, from her parents' point of view, he was Jewish.

She'd already been having thoughts about Israel when they'd first started going out. A turnoff, some might have thought, for a man but Neville liked an intelligent woman and respected her powerful drive. He could wait; she was young, not yet ready to settle, while he still had oats of his own to sow. They wrote to each other and occasionally phoned and meanwhile got on with their lives, until he met her plane and saw how much she had changed. She was older, slimmer, more confident; tanned like a gypsy, with her mass of wild hair restrained. Neville, knowing the time had arrived, proposed.

So here she was now, with her eighteen carat diamond, and there, after all these years, was Olivia.

Following the lunch, she had called him at the office, waiting, just as she used to with Gwen, for four days. 'Hi,' she said. 'It's Olivia Fernshaw. We met last Sunday at Deborah's.'

Neville, having forgotten her already, hastily ransacked his memory. There were so many other things on his mind – the markets, the wedding, his pneumatic new PA – that even a girlfriend of Debs came low on the list.

'We talked about my mother's money.' Now he

knew who she was. 'You kindly said you might help me invest it.' Her voice was low and melodious. She could turn it on when she tried.

Ah yes, the plain one; he had slipped her his card. He fleetingly cursed his own gallantry, induced by a rather good burgundy plus a strong desire to impress his future bride. Now he was stuck; there could be no backing off. He knew, to his cost, how tenacious such women could be. He agreed to meet her a week ahead; at five, before she started her evening shift. She told him she wouldn't be working that day; her job in the arts was accommodating though it did consume much of her time. Then she booked an appointment with a top hairstylist and threw in a manicure as well. Klaus would approve; he had liked her to look good and this, after all, was mainly because of him.

Neville forgot to mention it to Deborah; somehow it slipped his mind. In any case, she had quite enough on her plate.

Between her classes at Leo Baeck and fittings for her dress, Deborah's time these days simply flew. She was glad to have got away from the heat and a far more rigorous lifestyle than she was used to. It was good to be back in London again, with her own little car to drive around in as well as a lot of spoiling from her parents. Neville, too, when his thoughts weren't else-where, was excellent at smothering her with attention.

She preened, she pouted, did her little girl act; all she had learnt about equality went down the drain.

'He's an absolute dream,' she purred to Lisa. 'I've never had so much cosseting in my life.' Which had always come high on her list of priorities; right through school, she had wanted her own way, plus unending adulation. It came from being an only child and it would have done her no harm, thought Lisa, to have spent time with the Maguires.

Lisa herself was studying law and finding it hard to stay on top of her workload. Armed with an honours degree from Oxford, she had just completed the conversion course to train to become a barrister at Lincoln's Inn. Even thinking about all that studying made her tired but it was the one thing in life she had always wanted to do. From an early age, as a policeman's daughter, she had had respect for the law.

'You were a right little tearaway at school. Who'd have believed you would turn into such a prig.' Deborah reminded her of their escapades; it was quite extraordinary that neither had been expelled. Yet here they were, the rabbi and the barrister, only a few years away from their ultimate goals.

'Will you still know me when we're terribly distinguished?' Lisa shuddered at the thought.

'In hats and pearls and ageing tweeds? You bet.'

At university, they had missed each other, followed by their separate sabbatical years. But they'd stayed in touch as much as they could and got together in the holidays. Now they'd established monthly lunches which they did their best not to miss. Helen was at Harvard so they rarely got to see her, though Lisa had been to visit her several times.

'Boston's super. I half wish I'd gone there. Though the US legal system is different which might have been a problem.'

'You can always go there later,' said Deborah. 'Once you are qualified.' All she wanted right now for herself was marriage to Neville and a bunch of kids to keep her parents quiet. Her hell-raising days were a thing of the past. Her main worry now was losing weight in order to fit into the dress.

She looked different when he went out to fetch her, seated demurely in reception, flicking through a magazine. Her hair was glossy and beautifully styled and her eyes, when she looked up, were clear as glass.

'Neville,' she greeted him, rising to her feet and extending a beautifully-manicured hand. 'It is good of you to see me at such short notice.' Whatever she was wearing was understated but a perfect fit, he noticed.

Once she was settled in his office, he ran through the details again. 'Just to be on the safe side,' he said, to hide the fact he'd completely forgotten most of what she had told him at that lunch. Her mother had left her a small bequest, hers now she'd turned twenty-one. She wanted to invest it soundly and ensure that it would grow.

'I live very modestly in Covent Garden.' Though the chic exterior belied that fact. 'And there isn't anyone else that I can turn to.' The eyes beseeched him to treat her gently; he noticed a very slight trembling of her lip.

His sense of chivalry swiftly rose. 'Don't worry,' he said. 'Consider it done. I suggest a portfolio of bonds to spread your money and minimise the risk.'

She looked at him so trustingly that Neville's confidence grew. As green as they came, straight from finishing-school, with no male relative she could turn to, as well as very few friends. In his conceit, he'd forgotten how they had met. He glanced at the clock – it was quarter to six – and asked if she'd care for a quick drink.

'Just the one before I go home,' he said, not mentioning that Deborah would be waiting.

'I have to be at the theatre by seven,' she said. 'But that would be nice.'

She gave him her hand as she rose to her feet, smoothing her skirt as they'd taught her at finishing-school.

Sometimes Deborah and Lisa got together with Suzy, puttering along in her quiet life. She liked the college, had made a few friends, but the person with whom she spent most of her time was her mother.

'Gwen is divine, we all know that, but what on earth is Suzy up to? Sitting back and letting her life trickle

241

by.' Despite the mountains of work she got through, Lisa was rarely without a man and Deborah was still preoccupied with the wedding. Suzy, however, appeared content. Living at home was cheap and easy, the more so since her brother had moved out and she'd taken over his bedroom as a studio. Mother and daughter did things together; they had always got on well.

'Dad spends his evenings in front of the telly. So Mum and I go to pottery classes and are thinking of taking up yoga. I am also trying to teach her to paint. She spent all those years taking care of us kids with very little in it for herself. I'm hoping to help her compensate for some of the stuff she missed out on.'

'How is she?' Whenever she thought about Gwen, Deborah felt slightly guilty. All through her schooldays Suzy's parents had been more like family than her own. She must remember to invite them to the wedding; there was still so much to sort out.

'They're fine,' said Suzy, 'both of them. Fit as fiddles and relaxing more. Dad is slowly winding down the business. And playing even more golf.'

'And Kit?' asked Deborah, carefully casual, keen to know yet also dreading to hear.

'Good,' said Suzy. 'Enjoying the job. Seems to have fallen on his feet.' After a year at the Foreign Office, he was now in Strasbourg enjoying himself. His looks and charm were ideally suited to the career he had chosen. 'Not too much work and loads of play. Kit right down to the ground.'

'Does he have a girlfriend?' She could have kicked herself but the words were out before Lisa could bite them back. She was aware of Deborah's slightly slanted look but Suzy, noticing nothing, gabbled on.

'Loads, you know what my brother's like. Mum keeps hoping he'll settle down but I don't see much likelihood of that. At least not yet.'

'He's too young.' The words came out more sharply than intended. 'I don't think men should ever commit until they are thirty-five at the earliest.' But, then, her home had been awash with kids, rather like living in a zoo.

'Lucky for me Neville didn't think that way,' said Deborah smugly as she studied the menu. 'Is he still gorgeous?' she casually added, wondering what to choose that would have the least fat.

'So I'm told. Can't see it myself. Though when he's home, the phone seems to ring all the time.'

'This is cosy,' said Neville to Olivia, subtly pressing her thigh with his knee.

'Indeed,' she said, shifting slightly to avoid him. She knew what would come, though not quite yet; such things took a certain sleight of hand to arrange. Act too eager and the game could be lost. She didn't want to risk that.

The bar, in the City, was close to his office, light years away from the one where she worked. He'd get quite a shock if he saw her there, in fishnet tights and skimpy vamp's dress, with scarlet lipstick plastered across her face. Not that he'd be likely to object; she knew this type of sophisticated lout, suave and expensive on the surface but inside deeply corrupt. If she had the time, she would take him for a ride to pay him back for doing this to Deborah. But her own needs, right now, took precedence. What she was after was his expertise to help make her money grow.

'I cannot tell you how grateful I am,' she said. 'My mother died soon after I was born and I'm not sure where my father is right now.'

She let him take her hand, one step nearer to the inevitable pawing. Men were pigs, no argument about that; on the brink of marriage yet here he was, making a move on his fiancée's friend.

'The thing is,' she said, looking suitably abashed, 'I confess I am somewhat stuck for the readies right now. Don't get me wrong.' She saw his surprise. 'The job pays me a mega wage but until the quarterly cheque comes through, I'm a little strapped for cash.' She fluttered her lashes. 'And, of course, I'm closing my savings account so that you can take care of what I've got.'

Neville smiled and squeezed her elbow. Like most women, when it came to finance, the poor thing hadn't a clue. But she was rather sweet, he'd underestimated that; suddenly he felt protective. He pulled out his wallet, a gift from Deborah, and flicked through a fistful of notes.

'Fifty do you?' he asked her casually, expecting something in return.

'Make it a hundred. No, better still, two. That way you'll get it back all the sooner.' She didn't flicker as he counted out the notes, still not quite sure how she'd managed it. Somewhere nearby a clock struck seven. 'Gracious, is that the time?' she said. 'I must be there before the curtain goes up, am already running late. The producer has called a meeting of the angels. They're in a bit of a mess right now but nothing that fifty grand won't fix. That's what this business is about. I love it.' She smiled as she picked up her bag and accepted his peck. They would meet again very soon, she promised, as soon as she'd managed to get her hands on her cash.

'Call me when you need me,' he said, seeing her to the door. This pale, shy creature was starting to intrigue him; beneath the surface he sensed a darker spirit which, after Deborah's marshmallow charm, he found slightly challenging.

You bet she would call; she had barely begun, but Neville Hirsch was too self-centred to realise he was being taken for a ride. Vain and decidedly not too smart; for Olivia's purposes, the ideal combination. Once out of sight, she felt like dancing, knowing the game was now under way without the poor sap's having sussed. It also made her feel good to know she was cocking a snook at Deborah.

24

Often, early on, Suzy would wake and not believe she could possibly be so happy. She would turn to Andrew for confirmation and he would do what he could to convince her that he loved her as much as he said he did. More, even.

'Where were you all my life?' he would ask, nuzzling into her neck.

And she would reply with her customary frankness: 'Waiting for you to show up.'

They were living in Shepperton in his rented flat, right on the edge of the river, and Suzy would drift like a creature possessed, putting the makings of his breakfast together while Andrew did his early morning sprint along the towpath. There was a sheltered balcony on which they sat, eating their cornflakes and watching the boats, until it was time for him to go to Kew and her back to her painting.

'I can't believe it's so good,' she would say, burbling over the telephone to her mother. Since the day they first met they had never had an argument; if it ever came to a clash of opinion, he was the one to give way. Which wouldn't be natural in the normal course of things but for honeymooners was ideal.

'I'm so glad, darling. You waited so long. The least you can do for us now is live happily ever after.'

Gwen, Suzy sensed, was putting on a bit of a brave face. It couldn't be easy to be losing a daughter when she still hadn't quite got over the loss of her son. But if ever she attempted to raise the subject, Gwen invariably backed off.

'Nonsense,' she'd say, 'I'm not losing a daughter; merely extending the family.' But sometimes at night, when she thought Guy was sleeping, he would hear her muffled sobs. What worried Suzy was that Andrew had plans for imminent further travel. His branch of botany, propagating rare plants, took him, sooner or later, all over the world. It was something he had been honest about from the moment they'd first got together. The reason, he told her, that he'd not yet settled down was the peripatetic nature of his job. Which was fine with Suzy, who could paint wherever she liked, but was something she slightly dreaded telling her mother. Especially as Andrew was talking about China. She bounced it off her father first to see how he would react.

'Go for it girl!' He was all in favour. 'You have more than done your bit for the Aged Ps.'

But still she worried about breaking the news to

Gwen. Although externally her mother seemed resilient, she wasn't nearly as tough as she made out. She had done as she'd threatened on the morning of the wedding and requisitioned Suzy's bedroom as a workroom of her own. Suzy's own studio, stolen from Kit, remained untouched and uninvaded.

'Feel free to use it,' she had said. It seemed such a waste of space and excellent light. But Gwen was superstitious about that, preferring instead to make over Suzy's room. Guy stood back and let her get on with it, seeing it as displacement activity as she stripped the walls and painted them plain white. But to Suzy it still didn't seem quite right. Her mother should be relaxing as she grew older.

'Do me a favour,' she asked her friends when they met for a farewell lunch. 'And keep an eye on my mum for me after I'm gone.'

'Sure,' said Deborah, jotting it down. Visiting the elderly, counselling the bereaved were part of the regular parochial duties that mainly filled her days. Gwen, however, was quite apart from this. Deborah would be glad to stay in touch just as a friend.

'Any special reason?' asked Lisa. 'I hope she isn't ill.'

'No,' said Suzy. 'I just feel concerned.' And explained.

'Empty nest syndrome,' said Deborah knowledgeably. 'Sooner or later, I'm afraid, it will come to us all.' Luckily for her, her children were still small, though Abby was developing alarmingly fast and becoming the same sort of handful she'd once been herself. She hoped she'd cope better than her parents had done. These days she was a whole lot older and wiser.

'Not to me it won't,' said Lisa, still resolutely unattached. Though she was sympathetic if Gwen was feeling low. 'I'll try to give her a buzz myself. Perhaps invite her to lunch.'

'Be tactful, though, when you ring her,' warned Suzy. 'I'd hate her to think I'd been telling tales out of school.'

Kit had been part of their childhood, too, though Lisa had never known him well. He was tall and blond and intimidating to an Irish kid from a rough part of town who never quite knew how to hold her knife and fork. But the Palmers were all so relaxed and nice, she had rapidly fitted in. And learnt to look forward to their regular teas, the highlight before they went back to school. Deborah was always her special friend, since they lived in the same part of town, but the other three felt like sisters too, a blessed relief after all those small boys rampaging around her own home.

When she told the others, they were shocked. 'Fancy having to share a bedroom.'

'It's not that bad.' Roisin was just a kid and all the brothers were sharing too which meant that they all came out equal. But the Palmer house became Lisa's dream with its spacious rooms, its crooked beams and that wilderness garden that seemed like paradise. In place of the dangerous Kilburn streets, to be able to play unsupervised was more than she'd ever imagined. Sometimes Kit and his friends were there, too, so much older that they couldn't be bothered to talk to little girls. But when he was there on his own, he was totally different. Kind, considerate, always interested, with his lazy smile and compassionate eyes, never too busy to stop and chat or even take part in their games. Lisa had wished he was her brother, too, instead of those terrors at home.

The years had passed, and they had all grown up and gone their separate ways. Kit, five years older, had travelled the world before going up to Oxford. Lisa had almost forgotten him until that Boxing Day party, when she had just completed her first term and he had already graduated. She had been impressed at how he'd improved, no longer the easy-going, sports-mad schoolboy but a man now and handsome with it. She'd been flattered by the attention he gave her, dimly aware that Deborah was acting slightly oddly. He had talked exclusively to Lisa, keen to hear her impressions of Oxford for which he held a strong nostalgic yearning. She was at Lady Margaret Hall while he had been at St John's. But with just that one summer dividing them, it turned out that they had several people in common. He told her about his riotous life and what a ball he had had. And his flatmates embellished his scurrilous stories with relish.

* * *

At the end of the party, he ran her to the station; he and Suzy were staying on and Deborah was fully occupied in trying to impress the accountant with her father's posh car.

'Where are you living?' he asked her politely.

'Still with my parents in Kilburn,' she said. Though the house was crammed to the rafters with kids, she couldn't afford to move out. Besides, it would have offended her father who was fiercely proud of providing for them all.

'Mind if I call you?'

'Sure. Why not?' She acted cooler than she really felt. She scrawled down her number, devoutly wishing she lived at a better address. And then severely reminded herself he was only Suzy's big brother. Nothing to get worked up about; all he was being was polite.

She was surprised when he called her four days later to ask what she was doing on New Year's Eve. Nothing, she told him; she was always direct and didn't believe in the stupid games girls like Deborah played. He and his flatmates were giving a party and he wondered if she would come. Nothing special, he quickly explained; just a bunch of old Oxford pals and their dates which she might find amusing. She considered taking an escort herself, then dismissed the idea as silly. Should he turn out to have a girlfriend there, she would stay for one quick drink and then move on.

But when she arrived at the Baron's Court flat, he

was on his own and seemed pleased to see her. 'You look great,' he said as he took her coat and Lisa was glad she had bothered to make an effort.

'No Suzy?' she asked, glancing round the room. No, he said, she'd had something else on, a local do with her parents. No Deborah either, which was quite a relief. The accountant was there with another girl with whom he seemed suitably cosy.

They played loud music and drank a lot and danced to Buck's Fizz and the Police. When midnight struck and they all embraced, Kit surprised her by kissing her hard, then asking if he should run her home, as though she were nothing more than his kid sister's friend.

'No thanks,' said Lisa, suddenly withdrawing. She was old enough now to take care of herself. So he kissed her again and said, if she would like to, she could stay the night in his room. Taken aback, Lisa hesitated; at heart she was still a good Catholic girl, which she tried to cover up with a devil-may-care attitude. But she fancied Kit, had known him all these years. To back off now would lose her points and make her appear pathetic. Besides which, Lisa had never been a quitter. She accepted every challenge that presented itself.

'Okay,' she said, wondering what her pa would say. But that was something she'd deal with when she had to. She was grown up now and away at Oxford. And, with luck, he would be on duty tonight and never know.

By morning the balance of power had shifted and Kit no longer viewed her as a child. 'Whoever would have thought,' he said, kissing her gently, 'that the feisty little tyke would turn into you?'

Like Deborah before her, she never told Suzy or, for that matter, Deborah either. There were some things, she found, just too intimate to share with even your closest friend. And she didn't want to embarrass Kit, wasn't sure how he would feel. Her parents had not been aware she'd stayed out; her father, as she'd hoped, had been on duty and her mother hadn't even noticed. Even the kids for once didn't split; she had had a lucky escape.

They met a couple more times in London before the new term began. After which he drove up to Oxford at weekends and she smuggled him into her room. What had started as a casual fling became a raging passion; Lisa, eighteen, had been caught unawares and, before she knew it, was head over heels in love. Her studies suffered but she didn't care. This was far more important than any career. At Easter they made up vague excuses, both too shy to go public yet, and drove to Ireland in search of her roots, staying in small country pubs. But nemesis had been stalking them; you could not be raised the way Lisa was and hope to escape scot-free. When she missed a period, she couldn't believe it, assumed she had simply been working too hard. She waited another six weeks before she called him. She had to be in town, she said, and might they possibly meet? Of course, he said, sounding in tiptop form which made her feel warm and secure. They'd become so close, perhaps he already had an inkling. She made up her mind she would have the baby and postpone her bar application for a few years.

Kit suggested they meet at his flat and she went, expecting to stay. She wore an outfit that was not too revealing, telling herself that after this visit she would doubtless be engaged. She would still have to face her father, of course, but with Kit beside her, she wouldn't be afraid. Once he was over the initial shock, he was bound to see it was all for the best. They loved each other which was surely all that mattered.

The lights were all on and music was playing. Kit opened the door looking suave and composed, still wearing his Foreign Office suit.

'Great to see you,' he said, taking her bag. 'Everyone's here and we're opening champagne. Wait till you hear my news.'

After you, she thought silently; not wishing to steal his thunder but feeling a sudden qualm, though she didn't know why. Whatever it was, he was clearly on a high; she hoped her news wouldn't bring him down. He showed her into the living-room where everyone present hugged her. Some girls she didn't know were there and making plans for all going out for dinner.

'Can you stay?' Kit asked her. 'I'm hoping you will. We really have something to celebrate. My bosses say they are pleased with my progress and are posting me to Strasbourg.'

Ace! they all cried, and jolly well done, and one of the girls asked where Strasbourg was; wasn't it somewhere in Europe? Lisa smiled too and made the right noises but inside she was screaming and felt she might throw up. She said she was sorry but she couldn't stay, had an early tutorial she shouldn't miss and really ought to be going.

'Will I see you again before I go?' he asked, making no attempt to stop her.

'We'll see,' she said, quickly pecking his cheek, unaware that she'd never see him again.

Instead of Oxford, she went home to Kilburn, urgently needing the reassurance that only her mother could give. She hadn't told Kit about the baby; it wasn't the time and she sensed he would not be pleased. At this stage in his glittering career the last thing he needed was to be encumbered. She only wished the best for him but knew things were over between them. At least her mother would understand; babies were her stock in trade and there was nowhere else she could turn.

No-one answered when she rang the bell so she fumbled in her bag for her key. 'Ma,' she called in the unlit hall. 'It's me. I'm home. Is there anyone there?'

Normally she'd be greeted by a barrage of noise

but tonight everything was silent, no sound of children, not even the television on. She checked her watch; it was barely eleven. So where had everyone gone? She called again, then ran quickly up the stairs when a voice called softly: 'Up here.' A dim bulb was lit on the shabby landing and the door to her parents' bedroom stood ajar.

'Ma, are you there?' she said, suddenly alarmed, as she slowly opened the door.

'Lisa?' The voice sounded barely human and there lay her mother on bloodstained sheets, with something indescribable between her legs.

'What happened?' she cried as she rushed to the bed. Then saw it was a dead baby.

She wanted to call an ambulance but her mother was holding out her arms and all she could do was kneel beside her and offer what comfort she could. After she'd tidied her up a bit and wrapped the atrocity in a towel, Lisa held her mother and let her weep.

'Sure now, don't worry,' said Colleen in a broken voice. 'Our Lady decided it wasn't to be. So say a prayer with me before you go.'

Once she'd established the bleeding had stopped, Lisa rounded up the kids and brought them home to bed. She thought of calling her father but then didn't bother. Whatever had happened was between man and wife; these days she felt like a stranger. She sat with her mother until she slept, resisting the impulse to lecture her, knowing she now couldn't tell her about her own secret.

Her mind, by the time she got back to Oxford, was made up. She booked herself into the clinic vowing that, from this moment on, her career would always take precedence in her decisions. She was done with commitment and family life. Love was not for Lisa.

25

China was an eye-opener in more ways than one. Its wide horizons and breathtaking views stopped Suzy in her tracks. Till now her image of the vast sub-continent had been drab rows of faceless manikins, identically dressed in dark grey suits with matching expressionless faces. Nothing had prepared her for the actuality of such stupendous natural beauty. She was stunned.

'You see,' said Andrew, teasing her. 'Travel does help to broaden the mind.' He'd been on the road since his student days; there was very little of the world he hadn't seen. Even in the two years of their marriage, he had already dragged her to Osaka and New Zealand and now was in Sichuan again, hoping to finalise a quest he'd started just after the wedding. Then, for economic reasons, he had been compelled to leave her behind. Now, since the experiment was suddenly urgent and he'd no idea how long it would take, he'd insisted on bringing her too.

'Unbelievable,' breathed Suzy, feasting her eyes. 'It makes me feel that till now I've been positively blinkered.'

She was out with her paintbox for much of the day while Andrew was searching for the fabled tulip tree, the Chinese variety, imminently threatened with extinction. *Liriodendron chinense*, as he'd taught her to call it, a beautiful tree, growing in the wild, of which he had found a single example and taken a few of its seed-pods for propagation. Last time the experiment had failed so now he was really up against it. Far more exciting than working in a greenhouse; Suzy had to agree. She loved the area of China they were in, warmed to its people too. Pretty soon she cracked the veneer, started seeing them as individuals with a sharp and caustic humour with which she clicked. She no longer considered them an alien race but as cosmopolitan as Europeans. At times, for instance, in a busy marketplace they might just as easily have been Spanish or Italian with their bright black eyes and glossy hair, their open welcoming smiles. The children were especially enchanting and seemingly quite fearless. They crowded round her wherever she went, shyly trying to touch her face, as intrigued by her as she was by them. Sometimes they even gave her flowers. It caused her a pang which she couldn't quite define; some instinct deep within her was moved profoundly.

She steeped herself in Chinese culture and started planning an exhibition entirely Sichuan-based. Their silk-screen painting and fine embroidery inspired her to new heights of excellence. It was an influence that would never leave her, bringing out levels of talent she hadn't yet shown.

'I wish you could be here,' she wrote to Miss Holbrook, still her mentor and now a cherished friend. 'The light and colours are indescribable. Wherever you look is like a gigantic watercolour. Cézanne and Monet would have loved it.'

Maggie, who liked Andrew a lot, was delighted. Occasionally, over the years, she had worried that Suzy might somehow be missing out. This slightly late flowering was excellent news. She dared to hope it might also presage the patter of little feet.

In Suzy's absence Maggie had heard from Gwen who had talked to her at the wedding and mentioned she'd like to try painting herself, now that Suzy would soon be off and she'd have more time on her hands. Suzy had given her some rudimentary lessons but she found it hard to work with her daughter overseeing. Was there anywhere Maggie could advise her to go?

'Come to me,' said the teacher, delighted. Since her retirement and move to Hastings she had kept in her hand with a weekly class at St Martin's, where Suzy had studied. 'I can, at the very least, set you on the right track. After that we can probably find you somewhere a little closer to home.'

And so their Thursday afternoons began, three till

five at the college, painting, followed by a cosy hour in a wine-bar before Maggie caught her train back to the coast. Each of them grew to enjoy it immensely; they had more in common than they'd realised, and both were fundamentally lonely. Gwen found Maggie a marvellous teacher, which she'd heard from Suzy for twenty years, and Maggie delighted in Gwen's conversation which was sprightly, informed and to the point.

'To think,' said Gwen over a glass of wine, 'that all these years we've been on nodding terms when we might have become proper friends.'

'The school would not have approved,' said Maggie. 'Not that I ever gave a toss about that.' With her striking hair and imperious nose, she looked like some sort of celebrity which, in certain circles, she was. She always wore her carpet coat over a high-necked sweater, with her reading-glasses dangling on a beaded chain.

'I can't ever thank you enough,' said Gwen, 'for being so good to my daughter. She found you a total inspiration. We give you total credit for her success.'

It was not Maggie's style to display much emotion but she made it clear she was pleased. 'She always was a dear child,' she said. 'I couldn't be happier that things have worked out so well.'

They sat in silence, sipping their Merlot, and Maggie sensed Gwen had other things on her mind. She glanced at the clock; just twelve minutes to the train. 'I could catch one later, if you'd like,' she suggested.

'Perhaps you would care to join me for something to eat.'

Gwen was delighted and also grateful; Guy would not be home till late and, more than anything, she hated eating alone. After so many years of being full-time wife and mother, she found the emptiness of the house depressing. She talked a bit about Kit as they ate, still unable, after all these years, to understand how it possibly could have happened.

'He was always such a happy boy. I still can't believe he would take his own life.'

'So what do you think did happen?' asked Maggie, lighting one of her black cheroots after offering one to Gwen. She leaned both elbows on the marble table and tried to get Gwen to open up. They were an interesting family, the Palmers, but she sensed more complications than they showed. The husband seemed genial and easygoing yet this sensitive woman was by no means happy. Some hidden emotion emanating from her smacked slightly of despair.

When she finally realised what was going on, Suzy laughed at her own obtuseness. She had put it down to the diet at first, then to the climate change. But, when she was more or less certain, she went to a clinic and had her condition confirmed. Andrew, predictably, was overjoyed then immediately started to fret.

'I'm afraid I'm going to have to send you home. I daren't risk anything happening to you or the baby.'

Suzy roared; he was such a pet but a silly old fusspot at times. 'Come on,' she said, 'it will soon be the twenty-first century. And you can hardly call this civilisation backward.' Nevertheless, she was now thirty-six; medically speaking, 'an elderly primigravida'. 'Yuk!' she said when she read their notes. 'That really is a bummer. And here was I seeing myself as a slip of a girl.'

Andrew consulted his mother in Scotland who, level-headed though she was, came firmly down on his side.

'Better safe than sorry,' she said, offering to come to London for the birth, but that was something, said Andrew retreating, she would have to sort out with Gwen.

They got Suzy into Queen Charlotte's Hospital and, despite Andrew's protestations, she insisted on flying home alone, slightly resenting being treated like a child but excited at returning after so many months away.

'The second I hear, I'll be on the next plane.' But right now, she knew, Andrew's blasted seedlings took precedence over the baby.

Gwen's concern, which she didn't divulge, was what was happening with Guy. Lately he'd seemed not himself at all, had, in some intangible way, withdrawn from their usual close intimacy. She knew he had worries on the business front, at sixty-seven was facing the decision of whether to retire and shut up shop. He had run his own accountancy practice since the age of thirty-five and, though the work did not fully absorb him, not in the way that Andrew's did, it had managed to keep him lively and on his toes. Looking at him now from her workroom window as she tried her hand at sketching a laburnum that had erupted into full flower, he might still have been the lithe young man she had married forty-five years ago. She could hardly believe it had been so long, she still felt so youthful inside. As Suzy had logically pointed out, it was not unheard of for people to retire after they'd passed sixty-five but Guy hated being reminded of his age, still had the vanity of thinking he looked much younger. Once Gwen had lured him on a Saga holiday, a river cruise up the Elbe, but he couldn't stand the other passengers whom he'd lumped together as a bunch of old fogeys.

'Never again till I'm in my dotage,' he'd announced when they were safely home. 'And on a Zimmer like the rest of them.' Which wasn't quite fair, since some were early fifties, but Gwen got the drift of what he meant. And was glad. The romantic youth she had always loved was still there, under the skin. Though neither as tall nor as handsome as Kit, the family resemblance was still pretty strong. Suzy favoured her mother's side but the energy and leanness of the men was pure Palmer. Guy's regular golf games kept him fit and his brain was active because of his work. She sympathised with his current dilemma, didn't know what to advise that would be for the best.

Although they had always been virtually inseparable, preferring each other to anyone else, Guy seemed increasingly self-absorbed until she felt he was shutting her out and slipping into an inner world of his own. She knew she might not have been the easiest of company since Suzy had married and moved abroad. She missed her daughter's chatty company, her cheerful presence at meals. They had laughed and joked at the same trivial things, enjoyed the same soaps and those irritating ads, had even stood in the kitchen together and cooked. Guy was out for the working day, still travelling up and down to the City, but where once he'd come home full of news, these days he was silent and withdrawn. Sometimes he didn't appear till bedtime without a convincing explanation. She feared to probe; after years of harmony was reluctant to turn into a nagging wife.

'I think he's probably just worried,' she told Wanda, when they met for their regular coffee date. 'It can't be easy to face retirement and suddenly feel you're not wanted.'

Wanda, accustomed to having Cedric underfoot, understood absolutely. She and Gwen had been drawn together, despite having very little else in common, by Gwen's having been there the day Miranda died. Neither would ever forget the moment the police had suddenly arrived. It was still inconceivable that such an accident could have happened but, over the years, the Sinclairs had grown to accept it. Wanda, at first, had been virulently angry, accusing Olivia of shedding crocodile tears, and when it turned out she had not been working at her maths but simply skiving, the police had been to her home and questioned her. In the end the coroner had declared it an accident and the case was officially closed. Poor Olivia, had been Gwen's immediate thought. What a terrible thing to have had to go through after losing one of her friends. She had planned to make more of a fuss of the child but, very soon after, Olivia left the school.

And now Gwen had a grandchild on the way, though she tactfully tried not to say much because of Miranda. Wanda, however, already knew. Such news spread like wildfire through their circle.

'You must be thrilled,' she said, pressing Gwen's hand. 'I know I would be, in your position.'

Grateful and touched by her generous spirit, Gwen risked turning back the clock.

'How many years is it now?' she asked.

'Would you believe twenty-one? I can't believe she's been gone so long or that I am now so old.'

'Nonsense,' said Gwen, 'you've not changed a bit.' Though, in truth, poor Wanda was only a shadow of what she had once been. 'Kit's been dead twelve.' And they sank into silence, united by the intimacy of grief.

* * *

266

Guy wasn't clear how he'd allowed it to happen, this adventure on which he was embarked. One thing had led to another so quickly that now he was in too deeply to turn back. The kick he got was worth the deception though he dared not think what it would do to Gwen, should she ever find out. It made him feel like a player again, not just an ageing has-been, and for that alone he didn't regret it. In the street he walked taller, with a spring in his step, a man teetering on the edge of self-destruction. It was lunacy, she was half his age, but he'd long had a yen for much younger women and this one, when it came to the crunch, he had been unable to resist.

There hadn't been any special hidden agenda; it had caught him entirely unawares. But when she'd invited him out for lunch, as an elegant thank you for free advice, he had felt unnervingly drawn to her, for reasons he wasn't quite sure of. Guy, still missing his daughter badly, drew new strength from her youthful vigour and the undisguised admiration in her eyes. They lunched twice more, at his instigation, then, late one afternoon, she had called, said she had theatre tickets for that night and that someone had let her down. When he told Gwen he'd run into an old friend, she hadn't even queried it which made the next time easier. He was, he discovered, a natural liar; it wasn't a talent he had ever had to use and a sad indication of how he and Gwen had drifted apart.

From then on they met regularly. Gwen seemed

sunk in a world of her own so he gave up caring about alibis, certain she would never bother to check. Mainly they met for a quickish meal before going back to her place. She was warm, submissive and thrillingly erotic; restored his sexual prowess and made him feel young. By the time he got home, Gwen would be in bed, sunk into a book. She would ask politely if he'd had a good day without even bothering to listen to his reply.

Suzy lay like a queen against her pillows, proudly displaying her newborn daughter. Andrew had made it just in time but had now gone back to his hotel room to catch up on some sleep. The birth had been smooth and uneventful; she was ready to try it again, Suzy said. Gwen, unashamedly emotional, sat stroking one tiny finger while Guy fidgeted around the room, checking that all the technology worked and lowering the blind to protect the baby's face.

'Don't fuss, Dad,' said Suzy, the sudden expert. 'She isn't made of glass, you know. Babies are tougher than you think.' Gwen laughed; this was her daughter speaking who had, up till now, avoided babies like the plague. How rapidly natural instincts locked in; there had been a time, not so long ago, when she'd even had to tell her the facts of life. She wished this new tiny creature every blessing and silently vowed to watch over her. New life was the harbinger of new hope. A great dark weight started shifting from her heart.

'May I hold her?'

'Of course. She is your grandchild. And it's practically time for her feed. Might just as well wake her now before the nurse comes.' Suzy was watching her father pacing, unusually tense and ill at ease; she wondered what could be wrong.

'All right, Dad? You look as though you can't wait to get away.'

Guy, reminding himself sharply where he was, came hurrying back to the bed. 'I'm sorry, my dear, I was miles away. Can't quite get my head around the start of a new generation.'

'Your father's got a lot on his mind,' said Gwen, when he slipped out for a smoke. 'He is worrying about something, though I'm not sure what. He no longer confides in me the way he used to.'

Suzy, shocked, snapped out of her trance. She felt so secure, she could hardly bear that things might not be all right between her parents. Yet, now that she had a daughter of her own, she was suddenly aware of their mortality. In this small room were the people she loved most, other than Andrew who would also be with them shortly.

'What do you think it is?' she asked.

'Quite simply that he's scared of growing old.'

'Dad?' said Suzy, astonished. The thought of her father feeling insecure disturbed her. He was good old reliable, golf-playing Dad whom she and her mother had taken so much for granted. The only time she could remember him shaken was the terrible night they had heard of Kit's death. Then, for the one and only time in her life, she had seen her father shed tears. She devoutly hoped that never again would he go through anything that bad.

They waited till Andrew reappeared, showered and shaved in a crisp clean shirt, with a new light of love in his eyes. He carefully removed his daughter, now awake, from her grandmother's arms and held her tenderly against his chest, rocking her and patting her back like a pro. Guy had remembered to bring his camera and grouped them together around the bed while the nurse obligingly took snaps.

'You're not planning on taking her back to China, I hope.' Gwen was fearful of losing Holly before they were properly acquainted.

'Not for just now,' said Andrew mysteriously. There was something he needed to discuss with his wife but not till she had recovered a bit from the birth.

'Nice boy,' said Guy, as they left the hospital and went in search of his car.

It was almost twelve; Gwen felt like celebrating. 'Have you time to come and wet the baby's head?'

She saw his brief hesitation and felt her heart plummet. Whatever it was that was eating him these days seemed not to have gone away after all. Once she would have sat him down and demanded an explanation but they'd drifted too far in the past few months for her to take the risk. What if he'd simply stopped loving her? The thought was too dire to contemplate. She felt an urge to talk to Maggie who saw things as they really were and could usually sort them out.

'Why not?' said Guy, still feeling a traitor. 'Let me just call the office and check that there's nothing too urgent on my desk.' He would push the boat out and take her to the Connaught; his name still carried sufficient weight to get him in without a reservation. And Gwen was right, this was a red letter day which needed to be commemorated in style.

26

If Guy had lusted after Deborah as a schoolgirl, he was certainly not in a minority. From her earliest teens, she looked older than her years, was what in her grandparents' jargon was known as a tease. She was into boys in a major way when Suzy and Miranda were still riding their ponies, and interested in fashion from the age of eight. Though not her fault, her mother was mainly to blame. Her own involvement with trends and styles naturally overflowed into the home and the child had inherited her visual flair and always liked to look nice. Shopping with Mother was her biggest treat, after which they would indulge themselves and have lunch. Thus Deborah was as at home in Harrods as others of her age were at the zoo.

But she'd also inherited her father's brains and took to study like a natural. Boning up for exams was easy; she never even had to swot. Both Lisa and Helen worked harder to excel; Deborah sailed effortlessly through. And once she was over the silly phase, she became an exemplary student. All of which had helped contribute to her present state of eminence. Inevitably, she had passed her rabbinical exams and was now a highly respected functionary of the Jewish community.

So now, in turn, she was worrying about Abby who had reached the age that she had been when she first became interested in boys and, in her mother's footsteps, was now at the school. She had the same come-hither eyes and husky gurgling laugh. And her body was developing fast, ahead of the other girls in her class. It was history repeating itself but Deborah was a far more caring mother.

'I worry about her,' she said to Lisa. 'I see her turning out just like me.'

'Well, that's okay surely?' Lisa was surprised. To her mind, Abby could not have a better role model. Both of them were bright and sassy, like peas in a pod. The physical similarity was striking and made Lisa yearn for her teenage years when she and Deborah had been as thick as thieves.

'Not entirely,' said Deborah. 'There is much I regret.' Subsequent years had caused her to see the errors of her youth. Luckily, however, with two younger siblings, her daughter was likely to escape being spoilt. Luke and Daniel, though slightly younger, claimed as much attention as she did. And Neville, when he was home and had the time, was an enthusiastic father. His passion for football had always surprised her and now he was passing it on to the boys. Which meant that the males of the family had bonded and brought her full circle back to Abby. Worrying times.

'You are making a mountain from a molehill,' said Lisa. How she would have loved to have peace at home. 'She's a very bright kid and you've brought her up well. Leave her alone, for heaven's sake, and allow her to make her own mistakes.'

In theory, Deborah fully concurred, knowing Lisa was right. The other thing she was trying to teach her daughter was the lasting value of friendship. She encouraged Abby to bring friends home, though could never be the sort of mother Gwen Palmer had been to them all. There just wasn't time from her parochial duties to be as attentive to their needs. Although she cooked and was good at entertaining, she had rarely ever made a cake.

'Stop worrying. Times have changed,' said Lisa, amused to look back and remember how Deborah once was. Spoilt and capricious, with doting parents and a daddy who had always been like putty in her hands. She had dressed too old and pushed herself forward and flirted with all the boys. When Lisa remembered how they'd combed the nightspots, searching for suitable talent, she winced. What trollops they'd been yet they'd come through all right. By luck or instinct, she wasn't sure which, somehow they had survived unscathed. Apart, of course, from her own little hiccup which she still hadn't mentioned to a soul.

Deborah and Lisa remained best friends and their regular meetings were something on which both relied. Nothing could be so bad, they felt, that the other would not be able to help sort it out. Which was why they clung together now, hoping they could do the same for Suzy.

Cambridge had opened many doors for Deborah which had stood her in excellent stead. Always ambitious, she had flung herself into numerous social activities that had helped her in later life. At school she had always loved to debate so was naturally drawn to the Union, of which she eventually ended up president. That was when she had got her first taste of power; politics suited her, she loved a fight and felt herself guided towards a public career. Becoming a rabbi seemed the obvious next step; as a leading member of the community, she would quickly develop her own voice.

All of which had happened without a hitch and Deborah was daily rewarded by knowing that all the hard work she put into the congregation was worth it and doing real good. She was deadly efficient on the day-to-day stuff, ran her small office like a military campaign and was universally applauded for her fearless stance. The frivolity of her earlier life was replaced by a diehard attitude which meant she would fight to the end if the battle was worthwhile. The members of her congregation both loved and trusted her and her name became known in the world outside as someone who fought for her beliefs and always stood her ground. She took less care of her general appearance, though was always appropriately dressed, and tried not to mind about gradually putting on weight. It suited her, her girlfriends said, and did not detract from her looks. But her hair, which she kept cut short these days, had now become flecked with grey and she hated the circles beneath her eyes when she'd stayed up too late in her study.

'It's not important,' she told herself sternly. 'Vanity is unworthy.' Yet she yearned for her youth when she looked at her daughter and saw herself at the same age.

She won a number of public battles – better healthcare, crèches for workers, improved facilities for the disabled – which thrust her into the limelight and started making her name in the national news. Rabbi Hirsch had a reputation for fighting what seemed like hopeless causes and managing always to win. Her debating skills made her a natural for the media and she often appeared on television, forthrightly speaking her mind. The teacher who'd forecast that she'd end up Prime Minister was turning out to have had the right idea.

'You know,' said Lisa, hugely proud of her. 'You are the one who should have gone to law school.'

And Deborah, flattered, went on to do more, enjoying her public speaking role, still with an eye on

Westminster though she felt she was not yet quite ready. All was well in the Hirsch ménage; they had moved to a larger, more luxurious home, Abby was not yet out of control and both boys were doing well. Her parents flourished, she still had her friends and the BBC was proposing a radio slot. Everything in her life was near perfect. The one thing that slightly bothered her was her marriage.

Neville had always been entirely work-driven. It was one of the things that had first attracted her to him. She liked a man who knew his own potential and would go to any lengths to achieve it. Her father had always been her childhood idol. Neville was much like him. For the first few years, till the babies came, their marriage had been idyllic. Both were handsome and riding high, with plenty of money to supplement some really extravagant living. Deborah loved to entertain and it suited Neville's business ambitions to encourage her. On a regular basis, they had twelve for dinner with thirty or more for cocktails on Thursday nights. He encouraged her to spend money on her clothes and was openly approving when she showed them off. 'My wife, the rabbi' had become his catchphrase, spoken always with the utmost admiration.

But then she had fallen pregnant with Abby and after that the boys came along. And the usual things that erode relationships happened. Deborah was no longer free, on a whim, to fly to St-Tropez for the weekend. Or throw a party for a hundred bankers to help cement a deal. She was often tired in the morning, having been up all night nursing a child with a fever, and it took her several months to get back her figure.

'I don't think he finds me fun any more,' she started complaining to Lisa. 'When we do go out, he gets annoyed if I want to check in on the children.'

'I am sure he understands,' said Lisa, who privately had her own doubts. When Markus met him, he had not been impressed though had never said as much to her. But she knew Markus. And, more and more, was starting to appreciate what she'd got.

These days Neville had been getting home late, often in a foul mood. She usually sensed when he was playing away and had learnt to turn a blind eye. Nothing could be gained from a confrontation; he was a very accomplished liar, and it simply wasn't worth provoking a row. Deborah liked the life she had built and had no intention of wrecking things. Her work had become more important than her marriage, though she valued having the edifice to hide behind. They were viewed, she knew, by the world at large as being the perfect couple. Which, at least from a professional standpoint, was useful to them both.

She did a lot of counselling, was expert at lancing the wound and helping to draw the poison out. If she weren't a rabbi, she might have made a fortune as a private therapist.

'So explain to me Suzy's motives?' said Lisa, who was seldom off the case.

'How do you mean?' asked Deborah, whose mind had been wandering.

'First, if she did it, why?' asked Lisa. 'Second, since we know she didn't, what is she covering up?'

'I'm afraid I can't figure that out,' said Deborah. 'I've tried looking at it from every angle but only come up with blanks. If she did it, she's mad and we don't believe that. If she didn't, she ought to be fighting her corner instead of simply giving up. Yet the police, apparently, claim she confessed which is the bit that makes no sense. Whatever's going on?' And where was Andrew when they needed him? Why hadn't he been in touch?

Which was why she was still determined to go to New Orleans and hope to talk to Suzy face to face. She would be there now if Lisa would allow it but she kept telling her to wait. She couldn't help remembering what Neville had said, that marriage can often alter people; well, it had certainly altered both of them. Perhaps, after all, he had a point. Whatever his faults, he certainly wasn't a fool.

Helen's opinion was matter of fact; post-natal psychosis was all too common though doctors were inclined to overlook it. 'Especially down there in the south,' she said, 'where they may not have the mental health resources.'

'Well, suppose she did it.' Deborah was resistant. 'Why is Andrew acting like he is?'

'Probably in denial,' said Helen. 'Imagine losing both children like that then also having to face up to the cause. If she was stressed to that extent, her husband should have seen it. Considering how close they have always been it does seem unlikely that he didn't notice her tottering on the brink.'

'So you think we should go there?'

'Yes, probably we should. We, after all, are her closest friends who have known her for most of her life.'

'And you'd speak up in court?'

'I most certainly would. I'd do anything in the world to help get her off.'

Whatever it was that was wrong in Neville's life, he wasn't letting on. He came home late, increasingly tense, and snapped when she had a go. She had taken to gathering her papers together and moving upstairs at the sound of his key. Occasionally he slept in the downstairs guest-room in order not to disturb her, he said, when he finally came to bed. They should be talking it through together, which was what she would tell a parishioner, but the truth was, she didn't really want to know. She feared the marriage was in serious trouble but wasn't sure that she really cared any more.

For, if she were honest with herself, Neville had never come first. Despite the trappings and the money and glitz, she hadn't ever really loved him at all. Sex with him had been fine at first but once the wedding was out of the way, she had sensed his ardour rapidly wearing off. Surely it ought to last longer than that – or were the vows little more than a trap designed to ensure that the strain remained pure for the sake of future generations? Helen, again, was the expert on this; she had studied it at Harvard. How Deborah longed for a session with her, in person and not just by email.

Now she wondered what Markus was up to and slightly resented his being in New Orleans, especially since he hardly knew the Lockharts. Lisa had explained he was there quite by chance, as part of a combo performing at the Jazz Fest, and was only making marginal inquiries without ever revealing his interest.

'It can't do any harm,' she said. 'Markus is very discreet.' And he seemed to be getting on well with Nathan Blumberg.

The minute there's anything, she had told him, the three of them would be over like a shot. But she did see the point of not showing their hand until there was a reason for them to come.

'Leave it to the boys to handle,' she told a scandalised Deborah. 'Just occasionally, they can be more effective.'

27

Horace Cutts lived a quiet life, the more so in the last ten years since his wife, Eudora, had passed on. He still inhabited the same great cavernous house, with a wide veranda that ran right round it, wisteria dripping from the balustrades and his bentwood rocker in the porch. Before she died, he'd been thinking of retiring and doing a bit of barracuda fishing as he had done in his youth. But then the cancer caught up with her and Jared moved overseas with the children and Horace had to wake up to the fact that he was alone and lonely. He had been a lawyer all his life, like his pa and grandpa before him, and found he couldn't stop dabbling in the law. They came to him still in his book-lined study, the young attorneys of New Orleans, and stayed to talk even after they'd picked his brains. He also played the piano well so they'd linger as the light grew dim to hear him stroking his fingers over the keys. Chopin and Schubert were his favourite composers but he was also a mighty fine hand at jazz.

'No-one raised in this part of the world,' he'd explain to out-of-towners, 'can not get involved in the fine traditions of the south.' He liked his bourbon and tobacco, too, and would, of a night, sit outside on the porch and read until the nightjars started to roost.

'That's just old Horace,' the neighbours would say, seeing the glow of his paraffin lamp still burning as they turned in. He was such a fixture in the neighbourhood, the local women declared themselves safe as long as they knew he was out there, keeping watch.

When he read about the murders of those children, Horace was filled with revulsion. What kind of mother, was his first reaction along with the rest of the townsfolk, but then he got to thinking about it and decidedly smelled a rat. What kind of mother indeed, was his conclusion and he dialled the head of the New Orleans police.

'Now, look here, Horace,' said the police commissioner wearily. 'I thought you'd finally hung up your spurs long ago. Don't go meddling where you just ain't welcome. This little lady's gonna fry.'

Which naturally caused Horace a mild conniption so he put on his spats and laced his two-tone shoes and toddled down to the streetcar stop to take a ride into town. Retired he might be but his brain was still active and when he sensed an injustice in the making, there was just no keeping him down.

'Horace,' said Dee, when he turned up at the

courthouse. 'What are you even thinking about, coming here?'

'Justice,' said Horace, lighting his pipe. 'And how I am going to help that poor woman go free.'

Apocryphal, maybe, but that was the version that Nathan Blumberg told Markus, who then passed it on.

'You mean,' said Deborah, when Lisa called, 'that this guy is actually on her side?'

'So it would appear,' said Lisa. 'Markus swears to it. He is even hoping to get to meet the judge.'

'Brains as well as beauty, eh?' Deborah had to smile. So much, just now, was getting her down, it was good to know that something might feasibly go right. 'So does he think we should go over there?' She was still faintly miffed at his intervention. It had all been arranged behind her back; had she known, she would not have approved.

'It's Nathan who calls the shots,' said Lisa. 'And he's inclined to think we should still hold off.'

Deborah was itching to join the fight but Lisa was the legal brain. As long as Deborah knew there was movement there, she would try to curb her impatience. And she saw the point of Markus, an outsider, being a fly on the wall provided he did nothing to screw things up.

'Don't worry about it,' said Lisa shrewdly. 'It's a bit like the old boy network. When these jazz musicians get together, there's no telling what might emerge.'

28

As a result of his tulip tree triumph, which eventually resulted in an avenue at Kew, Andrew was approached by the city of New Orleans to become director of their botanical gardens, part of City Park. Since he'd always loved the American south, he instantly leapt at the chance. It fitted well into his area of research and would make a nice contrast to China. Suzy, amazingly, was pregnant again, two months after Holly's birth, but that did not deter her. Not at all. Having caught a big dose of Andrew's travel fever, she could hardly wait to be off again. And at least the States should be easier living, not least from the language point of view.

'Don't bank on it,' warned Deborah, who had been there. 'From what I know of that part of the world, the natives are barely comprehensible, though their accent is pure magic.'

'We'll manage,' said Suzy, 'and Andrew is thrilled. There are things he's been longing to do over there and anything that makes him happy suits me.'

The thought of two babies both under one year was a slightly daunting prospect but the thrill of being so blessed again more than made up for whatever qualms she had. As forty approached, she couldn't believe her luck especially after those anxious early years.

'I wish you were coming too,' she told Gwen, who was desolate at having to part from her again when Holly was still so young. All these years she had longed for a grandchild; now, on the brink of having two, she would miss their most interesting age. 'At least it's not as far as China. You'll always be welcome to stay.' Secretly Suzy was hoping her parents would be able to visit her regularly now that her father was finally thinking about retirement. Or even her mother on her own would do. She still sensed that things weren't quite right at home. Perhaps a break from their normal routine might help improve the situation.

'I promise I'll write often,' she said, as they hugged goodbye at the airport. 'And you definitely have to be there for the baby's birth.'

She was thrilled, though also somewhat surprised, by the blossoming friendship between Gwen and Miss Holbrook. She might have got them together sooner but the thought had not even crossed her mind. It had never occurred to her that her dynamic teacher would find anything at all in common with a staid suburban housewife. But the two had quickly become best of friends which made her feel slightly excluded.

Gwen, who had never been anyone's fool, picked up on this instantly. 'You don't understand what she sees in me. You can't imagine why she'd want to waste her time.' It amused her to see her daughter squirm but she knew she had got it spot on. 'What you over-look,' said Gwen, 'is that we are more or less the same age. And have shared experiences you cannot even guess at. Remember, I was a teacher too. We have quite a lot in common.'

In addition to which, she had loved the job and had given up only reluctantly when the children came along. These days the scenario would have been quite different but then it had seemed an imponderable dilemma. Guy could afford it, his business was thriving, and they'd both agreed that the babies had to come first. She had never really regretted that deci-sion and sensed her daughter would understand better once she found herself in a similar position. Suzy was fortunate in having a rare talent which meant she could work wherever she was, and even with two small chil-dren to look after, her art was unlikely to suffer much. Especially in the United States where people cared more about such things.

'Do you regret not having a family of your own?' Gwen asked Maggie after class one day as they sat in their usual wine-bar, sharing a bottle.

'Not in the slightest,' Maggie replied. 'Teaching the little blighters was enough. It gave me the framework to do my own thing and not have to worry about money.'

In a way, two sides of a similar coin. They realised they weren't so different after all. What Gwen had told Suzy turned out to be true; they had a fair bit in common. Gwen found Maggie a total inspiration, could understand why Suzy had been so fired. And Maggie, for her part, liked Gwen a lot and sympathised with what she was going through.

'Does Guy ever wonder what you're up to?' she asked. 'Two can play at that game, you know.'

'If he does, he never lets on,' said Gwen. 'Is just relieved I'm not drooping about, being a moaning Minnie.'

Nevertheless, Gwen didn't deserve it, being made to feel redundant at this stage in her life. Maggie wished there was something constructive she could do. What the husband needed was a kick up the backside; she usually found that sort of action worked.

'If you ever feel like a break from him,' she said, 'you'd be more than welcome in Hastings. A breath of sea air and some fresh fish and chips invariably does it for me.'

Gwen was touched; she liked the idea. Guy had his golf and his secret life; it was high time she started doing things on her own. It would do him no harm to fend for himself. She had been his minion quite long enough. Time to get out from underneath and start living.

'Smashing,' she said, 'I would really like that.' And started to feel much better about herself.

Holly was still not quite a year when her brother, Jonah, arrived, a sweet little baby with a smudge of dark hair and a thoughtful expression in his eyes.

'He is clearly an ancient soul,' said Gwen, who had flown over on her own to witness the birth. Guy was tied up with other things; he sent his apologies and love. She gently lifted her grandson from his cot; at last another Palmer male. She prayed that his life would turn out well, better than Kit's had done.

'What's Dad up to?'

'Just working,' said Gwen. Despite her hopes that he'd soon retire, he was still up and down to the City. She was aware that Suzy was growing suspicious but what was she going to tell her? That her father appeared not to love her any more and was possibly looking elsewhere? She firmly pushed it out of her mind, would put it on hold for later. Now she had one predominant desire, to welcome Jonah Lockhart into the world.

Holly, at eleven months, was enchanting and reaching the toddling stage. With their great solemn eyes and wispy hair, each looked the image of the other and, with luck, because of the closeness in age, would grow up to be good companions. The Lockharts lived in the Garden District, one of the nicest areas of town, with wide tree-lined streets and imposing homes, set in spacious grounds.

'What are the neighbours like?' asked Gwen, as they sat outside on the porch.

'Nice,' said Suzy, 'the few we have met. We haven't been here long enough to socialise much.'

'That will start happening automatically as the children grow and you get around a bit more.' She was staying for only a week this time, keen not to come between Suzy and Andrew. She knew from experience what sleepless nights could be like.

'But you'll come back soon?'

'Whenever you need me. And next time I promise I'll bring Dad.'

Suzy adapted to motherhood more easily than she'd expected and didn't resent the time it took from her painting. In a way, it made sense to get it over in one go, though she did find the broken nights extremely exhausting. Andrew was always willing to help but she felt it was really her role. He, poor man, had a new department to run whereas all she had to do was manage the home. Or so, not wishing to upset him, she let him think. They were fine when they were asleep, she said. She could put her career on hold.

The girls pored over the jpegs she sent and cooed at the babies' beauty.

'I'll say this for Suzy,' said Deborah, admiringly. 'When she chooses to do a thing, she does it well.'

Her China exhibition would be opening soon but she felt she couldn't tear herself away to go over.

'The nanny can easily cope,' said Andrew, dreading to think she might really go but anxious not to appear to stand in her way. These days she was a celebrated artist while he was little more than a jumped up gardener.

'No way, she can't,' objected Suzy, playing at being outraged. 'I'm not risking leaving you alone with her. It's more than our marriage is worth.' The pictures would sell themselves, she reasoned, while to miss one second of her children's first months was simply not an option. The nanny was great but not living in. Suzy wasn't quite ready yet to have interlopers in her home.

'Where did the talent originate?' asked Maggie, out on the terrace in Spain where Gwen was painting a land-scape while the others had gone into town. They were on a week's painting holiday with Maggie as tutor.

'Hers or mine?' Gwen narrowed her eyes and held her brush at arm's length to judge the perspective. Her feet were bare and her legs well-tanned. Her greying curls were concealed by a wide-brimmed straw hat.

'You're right. That's the answer, she got it from you. Please forgive me for not having seen that before. Do you regret now that you didn't start sooner?' Maggie relaxed in a basket chair and basted her face in the sun. She liked all the group but was most at ease with Gwen whose company she found so empathetic.

'Nope,' said Gwen, not having to consider. 'I have always believed that things like painting happen when you are ready. Even if I'd had Suzy's chances, it doesn't follow I'd have been any good. Creative things, of whatever kind, develop mainly out of life's experience. The rare exceptions are freaks in my opinion.'

Maggie laughed. 'You can learn the techniques. That's where I come in.'

'But not the vision. You can't teach heart. Not what lies within.' She squinted up and caught Maggie's eye. Both of them burst into laughter.

'Wise words indeed. Shall we break for lunch? You don't want to overdo things, not in this heat.' And at any minute the others would be back, expecting a meal on the table.

Guy had been left to fend for himself; Gwen felt little remorse. But, being the consummate wife she was, before she left she'd arranged for him to eat out almost every night with neighbours.

'They all adore him. They always have. Something about the Palmer men makes them irresistible.' She wondered about baby Jonah; too early to tell. 'The secret is, I've done everything for them. Women can rarely resist a helpless man.'

Maggie opened a bottle of Rioja, happy to see Gwen so relaxed. The worry lines had gone from her eyes and her appetite seemed back to normal.

'And you don't miss him?'

'Not a bit.' Which, for the first time in her marriage, was true.

*　*　*

Things in Guy's life were far less simple; she had vanished, just like that. Off to pastures new, he assumed, the day he desperately rang her bell and found she'd gone and left no forwarding address. She had not been returning his calls for two weeks but he'd put that down to work pressures. At half his age, she was right in her prime and the job, about which she'd said very little, was making increasing demands. Now there was nothing more he could do, he realised that right away. He had known from the start he was taking huge risks, gambling with everything he held most dear for the sake of his ageing vanity; truly pathetic. He hadn't loved her but had grown to think he might simply because of the way she made him feel. He only rarely took her out so it couldn't have been his money, unless she was a lot subtler than he'd thought. Which didn't explain why she'd scarpered now unless she was simply after better pickings. All he could do was lick his wounds and crawl home to his patient wife. One thing he knew was, no matter what happened, neither Gwen nor Suzy must ever find out.

The thing was, Gwen wasn't there any more, not in the way she had once been. Since Suzy's wedding, he had noticed a change. After moping around for a while, she had suddenly jerked herself back into life, had taken up painting, enrolled in a course and now was seeing a lot of Suzy's teacher. All of it commendable, yet he found it disconcerting and it didn't help his feeling of impotence. Now Gwen was the one with the alternative life while Guy had to turn to his neighbours' wives for the admiration he had always relied on.

One night a week she came home late, though he'd understood the art class started at three. What went on in the intervening hours she hadn't bothered to tell him or else, which was more likely, he hadn't listened. All he knew was she was suddenly much brighter and the laughter that seemed to have left with Suzy was back. She spent long hours alone in her workroom, emerging in excellent spirits to cook him a meal. She still gave him her full attention and listened to what he said, and yet, in some subtle intrinsic way, had changed. And now she was off on her own in Spain with a bunch of new friends from her class. Guy, who'd never been a worrier before, poured out his woes to Wanda.

'You're a bit of a dark horse,' she said, next time she met Gwen for coffee. 'Giving the old man the run around. I only hope it is worth it.' Gwen sensed disapproval under the smile.

'You give me too much credit,' said Gwen, attractively tanned and fit. Though hugely amused at Guy's anxiousness, she thought she had better come clean. Couldn't risk letting the neighbourhood get entirely the wrong impression; Wanda, for all her charm, was a bit of a dope. 'All I'm up to is my art class,' she said. 'After all these years waiting on him hand and foot, I need to do my own thing. Life is short, there's not a lot left. I want to do my bit while I still can.'

She sensed that Wanda was disappointed, could see it in her eyes. A bit of scandal was grist to her mill and she always flirted with Guy, it was how she was.

'And now,' said Gwen, 'I must get on with my shopping. Tonight is the opening of Suzy's exhibition.'

The exhibition had shining reviews and the paintings were rapidly snapped up. The artist's absence, as Suzy had foreseen, seemed not to make a difference. Maggie remembered the Finchley Road days and the prediction she had made. The name Suzy Palmer was becoming well known sooner even than she had expected. The Cork Street gallery was very prestigious; the art world was there in force.

Gwen had invited her to the Private View and afterwards to dinner with her and Guy. Maggie had never really talked to him before, had only exchanged passing words at the school and later at the wedding. She was glad of the chance to know him better and assess what made the relationship tick. She liked him enormously, had done so from the start, was charmed by his unassuming candour. Some men found her over-assertive but Guy took her in his stride and made her feel very welcome indeed at the meal. Naturally, their main talk was of Suzy and how New Orleans was suiting her.

'To start with, she wasn't sure,' said Guy, 'how they

were going to fit in. China was one thing but only short term. Here they are going to be settling for a while.'

'The house is truly gorgeous,' said Gwen. 'And the town is right up your street. Some time you ought to go over and see them. I know she would love it if you did.' Suzy still looked on Maggie very much as her mentor even now her own work was so acclaimed.

Maggie, despite her nomad spirit, had not yet done the American south. She had always planned to go there, so promised she would. 'I'll wait till the children are a little bit older. I'm sure she's far too pressured for visitors now.'

They chatted on about other things, then went their separate ways.

'Nice woman,' said Guy on the journey home. He had left the car at the station. 'I like that strong outspoken type. You know where you are with Maggie Holbrook. And you must admit she does make a change from poor Wanda.'

29

Jackson came to hear Markus play and was suitably impressed. He invited him back to hear him sing on the Sunday.

'Will your wife be there?'

'Well, of course,' he said. 'But before that there's someone else I think you should meet.'

It was after ten when they reached the house where a mellow light showed through the open front door and a respectful gathering was listening in silence to a pianist playing honky-tonk. He raised one hand in casual greeting and a white-coated waiter slipped across and offered them each a drink. Jackson and Markus found seats at the back and settled down to listen.

He was quite an elderly silver-haired man but, boy, could he play piano. Markus was quite electrified by the ease of his performance. All the old tunes came rattling out, the spirit of the deep south, and when people began to call out requests, he effortlessly slid into each new number without having to pause or look for the sheet music. When he finally stopped, the applause was deafening and he laughed and left the piano-stool and came across the room to welcome Markus.

The hand he offered was firm and dry. 'Horace Cutts,' he said. 'I understand you're a fellow performer. Welcome to New Orleans.'

He must have been in his seventies, reckoned Markus, but it didn't show in his playing. 'That was some performance,' he said. 'We ought to be seeing you down at Preservation Hall.'

Horace laughed. 'Those days are way behind me, though I've done my bit in my time. You can't live here and not play jazz; they would run you out of town.'

The audience, who were mainly young men, started to slip away. 'Lawyers mainly,' their host explained. 'They like to drop in here after work and use me as a kind of sounding-board.'

He led them on to the lamplit porch and called for another round of drinks. Markus preferred to stick with beer but the older men drank bourbon.

'So what are you doing in these parts?' asked Horace.

'I am here for Jazz Fest,' Markus said.

'Apart from that?' The eyes behind the lenses were sharp; this was a man who rarely missed a trick. It was obvious Jackson had not been discreet, so Markus thought what the hell. If he didn't seize the moment right now his whole expedition might have been in vain. So, hoping that Lisa wouldn't object, he told him he knew Suzy Palmer.

For a while Horace sat in contemplative silence, visibly marshalling his thoughts. Markus could not make out his expression; all he could see was the light glinting off his glasses.

'An interesting case,' he said at last. 'With plenty of missing pieces. They say she killed her children but I don't believe it.'

Another long pause while the sounds of the night assailed them from all sides; the restless clicking of the cicadas and the distant honking of frogs. It was a lush, moist atmosphere packed with movement and the turbulent magic of the south. Markus slowly relaxed his muscles; it had been an exhausting day. Six hours playing on an open air stage, with only occasional breaks, had done him in. It was good at last to sit back and loosen up and try to get the music out of his head.

'How well do you know her?' asked Horace suddenly.

'I have only met her once,' said Markus, 'but I know a lot about her.'

'Including that you don't think she could have done it? Else, it goes without saying, you wouldn't be here.'

Markus nodded; he had got it in one. This was a very astute man.

'These are the facts as presented,' said Horace, talking as if to himself. 'A neighbour reports raised voices late at night, followed by a slamming door and, much later, a car driving off. The workers at the botanical gardens confirm the husband was there all night or, at least, since the early morning, which gives him some sort of alibi. Meanwhile, she goes there to remonstrate, leaving the children in the car. And when they fail to resolve their quarrel, she drives the car up to Riverbend, stopping on the way there to drop off her laundry, and drowns them both in the river. Then she goes home and prepares her husband's supper.'

Put like that it did sound absurd but the facts were as Lisa had said. The police had not yet come up with another suspect.

'But why would she do it?'

'I'm asking you. You have come here from London to pick my brains.'

Markus shuffled his feet in the darkness and accepted another beer. Horace Cutts was testing him and he didn't know how to respond. Except he knew that this meeting was vital and somehow he must do his best to persuade him to get her off. Not that he needed persuading, it seemed. The lamplight showed that the eyes were benevolent.

'The fly in the ointment,' said Horace next, 'is that she claims to have done it. Now, young man, can you explain why she'd say a thing like that?'

'You don't think she's telling the truth?'

'No way. I have only met her a couple of times but I'd stake my reputation on her innocence.'

Well, that was something; Markus was relieved. At least Lisa couldn't accuse him of screwing up. But it still didn't get him off the hook; why would she claim to have done it if she hadn't? And if she didn't do it, who did? Could she be covering up? And, if so, on whose behalf – it was still going round in circles.

'I have taken her through all of this,' said Horace, 'and the lady is mightily confused. As you might guess, the death of her children has temporarily driven her out of her mind. She no longer has any idea what happened and, furthermore, doesn't care. In her own eyes, her life is over. She's indifferent to what the law decides. So now it is up to me.'

'And what do you think?' asked Jackson, intervening. He'd been sitting in silence all this time, soaking in information. The fact that his wife would be judging this case had, so far, not been mentioned. 'You're a wise man and you've chosen to defend her. You must have a pretty strong case to be doing that.'

'You want the truth?' said Horace wearily, suddenly looking his age. 'I can't be sure I have a hope in hell of getting that little lady off the hook. All I can guarantee is that I will try.'

'I think,' said Markus, as they rose to leave, 'that what you are looking for here is the missing link. If it wasn't her, then someone else did it and that's the person we need to find.'

'Exactly,' said Horace, shaking his hand. 'The more you can tell me, the easier it will be.'

30

That night, Lisa had been so exhausted she couldn't even face the tube-ride home, so wandered into Soho instead, in search of some good Thai food. The other option would have been a taxi but Rotherhithe was a good way out and her working-class roots rebelled against needless extravagance. She had been in a four-hour meeting in chambers with a would-be client she found obnoxious, about whose business ethics she had strong doubts. She didn't like his solicitor either, found the whole matter unpalatable, but couldn't turn him down without solid reasons. Finally, after four hours' sparring, she'd convinced him he hadn't got a case. Had put it on hold, pending further inquiries, and succeeded in getting rid of both of them by ten. By which time she was dead on her feet and craving only sleep. Until she realised that she was also famished.

The sounds from Ronnie Scott's, next door, began to be enticing once she had had her fill of jungle curry.

It was late but why not, she could still take that taxi, and no-one was waiting up for her at home. Although she loved the solitary life, there were times when she needed people, and the famous jazz club was just what she felt like now. Lisa paid her entrance money and was shown to a table in the dark interior where a performance was already under way. She ordered a whisky, then sat back to listen and found herself instantly entranced.

A saxophone player was performing solo, lit by a single silver beam. Because he was dressed entirely in black, all she could see was the gleam of his instrument and the shine on his flaxen hair. He was playing something eerie and disembodied that touched on her sensibility like a nerve. At the end of the number, when the lights came up and the audience gave a resounding cheer, Lisa saw he was young and good-looking, lithe with a muscular bum. She felt the familiar quaver lower down and decided to stay for another drink. All of a sudden her energy returned; the night was young and, what the hell, tomorrow was the weekend.

She stayed so long that she caught his eye and he casually wandered over.

'Drink?' she offered and he asked for a beer. That was the night she met Markus; they never looked back. At 3 a.m., when Ronnie Scott's closed, he came home with her in the cab, bringing only his instrument case and a battered leather jacket.

'You travel light.'

'It is all I've got. I can pick up a razor in the morning.'

Deborah and Helen were fascinated; emails flew.

'How old did you say?'

'Twenty-three, I think. Old enough, at least, to stay up with the grownups.'

Twelve years difference; Deborah was shocked but Helen was philosophic. Since meeting Piet, her life had turned around; she only wished as much happiness for Lisa.

'How come she didn't settle down before?' At school she had always been very much into boys.

Not even Deborah, Lisa's principal crony, knew the answer to that. 'It certainly wasn't through lack of choice,' she replied.

She was pleased for Lisa yet still surprised that she continued playing her cards so close to her chest. When cross-examined, which she often was, she would laugh and joke, then flippantly change the subject. No, she refused to be drawn about Markus; he was great, they were good together was all she would say. Deborah tried hard to conceal her envy but, all the same, felt somehow let down. It was part of a Best Friend's function to spill the beans.

The fact was, Lisa had never experienced anything quite like this. He had the unflagging energy of his age and wanted to do it most of the time until she was pleading for mercy.

'Whoa, slow down! We have got all night. Controlled is often better.' He was such a boy which was what she liked. Apart from his sexual agility, she found his outlook on everything refreshing. He was here, in London, on his way round the world, paying his way with his virtuoso playing before returning to Hamburg and the bank.

'What do your parents think about this?' From what she'd heard of his father, in particular, she couldn't imagine him wanting his son to be just an itinerant musician.

'My mother's all for it. My father needs slightly more convincing.'

'Do they know about me?'

'Not yet.' He seemed embarrassed. 'They know there's someone, that's all.'

'But not the details?' She laughed and ruffled his hair. 'Don't worry, in their position I'd be appalled too.'

Markus was unusually easy to have around. Up till now, Lisa, whoever she was seeing, had managed to maintain full independence. She liked male company, was addicted to sex but also valued her privacy over all else. The job she did was so taxing to the brain that she had to have no distractions as she burrowed through files, made copious notes and put her sharp, analytical mind towards seeing all sides of a case. Alone, with only soft music playing, she was in her element. Any other human presence set her nerves on edge; just listening to someone attempting to be quiet destroyed her concentration in a flash. The furtive creeping in another room, the muffled sound of the television, turned low. The sound of the kettle being boiled, even the click as it turned itself off, was sufficient to drive Lisa nuts.

Markus, however, had a soothing presence which made her feel comfortable and rested. She liked to know he was there in the next room, reading quietly while she worked, or sleeping like a baby on the comfortable couch, ready to spring into action when she was done. Unlike most other men she had known, Markus was totally adaptable. If she needed, last minute, to cancel a date because of an unexpected work crisis, he never showed any sign of minding at all.

'Okay, babe.' There were other things he could do but mainly he stayed around the boat and simply kept out of her way. His cooking had improved since they'd come here to live and she'd be rewarded by a really good meal as well as a backrub when she was finally through.

She had bought the houseboat on a whim because they both fell in love with it and she felt it was time to move on from Rotherhithe. Also it was more convenient for her work. She could cycle to her chambers along the towpath.

'What do you talk about at breakfast?' asked Deborah, to her mind always the acid test.

'We don't,' said Lisa, 'he is usually still sleeping. Which is, I have to confess, a bit of a bonus.'

When Suzy returned from China to give birth, Deborah and Lisa went straight to the hospital to give support and also view the baby. Helen sent her love and wished she could be there too. In her customary open-handed way, Suzy appointed all three as joint godmothers; they solemnly pledged to take their duties seriously. Strictly speaking, Deborah wasn't eligible but Suzy liked the idea of a rabbi on her team. The more the merrier and better for the baby; this way she would be covered from all angles.

'I'm calling her Holly Miranda,' she told them. 'Which seems appropriate, don't you think? By rights, Miranda should by now have children of her own.'

'Well, it's better than *Carmen* Miranda,' quipped Lisa but neither took any notice. Their thoughts were back with their own Miranda now.

'Twenty-two years,' said Deborah in wonder. 'It doesn't seem nearly as long as that.' To think, she now had a daughter of her own at the school.

All fell silent, remembering the day they'd heard the news about the macabre accident.

'I often still wonder what actually happened.' Lisa was no longer joking; her barrister's sharp intelligence had cut in.

'Precisely what do you mean?' asked Deborah, suddenly alert. Lately she had been thinking about it too.

'Well, they said it was an accident but the facts never quite added up. Nobody seemed to take it sufficiently seriously.' The others stared but Lisa meant it; she had been unable to get it out of her mind. 'In a way, I feel partly responsible,' she said. 'If it hadn't been for the skipping games and me showing off, doing Irish jigs, she wouldn't have been in the gym on her own in the first place.'

'Of course it wasn't your fault,' said Deborah. 'You are overlooking one crucial fact: the way Miranda was brought up. Where the rest of us might have just muddled through, she had to get it perfect. The tragedy was, there was no-one else there to catch her when she fell.'

'Olivia should have been there,' said Suzy, whose mother had had to console the stricken girl. 'She blamed herself, feeling she had let Miranda down.'

'Typical Olivia,' said Deborah with scorn. 'Always snivelling about something and making a fuss.'

'Be fair,' said Suzy, leaping to her defence. 'Don't forget what a rotten childhood she had.'

'Which one is Olivia?' asked Markus when Lisa ran some of this past him when she got home. Another thing Lisa liked about him was his fascination with all her friends. Unlike most men, he had a keen interest in gossip.

'You haven't met her. She hasn't been around. These days, I gather, she travels a lot with her work.'

'Which is?'

'A singer and entertainer. It's really odd; at school she was such a mouse. Small and scrawny with glasses and spots. The talent only really surfaced after she had left.' Poor Olivia, her timing had been dreadful. She had let down first Miranda and then the school.

'I haven't met Suzy either,' said Markus. 'Nor South African Helen.' But he'd heard a lot about all of them, bit by bit.

'Well, maybe while Suzy and Andrew are still here.' It all depended on their travel schedule and whether they'd feel comfortable leaving the baby. She curled up next to him on the couch and they watched the news together. She liked to find him here when she got home.

'Tell me more about Olivia,' he said.

'What do you want to know?'

'Everything really. You rarely mention her. And yet she used to be part of your tight little set.'

'Only ever marginally. She was little more than a hanger-on. When Miranda died, she left the school so never even properly took her place.'

Markus laughed and kissed her neck. It was all so English, the stories about her schooldays. Lisa was wonderfully intense about her friendships; he truly admired her for that.

'Time to turn in,' she said, looking at the clock. 'I'm in court tomorrow so need my beauty sleep.'

* * *

The case, concerning a battered wife, dragged on for several days. Lisa, who was fully on the poor woman's side, finally got her off. She had killed her partner in self-defence and had served several years of her sentence before an appeal had brought her back into court. By the time the judge had reversed the verdict, the press were crowded outside. Lisa, still in her wig and gown, stood on the steps of the law-courts to make a brief statement. She was dying to change her clothes and go home; the energy drain had taken its toll and she couldn't wait to get out of this itchy wig.

Someone tapped her gently on the shoulder and when she turned, expecting another camera, she came face to face with a smartly clad woman. Olivia.

'I read about the case,' she said, 'and wanted to see you in action. I have been up there in the gallery all week.'

'Good heavens,' said Lisa, 'how extraordinarily odd. I was talking about you just the other day.'

31

'I couldn't believe it,' said Lisa on the phone. 'I turned my head and there she was, standing there grinning like a Cheshire Cat, as large as life and, I must say, looking terrific.'

'Straight after we had been talking about her, too.'

'Exactly. As though it were meant.' Her initial reaction had been surprise, followed by genuine delight. Of the five of them, Olivia had always been the most elusive. The two hadn't met since Suzy's wedding, a good four years before.

'How did she seem?'

'Relaxed and happy. Life appears to be treating her well. She has been in London on and off but never had time to call.' Or so she said. About that Lisa still remained dubious though she had, of course, recently moved home. 'Anyhow,' she continued, 'the point of this call is to invite you and Neville to supper at my place on Thursday. I hope you can make it. Olivia will be there. I am hoping to get the Lockharts too before they disappear again.'

'And Markus?'

'Markus, indeed,' said Lisa. 'The poor boy gets lumbered with the cooking.'

Lisa remained slightly mystified as to why Olivia had suddenly reappeared. If she'd been in London on and off, as she'd said, she could surely have called before now. But maybe that was too cynical; being a barrister had sharpened her nose for deception. She determined to give her the benefit of the doubt. And was dying to have a proper catch up on the recent missing years.

'Will I like her?' asked Markus.

'Judge for yourself. One thing I do know, you'll certainly like Suzy and Andrew.'

Suzy and Andrew were the first to arrive, soon after Lisa got home herself, Suzy, exuberant with happiness, clutching the baby.

'You brought her!' Lisa was a little surprised; Holly was still so young.

'Had to. I'm breast-feeding,' said Suzy proudly while Andrew, carrying the Moses basket, simply smiled.

'Stick that in the bedroom,' Lisa told him. 'And then she can have a nap when she gets tired.' Holly, however, was wide awake, with great dark sparkling eyes and a happy smile. 'She's the image of her mother,' said Lisa, holding her tiny hand.

'Only with Andrew's eyes,' said Suzy. And Kit's smile.

Suzy looked radiant and fully recovered, glowing with health and wearing a maternity smock. Andrew stood shyly behind her as both girls cooed. Markus emerged from the galley kitchen and Lisa introduced him. And just at that moment the doorbell rang and in walked Deborah and Neville.

'Is she here?' muttered Deborah, embracing Lisa and furtively glancing around.

'Not yet. Relax.' She was curious to find that Deborah's old antipathy still existed.

Deborah crowed and cuddled the baby having snatched her from Suzy's arms. The others sat down and Markus offered them drinks.

'Well, here we all are,' said Lisa in triumph, having got them all together after so long. Later she'd put in a call to Helen; Cape Town was only one hour ahead of London time. 'Welcome to our ark.'

'Here's to us all,' said Neville, raising his glass, and the others all clinked with each other. Markus disappeared back into the kitchen and Deborah and Suzy widened their eyes in approval. Trust Lisa to have got the lot; the career, the fame, the enchanting houseboat and now this delectable young man. Well, good luck to her; she had worked hard enough. The doorbell rang. Olivia had arrived.

'Well,' she said, smiling around at them all. 'What a surprise and what a great place to be. I have always wanted to live near water; you must tell me later how you did it.' Then she crossed to Suzy, pecked her cheek and asked if she could hold the baby. The rest of them sat and watched her as she cooed.

Olivia was dressed with the neat simplicity that seemed to be her style. A narrow skirt and a cashmere sweater, both in a flattering shade of dove grey with the understated chic of a top designer. Her hair was streaked and expertly cut to fit, cap-like, around her small, oval face. And when she smiled, her teeth were even and perfect. She looked far less than her age.

Markus appeared again, like a genie, and poured her a glass of white wine. 'I'll be with you soon,' he promised, and vanished again.

Everyone sat around and relaxed and Olivia handed the baby back and went to sit on the couch between Andrew and Neville. Lisa saw Deborah watching her, as alert and tense as a cat. She clearly knew Neville but they said very little; instead she turned her full attention on Andrew.

'Tell us what you've been up to,' said Lisa, extending the conversation to include them all. 'None of us has seen you in quite a while.' They knew about the marriage, of course, which wasn't something, it seemed, she cared to discuss. She wasn't wearing a ring or using his name so Lisa decided diplomacy was best and left it for her to bring the subject up. They only knew from Helen, after all; perhaps it was still supposed to be a secret.

'Helen told us you'd been in Cape Town. Straight after our wedding, I believe.' Suzy was genuinely pleased to see her. Any reservations she might once have had had gone since she'd met Andrew. She valued her girlfriends even more now they lived so far away, was grateful to Lisa for bringing them all together.

'Yes,' said Olivia, 'I've been travelling a lot. I feel guilty at being such a lousy correspondent. I never seem to have time.'

You have time to flirt with other people's husbands; Deborah was watching her like a hawk. Neville was giving the distinct impression of a man whose collar was a shade too tight. After a while he rose abruptly and went to join Markus in the kitchen.

'But what exactly are you doing?' Lisa persisted.

'This and that in the theatre,' said Olivia, vaguely waving her hand. 'Voice-overs, radio, you name it, I've been there. Now and then I do a cabaret act.' She still seemed oddly unsure of herself when faced with a battery of questions. No-one would guess what she did for a living; she still seemed far too reserved. She wasn't pretty though certainly made the best of what she'd got. Her nails were immaculately manicured; everything about her was clean and neat.

Markus stuck his head round the door and announced that dinner was served and they all trooped through to the dining alcove to be seated.

* * *

To Suzy, who'd been away so long, the reunion was perfect. Her closest friends and the man she loved all grouped around the same table together, getting on. Soon they would put in a call to Helen and then it would be complete. 'I think we should drink to Miranda,' she said, so they did.

Olivia seemed much nicer these days, softer somehow and sweeter. She had always been slightly on her guard but now appeared much more relaxed. She sparkled as she chatted to Andrew and Suzy could see that he liked her. She was glad; he was such a diffident man that she loved to see him getting on well with her friends.

'When are you going back?' Deborah asked her. 'I hope you're planning to stick around for a while.'

Suzy looked across at Andrew, sending him some silent signal, so he broke off talking to Olivia and announced their latest news.

'We are leaving China for good,' he said. 'And moving to New Orleans.'

'Wow!' said Markus. 'That's a really neat place. I've been meaning to go back there myself for years. Only something got in my way.' The look he gave Lisa was full of such love that Deborah felt a sudden twinge of jealousy. It was years since Neville had looked at her that way. When once she had liked to hold centre stage, these days he made her feel that she didn't exist. Even now he was silent and withdrawn, no doubt thinking about the money markets. Whereas Andrew was clearly besotted with Suzy and Markus had the look of a man who couldn't wait to get Lisa out of her clothes.

'You will all have to come and visit us,' said Suzy. 'We plan to keep open house. No-one but Mum came to see us in China but there's far less excuse with the States.'

'How is your mother?' asked Olivia on cue so Suzy moved over to sit beside her and fill her in on them both.

'She would love to see you. Why not give her a ring? I know she was disappointed when you lost touch.'

'I'm sorry,' said Olivia. 'I've been very remiss. Tell her I promise to call her very soon.'

'What did you think?' asked Lisa later, when the guests had gone and they were tucked up in bed. Because of the baby, the Lockharts had left first, followed soon after by the Hirsches. They had offered Olivia a lift which she had declined.

'I am only going to Covent Garden,' she said, 'and can easily take a cab.' She was clearly in no hurry to leave herself. 'Tell me,' she said, curling up next to Markus after he'd poured them another drink. 'How do you make it as a jazz musician? I would guess it is pretty hard.'

'Not if you have the right contacts,' said Markus, 'and are in the right place at the right time.' He told her about his forthcoming recital, at St Paul's Cathedral the following week, and Lisa, as she cleared the dishes, heard Olivia telling him how much she would like to come. She grimaced to herself a little; why didn't that surprise her? But was pleased to hear Markus offering Olivia a ticket because it showed how much he must like her friends.

'I liked them all,' said Markus, 'more or less.' He had never taken to Deborah's husband, had seen at a glance how untrustworthy he was and how he neglected his rather wonderful wife. But he wouldn't say as much to Lisa because he knew how she doted on them all.

'What do you mean by more or less?' Lisa was nobody's fool. She had sensed a distinct reserve between the two men.

'Just as I say, I liked them all. Especially Andrew and Suzy. At a glance, I would guess they have a really solid marriage. I hope I'll get the chance to see more of them.'

'And Olivia? What did you think of her?' She had seen the way she had hugged him when she left.

'An interesting mix. On the surface a flirt, but that is mainly a cover. Beneath it I'm not even sure if she likes men at all.'

St Paul's Cathedral was fully booked, the audience seated in the nave. Unfortunately Lisa was working late so Olivia went there on her own. Her seat was right underneath the dome; the acoustics would be perfect. She was proud of being a VIP, had a sneaking look around her to check if anyone she recognised was there. The singing started from way off, a muted mediaeval chanting that echoed around the vast edifice so at first it wasn't clear from where it was coming. Olivia, like everyone else, craned round but was right in the fulcrum of the sound. Then the voices were joined by the distant lament of a soaring tenor saxophone and slowly, up the centre aisle, processed five singers in surplices, followed by a solitary musician.

The whole effect was electrifying; Olivia, with her perfect ear, was pulverised by the sound. Not the jazz she had been expecting but something far more spiritual, like Pan pipes in a temple. Her whole scalp prickled as the music soared and she sensed she was not alone in her elation. She turned to look and there was Markus, tall and graceful in a stark black suit, matched by a plain black shirt. The contrast with the choir's surplices was dramatic. For two hours the audience was mesmerised, until the concert reached its climax and the singers, followed by Markus, filtered out. You could cut the emotion but nobody spoke; nor, because it was a cathedral, did they clap.

Not quite certain what to do next, Olivia hung around. The rest of the audience were quickly gone till she stood alone beneath the dome and watched the verger slowly extinguishing lights. Since Markus hadn't been in costume, he wouldn't have to change.

He hadn't asked her to meet him after, so maybe he'd slipped away. Then suddenly there he was on the steps, shaking hands with the choristers, and when she went to join him, he turned and smiled.

'Well,' he asked her, 'what did you think? Didn't you find it effective in that great space?'

'I found it stunning. It blew my mind. Now I can understand how you live off your music.'

'Off my music and for my music. The only thing I care for, other than Lisa.'

It was almost like a reprimand which Olivia chose to ignore. He was not Lisa's husband, therefore up for grabs, and she'd always enjoyed a good fight. Neville had been easy, likewise Guy Palmer, though she tried not to think about Klaus. Nor, indeed, the other one who had cruelly laughed in her face.

'Come on,' she said, slipping her hand through his arm, 'I am taking you out to dinner to celebrate.'

They ate at the Ivy, which she'd booked in advance, presuming she'd get her way. She was paying, would not hear no; besides, she was considerably older than him. He hadn't needed to check with Lisa; when she was up to her ears in a case she preferred it if he stayed out. Besides, he was curious to know more about Olivia.

He got her to talk about herself and her burgeoning singing career. She was, she admitted, a natural mimic who could imitate almost any voice that came within her range. 'I'm not original, not like you. What you hear when I do my thing is little more than karaoke.'

Markus laughed. He liked her style. She was sharp as a blade and witty with it. So why, he asked, was she on her own? Or did she have a fella tucked away somewhere?

'I've always been alone,' she said. 'Right since the time I was born. My father rejected me, though I don't know why, and nobody else has ever really cared.'

She wasn't sympathy-seeking, he could see, just telling it as it was. Her eyes were clear and looked straight into his. She could not have been more honest if she tried. But still he didn't like her.

32

Jackson dropped him at the hotel. He was staying off Decatur. The room they had given him had no windows. A sumptuous suite with amazing décor, a spacious bed with brocade hangings, a television and a whirlpool bath, a mini-bar but, on investigation, no windows. And Markus, who lived on a boat, couldn't stomach that.

'My room has no windows,' he told them at reception. Impassively, they checked the computer and told him he had no other choice. The city was packed to the gunnels with tourists; they simply did not have another room.

'Most people, sir,' the porter confided, 'use that room only to sleep. They come to this city to hear the jazz, are up all night listening to the music, and when they finally come back here, they sleep.'

Markus, by that stage too tired to argue, found it was just as he said. After all that playing he was drop dead exhausted and all he wanted to do was fall into bed. But his brain was buzzing with what Horace had said; the first thing he would do in the morning was call Lisa.

'I think you ought to come,' he said. 'As soon as you possibly can.'

'Wait,' she said, 'what's going on? What does Nathan have to say?'

'Nathan doesn't know,' he said. 'And, besides, I am not entirely sure he is on our side. Two small children; no, there's no way he could be.' And the baying of the wolves was growing louder.

'Are you winding me up?' asked Lisa sternly.

'No,' said Markus. 'Just come.'

'All of us?'

'Why not?' he said. Hell, they might as well do it in style. The case, as it stood, was a joke charade with no evidence worth presenting. Any minute now, the tumbrels would roll. And the more ammunition they could provide . . . well, Lisa had said it herself. Rally the troops, including Miss Holbrook. Let anthropologist Helen off the leash. Get the rabbi to preach a sermon. Stop holding fire because of some lawyer who didn't even believe she hadn't done it.

'Wait,' he said. 'Just one more thing. Did you manage to contact Olivia?'

* * *

No, she had said; why did you ask? But Markus was working on overtime. Something had clicked, though he wasn't sure what, and, one by one, the pieces were falling into place.

33

Helen had been a little concerned when she heard from Deborah that Suzy was pregnant again. They had only just settled in New Orleans and Holly was still barely crawling. Two within a year; it would be tough for even the youngest mother but Suzy was almost forty.

'I hope she knows what she's doing,' she said. 'Though I guess by now it's too late.'

Deborah, startled, asked what she meant. Surely a second pregnancy could only be a matter for rejoicing.

'But you had yours at a much earlier age and also at healthy intervals. With time to adjust to each new birth without producing them like a conveyor belt.'

'All of a sudden you're the expert?' said Deborah, recalling Helen's consistently feminist views. For years she had sworn she would never have children, and now here she was lecturing Deborah on the subject of childbirth.

'I may not ever have been pregnant,' argued Helen,

'but the boys have taught me a lot. And you must also take into account my qualifications.'

After she'd finished her Ph.D., she had specialised in her chosen field and written a couple of highly-regarded books. Piet was now heavily into politics, researching the causes of the AIDS pandemic in an attempt to persuade President Mbeki to alter his stance. It was comfortable still to be working nearby, no longer on the same corridor but part of the same campus. They rarely drove to work together because their timetables were so erratic but she liked to know he was there, not far away.

Now she confided her fears about Suzy; Piet, after all, was a bona fide parent whose sons had been born close together, then rapidly bereaved. He understood the inherent perils of starting a family later in life.

'But you turned out all right,' he said, the humour apparent in his eyes.

'Yes, but largely from luck,' she said. 'The biological odds were against it, the age gap far too large.' Her mother might as well have been a single parent for all the involvement her father showed. And the solitary life she had led as a child had helped form her strongly held beliefs. None of which had altered when she got married.

'But what's this to do with Suzy?' asked Piet.

'I'm not entirely sure. I'm just concerned.'

* * *

Gwen was slightly worried, too, that Suzy might find it hard to cope. She had been aware, on that fleeting visit, that she was already very weighed down, though reluctant to let the nanny take over too much. That part Gwen understood; it was only natural, and she was pretty sure that she would have felt much the same. But Kit and Suzy had five years between them and Gwen had looked after them both full-time. Suzy's situation was entirely different; her career had suddenly taken off and there were pressures on her to do a lot more work.

'Can't you take a sabbatical?' Gwen wrote.

'No way,' replied Suzy, 'that's not how the art world works.'

Gwen would have liked to be out there herself, lending a grandmotherly hand, but things at home were at a delicate stage. Guy had finally made his decision and was winding up the business. He needed the emotional support that only a wife could supply.

'I don't want to leave him,' she said to Maggie. 'I feel he needs nurturing at this stage.' Whatever had been going on had apparently passed but she felt the marriage was still shaky. Slowly they'd embarked on rebuilding bridges; she hesitated to provoke another crisis.

'Suzy can handle it,' said Maggie firmly. 'Remember, she's grown up now.'

And with an admirably solid marriage. Andrew was a saint; that had never been in doubt.

* * *

With her girlfriends Suzy was a lot more direct. 'I no longer have any energy,' she emailed Deborah. 'And am losing weight faster than I should. My appetite has disappeared completely.'

'Lucky you,' was Deborah's response. 'Pregnancy had the reverse effect on me. But it's only natural to experience some changes. Your hormones are all shook up.' Helen had not been wrong; two as close as that must be pure hell.

'I can't stop crying,' Suzy said to Lisa, who was more hard-headed about such things. 'And I often feel scared of dropping the baby or doing him some other harm.' The nanny was black, with the sweetest smile and a bunch of grown children of her own. She doted on Jonah but Suzy was suspicious and hated it when she took him out in his pram.

'Calm down,' said Lisa, 'she won't abduct him. I presume you checked her out before you hired her.'

'Andrew did. And met her last employer. But what does a father know about such things?'

She also told Lisa she had lost her libido and didn't want Andrew to touch her. He took it well but it made her feel bad; she no longer even wanted him in her bed.

'I am certain that will sort itself out as soon as you stop breast-feeding. Don't be so hard on yourself,' urged Lisa. 'So much has changed in the past twelve months, it's no wonder you feel overwhelmed.'

'Work is the greatest panacea,' wrote Maggie.

'Whatever you do, make sure your work doesn't suffer.' Privately, in her own opinion, art should come before children every time.

'Women are voting with their ovaries,' said Helen, 'by refusing to have so many babies.' At the university she was viewed with mistrust; many of her male colleagues resented her presence. The widely-held opinion, which they never failed to share, was that she should spend more time at home with the kids.

'Think of your husband,' one even dared to say. 'Wouldn't he prefer a larger family?'

Helen disliked the implication that her field research didn't count. At least at Harvard she had put across her point until they'd started to treat her with more respect.

'They consider women to be second-class here,' she regularly grumbled to Piet. 'One reason this country lags behind most of the world.' Five million South Africans were living with AIDS because the government chose to ignore its existence. The townships, in particular, were nurturing a rapidly-growing plague. Piet's commitment to his homeland was sorely needed.

'I have every confidence you'll convince them in the end.' He had absolute faith in Helen's campaign and no complaints about things at home, was grateful and impressed by how she coped.

It had taken her a year or two but Helen now doted on the boys. They'd been five and six when she'd taken them on but now were so much a part of her, she looked upon them as her own. Scott, the older, was studious like his dad while Gary was the athletic type, with a sunnier, more outgoing nature. To start with, Helen had found it hard to empathise with their needs. Her own mother was of the school of thought that held that babies should be left to cry instead of being picked up. As a result, their relationship had never been tactile; to this day, her mother found it hard to kiss her on the cheek. And that, when she'd first got together with Piet, was something he'd had to overcome.

But once she was used to the little boys, maternal instincts came bubbling up. It was easier to let her emotions show when dealing with children who were missing their mother, with the result that their father shared in the benefits too. It had been a period of growth for them all which they'd come through with flying colours. Although Helen worked hard, she had learned to give way and allow the family sometimes to take centre stage.

'Which is really what Suzy should be doing now, putting the babies first. If I can cut down on my workload, so should she.'

But Suzy's depression was rapidly worsening, though she tried not to let it show. If she was fractious with the nanny, she compensated with extra wages and afternoons off that she couldn't really afford to give.

Holly, no longer the centre of attention, instantly played up, which only aggravated Jonah so that he cried too until Suzy was tempted to knock their heads together.

'I never realised how bad it could be,' she plaintively wrote to Deborah. 'How you coped with three, I cannot imagine.'

'Don't panic,' Deborah replied. 'It doesn't last long.' She dared not tell her about the Terrible Twos. She wished there was something constructive she could do but was far too busy to take time off and go out there.

'I'm the one who should really go,' said Gwen. 'But at the moment I feel my husband comes first.' Lately he'd been subdued again; he didn't want to stop working. The least she could do was be there when he came home.

Andrew was putting in long hours at his new job, loving it but finding it fairly stressful. The heat was oppressive at this time of year and there'd been a backlog of stuff to sort out, left by the previous director. He was grateful when he finally got home to find it a haven of peace, with both babies fed and tucked up in their cots and a meal all ready, waiting to be served. He did notice Suzy was pale and thinner but put it down simply to motherhood and natural biological changes. Because she never spoke a word of complaint, he had no idea what she was going through.

Helen liked to describe herself as an expert on infanticide. At cocktail parties or faculty functions, at which she was usually bored to tears, she used it as an answer designed to shock. Some of the wives resented her as virulently as their husbands did and, far from being sisters under the skin, could turn quite hostile on meeting her when she preferred to talk about work instead of her husband's children. Seeing her engrossed in earnest debate, Piet would look across at her and wink. And Helen would flash him a radiant smile to show she was hugely enjoying herself. She loved it when their hackles started to rise.

Cape Town women, on the whole, had hobbies rather than jobs. She didn't consider selling real estate or choosing fabrics for richer women more than something to fill in time and earn them a little pin money. Mainly they shopped and lunched and kvetched, about property values and lazy maids and the latest trendy health club to open in town. People like Helen they found unnerving, with her doctorate and her published books and habit of talking above their heads about science.

'They really hate you.' Piet was amused. Nothing she did could stem his admiration.

'I know,' she said, quite gleeful with joy. 'They find it shocking I even know about such things.'

'They'll never admit you to their club.'

'Don't care. I've got my reading group which is more than enough for me.'

Annie and Jackie and Shirley and Pat remained her real friends and the more she saw them, the more she relied upon them. These were women she could really relate to, who found her scientific theories fascinating. Two had children, two did not, yet all were united by their gender and being financially independent. Not for them the spoilt complaints of the boring faculty wives. Helen's group were all self-supporting, even Shirley with her brand new husband, as, indeed, was Helen herself, to her pride.

She told them a little about Charles Darwin, whose work was deeply relevant to her research. A lot of his theories were influenced by his own relationship with his mother who died when he was eight. After her death, her name was not mentioned within the family again and, in later years, he could not recall her except for her black velvet funeral gown. Shortly after her death, he was sent away to school.

'You see,' said Helen, 'his entire philosophy was derived from the loss of his mother at an impression-able age. He was the father of evolutionary theory yet fundamentally a very damaged child.'

She told them about attachment theory and how human babies, deprived of such love, can suffer irreparable damage. She thought immediately about poor Suzy and how her threatened withdrawal from her children could, though highly unlikely, have a similar effect. What was starting to look like post-natal depression could, unless effectively stopped, possibly advance into psychosis.

* * *

'You can't be serious.' Deborah was appalled. Helen had got to thinking about it and decided, as a precaution, to bounce her theory off her friends. Not that there was anything much they could do.

'Whatever you do, don't tell Gwen,' she said. 'We can't have her getting worried. She has been through enough in her life already, without unnecessary alarms.'

'Should you talk to Andrew perhaps?'

Helen was doubtful. 'I hardly know him. He might think I was merely meddling and resent it.'

'So what can we do?'

'Just be aware. And keep in touch with her as much as you can. If my theory is right, it should pass in time. Before we know it, she'll be right as rain.'

But it was a worry to someone like Helen who steeped herself in behavioural problems and their anthropological roots. Poor Suzy; her happiness had been so complete, she didn't need a glitch like this to spoil it.

Which was why, when Helen first heard the news, she was shocked but in some ways prepared.

34

Markus was watering the geraniums on the deck when somebody whistled from above him. He looked up, startled, to see who it was. Few people knew of their recent move; they had hoped to keep it quiet. Due to the nature of Lisa's profession, with all its inherent dangers, both were keen that the public at large shouldn't know where to find her. Besides which, they valued their privacy. The relationship was still at the honeymoon stage.

A small, slim woman in T-shirt and jeans was waving vigorously from the bridge.

'Yoo hoo, Markus!' she called. 'How are you? Is it okay if I come down?'

His spirits dropped. Olivia. He'd had a hunch that he'd not seen the last of her.

'Sure,' he said, emptying the watering-can and hanging it back on the hook. 'But before you do, I should warn you Lisa's not here.'

'It's you I want, in any case,' she said as she tripped

across the gangplank. She was wearing sandals with spiky heels, hardly the footwear for a boat. Markus checked the time – it was just past eleven – and wondered what he could do to get rid of her fast. He had no fixed plans at all for today except he usually spent the afternoons practising. Still, since Olivia was Lisa's friend, he would have to be polite and go through the motions without appearing to snub her.

'Will you join me for a coffee?' he asked, leading the way inside.

Once she was settled and he'd made them both coffee, Olivia positively radiated charm. She had the ability, which slightly unnerved him, of totally transforming herself. He wasn't at all sure that, had he met her in the street, he'd have recognised her today. Her casual gear was in total contrast to how she had looked the other night but, in its way, equally arresting. Her hair was glossy and superbly cut with perhaps a subtle change in its basic colour. Markus, unused to observing such details, was nevertheless alert to her altered mood. Chameleon-like, that was what she was. The shy little thing he had dined with at the Ivy, today had turned into a dangerous vamp.

'Dear Markus,' she said. 'I've been thinking about you a lot. I can't get that music out of my head.' Her eyes were translucent and as clear as glass, seeming to have no colour. Something about them reminded him of a wolf; he wondered how she described them on her passport. She wriggled enticingly on the couch and kicked off her killer heels. Small but perfectly formed, she was. He was slightly surprised that he hadn't noticed before.

'One of my ambitions,' she confessed, 'is to be a torch singer. Dark and sultry and ever so slightly bad.' She giggled. 'Can't you just see me at the Café de Paris, giving it all I've got?'

Markus smiled politely. Since he had never heard her sing, he couldn't really comment. She looked good in jeans, but not that good, and her face was scarcely unforgettable. Also, in his opinion, she was too small.

Seeing the undisguised doubt on his face, Olivia leapt to her feet and started parading. She slipped back into the extravagant sandals and strutted and pranced with arms upraised as she swung into Billie Holiday mode and astounded him.

'*Oo-oo-oo, what a little moonlight can do-oo-oo,*' she crooned, instantly becoming the ill-fated singer. Markus sat there gobsmacked with amazement; before his eyes she had actually changed her persona. Aware of his unguarded admiration, Olivia swung into Ella Fitzgerald, appearing to grow in size and bulk as she sang.

'*A-tisket, a-tasket . . .*' She shimmied and wiggled her sizeable rump and Markus's admiration knew no bounds. The girl was terrific, there was no denying that. How could such a colourless person possess such a towering talent?

Olivia saw that she had him intrigued. 'We'd make a great combination, you and I.'

Just like that, as cool as you please. For a moment Markus was lost for words then, assuming she only meant musically, acknowledged that might well be so. The cathedral gig had deliberately showcased his more classical side but where his passions really lay was in jazz. Still saying nothing, he left the room and returned with his saxophone. He lifted the instrument reverently from its case, blew a few tentative trial notes, then broke into 'Blue Moon'. And Olivia, accepting the challenge like a trouper, segued in with the lyrics.

They jammed for forty minutes or so and when Markus stepped outside for some air, the bridge was crowded with passers-by, listening with rapt attention. On seeing him, they started to clap and Markus laughed and saluted them. He turned and beckoned Olivia out and she dipped into a graceful curtsey, holding out an invisible skirt with her hand.

'Olivia dropped by earlier,' he said carefully, once Lisa had had her shower and he'd poured her a drink.

'Yes?' she said, expressing no surprise. 'How was she?'

'She was good,' he said thoughtfully, gazing into space, uncertain what to make of the odd encounter.

Lisa, skimming the headlines of the paper, was only partially listening.

'Very good, in fact,' he said. 'Have you ever heard her sing?'

'She sang?' He now had her full attention. She put

339

aside the paper and stared in surprise. 'Only years ago at school. Shortly before she vanished.'

'She wanted us to make music together. I have to tell you, she was bloody good.' Better than that; she was fabulous. He still couldn't get her vibrancy out of his head.

Little Olivia, who was always so shy and wouldn't say boo to a goose, coming here of her own accord, apparently to show off. Lisa laughed. 'I can't turn my back for a second,' she said, 'without some predatory woman coming on to you.' But, unlike Deborah, she wasn't jealous. Flattered, in fact, when she thought it through, but also hugely surprised.

'I guess she must be lonely,' said Markus. 'Because when we finished jamming, she just went off.'

'Is she coming back?'

'I would think so. I doubt we've seen the last of that little lady.'

'Bloody nerve,' said Deborah predictably. 'Can't she keep her hands off anyone's man?'

'I don't think she's after Markus,' said Lisa. 'If she is, it is only that sad little waif, out to grab anything good that somebody else has.'

'The cuckoo syndrome.' Deborah remembered.

'Precisely.' It fitted with what Helen had said. Starting with Gwen when she first came on the scene; her neediness then had driven the Palmer children wild.

Helen had talked about deprivation and the lasting

effects it could have on a child. Listening to her, Deborah had worried in case she was harming her own kids in any way. Helen had reassured her.

'You can't go far wrong with two loving parents and a stable home,' she said. Which was what she fervently hoped she was giving the boys.

'Can't she find a man of her own? She's far more presentable now.' Rabbi or not, Deborah couldn't resist those sharp little digs of her schooldays.

'Miaow,' said Lisa. 'You still don't like her. I have never really been able to understand why.'

Deborah shrugged. 'I no longer remember. For some weird reason she always got up my nose.'

'She's harmless really, I promise you. Desperately longed to be one of us but somehow never quite fitted in.' Even the accent had been assumed. At times of great stress, like Miranda's death, the patina had audibly slipped. And yet she had perfect pitch, it appeared. What an odd little paradox she was.

He had forecast it so wasn't surprised when Olivia turned up again. This time she phoned first to speak to Lisa, doubtless checking that the coast was clear, and half an hour later there she was on the gangplank.

'I've brought some music,' she said with a smile. 'Plus a bottle to keep our energy up. It's thirsty work, this session stuff. Can't have you drying up.'

She was still in jeans but with a tighter top and wearing considerably more makeup. From her bag she produced an armful of sheet music plus a bottle of expensive Italian plonk. She kicked off her shoes, clearly feeling at home, and settled herself on the couch without being asked.

Markus thought hard and made a fast decision. He was not a prude, but this had to be nipped in the bud. The best thing ever to have happened to him was Lisa. He couldn't have this stranger doing a spoiler.

'I'm sorry,' he said, 'if you've had a wasted journey but today I have to do some serious practice.' He was back at Ronnie Scott's the following week and wanted to ensure a peak performance. He offered Olivia coffee but she declined.

'You don't mind if I hang around,' she asked casually, 'and listen?'

There she had him. Since she'd come all this way he could hardly say he preferred to be alone. From a professional performer that wouldn't ring true and it was arrogant to assume that she wanted more.

'Up to you,' he said, taking out his saxophone, 'but you might get very bored with the repetition.'

'I know I could never be bored by your playing and maybe could also pick up a few tricks.' She meant it about the cabaret career and when she set her mind on something, she almost always got it.

Markus couldn't argue with that so he settled down to his practice while Olivia simply lay on the couch and listened. After a couple of hours, he opened the bottle and they sat outside on the deck together and drank it. She'd been good as gold, hadn't interrupted, nor had she tried any vampish tricks. His first impression had probably been right. She travelled so much and lived on her own; all she was really lacking was company.

'So she's been here again. You didn't tell me.'

Markus positively jumped with guilt though nothing remotely had gone on. He looked up warily, wondering how she knew, and there stood Lisa in the bathroom doorway, triumphantly holding a lipstick like a trophy.

'Gotcha,' she said, grinning broadly. 'The least you could learn to do is cover your tracks.'

'She turned up unannounced,' he said, 'after ringing first to check that you weren't here.'

'And you were too kind to turn her away. Quite right. She is fairly pathetic.' It was the oldest trick in the world to leave traces, like an animal marking its territory. Only a man as decent as Markus could have failed to suspect an ulterior motive. But enough was enough; even Lisa's patience had limits. And if Olivia was going to abuse her friendship, it was time she was given her marching orders fast.

'Did she leave a number?' she asked. It was symptomatic of Olivia's lifestyle that no-one ever seemed to know where she lived.

Markus, feeling incredibly foolish, shook his head. He'd enjoyed her company and admiration, had been stimulated by her hearty applause. From a music angle, she knew her stuff and her suggestion that they try working together was not entirely far-fetched. Not unless it would upset Lisa; that was the very last thing in the world he would do.

By lucky chance, next time she phoned Lisa was working at home. 'Olivia,' she said, as friendly as ever. 'I'm glad you called. You left your lipstick here.'

'No problem,' she said, sounding equally unfazed. 'I'll pick it up next time I drop by. May I please speak to Markus?'

For a moment Lisa was lost for words but quickly regained control. 'I'm afraid he's having a nap,' she said. 'And I don't want to wake him because he's playing tonight.'

'Oh, where?' asked Olivia, sounding eager. 'Perhaps I'll go along and catch the show.'

'It's a sell-out,' said Lisa, gritting her teeth, the friend-liness draining from her voice. 'If you leave your number I'll tell him you called. We must all get together again some time. I know that Markus would like that.'

Just for a moment Olivia paused. Then: 'I'm moving around quite a bit,' she said. 'I'll check in again next time I'm passing through. Do give Markus my love.'

'I hate to admit it but I fear you might be right,' said Lisa over lunch. 'I think she may have more on her mind than simply catching up with old school chums.'

Deborah, glad not to seem a bitch, nodded her

head in agreement. 'Not that you've anything to worry about. Markus quite obviously adores you.'

'I'm not worried,' said Lisa truthfully. 'But I do find her behaviour odd and, frankly, not very friendly. I don't know what she hopes to achieve by blatantly butting in on our lives as though she had some sort of entitlement.' That's how she'd always been at school and they'd put it down to insecurity, having no immediate family of her own. But husbands and boyfriends were another matter; she was overstepping the boundaries of friendship. 'You never did tell me what happened with Neville.'

'Not a lot,' said Deborah cagily. 'Nothing I couldn't fix.' The truth was she still didn't know for sure, just that Neville had acted evasive while Olivia seemed like the cat who had got the cream. Deborah had put a stop to that by not inviting her to their wedding. What, if anything, had happened after that, she had no way of knowing for sure. But in her heart she would never forgive Olivia.

'Do you know if she ever called Gwen?' asked Lisa.

'She certainly hasn't said so.' True to her word, since Suzy left, Deborah had stayed in touch with her mother. 'That's another peculiar thing. The way she used to cling to Gwen was positively manic. Yet she dropped her the instant she went away and hasn't been in touch with her since. Gwen never says a word about it yet I know how hurt she must be. Even at Suzy's wedding they barely spoke.'

'An opportunist is what she is. After whatever she can get.' Lisa was used to assessing people and Olivia was a classic case. Though it wasn't a mother she was after these days but somebody else's man.

A few weeks later she called again, but only to say goodbye. She was off to the States, she told Markus, for a gig and would be in touch when she returned, to talk about working together.

'She doesn't give up,' said Lisa, relieved. Then put her out of her mind.

35

'Good heavens!' said Suzy when she opened the door. 'What in the world are you doing here? What a delightful surprise.'

'You said you were planning to keep open house so I took you at your word.' Olivia hefted her suitcase into the hall and dropped her heavy shoulderbag with a sigh. 'The rest of my stuff is still at the airport. I thought I'd better check first that you were around.'

'How on earth did you find us?' asked Suzy, following her through the spacious hall into the kitchen at the rear. Olivia acted as though she knew the place and seemed to take her welcome entirely for granted. But, then, she'd always possessed a degree of gall, right from the Pinner days.

'I'd kill for a cuppa,' she said, looking around. Suzy lit the gas under the kettle and took down beakers from the shelf. 'I spoke to your mum,' said Olivia casually. 'Said I might be passing through and asked her how you were.' The fact she'd flown here from Santa Fe purely to stay with the Lockharts went unsaid.

It was odd Mum hadn't mentioned it but lately she'd been preoccupied with Dad's retirement plans. And Suzy's welcome was genuine; since they'd relocated, she'd been virtually a recluse and wasn't even keeping up with her friends. The pressures of two small babies and trying to cope with a brand new life were taking their toll on her nerves. Placid by nature, right now she was fraught though she tried very hard to disguise the fact and to act as though everything was normal. Andrew, bless him, was such a brick she'd do anything in her power not to alarm him.

'How is it going?' Olivia was shamelessly snooping, opening and shutting doors and peering around. The Lockharts had certainly done themselves proud with a house this size in a really classy enclave. The Garden District, she had read in the guidebook, was one of the best neighbourhoods in town. Smiling brightly, she turned to Suzy and gave her an unexpected hug.

'It's great to be here and I can't wait to see the kids. I hope it's okay if I stick around. At least you've got plenty of space.'

Bonnie had taken the children out and Suzy had been working in her studio. She was wearing a paint-smudged overall which she now quickly removed. It was true she didn't get out enough and Olivia's arrival was a welcome relief. More than anything, she realised now, she needed someone in whom she could really confide. And who better than a friend from the old days who had, at one time, practically been part of her family? She carried the tea-tray on to the porch and they settled down on the swing. At this hour in the afternoon the street was silent and abnormally still with not so much as a leaf stirring in the trees.

'Make the most of the peace,' warned Suzy. 'Before the kids get back.'

Olivia talked about Santa Fe and how she had come here on a whim. 'You made it sound so inviting,' she said. 'That night we were all at Lisa's.'

After almost a year, there was much to catch up on so they lingered over their tea. Olivia told Suzy about Markus's concert and that they were planning to perform together.

'I hadn't realised you knew him that well.' Suzy's recollection was that they'd all met him at the same time.

'Oh, me and Markus are just like that. We clicked the minute we met. And you really ought to hear him play. He's fantastic.'

Suzy agreed he was nice and very dishy. 'Lisa certainly seems happy,' she said. 'I do hope it all works out. I tell you, marriage is the best thing that's happened to me.' She looked slightly strained and had lost too much weight but her eyes lit up whenever she mentioned Andrew.

'Better even than motherhood?' The last time they'd met she had been ecstatic.

Suzy groaned and rolled her eyes. 'Two pregnancies in such a short time was madness but it's starting to improve. Finally we are getting a bit more sleep.' Suzy was understating it; most of the time they had lived here had been a nightmare.

On cue, from the street they heard little voices and through the gates came Bonnie, pushing the stroller. She was stout and black and immaculate, in a crisp blue and white uniform. The minute they came into sight they started waving and Suzy, with considerable effort, dragged herself from the swing to welcome them home.

'Hello, darlings,' she called from the porch and ran barefoot down the steps. 'How've they been?' she asked the nanny and Bonnie, with an expansive smile, told her, as good as gold.

'We've been feeding the ducks in the park,' she said. 'Jonah is getting to love them as much as she does.'

Holly had grown a lot in a year and was now a real little girl. The baby, Jonah, was her spitting image, though just at the gurgling and waving stage.

'You're a regular little cutie-pie,' cooed Olivia, picking him up.

'Not so,' warned Suzy. 'Wait till he wakes you in the night. I'll put you in the garage flat. That way, at least, you stand a chance of some sleep.' And there wasn't a hint of humour when she said it.

While Bonnie was feeding and bathing the babies,

Suzy showed Olivia to her room. The garage block, which had once been stables, was apart from the house, set back among trees like the lodge of a stately home. A wooden staircase ran up the outside to a self-contained flat above. What once had been the chauffeur's quarters was now an elegant guest-suite.

'You should find you have everything you need,' said Suzy. There was even a television and tea-maker there. She left Olivia to settle in and told her to come across to the house when she was ready.

'Andrew gets home around seven,' she said. 'And we eat when the babies are asleep.'

Nice one, thought Olivia, looking round; again she had fallen on her feet. Far enough from the house to be private yet close enough for her not to feel cut off. I think I could be very happy here, she decided with satisfaction. And felt no immediate need to be moving on.

Dinner was late because Andrew was tired so they sat out on the porch until it was dark. He made mint juleps which he insisted Olivia try. 'You haven't experienced the real south till you have had one.'

Even in April the air was humid and at night the heavy scent of flowers was almost overpowering. There was the steady hum of cicadas all around and the eerie cry of the occasional exotic night-bird. New Mexico had been too arid; this luscious terrain was more to Olivia's taste.

'You must make Suzy show you the cemetery. Lafayette is just up the road and totally fascinating.' Andrew had been here long enough to feel it was now his city. He got an obvious kick out of showing it off. 'Since New Orleans is built on a swamp, they have to bury them above the ground. And because of the tropical heat, they self-cremate. Within a year the bodies are gone, leaving room for a new incumbent. It effectively solves the housing problem for the dead.'

'What a novel idea,' said Olivia, sipping her second mint julep. 'And an ideal way, I would think, to conceal a crime.'

Andrew was an absolute dear; the more she saw, the more Olivia liked him. She found his presence quiet and restful; he could sit for hours playing with his children or wandering round the garden, showing her plants. He was loving the challenges of the job and offered Olivia a guided tour whenever it suited her.

'I think you'll be impressed,' he said, 'at what we've achieved so far.' He had soft brown eyes and a hesitant smile which broadened instantly the moment his wife appeared. Nice, thought Olivia, with the familiar pang. Why did things like that never happen to her?

With Olivia there, Suzy started to revive. She'd been tense and irritable far too long which had worried Andrew profoundly. Now, with someone around to talk to, some of the old joie de vivre came bubbling back. Leaving the children for Bonnie to mind, they would ride the streetcar down St Charles and stroll through the French Quarter. Olivia loved it.

'It's all so over the top,' she said, 'with streetlife on every corner.' Jackson Square crawled with jazz musicians performing in the open air. They sat and listened for hours on end, drinking coffee and occasional glasses of wine. The weather was balmy and it rarely rained, except in short heavy bursts.

'You should stay at least until Jazz Fest,' said Suzy. 'Apart from Mardi Gras, which you've missed, it's the social highlight of the year.'

Which was fine with Olivia, who felt thoroughly at home. The house, which was vast and Victorian, was reminiscent of Suzy's childhood, strewn with comfortable sofas and inglenooks. The babies were sweet, if a little noisy, but the nanny looked after them well. Occasionally, on Bonnie's afternoon off, Olivia volunteered to stand in. Once she had got the hang of it, they were easy enough to entertain and it gave her a sense of belonging, which she liked.

'You're sure you don't mind?' asked Suzy gratefully, itching to get back to work.

'I love it,' said Olivia, 'they are both so sweet. And it makes me feel that I'm not entirely redundant.'

'I can't see what all the fuss was about,' said Andrew, who'd been in the family long enough to have heard the Olivia stories. 'To me she seems perfectly sweet and rather wistful.' There was something about her that touched his heart, the way he saw her looking at his children. As though she lacked something integral from her life, someone to love of her own. And having her there had done wonders for Suzy. She was slowly becoming her old happy self and the tortured harpy was gone, he hoped for good.

'Oh, she's okay,' said Suzy, laughing. 'It's just that when she was young she was harder to take.' There was no trace left of the anxious child who had followed her mother around, hanging on to her words as though they were gospel. These days Olivia was very self-possessed, with the tact to make herself scarce in order not to crowd them. Today she had gone into town on her own, chasing up contacts, she said, in the hope of getting some singing engagements. It was an opportunity not to be missed, here in the centre of the jazz world.

'Does that mean she'll be staying on?' asked Andrew, when they were alone.

'Don't know but I rather hope she does.' She fitted in well, the kids adored her, even Bonnie seemed unusually content. Olivia was working her charm on them all, most especially Andrew. Which didn't bother Suzy in the least; she was used to her friend's funny little ways.

'May I talk to you frankly?' asked Olivia, strolling with Andrew through the gardens. He had taken off a couple of hours to show her around his place of work, of

354

which he was justly proud. A tourist attraction combined with a study centre; better even than China had been from Andrew's point of view. Here there was wider scope for his area of research.

'Sure,' he said, 'you can tell me anything.' Even in the short time she'd been there, she'd become a trusted friend. He had liked what he'd seen of all of Suzy's set but the only one he'd had time to know was Olivia. She was a quiet and considerate guest who made him laugh and had the good manners not to be always underfoot. The last thing he needed, after a day's work, was a house-guest who needed entertaining. Olivia was either out in the kitchen, helping Suzy with the meal, or else in the nursery singing to the children, which worked like a charm as it sent them both straight off to sleep. 'She is great,' he said more than once to Suzy. 'Perhaps we can persuade her to stay on.'

Remembering Olivia as a clingy child, Suzy doubted that she'd need much encouragement. She was comfortably entrenched above the garage and treating the place like her own. But whereas in the old days she had got on Suzy's nerves, now she was much more diplomatic. She had developed an awareness of other people's needs, especially the value of privacy between couples. At the slightest sign that they would like to be alone, Olivia was out of there like a shot. She was happy to go into town on her own and was spending more and more evenings listening to jazz. Occasionally Suzy went with her while Andrew happily baby-sat.

He was grateful to have his old wife back, the one who perpetually smiled.

Now, as he waited for Olivia to speak, he did so with sudden apprehension. From the look on her face and her hesitation, he sensed he might not like what she had to say.

'It's Suzy,' she eventually told him, choosing her words with care. 'I am slightly worried about her state of mind.'

'Really?' said Andrew, reacting with shock. 'She seems to have been so much better since you've been here.' There had been months when she hadn't slept at all and dragged herself around all day in a grubby bathrobe. He had thought about asking Gwen to come back, then decided that might make things worse. Two women acting mother to a baby could result in the pair of them falling out. And, much though he liked his mother-in-law, he found her constant presence a bit overwhelming. He was a quiet man of simple tastes who preferred to be alone in his home with his wife. He could only tolerate having a nanny because she didn't live in.

But now Olivia had startled him. Just as he'd thought things were back on track, this bolt had come out of the blue. She saw his concern and apologised. She would never have brought it up, she said, if she hadn't thought there were things he ought to know.

'Like what?' asked Andrew, slightly aghast, yet grateful that she'd had the courage to speak. It was an awkward situation for her, especially since she didn't know him well. But he saw she had Suzy's well-being at heart, so gave full attention to what she said.

'It's hard to pin it down,' she said, fingering a delicate plant. 'It's nothing exactly that she does or says, more the way she looks at them with a coldness in her eyes.'

'Go on,' said Andrew, increasingly alarmed, fearful now of what was coming. Could he have possibly misread the situation? What a stroke of good fortune it was that Olivia had happened to turn up.

'The one I worry about most is Jonah. When he cries, it seems to drive her mad. I realise what a strain it must be, with his persistent earache. Poor Suzy, having to cope with two when Holly is only beginning to toddle. But it frightens me, frankly, the way she shakes him to try to shut him up.'

Andrew passed a hand before his eyes. This was worse, far worse than he had feared. 'You don't think she'd damage him, do you?' he said. The idea was unthinkable yet had to be confronted.

'I really don't know. I didn't want to tell you but your children's safety is paramount. I hope you don't think I have spoken out of turn.'

'What should I do?' he implored her, his eyes brimming suddenly with tears.

Olivia pressed his hand with both of hers. 'Well, to start with, please don't panic. I am only alerting you to certain signs. Provided she's not alone with them, I'm sure there's nothing to worry about and we both agree she is coping much better these days.'

'You don't think there's anyone I ought to alert?' That scenario was chilling.

'Like who?' she asked. 'The authorities? No, I most certainly do not. Look, if you'll let me, I would like to stay on and do whatever I can to lessen the strain. I've been looking around for work as it is, so it shouldn't make Suzy suspicious. And once she is totally better, I'll clear off.'

Andrew wiped his eyes with the back of his hand. 'You're a truly wonderful friend,' he said. 'Is there anything at all I can do to repay you?'

'You're already providing bed and board. Now all I need is a job.'

'I'm afraid I don't have those sorts of contacts.'

'That's not important. Any job will do. I can't go on living here as a guest and my money is fast running out.' She could turn her hand to anything, she said, had supported herself since the age of sixteen. 'Just something to keep me occupied during the hours that the nanny is here. We don't want overkill.'

So Andrew came up with a simple solution without Suzy's being aware there had been collusion. They needed part-time help in the garden gift-shop which was perfectly placed for where they lived. It would not stand in Olivia's way, should anything musical come up, and would be a perfect cover for watching Suzy.

'But why would you want to work there?' Suzy

asked. 'You are more than welcome to stay as long as you like.' Reflecting back to those weekends in Pinner, she marvelled at how her friend had changed. The needy child had become a pillar of strength.

'Because,' said Olivia, 'you've been more than kind. I'd like to contribute something towards my keep.'

36

They were out in the garden, beneath the trees, the babies playing in their paddling-pool, Olivia doing needlework, Suzy sketching. It was Monday so the gift-shop was closed and Olivia had the afternoon off, though Andrew was working as usual in his office. The heat was heavy and the trees were still. Time had done one of its concertina tricks; they were back in their childhood again.

'This reminds me a bit of your mother's garden. Only tidier,' said Olivia. Suzy agreed.

'She's always preferred the wilderness look though she still has a lot of gardening to do. That casual appearance has all been craftily planned.'

'It was in that garden I first met her,' said Olivia, 'when I was all decked out in that ghastly dress.'

'My thirteenth birthday party. I remember it well. You'd just arrived at the school.'

'And was frightened out of my wits by the lot of you.'

'Really?' said Suzy. 'I don't recall it showing. Though my mother must have detected something because she immediately took you under her wing.'

'What do you hear from her?' asked Olivia, secretly guilty that she still hadn't been in touch. Her story about the phone call was false. She had wangled the Lockharts' address from Information.

'I haven't heard much from her recently. Dad's in the process of winding down the business and she's concentrating all her attention on him.' Maggie reported he was in a shaky state, finally facing the inevitable though still hating the thought of retirement. They had weathered whatever the crisis had been, about which her mother had not said a word. She suspected Maggie knew more than she let on and found it sad that, even at this age, parents still kept things from their children. She looked across at Holly and Jonah and wondered if she would feel the same when they were fully grown-up.

'Do you ever think about Miranda?' she asked.

'These days, hardly at all,' said Olivia. 'It all seems such ages ago.'

They worked in silence with their separate thoughts till Holly toddled over to interrupt them. Suzy, with a sigh, laid down her sketchpad and gathered the child into her arms.

'I can't believe we're so old,' she said, a thought she'd been having quite frequently lately. 'Verging on middle-aged.'

'Don't say that,' said Olivia with a shudder. 'I still have the best of my life ahead.' In her shorts and T-shirt, without a scrap of makeup, she certainly didn't look remotely her age. One of the advantages of being small and thin; she still had the slightly undernourished look she had had at age thirteen.

'Wouldn't you like to have kids of your own?' Holly, sucking her thumb, was falling asleep. Olivia was always very cagey about her life; she still hadn't told Suzy about Klaus.

'One day,' she said, as she carefully stitched; she was making a tapestry cushion cover as a hostess gift for the house. The finishing-school had not been a total waste of time. 'Though I suppose, now you mention it, I don't have that much time. Forty marks the start of the big decline.'

They sat and pondered and Suzy felt sad; she hoped her parents were coping all right without her.

Gwen was standing in Suzy's studio, which had formerly been Kit's bedroom. Now that Suzy had children of her own, she doubted she'd ever be back to claim it and was contemplating taking it over herself. Suzy was right: the light was perfect, and her own skills had improved so much, she felt she needed a more professional space. Suzy's old bedroom, which she'd requisitioned, could now be converted once again, into a study for Guy. With both of them going to be home all day, he needed somewhere of his own to withdraw to. In the old days, wives had sewing-rooms while their husbands went to their clubs. Guy still had the golf club, of course, but mustn't be made to feel in the way if he wanted simply to potter around the house. It would mean a new paint-job and rearrangement of furniture but this time he could do it himself. It would make a nice new project to keep him busy.

'I am worried in case he gets bored,' she told Maggie, 'and loses the will to live.' In the past few weeks, since he'd made the decision, he seemed to be slowing down just as she, conversely, was growing more involved with her art. Maggie, by now her most inti-mate friend, thoroughly understood. Late sixties was the danger age and men had a habit of popping off when they felt their usefulness waning.

'What he needs,' she said, 'is a hobby too. There must be something he's always wanted to do. Wine-tasting, fishing, even stamp-collecting; anything to stop his mind atrophying.'

'I don't see him fishing,' said Gwen with a laugh. 'He'd be far too squeamish to remove the hook and I'm not having maggots in my fridge. But wine-tasting might keep him occupied; he could start to lay down his own cellar.' She would approach it subtly and let him believe the idea had always been his. But first he might as well start clearing out the room.

She removed all her canvases and painting gear and stashed them in Suzy's studio. She would need extra space to store it all; she didn't want to disturb Suzy's things but hated working in a mess.

'Before you start rubbing down the walls,' she said to Guy, who was reading the paper, 'you might have a look in the cupboards upstairs and see what can be disposed of. Most of it, I'd imagine. It's probably all junk.'

Suzy was thinking of Miss Holbrook's flat which she used to visit so often while still at school. She remembered its smell of turps and paint that, even to this day, took her back in time. Her green-flecked eyes sparkled with nostalgic longing; in some ways those had been her happiest days. She told Olivia of those magical Saturdays and the conversations they'd had over afternoon tea.

'She taught me so much about life,' she said, 'and how to follow your wildest dreams and never admit defeat nor ever give up.' Without Miss Holbrook's acerbic tongue she might never have been where she was today, an esteemed water-colourist with a solid following whose biennial exhibitions always sold out. 'She taught me how to paint,' she said, 'and now she is teaching my mother.' And Gwen, she knew, was enjoying it, just as she had.

'Which, would you say, came first?' asked Olivia. 'Your art or your lovely family?'

'Don't be absurd, there can be no comparison. I could never be without my babies or Andrew.'

'No, but seriously, if you had to choose. I am being entirely hypothetical.' Olivia seemed curiously keen to hear her answer.

Suzy gave it considered thought. 'I hate to say it but – hypothetically – I suppose it would have to be my art.' Her mind had been set on being a painter right from her earliest years whereas finding a husband and settling down was something she'd given little thought to. Which was odd considering her parents' happy marriage and how harmonious things had been at home.

They sat in silence; it was a shocking admission but one of Suzy's most valiant qualities was that she was literal with the truth.

Guy had been upstairs so long, Gwen suddenly started to miss him. What had started reluctantly as a household chore seemed to have taken him over. He appeared for lunch when she summoned him but made short shrift of the veal and ham pie, swallowed his beer and prepared to go back again.

'No coffee?' she said and he shook his head.

'Later.' And he was gone.

'Well,' she reported to Maggie on the phone. 'Goodness knows what I've started now but it seems to be doing the trick.'

She decided to let him get on with it. There was a landscape she wanted to finish. Normally, about now, he'd be dozing off or nagging her to go for a walk.

Instead there was silence from upstairs so she slipped into the garden with her paints. The past few weeks had been turbulent; having made his decision about retirement, he was not intending to go without a fuss. It wasn't as though they still needed his earnings; after all those years of accountancy, they were more than well taken care of for the future. It was all laid down in pension plans and annuities for the family; should anything untoward ever happen, Suzy and her children would be all right.

'Love, she has a husband now,' Gwen had said when he'd explained it to her but Guy had been adamant that his daughter came first.

'We are well enough off as it is,' he said. 'My investments will more than see us through. And even though Andrew's a lovely lad, I wouldn't feel right retiring without knowing that her inheritance, and the children's, was tied up and watertight.'

Gwen had said nothing; he must do it his own way. But, inside, her heart swelled with pride that the man she had chosen and loved all these years was doing so well by them all.

'Maybe now,' she confided to Maggie, 'he will at last be able to relax.' And, come the summer, might even be persuaded to go with her to the States to visit the Lockharts. When Jonah was born, he had been too busy. Pressures of business and something else had made him constantly moody and withdrawn.

'When a man gives up his business,' Maggie said,

'he feels as though his manhood has been cut off.' She should know; she had fought against retirement and successfully stayed the course and continued to work.

'How's your dad taking retirement?' asked Olivia, surprising Suzy who hadn't expected her to remember, let alone care. She was wrestling now with Jonah, who was crying and fast reducing her to an ugly mood. It must be that blasted earache again; nothing seemed to make it go away. Olivia, seeing the danger signs, tried to take some of the pressure off by giving Holly a piggyback ride, then tickling her tummy on the grass.

'I expect he'll be over to see you soon.' It was a statement, not a question. The thing Suzy had that Olivia most envied was the strong, unconditional love she got from her parents. Nothing she ever did could put them off. They had been the same with Kit.

'I must have been about Holly's age,' she mused, 'when my mother died. The love you are giving your kids I never had.'

'What exactly happened?' asked Suzy now that the baby had stopped crying. In all the years they had known Olivia, she had never been forthcoming with the facts though Gwen had tried repeatedly to get her to talk.

'She is hiding something, I would swear to it,' she'd say. 'The child has a tormented soul.'

Now Suzy waited expectantly; perhaps the moment had come. At almost forty, there could surely be nothing that could do any harm by bringing it to the surface.

'To tell you the truth, I really don't know. Both my dad and my aunt refuse to discuss it.' All it had ever been was a distant blur; Olivia's conscious memories seemed not to have started until three.

Poor Olivia, it helped to explain a lot. Now that she had babies of her own, Suzy was growing to realise the full strength of the maternal bond and that she would kill without hesitation in order to protect them. Olivia had never experienced such love which was why she had felt an outsider all her life, condemned to travel constantly on her own.

Guy was sitting motionless on the couch when Gwen took him up a cup of tea. Around his feet were piled heaps of things unearthed from the drawers of the chest that had once been Kit's. Gwen was stricken with sudden guilt; she should have sorted it out herself years ago.

'All right?' she asked brightly, looking swiftly round the room, still a model of tidiness apart from the things on the floor.

'No, not all right,' replied Guy in distress, and when she looked she saw that he was crying.

She crossed and placed a hand on his shoulder; she hadn't known him shed tears since that terrible night. Around him was neatly stacked Kit's past, all the stuff from his schoolboy years before he finally left home. Framed photographs of the teams he had played in, too many to hang on the wall. And every issue of the school magazine since he'd gone there at thirteen. Kit had always been a hoarder; on his death she had shut it all away untouched in a fruitless effort to help her forget. And now it was open again, like a wound, and at last, after all these barren years, they were forced to confront it head on.

37

Maggie decided not to join them after all. She thought she would be more useful at home, providing moral support to Guy and Gwen. Helen arranged to fly direct and they'd all meet up in New Orleans at the hotel Markus had booked for them in the French Quarter. Deborah and Lisa flew via Washington; on a happier occasion they might have stopped over for a weekend.

'Perhaps on the way back,' said Deborah but Lisa was not convinced. She was hugely cheered by Markus's report that Horace Cutts was fired up to take the case, but quietly worried that Nathan wasn't behind them.

'You have to see his point of view.' Deborah was always rational. 'With children that small, it's no wonder he finds it distasteful.' Besides, he wasn't directly involved. Horace Cutts was their champion now; all of them were banking their hopes on him.

The ride into town took twenty minutes; Markus

was waiting for them at the hotel. Lisa ran to him and he swept her off her feet; they looked a perfect pair, thought Deborah, envious of their happiness. Helen had arrived already and Markus had introduced himself and given her an update on his findings. Later, when they'd revived a bit, he had fixed a meeting with Horace Cutts. The court would call the final witnesses tomorrow; they had arrived only just in time.

Helen and Deborah were sharing a room; they found it more comfortable that way. It took them back to their teenage years and the many hours they had spent together, sorting out the problems of the world. So much had happened to both of them yet underneath they were still the same, high-achievers with similar values united in their commitment to rescuing a friend.

'Do you want to use the bathroom first?' asked Helen politely.

'No, go ahead.'

They had slipped back into the easy friendship they had always had since school. With the door propped open while she dried her hair, Helen explained her academic view of the chances that Suzy was suffering post-natal psychosis. Deborah, reclining on the bed, jerked up in sudden horror.

'Are you suggesting she did it?' she exclaimed.

'Only that if she did, she was temporarily insane.'

'Which is, perhaps, why Andrew won't talk.'

'That's precisely what I've been thinking.'

It was a shocking idea but they needed to confront it, especially before their meeting with Horace Cutts.

'That's why I came,' said Helen, 'to lend a voice. My last book leans heavily on the subject and has been widely reviewed.' *The New York Review of Books*, in particular, had given it star billing. Within her own academic field, Helen was greatly revered.

'What are her chances if they find her guilty?'

'A lot more hopeful if they will listen to me.'

Markus was thoughtful as he waited for Lisa to finish unpacking and freshen up. They had been apart for only four days but he'd missed her even more than he'd expected. She stood there in her satin slip, debating what to wear.

'Do you think, for a lawyer, I ought to dress up? Or go the other way and be dead casual?'

'Smart but demure,' said Markus with conviction. A southern gentleman like Horace Cutts would expect that of a lady. They were due at his house at six p.m. but first there was something else Markus wanted to do. Throughout the night he'd been kept awake by a sneaking suspicion that refused to budge. And the more it nagged, the more he was certain he was right. He wouldn't share it with the others just yet but would make a minor detour to explore his hunch.

'Where are we going?'

'You'll see very soon.'

They were all crammed into a Checker cab with Markus seated at the front. The Garden District was not far away and directly en route to Horace's house, which was convenient. The women twittered and craned their necks, despite their anxiety keen to see the sights. It was light and bright in the late afternoon and the heat was oppressive. All were wearing stylish clothes out of deference to the lawyer and Helen was clutching a copy of her book to impress him.

But first they had a call to make. Markus remained inscrutable; he had briefed the driver before they set off and refused to say another word about their destination. The streets grew wider and were lined with trees and the houses were substantial, many of them set in acres of grounds, well back off the road. The driver swung through wrought iron gates and up a curving drive to a spacious porch.

'I won't be a second. Please wait here,' said Markus, as he climbed the steps and pounded the heavy knocker. The house looked dead and unoccupied with most of its shutters closed but somewhere inside was a broken man whose life had been suddenly destroyed. The very least Markus could try to do was save him.

He stood on the porch and looked around, then risked the knocker again. A child's broken toy was lying there discarded and it wrenched his heart to see it. The girls were waiting patiently in the cab, still unaware of where they were. They admired the sweep of landscaped garden and the curtain of wisteria that swathed the house.

He might be horribly wrong, he knew, but even if he was there was little to lose. From this point on it was life or death and time was running out fast. Then he saw movement behind the glass and the door was slowly opened. The woman who stood there looked entirely at home, in Capri pants and a halter top, a glass of champagne in her hand. She stared at Markus, immobilised by shock.

'Hello, Olivia,' he said.

38

The news had come as they sat down to supper, a call from the Strasbourg police. Suzy was home and laughing her head off at something stupid her mother had said when her father came blundering into the room, ashen-faced. At first he couldn't find the words; then, when he did, they didn't add up or make sense.

'What?' asked Gwen, searching his eyes for the truth. 'Repeat it slowly. I don't think I quite understand.'

An accident, the police had said; a gun had gone off in his rooms. There was no-one else there so the verdict was open, but it looked very much like suicide. They weren't, for the moment, looking for anyone else.

'But he didn't even have a gun,' said Suzy. 'Never learnt to shoot.'

'You don't need to be an expert shot to put a gun to your head.'

* * *

'To this day, I can't really believe it,' said Guy, burying his face in his hands. 'The words were flying around in my brain but not making any sense.'

Gwen came to sit beside him on the couch and gently stroked his head. 'You've never really talked it through,' she said. 'Not in all this time.'

Fifteen years, in fact, it had been, though in some ways it seemed far less. Guy had left for Strasbourg a loving, grieving father but returned a virtual stranger. It had taken him months to face up to what had happened; for a while he had moved into the spare room because he couldn't bear to be alone with her nor allow himself to touch her. It could have destroyed their marriage but it didn't; they had lived through too much together. By the time he was able to sleep again and the nightmares began to recede, he could look at the facts more rationally and acquit himself of the full blame.

'All I could think of, at first, was that I had failed him. That fearless, happy-go-lucky boy with most of his life still ahead of him. Somehow I'd let him down as a father. I simply couldn't handle it, kept wondering where I went wrong.'

'Dearest, he was twenty-eight,' she said, resting her hand on his shoulder. Guy had been in some inner turmoil for months; it came as a huge relief now to know it was this. But she wished they'd been able to talk about it sooner. For a while she had felt that the marriage was falling apart.

* * *

They had managed to get on a flight that night. Guy and Suzy; Gwen was too shattered to go. A respectful policeman had met them off the plane and transported them to a hotel. Strasbourg was a small and compact city; Kit's flat was right in the centre, by the cathedral.

'I don't recommend that you go in there, sir.' His manner was firm but kindly. 'We have taped it off to keep sightseers out while the forensic team is in there, doing their stuff.'

'I have to go,' said Guy. 'He was my son.'

The next part was something he'd never told Gwen, or anyone else, for that matter. Words could never describe the scene though the images lived in his head. A spray of blood across one whitewashed wall though, in view of what had happened, surprisingly little.

'A bullet between the eyes,' said the policeman. 'He certainly knew what he was doing. And must have had nerves of steel to have pulled the trigger.'

They had taken him next to the mortuary, where he formally identified the body. He remembered the small, neat bloodless hole and the look of faint surprise on the handsome face. He'd been due home shortly for a long weekend; Gwen had already baked his favourite fruit cake.

'It was,' said Suzy, as they lingered under the trees, enjoying the slumberous heat of the afternoon, 'the single worst episode of my life. Listening to Dad going over and over what possible reason he could have had to do such a terrible thing, all the while blaming himself, of course, as any caring parent was bound to.' She looked at her happily paddling pair and the thought of anything happening to them clutched at her heart like a claw. Just remembering, after so many years, brought all the horror flooding back. It was the first time Suzy had talked about it. Olivia sat quietly and stitched.

'And your mother?' she asked, still keeping her tone light, though guilt at her neglect still nagged at her.

'My mother was annihilated. For a time we feared she'd go out of her mind. She took to her bed for a couple of weeks and refused to eat a thing. You'll remember how much she idolised my brother.'

They had fooled around like a couple of kids, playing silly games over the washing-up, which Gwen would start by flicking him with her dishcloth. Then Kit would sweep her up over his head while she hammered his back with her fists. At six foot four, he topped her by ten inches but somehow Gwen always managed to win. Olivia, watching, had always felt shut out. No-one had ever engaged her in horseplay like that.

'And how's she coping now?' she asked. At the wedding Gwen had treated her like a stranger.

'Now she's fine though it took some years. In her eyes, the best thing I've done is produce these kids.'

* * *

Next morning Guy had returned to the flat, insisting that Suzy remain at the hotel in case her mother called. Although she begged to accompany him, he didn't want her to see the gut-churning scene. He knew they had done a thorough search but needed to visit the place again. Some detail might have been overlooked; Kit appeared to have left no note which, in such circumstances, was unusual. Although Guy knew nothing about suicide, he had thought he'd known a little about his son.

'Would you mind waiting outside?' he asked. 'I would like to spend some time here on my own.'

The man understood; he had sons of his own. And couldn't imagine how anyone sane could survive such a shattering experience. Apart from the blood, not yet cleared away, the flat appeared much as it had been. Very much a bachelor establishment with sports gear littering the bedroom floor, a power shower and rowing-machine and cases of well-chosen wine. The only items the police had removed, apart from the gun, of course, were two crystal glasses with traces of champagne and a smear of lipstick on one of them. But they might have been there for days already; no-one appeared to know Kit's recent movements. The forensic people had dusted them for prints but not found any that matched.

'And the gun?'

'The only prints on that were his.'

'Where did it come from?'

'That we don't know. Can only assume he bought it for the purpose.'

But there must be something. Guy cased the place, opening drawers and fingering through his things. Rows of suits, all tailor-made and bearing upmarket labels, with shirts to match and shoes and ties; in any other circumstances, Guy might have found it amusing. His son, the slob whom his mother had constantly nagged, had metamorphosed into Christopher Palmer, the dandy.

The desk was unlocked and held just unpaid bills and boxes of business cards and personal stationery. He found an engagement diary there, too, filled with Kit's familiar scrawl but revealing nothing of any significance, certainly not to Guy. Cocktail parties, formal dinners, endless sporting engagements. But nothing at all that leapt out at him or instantly rang any bells. Without someone there who could guide him through it, Guy was completely at a loss.

'Why?' he kept asking himself as he searched but failed to come up with any plausible answer.

They stayed on in Strasbourg a couple more days and met up with some of Kit's colleagues. At the consulate he appeared well-liked and seemed to have numerous friends. One of them took them into his office where family photos were prominently displayed.

'He talked about you so much,' he said, 'that I used to accuse him of being homesick. I don't think he was, though. He fitted in so well. He liked the work and the social life, played squash and tennis and cricket, of course, and was highly successful with the ladies.'

'Anyone special?' Suzy wanted to know. Kit had always been cagey about his love life but if there'd been anyone particular on the scene, she would very much like to meet her. As brother and sister they had always been close and it might throw light on his state of mind. Well, he couldn't swear to it, said the colleague, but he had suspected in the past few weeks that something important was happening in Kit's life.

'You know, better than I, what he was like, making a joke about everything and never taking any of these women seriously. He went to so many social functions and was always picking people up. No offence,' he glanced worriedly at Guy, 'but he could have had anyone he wanted and not, by any means, just single either.'

Suzy laughed. 'That sounds like my brother. Should anyone surface, please let us know.' There wouldn't be a funeral, not in Strasbourg. They were taking him home, to bury him in Pinner. But among these hordes of people they hadn't met, maybe someone was nursing a broken heart. That was the person Suzy wanted to meet. Guy handed over his business card, with their home number scribbled on the back.

'And did anyone ever turn up?' asked Olivia, by now transfixed by the story. Suzy assumed that she'd never really known him but overlooked those many week-ends she had been there in the house.

'Nobody,' said Suzy. 'Apart, of course, from the hundreds of letters of condolence we received. My brother was very much loved all his life and when he died, the grief was overflowing.'

The girls had taken it surprisingly hard; she remembered Deborah blubbing on the phone, then driving straight over to Pinner to console her and crying again in her arms. Suzy had been both touched and impressed; only months before, Deborah had married Neville. She'd had no idea all these years how much she had cared.

'I always felt he was my brother, too,' said Deborah unconvincingly. 'He was everything I ever wanted in a man.'

In circumstances less harrowing, Suzy might well have probed; as it was, they were both too weepy to say much more. They clung together like the sisters they were and consoled each other by sharing their terrible grief.

Lisa had handled it entirely differently; her reserve had made it seem that she didn't care. She had taken time off for the funeral and stood stiffly in the crowded churchyard, looking oddly detached in her barrister's stark black. Naturally, she had said all the right things, had clung to Gwen and shaken Guy's hand, but had hurried away as soon as she could and hardly mentioned him since. Deep in her heart,

Suzy had been hurt. Even Helen had taken the trouble to send flowers.

'Everyone loved him,' she told Olivia now. 'I guess people have different ways of expressing their sorrow.'

There was a pause while Olivia selected another colour, then sucked the end and threaded it through her needle.

'I never loved him,' she said, after a pause. 'If I felt anything for him at all, it was hate.'

Unable to believe she had heard correctly, Suzy turned to stare at her. Olivia was staring straight back with ice in her eyes.

'Yes, you heard right,' she said challengingly. 'All he ever did all those years was put me down.'

'Oh, come now,' said Suzy, recovering from the shock. 'He treated us all exactly the same, as kids too young to take seriously. He was nice enough when he had the time but otherwise, you could forget it. I must have been twenty before we ever really talked.'

Olivia, however, remained unconvinced. He had had a profound effect on her teenage years. She had never forgotten how he'd flirted with Miranda yet, when he came to look at her, couldn't even remember her name.

39

Strasbourg in spring was at its best, awash with blossom and sunshine and tourists. The European Parliament was in session which meant a burgeoning social life since the consulate staff were always expected at functions. Kit, who was now in his fifth year of duty, was a well-known fixture on the circuit and out on the town almost every night. In the years since Oxford he had filled out a little and was now even better-looking. Some of the boyish raffishness had gone so that, with his height and imposing presence, he dominated any gathering and everyone knew who he was. At the Foreign Office, he was highly thought of; his future prospects were good.

Women adored him, as they always had, and it was quite an achievement, at twenty-eight, to have managed to keep himself unattached, though there had been some narrow shaves. His mother kept urging him to settle down; she would like some grandchildren, she said, and Suzy showed no signs of settling either.

But Kit, at heart, was very much a man's man whose sporting interests came first. He liked the job and his bachelor existence and was in no hurry at all to give it up. His parents' marriage was an inspiration yet he felt no pressure to emulate them yet. He had time enough in the future for being adult; all he wanted right now was to have fun.

Until he went to a cocktail party and met Désirée, a French translator, and suddenly found himself smitten. She had doe-like eyes and a fabulous figure and, from the moment she caught his eye, Kit Palmer was a marked man. He fought his way through the crowd to her side and made his own introductions. She was new in town, just arrived from Geneva, and he wasted no time in getting her number and asking her out on a date. Then he went home and vacuumed his flat and sent all his sheets to the laundry. The single life had much to recommend it but the time for serious changes had arrived.

The Swiss Embassy was throwing a lavish party and Kit had arranged to be there. She would come, she had said, if she could get away. Because the assembly was still in session, her working hours were erratic and she'd no way of knowing until the last minute when she was likely to get off.

'Don't worry,' he'd said. 'I shall be there anyway. And perhaps if you make it, you'll allow me to take you to dinner.'

So there he hovered in his very best suit, making sporadic conversation, his restless eyes raking the company and constantly checking his watch. So that when someone tapped him on the shoulder, he spun round with relief.

'Hello, Kit Palmer,' said a voice. 'How are you? Long time no see.' And he found himself face to face with a woman he had no recollection of seeing before, let alone ever knowing. She was smallish and thin and neatly dressed in plain, unassuming beige silk, which blended effectively with her face and hair and gave her an aura of total anonymity. She could have been anyone, he met so many, but she clearly thought she knew him.

'You don't remember me,' she said and Kit had to confess that he didn't. And just at that moment, as he was making excuses and someone was mentioning the Countess von Richthofen, a hand was waving and Désirée had arrived.

'You'll have to excuse me,' he said to Olivia, shoving his business card into her hand. 'But my date is here so I really have to go. Call me at the office some time and maybe we can catch up. Good to see you after so many years.'

And off he went, shouldering his way through the throng without so much as a backward glance. The man who had regularly ignored her as a schoolgirl clearly hadn't altered in any way. She watched him as he greeted his date, kissing her effusively on both cheeks. She was dark and soignée and quite obviously French but otherwise nothing very special. Nothing that, had he cared to find out, she couldn't have offered him herself.

Right, thought Olivia, pocketing his card. The time has come for a showdown. We will get together, Mr Christopher Palmer, and then see who has the last laugh.

It was Thursday evening and the bells were ringing as Kit put the finishing touches to the room. Shop-bought canapés and Bollinger on ice; it mustn't look too contrived yet hit the right note. He had booked a table at La Maison Kammerzell, which was just across the square from where he lived, but first they would have a leisurely drink and, if all went according to plan, he would hope to bring her back later. If only those damned cathedral bells would shut up.

She was due at eight and at twelve minutes to the doorbell rang from below. Kit passed his hands rapidly over his hair, checked in the mirror that his teeth were clean and pressed the entry button. It was four floors up and she'd have to walk so he'd just got time for a final flick round. His palms were sweaty so he wiped them on his pants. He couldn't remember being this nervous, not since he left school.

By the time the knock came he was calm again and swung the door open in welcome.

'Oh,' he said when he saw who it was. 'I was expecting somebody else.'

'That's all right,' said his visitor calmly. 'Mind if I come in anyway?' And passed him in the doorway before he could answer.

Kit thought fast; there was nothing he could do except be gracious and wait for Désirée to arrive. At which point the visitor would have to leave; in the meantime there was no harm in being civil. He had racked his brains but still didn't know who she was.

'Champagne?' he offered. He had excellent manners and slipped a second bottle into the fridge. He left the canapés in the kitchen; the less he offered, the sooner she would depart. And in the meantime, perhaps he'd remember her name. The foreign-sounding title told him nothing but here, in Strasbourg, you met all sorts.

'Well,' he said, raising the crystal glass. 'It's certainly been a long time.'

'Too long,' she said, fumbling inside her bag.

He hoped she wasn't thinking of smoking; he didn't want her polluting the air. 'We will have to catch up when I'm not quite so busy. But right now I'm afraid I have a date. Who is due here just about now.'

The bullet caught him between the eyes. Within a blink he was dead.

40

It was hotter than ever so Dee gave in and swapped her tailored suit for a linen dress.

'You look like Oprah, only better,' said Jackson, kissing her before they got into the car. Today he was coming with her to watch the climax of the trial.

They were all there on the courthouse steps; Deborah, Helen, Lisa and Markus, Markus and Lisa holding hands. Last night's meeting with Horace had gone well. They now had a modicum of renewed hope for Suzy and Horace had plans up his sleeve which he wouldn't divulge.

Proceedings started, and the defendant was sworn in. Suzy, looking, if possible, even frailer, managed to walk unaided to the dock. She glanced to neither left nor right when the usher called out her name.

'Do you think she knows we are here?' whispered Helen. It wasn't clear from the public gallery, where they were seated as a group.

'It's hard to tell,' said Deborah, 'but I hope so.' The

Suzy she was looking at now was a shadow of her former self. Gone was the sparkle and happy-go-lucky smile. The eyes were sunken and the mouth tight-lipped; she had been to hell and back.

The first witness Horace called to the stand was Bonnie, the children's nanny. Using his courteous, old world charm, he led her skilfully through her responses and everything she said was in Suzy's favour. A good employer, generous and fair, who allowed her as much time off as she needed and occasionally took the children off her hands. A closeknit family with devoted parents. Whatever had happened could only have been accidental.

'So how *did* it happen?' oily Orville asked, his smile fixed and his condescension showing. Bonnie mumbled and shook her head, instantly losing her confidence when he grilled her.

'Were you there that day?'

'No,' she replied. She had had to go to the hospital for tests.

'And would you say Mrs Lockhart had an equable temperament?'

Again the nanny looked at a loss.

'Objection,' Horace interjected.

Next on the stand was Rabbi Hirsch, called as a character witness. She had taken great pains to dress the part and was sweltering in her tailored suit. She looked at the judge and wished she had thought of wearing linen. Horace led her through her replies and she briefly sketched the history of their friendship. She could, she told the court, speak as a sister as well as a professional spiritual adviser.

'Would you say she has a violent temper?' Orville was refusing to let that one drop.

'Absolutely not,' said Deborah. 'In the twenty-eight years we have been close friends, I have never so much as heard her raise her voice.' Her mind flashed back to the grieving parents who were too distressed to have made the journey here. 'She comes from a loving, united family who raised their children to be tolerant and forbearing. Any kind of violent action would be anathema to them all.'

'So tell us about the older brother.'

'Objection!' bellowed Horace.

Helen looked poised and also well-dressed, though in a minor key. She held in her hand her motherhood book which Horace had insisted she use as a prop.

'I can't do that,' she'd objected, 'it's showing off,' but he had managed to convince her. All his stagecraft – his Phi Beta Kappa key, his spats, the old world charm – were professional aids. In another life he might have been an actor, a vital component of the advocate's role.

'You have to convince the jury you're bona fide. A weighty tome like that should help make the point.' He introduced her as a world class academic then left her alone to give her views on the chance (one in three hundred) that post-natal psychosis would affect someone like Suzy to such a degree.

'I hope she's not leading them to convict her.' Deborah was suddenly alarmed.

Lisa silently shook her head and continued listening intently. Helen was the voice of scientific reason as she spoke of Darwin and the genesis of man and boiled it all down to a matter of hormones and genes. 'The worst that can happen,' Lisa whispered to Deborah, 'is that Helen will convince them that she wasn't of sound mind.'

'Which means they'll let her off?'

'Well, not entirely.' But anything would be preferable to the chair.

This time Orville had no questions. The cool professor, with her neatly turned back cuffs, read them extracts from her own research and managed to keep emotion out of her voice. Horace nodded as she left the stand and Deborah sensed he felt things were going well. She looked at the judge who remained impassive. There was no way of telling from her what the outcome would be.

Next came a prosecution witness, the nearby neighbour who had reported the row. A writer, well-known in the local community, she'd been reading by her open window when she heard raised voices from the Lockhart house which was just across the lawn from where she lived.

'Could you hear what they were saying, ma'am?'

'No. But I also heard the children crying. Normally by that hour they are both asleep.'

'At what time approximately would that have been?'

'Well, certainly well after supper. Around ten-thirty or eleven, I'd say. I was thinking of turning in.'

'And do you make a habit of eavesdropping?' Horace was on his feet again and fixing her with a penetrating stare. 'I would have thought the properties were far enough apart to allow complete privacy. Surely that's why you pay those real estate rates.'

The woman, flamboyant in head-to-toe mauve, flushed, which didn't become her. 'I assure you I wasn't eavesdropping,' she snapped. 'They were making a great deal of noise.'

'Order!' barked Dee and banged her gavel. Jackson, up in the gallery with Lisa and Markus, smiled.

All eyes swivelled to peer at Suzy when Orville called her to the stand. She looked not entirely compos mentis but in a perpetual daze. The hearts of her friends overflowed with protective love. She had lost her children and now her own life was at stake. Deborah, Lisa and Helen held hands. At last they were about to hear the crucial part of the evidence.

Suzy, it seemed, had been cooking for hours, slowed down by the baby's constant bawling. Despite the prescription from the doctor, his earache refused to go away which meant he was tired and cranky much of the time. Added to which, Bonnie had health problems too and had taken a full day off for medical tests. Suzy was facing an urgent deadline but was unable to do any work because she couldn't leave the children on their own. So she'd dumped them both in Jonah's playpen, in order to keep an eye on them as she cooked. She was making Andrew his favourite supper, lamb and tomatoes with flageolet beans, which took five hours to cook but was delicious. Meanwhile, she had baked brownies for the kids and was making onion marmalade to put down. Since she couldn't get on with her painting, the constructive thing was to catch up on household chores. Her mother would have laughed to see her; she was turning into a regular little hausfrau.

She set the table and looked at the clock; Andrew was already a full hour late. It was time the babies went to bed so she turned down the heat, to let the jam simmer, and carried them both upstairs. After she'd bathed them and tucked them in, she read them both a story. One advantage of the closeness in age was that they liked the same things. Except that after Holly had dropped off, Jonah continued fretful and resumed his grizzling the moment she switched off the light.

If Andrew would only come home and take over, she could finish the marmalade, seal it in jars and put the last touches to the meal. It was most unlike him not to be on time; the least he could have done was let her know. By the time she heard the car, she was grumpy herself and when he strolled in with Olivia in tow, it was all she could do not to make an acid remark.

Both appeared in excellent spirits and were laughing

at some joke. Since Olivia had started working at the gift-shop, the two had become as thick as thieves so that Suzy, in her frazzled state, increasingly felt left out. Ignoring the fact she was barely civil, Andrew invited Olivia to stay.

'I'm sure there's enough for all of us,' he said. 'Suzy usually over-caters.'

Which didn't help to improve her mood even though it was true. Ungraciously, she set a third place, even before Olivia had accepted, and meanwhile upstairs the babies had started to cry.

'So,' said Orville, after Suzy's stumbling testimony. 'You are telling the court that you were extremely stressed out.'

'Objection,' said Horace, 'you are leading the witness. She is simply setting the scene for the later row.'

Suzy, still looking shell-shocked, didn't react. Her eyes were lifeless, her delivery flat; she barely seemed to know what she was saying.

'Poor darling,' said Deborah, agonised, though dying to know how Olivia fitted in. Until last night they had not even known she was here.

Olivia had been at her most coquettish which didn't exactly improve Suzy's mood. When Andrew went up to settle the children, she insisted on going with him. Suzy, as she dished out the stew, could hear her girlish laughter. Tonight she was playing the ingénue, which particularly grated. Fish and house-guests, the same old story. Deborah caught Helen's eye and she nodded her head.

Olivia chattered all through the meal, more or less ignoring Suzy but openly flirting with Andrew. And when, eventually, she got the message and took herself home to the garage flat, Suzy turned on him in a rage and accused him of leading her on.

'Don't be ridiculous,' he said. 'You are simply overreacting.' At which point both babies resumed their screaming and Suzy threw an iron ladle at his head.

'And then what happened?' Orville was setting her a trap. He was openly triumphant.

'He left the house and slammed the door. I didn't see him again all night. Much later I heard a car engine starting up.'

Suzy, having been up all night, trying to calm Jonah and worrying about what she had done, walked across the lawn at five to check if Andrew's car was back in the garage. It wasn't, which came as a slight relief until Olivia appeared at the top of the steps, barefoot and wrapped in a fetching negligee.

'He isn't here,' she said with a smirk. 'Though he was for most of the night. He has gone for a drive in order to clear his head.' No longer the quiet, supportive friend, now she was positively gloating, flaunting her sexuality at Suzy, claiming the upper hand.

'And what did you do?' The court held its breath.

Suzy looked confused. 'Returned to the house.'

Later she bundled up the children – Bonnie had asked for another day off – and drove to Andrew's office to have things out. Because of the kids, he had come out to the car and when she'd accused him of having an affair, he had ordered her sharply and coldly to calm down.

'For Christ's sake, get a grip,' he had hissed. 'You're making an exhibition of yourself.'

'So then what did you do?' asked Orville.

'Drove to the mall to buy groceries.' If it hadn't all been so horribly tragic, Deborah might have laughed. Only Suzy, at such a time, could get on with the mundanities of life, though it did also hint that she might have been slightly deranged.

The rest of the story they knew already. She had taken the sheets to the drive-in laundry and had to get out of the car for a minute to drag the heavy bag to the automated slot. Leaving the kids in the car with the engine running.

'You know, in this country, that's illegal?'

'It was only for a couple of seconds.'

'And somebody drove the car away?'

'Just in the time my back was turned.'

'Someone who happened to chance along?'

'Someone, almost certainly, following me.' There had been another car parked nearby but she'd been too distraught at the time to take it in.

'So then what did you do?'

'I cried.' And ran around like a headless chicken, screaming and thrashing her arms about, begging for someone to help her find her children.

'Why didn't you call the police?'

'I couldn't. My phone was still in the car. And the drive-in laundry was automated. There wasn't anyone there.'

In the end she had flagged down a passing motorist and asked to borrow his phone. But someone had already reported the theft and when he dropped her off at the precinct, they held her for questioning. The caller on Suzy's phone, which they'd checked, had spoken in an English accent, said she was sick of the baby's crying and her husband's infidelity and was on her way to Riverbend to end it all.

'Which was where the abandoned car was found?' And the sad little bodies of the babies. Though not the driver of the car. Nor Suzy.

By the time the cops came to take her in she had lost all touch with reason. She only knew that the children were dead and that it was somehow her fault. Since when she had been in perpetual shock and entirely convinced that she'd done it.

'She'd believe almost anything,' Horace said, 'that anyone put in her head.'

Suzy was led away and they broke for lunch. The others crossed the street to a bar and settled, in a gloomy group, around a corner table.

'Old Horace had better have something up his

sleeve.' Lisa was starting to sweat. Because of her knowledge of the defendant, she believed her story implicitly but couldn't see the jury doing likewise. 'It still doesn't quite add up,' she said. 'Whoever would do a thing like that?'

'Wait till this afternoon,' said Markus. 'When, I suspect, you'll find out.'

The courtroom was packed when they returned but their seats had been reserved. Just before the judge walked in, someone entered the rear of the gallery and the spectators had to squash up to make more room. Deborah turned to see who it was but her view was blocked by a bailiff. She settled back to concentrate on the proceedings.

It was Horace's turn to call a witness and the name he gave surprised them.

'Call Olivia Fernshaw,' he said and the friends looked round in surprise. They hadn't realised she would be involved, just fancied her a pawn in Suzy's story. Surely her presence in town was coincidental.

Today Olivia was dressed like a nun in plainest, starkest grey. She wore flat pumps and no jewellery and looked subdued and suitably chastened at having to be there at all. She was really just passing through, she explained, and hadn't intended to stay but was doing a favour for Suzy's husband by running the gift-shop in the gardens until he could make a permanent appointment. She gazed at Horace appealingly but it failed to cut any ice. All traces of old world charm were gone; now he was starting to show his teeth and what that revealed wasn't pleasant.

'So, Miss Fernshaw,' Horace addressed her. 'What have you got to say for yourself? You have told the court you were just passing through. From where to where, I would like to know, and, indeed, with what intent?'

Her clear candid eyes implored him to be gentle but the lawyer was having none of it. He paced up and down and swung his key, his steely eyes clashing with hers.

'I came because Suzy is my friend,' she said. 'And they'd both invited me to visit. Then once I got here, I saw they were in trouble so volunteered to stay on.'

'What sort of trouble?'

'They were not getting on. I could see she was on the edge of losing her wits.' She looked like the friend she purported to be, upset and embarrassed by her frankness.

'Traitor!' hissed Deborah, up in the gallery. 'I always knew the bitch could never be trusted.'

'And then what happened?'

'The next bit's hard. I'd prefer not to have to say it in open court.'

The judge invited both lawyers to confer and then directed Horace to proceed.

'What happened?' he asked again and she visibly squirmed.

'He came on to me,' she said in a very low voice. 'I swear I never intended it to happen.' She looked round the courtroom, beseeching their mercy, a stalwart friend who had been unjustly abused.

'Liar!' roared a voice from the gallery and Andrew Lockhart came pushing his way through the crowd. Leaning forward as though he might jump, he drilled Olivia with hate-filled eyes. 'You murdered my children,' he said.

Commotion broke out throughout the courtroom and Dee had to bang her gavel many times before she could bring them to order. In the dock the prisoner was showing signs of life as dawning understanding crossed her face.

'I trusted you,' was all she said and then broke down in tears.

'I didn't mean it,' pleaded Olivia as two bailiffs led her away. 'All I wanted was the life you had. I had nothing while you always had it all.'

Still seated in the gallery, Deborah remembered the afternoon she had started off visiting Suzy's parents and ended up pursuing Olivia's aunt. In Stanmore, just up the road, because of a hunch.

The house, when she had approached it, had been quiet and Sarah Standish, when she opened the door, seemed very much on her guard. She showed Deborah in, as though almost expecting her, listened while she asked her questions, then gave a sad little shake of the head and told her all she knew. Not a soldier, not for some years, but a conman, in and out of jail, who had ruined her sister's life and then his daughter's.

'She isn't intrinsically bad,' she had said. 'All she ever lacked was genuine love.'

41

It was late but the child couldn't sleep; there were voices below. She climbed out of bed and tiptoed to the landing, trying to hear what was being said, hating, as always, not to be included. The light was on, though not on the stairs, and the door to the lounge stood enticingly open a crack. She could hear the laughter and the smell of cigar smoke, then the clink of a bottle against glass.

Someone was down there, presumably her daddy. He'd been gone so long, she could hardly recall how he looked. She remembered his hugs, though, and the bristles on his chin and the way he called her Princess and gave her sweeties. She moved a couple of steps further down and could see his luggage in the hall. A khaki kitbag and an overcoat, while his army beret, with its polished badge, lay on the telephone table by the front door. Now they were starting to move about and the laughter ceased abruptly. She could hear her mother crying out and then more muffled scuffling in the room. The child crept closer, longing to join them but fearful of letting them know she had come down. Her daddy was always kind to her but her mummy quite often was cross. She wasn't supposed to get out of bed until morning.

Under the cap was a pair of leather gloves and something the child had not seen before. Barefoot she tiptoed along the hall and pressed her face to the narrow gap in the doorway. Her mother was on the floor with her father on top. She could see from her mother's frantic wriggling that she was trying to get away but the more she struggled, the more he panted and pinned her down with his weight.

'No,' she was saying, 'not yet. Let me breathe.' But he covered her mouth with his hand.

'The child,' she said, shaking him off. 'Don't wake her.' And she flailed with her arms and tried very hard to escape.

The child looked around. She must help her mummy; she had seen him do this before. The closest object that she could lift was under the leather gloves in the hall so she pulled it carefully from its holster and brought it back to the doorway.

'Yes,' she was saying now, 'yes, yes, yes' and, as he rolled off her, she turned her head.

'Olivia?' she said just a fraction too late. The bullet caught her squarely between the eyes.